When a troubled young woman's body is found on a riverbank hundreds of miles from home, detective Luke Lennox battles small town politics, old loyalties and the temptation of the deceased's hauntingly beautiful identical twin to bring a killer to justice.

PRAISE FOR NORA LeDuc

MURDER CAME CALLING: "A Night Owl Romance Book Review TOP PICK!"

~*~

"*STAGING MURDER* absolutely kept me glued to my ereader. I was caught up in the suspense, quite curious about the murder, the threats and what they all meant for Ava."

~Jennifer Porter, Romance Novel News

~*~

"Impressively crafted, *PICK UP LINES FOR MURDER* is an enjoyable suspense thriller."

~Josee Morgan, Apex Reviews

~*~

MURDER BY HEART: "Tension begins on the first page and doesn't end until an unexpected culprit is revealed in the last few pages. This cleverly crafted story is filled with sexual tension that neither the hero nor the heroine wants to recognize and an abundance of action as they try to outwit a vicious killer."

~ Donna M. Brown for Romantic Times Book Reviews

~*~

LOVE'S WICKED JEWEL: "Several of the scenes contain wry humor that binds all into a tidy bundle of compelling and suspenseful romance."

~Faith V. Smith, Romantic Times Book Reviews

DEAD WOMEN
TELL NO LIES

NORA LEDUC

DEAD WOMEN TELL NO LIES

Copyright © 2013 Nora LeDuc

Contact Information: NoraLeDuc@yahoo.com

Cover Art by Niina Cord
Interior Formatting by Author E.M.S.
Edited by Caroline Tolley

Publishing History 2013
ISBN: 0-9892090-1-6
ISBN-13: 978-0-9892090-1-4

Published in the United States of America

DEDICATION

To Anita, breakfast companion, supporter and dearest friend. I
thank you for all of it. Here's to our next time together.

A special thanks to all my readers. Nora

.

PROLOGUE

Brattleboro, Vermont
February 25th

A chill seeped into Rose Blue's hands, through her jeans and stocking feet on the wooden kitchen floor. She paused over her unmade sandwich and stretched the cuffs of her navy turtleneck downward.

The rip of duct tape echoed in her ears. Footsteps crunched against the stones. Closer. Closer.

The granite counter blurred and warped into a granite ledge overhanging a river.

The vision sucked her in.

A shadowy figure hovered over a petite woman wearing a pink parka and lying on the ridge. Clammy strands of blond hair clung to a heart-shaped face, a face the mirror image of her own.

"Dahlia!"

Oh, God! Gooseflesh rippled up Rose's spine. The shadow bound Dahlia's hands and feet with gray tape, round and round. Terror flooded Rose's chest. Goose flesh ripped across her arms.

"Help!" she screamed before the duct tape silenced her sister's last cry.

Rose gasped and turned over. She was lying on the planked floor in her one bedroom apartment. What happened? The hum of the furnace kicked on followed by a flash of heat that filled the first floor apartment.

Her head ached like someone had slugged her. Near her hand,

she spotted the butter knife. She grabbed the weapon and crawled toward the granite counter. Gripping the edge, she hauled herself to her feet. She held the blade in striking position while she tossed frantic glances over her shoulder to search the area.

Was she suffering a migraine, going crazy? She listened for the creep of a footstep, the sound of breathing, any noise in her apartment. "Who's there?"

Silence answered. She raked a gaze over the table, trying to ground herself. Her store's printed balance sheet leaned against her open laptop, the way she'd left it a few minutes ago. The sun's dying rays shone through the small window above the porcelain sink and slanted downward onto the hardwood. Nothing seemed disturbed.

Near her elbows, the jar of peanut butter rested by the loaf of bread. One slice of wheat lay on the dish smeared with the brown spread.

What was going on? She shuddered with horror at the memory of her sister lying on the ground. Rose had once experienced her sister's pain when Dahlia broke a foot at soccer. When the X-rays revealed Rose's bone intact, Gram had ripped into her about faking it to gain attention. After that, Rose censored all her aches and pains, especially if Dahlia had the same problem.

Was something like that happening again? The stove clock showed she'd lost fifteen to twenty minutes of time. Her head throbbed, and her brain refused to work. One idea broke through her frazzled thoughts: Dahlia was in trouble now.

"Rose...help!"

Her sister was calling her. Where was she? A sense of breathless urgency grew in Rose's chest. She sprinted across the floor to the house phone and hit the speed dial for her sister's landline even though she doubted her twin was home. Dahlia's home phone rang over and over. "Answer. Answer."

Her voicemail responded. "This is Dahlia. Leave a message."

Rose hung up and tried her sister's cell. She listened to the beginning of the recorded greeting before she hit the end button. With a growing premonition of something deadly, she shoved her feet into shoes and threw on her gray parka. Her sister needed her.

CHAPTER 1

Friday, March 23rd

At 11:00 am, Detective Luke Lennox drove through the bustling center of Ledgeview, New Hampshire. He stopped for the octogenarian crossing the street to enter Joe's Coffee Shop where the retired crowd hung out. On the sidewalk, a group of women pointed at the Made in New Hampshire jewelry and crafts in the storefront window. The downtown had embraced the slogan, "Buy Local," and for a small city of thirty thousand, the business section seemed to be thriving. He hit the accelerator and passed the white steeple church at the head of the block. Two miles out, he drove past the popular shopping plaza with Egore's Electronics.

From there, Luke headed north, past refinished farm houses, dilapidated barns and newer homes separated by acres of land and old stone walls. He pulled over and parked near the swamp where the man walking his dog had found the missing woman's wallet two days ago. The billfold was located about six feet from the roadside. A good throw from a passing car would hit the spot. If the woman was alive, why hadn't she reported her possessions stolen or lost? The answer was not one he liked.

Ledgeview had grown in the last few years, but the population clustered around the city center. On the outskirts, buildings fell away to long stretches of woods. Places perfect for illegal activity.

He hopped out of his car, Old Charger, and cool air whirled around him. He buttoned up his dad's worn, leather jacket and focused on what he'd learned about the case. The twenty-seven-year-old, Vermont female, Dahlia Blue, disappeared from her home almost a month ago and was reported missing by her sister. At the moment, the wallet remained their sole clue. It drew him to the marsh, though yesterday's organized search of the locale revealed nothing.

From inside his trunk, he removed his size twelve hiking boots and snagged a couple of evidence bags. He probably wouldn't use them, but solving crimes taught him to always travel prepared. Luke stuffed the bags into the back pocket of his jeans and switched his footwear. Set, he tramped off. Tomorrow he'd meet the woman's twin, Rose Blue. The Vermont Police had been handling the case up to this point, based on the theory the missing woman remained somewhere in state.

Now, Luke wanted a face-to-face interview with the only living family member. He also wanted, no needed, to find a lead. He raised his shoulders against a blast of wind and tugged on his blue knit hat. A few stray blonde hairs clung to the fabric. When he worked a case, he never stopped for mundane time suckers like haircuts.

The water's hum grew to a roar as he approached a copse of pines. The ice on the lakes and streams was out early this year and fed the bodies of water. He trekked under protruding boughs. His large form hit and snapped the branches. The evergreen's fragrance followed him to the other side of the trees where he searched for an obscure footprint or a discarded item.

A stab of gray on the tip of a barren branch waved in the air. He started forward when his boot slipped. He regained his balance with a glance at the river a few yards away. One fall on an icy patch and chances were good he'd slide down into the fast moving current. He wouldn't last long in the sub freezing water.

Sidestepping, he approached the scrub until he stood beside the silver fabric. Duct tape. It might not have been here when the searchers plodded through, or they simply missed the tape. Even if the gray fabric had gone unnoticed, the tape could have been left by a hiker or hunter and not connected to the missing Dahlia Blue. He removed his jackknife and prayed this was his break. Luke sawed through the tip of the limb, stuffed the evidence bag and walked up toward his car. Three feet from the road, his cell rang.

"Hey, we're behind the *Smith Plaza* on South Main, near the interstate," Detective Mike Conroy announced in his thin voice. "A couple of teens got a surprise when they thought they'd get in a little privacy down by the water. Turns out, they were almost able to make it a threesome."

"Is this a vice call, Conroy? What's your point?"

"The kids found a woman tangled in the brush on the riverbank, only she was dead and not up for their ideas. From her condition, I'd say she didn't wander into the undergrowth on her own. I've cordoned off the area. Vic appears to be the Vermont woman reported missing last month."

Dahlia Blue? Damn. "I'm on my way."

As he sped to the scene in Old Charger, Luke searched his mental list of homicide cases involving dead ringers. He'd read about two identical sisters who murdered their mother in Georgia, and he couldn't forget the Han twins in California. Two bright, inseparable young women whose bond was broken when one attempted to murder the other. The good twin versus the bad played big in the press.

Was the surviving Blue sibling an evil, vindictive killer who'd murdered her sister? She better have a lot of answers for him. Luke hit the gas. A lot was riding on this investigation. He'd overheard the grumbles at the station that the chief hired him back because of Luke's father. He'd been a lifer in the department and an old pal of the chief's.

Plenty of gossips would love Luke, who'd left them behind for bigger and better in Buffalo, to screw up his first case as Ledgeview's head detective. He shrugged to ease the cramping muscles in his upper back. He'd proved them wrong and knock their duty boots off too.

From Main Street, he turned into the shopping plaza that edged the abandoned railroad tracks. He cruised down the fire lane, circling around the back of the two anchor stores, Babyland and Jumbo Mart. The New Hampshire Liquor Store stood on the side of the lot, tempting buyers with weekly specials posted in the window. As he sped past the delivery dock and over the tracks, he spotted four cruisers, an ambulance and a small crowd congregated on the hill crest. The news van for Channel 23 was parked to the side.

He flashed his dome light and drove toward the scene. The uniforms stepped in front of the gathering, pushed the gawkers back and waved him forward. He hopped out of Old Charger. While his men held the crowd away, Luke met Detective Conroy. At six foot-two, the man was one of the few on the force who could stare Luke in the eye. True to form, Conroy never wasted a second on a smile or a greeting. Today was no exception. His navy parka hung open, revealing the badge on his belt and his protruding stomach. The odor of fried onions clung to him. "Our victim is below on the bank."

"What's happening with the photos and measurements of the area?" Luke scanned the hilly terrain of dead grass and shrubs. "Have you separated the teens to take their stories?"

Conroy's brown eyes flashed behind his dark framed glasses, and he raked a hand through his short-cropped hair. "We've done our part. We're working on pictures, measurements and have separately interviewed the teenagers who found the body." He put one hand on his belt and glared at Luke. "We're capable of conducting a homicide investigation even though our city's a lot smaller than Buffalo."

"Good start for a homeboy," Luke snapped. "Now cut the crap and get down to business." Conroy refused to let go of the fact that Luke snagged the job Conroy wanted.

"Any drag marks, footprints or pieces of clothing found?" Luke asked.

"No marks or prints found near the body. The men are working the hill. The ground is too frozen to give us much. The remains of her clothes are shredded. Pieces of duct tape trussed her wrists, ankles and mouth."

Maybe the forensics techies would connect the tape he'd found to the pieces on Miss Blue.

"It's difficult to judge if she was assaulted," Conroy said. "I'd guess she's been in the water for a while and did a job on the forensics. The new ME will help us there." Conroy shook his head. "No personal belongings found yet. Oh, and for the record, we're videoing the scene. You did want us to do that, right, or do you do it different in the big city?"

"Listen, Conroy, do the job and save the attitude for whoever tied up the woman and disposed of her like trash." Luke tamped down on the urge to tell Conroy off further. "If the videographer hasn't already, have him shoot the crowd. You never know if our killer is standing around watching us."

"Got it. Follow me." Conroy trudged parallel to the river and stopped to speak to the slim, young man with the camera. After that, he continued with Luke downward toward the bank.

Luke's boots thudded across the lifeless grass while the sound of the gushing river below grew louder the closer as they hiked to the waterway. His gut clenched. A few techies threw cool glances at him, the big shot detective. Many of them remembered his excitement when he left to join a "better" force.

Ahead, Conroy slowed at the edge of the gray water. Unkempt brush and litter covered the ground. An overgrown shrub wagged a warning in the breeze and bit into Luke's pant legs. With a curse, he freed his clothing.

"Enjoying yourself, detective?" Conroy tossed over his shoulder.

"Yeah, it's as much fun as watching the Yankees pound the Sox at Fenway." Luke picked his way through the bushes to join the detective near two uniforms. By Conroy's feet, he found the woman.

"The last break in the temperature melted most of the ice and raised the water level," Conroy told him. "She was a floater who got caught in the brambles."

Luke crouched beside the woman, who rested in a semi fetal position. She appeared small, about five-feet, and helpless. Her arms and legs were twisted and held prisoner in the wild rose's thorns. A tattered white shirt lay open around her thin body, exposing bare breasts. A shredded bra was pushed up toward her throat. Her lower torso was nude, and she wore no shoes. Wet blonde hair hugged her cheeks. Tape wound around her mouth sealed in her secrets. Her open hazel eyes glistened lifelike, staring up at him. Death couldn't hide the fact the woman had been attractive.

"Spooky, isn't it?" Conroy grimaced. "Her eyes make her look alive. I almost expect her to try to speak."

If only they'd found her before the scumbag left her like this. Luke swallowed the bitter taste and straightened. "Her sister mentioned a butterfly necklace when she filed the missing person's report. Anyone locate it or come up with a reason for her to be in Ledgeview?"

"No jewelry found on the body or near the scene. No one's discovered a reason for her move from the Vermont border where she ran a business and rented an apartment. It's a strange one," Conroy conceded.

"We'll find out what happened to her." No one deserved to die this way. Luke's wall of self preservation slammed shut, cutting him off from her pain. "I'll contact the sister."

What or who ended the young woman's life with such brutality? He turned and headed up the bank to speak to Rose Blue in private.

* * *

No one knew who killed the woman. They'd kept their meetings secret. She'd smiled that trusting smile and followed like an innocent follows the devil and his promises. How she regretted that before her death, begging and crying.

The best part was the final moment when she realized she'd never escape. The fear on her face....an adrenaline rush with no comparison!

Today her sister had come looking here, looking there. Keep searching, sister. You'll find me. Until then, I'm watching. My pretty Rose, you were meant for me.

* * *

Rose stared through the morgue glass at the inert body. Her sister, who always had a hint of laughter in her voice and a ready smile, was a corpse. Her wild, out-of-control hair that she fussed over lay limp and lifeless. Rose's chest tightened and she caught only short breaths. The room dipped under her feet. She silently prayed she wouldn't get sick.

"Are you okay?" Detective Lennox stepped forward and guided her away from the glass with a gentle, but firm grip and then released her. "Do you want me to call a friend or relative?"

Who would she call in Ledgeview? Besides the police, she'd only spoken to Dahlia's landlord, and he barely knew her. She gulped in air and the dizziness eased. "No, sorry, I needed a moment. I tried to prepare myself, but staring at my sister on the metal tray like a specimen was worse than I expected." She turned to the six-foot-plus detective in washed out jeans and scuffed leather jacket.

He stared at her with intense, blue eyes he most likely used to intimidate his suspects. A few days' growth of blonde whiskers marked his lean jaw. He hovered at her elbow as though he expected her to faint. His mouth softened, and she swore she heard a touch of sympathy in his voice a moment ago.

"Are you confirming it's your sister, Dahlia Blue?"

"It is." She tugged out her chain from inside her white button down shirt. She held up the silver butterfly pendant with a ruby on each wing. "My sister created identical necklaces for our birthdays with our birthstone. The jewelry's not worth much. But it meant a lot to her, and I'd appreciate it if you passed the jewelry on to me."

"No necklace was found. My men recovered two personal items, a torn blouse and a bra. You're sure she was wearing the butterfly when she disappeared?"

"She never took it off." Rose remembered the day her sister had given the chain and pendant to her.

Dahlia grinned her lopsided smile. *"Happy Birthday, twin of mine. Wait until you open your present. You'll love it. I know because I do."*

"I apologize in advance for bringing up the subject," he said, returning her to the present, "but your sister was awaiting a court hearing on a shoplifting charge."

She flinched and tilted her head to reassess him. Why did he bring that incident up now? Was he fishing for some flaw in Dahlia? "You mean the engagement ring from her ex, A.J. Edwards. Her lawyer worked out the legal matters, and the theft charge was dismissed. The incident was a mistake in the first place. She's not a thief."

"She rented a place in Ledgeview. I'm trying to understand why she left home and moved to a new city. Was she running to avoid court?"

"My sister didn't really move. Most of her belongings are still in Vermont, and she wouldn't take off because of a false charge. She believed her lawyer would prove her innocence. Besides, when Dahlia was upset, she'd lay low, but she'd never leave town. My Gram instilled in us the belief we should never run away from our problems. She was very strong in her convictions, and Dahlia and I loved our hometown. So to answer your question, I've no idea why she came to New Hampshire."

"Did your sister own a cell phone or laptop? I'd like to look at her phone records and emails."

"She was using a prepaid one, temporarily, until our boutique earned out and freed up her money. I don't know what happened to her laptop. She must have taken it to New Hampshire with her, but she was much more a phone person. It was faster and she liked fast."

"I'd guess her laptop is in a landfill in New Jersey or some other unsearchable site. We can look into her ISP, but sometimes their storage is brief."

Rose darted a glance at her sister's body. Her stomach dropped with a sickening wave. "I'd like to leave now."

"I'm sorry for your loss, Miss Blue." Lennox escorted her toward the exit. "Are you registered in a hotel or driving back to Vermont?"

"I'm staying in New Hampshire until you arrest her killer. I drove over from Dahlia's apartment."

His stare bored into her. "Are you sure you want to stay at her building? You're lucky if your sister's rental provides any security. It's an old structure without the safety updates offered in modern apartments."

"I don't need a five star hotel. I'll be fine." *Keep moving through the door. Don't picture Dahlia lying on the table in the morgue. Block the image.*

Outside, she pointed at her vehicle. "My car's the green compact parked at the curb."

He walked her to the edge of the sidewalk and paused. "Miss Blue, I have to ask you a favor. Keep the fact your sister's necklace is missing to yourself."

She nodded. At any minute, she'd break into tears or collapse. She wanted to get away before either happened.

He held out his card. "Here's my number. Call me night or day."

"What about your family? I don't want to intrude."

"You won't bother anyone. Call."

At his last clipped word, she looked closer. An air of

authority that breathed confidence rolled off his broad shoulders. She wished it would land on her.

"I'd like to discuss the progress of the case when I'm more on top of everything."

"I'll keep you up to date," he promised, gentling his voice. His blue eyes met hers. "Don't worry. We'll arrest the person who did this to your sister. She won't be forgotten."

The forceful, steady light of certainty shone through his gaze, and the strong line of his whiskered jaw tightened. She believed him. A sense of relief and assurance poured through her. Palming his card, she slid inside the front seat. She'd meet with Detective Lennox again soon. She keyed the engine of her vehicle and merged into the traffic.

"I won't forget, Gram," she whispered, blinking away tears. "I'll keep my promise to find Dahlia's killer." Her hand went to the weapon's bulge in her pocket.

CHAPTER 2

Monday, Dahlia was buried with her First Communion rosary next to Mom and Gram in Brattleboro's Village Cemetery. Father Mark bent his balding head and said the final prayers in the shadow of the mountain, just beyond the moss covered markers. Several church members, a handful of neighbors and Gram's co-workers from the diner listened to the pastor's words. With the murmur of one final rest in peace, they disbanded for refreshments in the church's basement.

As children, Rose and Dahlia had always whined about attending Sunday Mass, and as they grew independent, they skipped the weekly ritual. Today, the familiar faces added a sense of support and consolation.

Rose accepted condolences and answered the discreet inquires about the investigation into Dahlia's death. Time seemed to drag, and Rose longed to escape. When the last mourner left, she swallowed the lump in her throat and caught up with her friend, Cassie, to discuss arrangements for keeping her store open. A friend since kindergarten, Cassie accepted the job of holding down the boutique until Rose returned.

The next day Rose drove to Ledgeview to follow through on her promise to Gram. She locked herself away in Dahlia's apartment and pulled out the photo album she'd brought back. The pictures always gave her the feeling that she belonged to a real family.

She opened the worn cover and flipped to the first photo of her always sober, gray-haired grandmother. If only her sister paid attention to Gram's favorite warning: "Always work hard and remember the only free lunch sits in the mousetrap."

It was advice Dahlia ignored and her mother botched by giving birth to them at age seventeen. On the next page, Dahlia had inserted a magazine picture of George Clooney with the label "Father" printed underneath.

Rose shook her head and turned to the photo of her mother who could now pass for her sister. The camera's eye preserved her mom's youth at age twenty-five. In her short life, her mother had several boyfriends but never met a man who cared for her beyond a month or two.

Maybe the Blue women weren't born for love. None of them had found it. Not that it mattered. Tomorrow she'd meet with Detective Lennox. She prayed he was about to make an arrest. His intense stare and sharp questions left her on edge, yet his decisiveness drew her to him. She liked the fact a strong man was working her sister's case. He'd find Dahlia's killer.

The memory of Dahlia lying in the morgue hung in her mind. Her lifeless eyes stared forever upward. Her blue lips frozen open in a last gasp.

Rose tossed the album aside, threw on her winter wear and fled the apartment and the painful memory. The cold soon invaded her boots and gloves, but she welcomed the fresh air. She wandered the well–lit sidewalks of the clapboard homes reminiscent of houses from the turn of the century. Their carriage houses now used as garages or altered into small apartments stood a short distance from the main buildings. A variety store and a Laundromat occupied the corners of the next two blocks. As she walked, her mind retraced the last couple of weeks until she stopped.

Where was she, a park? To her left was a fenced-in tennis court without a net and, most likely, abandoned for the season. Ahead a sign stapled to a stake announced the skating hours and rules for the ice.

The wind whistled for a second before dropping to a whisper and transformed into Dahlia's voice calling to her, coaxing and pleading somewhere near the water. Rose hesitated then drew closer to the frozen pond. She peered downward where blond hair lighter than her own floated weightless toward the ice. Her sister's face, a face like her own for twenty-seven years, tilted up, revealing the birthmark under her chin, their one difference. Her bound hands pressed against the invisible barrier. Her hazel eyes screamed for someone to listen. The duct tape over her mouth strangled the last plea for mercy, but the muffled desperate cry reached Rose.

"Help me!"

Oh my, God! "Dahl-ia? Dahl-ia!" Rose's heart jumped into her throat, making her voice shake. She lunged toward her sister, and the crack of the thin ice under her feet warned her away. She retreated to the firm ground and shivered in the frosty air.

In the water, Dahlia's form dissolved and disappeared.

This was how her sister's life ended. Her mouth taped, her limbs bound, she'd been left to drown, to die without hope. Rose swept shaking hands over her face and tried to wipe away the terrifying vision.

"Dahlia, who did this to you?" Chills swept over her. She fumbled with the jacket zipper, pulling the tab up to her chin while a myriad of emotions, shock, terror, and grief left her frozen to the ground. "I'm sorry we fought. I'm sorry I yelled at you."

She shoved her hands into the pockets of her gray parka, hunched her shoulders and struggled with the tears until someone shouting and whistling for a dog brought her back to the surroundings.

How late was it? She'd lost sense of time and place. Shuddering, she grabbed control of herself. Now, she craved traffic and noise, not the solitude of the park where she'd attempted to seize a few seconds of peace. She had to escape her twin's ghost.

Near the plaque for a historic trolley stop, she emerged onto the empty sidewalk. Across the street, large houses with wraparound porches rested dark and silent. It must be close to eleven o'clock. She cut across the street, putting distance between her sister's spirit and herself. Why had Dahlia appeared to her? Was she trying to tell her something, or did she think Rose didn't care about her after their last big fight? How many times during their lives had she given Dahlia one more chance to change? Sharp regret bit into Rose. "I know you were a good person, Dahlia, but you sometimes seemed to lose your way. I'm sorry I wasn't there for you."

"I'll make it right. If it takes everything I own, I'll make sure the monster who killed you is found and punished. He'll never hurt anyone again. I promise."

Rose trotted down Main Street with its two and three story clapboard facades and mixed brick fronts. She passed the dark store windows and locked doors of Minicake Bakery and Joe's Coffee. Above the shops, unlit apartments reminded her of the late hour. At least the city salted and sanded the main sidewalks, but no one else seemed inclined to enjoy a stroll in the late March night air. In their homes, people snuggled in their beds or wound down in front of the television. She was the only one foolish enough to wander out this late. The cold stung her fingers and toes, pushing her forward.

Suddenly the sound of footsteps prickled her skin. She peered over her shoulder. An unfamiliar figure dressed in black trailed less than a block behind. The figure's height and stride suggested a man.

Two more blocks to her sister's place. Throwing back covert glances, she picked up her pace. She'd learned basic self-defense moves but at a lean five feet, she was hardly a match if her might-be pursuer turned out to be a wrestler from a Friday Night Smackdown.

The sound of the shadowing footsteps increased. Was it a coincidence? She broke into a jog. The man's steps pounded behind. Her jog changed to a flat out run. He mirrored her movements. Adrenaline shot through her body.

Across the street, Dahlia's two story apartment bounced into sight. *Hurry. Faster.* She forced her legs to move at breakneck speed. The thud of boots told her the pursuer was closing in. *No!* Her lungs burned from the effort to breathe. Her gasps of breath shot out and trailed behind in the frigid air. She fingered the trigger of the pistol in her side pocket. A stolen glimpse over her shoulder confirmed he'd narrowed the distance between them. A ski mask concealed the pursuer's face. He kept one hand inside his jacket. Was he carrying a weapon?

I'll never make it. She yanked out her gun and peeked behind while swerving into the street to cross.

Brakes squealed. A vehicle's horn blew. Her pistol tumbled

to the ground. A black car squealed to a stop, its hood inches from her legs.

She scooped up the handgun. The driver pulled to the side and slammed the door. Rose clutched her weapon with both hands and met the anger in the six-foot-plus driver's familiar, sharp blue eyes and shadowed jaw.

"Detective Lennox, someone is chasing me." She gestured toward her stalker without taking her gaze from the detective.

"Stay here." Without another word, he took off down the street.

She watched his form grow smaller on the sidewalk. No signs remained of the pursuer. Her breathing evened out. She slid the gun into her jacket pocket, safe for the moment, but her tail could be hiding nearby.

Across the street, her building's main entrance lured her with promises of security. No reason to stand around. She'd speak to the detective later. She headed for the front door and paused to jam the key into the keyhole.

"He's gone."

She whirled around at the voice and stared into the detective's large chest. She backed a step, and her hand tightened on the butt of the gun in her jacket.

"I hope you're familiar with that Thirty-Eight Special." He nodded at her pocket.

"Of course, I legally bought it after my sister went missing and I was out searching for her." Rose wasn't about to admit she intended to wave the gun around and never take off the safety even though she'd taken a crash self-protection course. What are you doing here? You couldn't have just happened by."

"I finished a call and was on my way home. Who chased you?"

She stared up at the towering man in the leather jacket. He was dressed in jeans and running shoes. He watched her closely, and her heartbeat picked up. Was she lucky or unlucky? Had he really been driving past, or had he parked nearby to scope her out?

"Miss Blue?" He wagged a hand in front of her face.

"Sorry, I've no idea who followed me or if he was someone out for a jog." Had she imagined the man pursued her?

16

"Has anyone tailed you before tonight?"

"Never."

His grim façade fell away. "I'm relieved you're well enough for a run, but exercising late at night isn't anything I'd recommend. A young, pretty woman alone in the dark can attract attention she doesn't want."

"I wanted some fresh air. It usually helps my migraines. I can't predict them, and emotional stress doesn't help. Don't worry, I won't repeat my mistake."

"Good to hear. Rest up and come down to the station tomorrow. I'll take your statement then." He stepped forward. "Let me escort you into your apartment."

Without waiting for her answer, he pushed the entry door wide and walked across the threshold. Inside, he paced around the hall, examining the shadows in the corners, and finally yanked on the door leading to the vacant, first floor restaurant. It was locked. She shut the main door and turned the bolt. Safe.

"How long did the man follow you?" His voice held a tone of authority.

"A few blocks." For once, she welcomed the familiar first floor mustiness.

"How often do you go for a run at night?" He seemed to watch her with a calculating expression as though he was judging her.

"The workout helps my insomnia. If you'll excuse me, I'd like to go upstairs to my place. Like you said, we can talk tomorrow."

"I'll go with you." He placed a foot on the first step and gestured upward.

He seemed overeager to accompany her. Did he want to poke around her apartment or had fear warped her perceptions? "I can manage the stairs by myself."

"Humor me." He peered at her like she was a convicted felon. "Migraines, insomnia, and the need for exercise, what else ails you, Miss Blue?"

Killers and ghosts. "You know me already, Detective Lennox," she said, forcing a smile. "I'm ready." She nodded upward.

The detective shadowed behind, never allowing her to get

ahead. Their footsteps echoed in the empty vestibule. She stopped outside her apartment. A piece of newspaper was jammed inside the doorframe crack.

"Wait a minute. Don't open up yet." He wriggled the paper out of its spot.

"Really, I don't care about an ad."

He unfolded the clipping and held the piece of paper in his gloved hands.

She leaned forward. The picture of her murdered sister stared back from the newsprint. Underneath Dahlia's photo, someone had altered the caption with a black marker. Her name, Rose Blue, replaced her dead twin's.

Who'd done this? Was it the stranger who'd followed her tonight? If he left the clipping, he knew where she lived and how to get into her building. *No!*

"I'm going in. Stay put." He swiped the key from her hand and opened up. He snapped on the overhead light and removed his weapon from the belt under his jacket. The sound of his footsteps growing and fading told her where he was in the one bedroom. "All's clear," he said, reappearing in the narrow hallway without his gun visible.

She entered eager to be alone and deal with her raw nerves. "Thanks again, Detective Lennox. I bet you need to get home."

"No one's expected me there for years." He studied the door frame and handle. "No signs of a break in." He faced her. "You should move out of this place. It's not safe." His stare drilled into her, daring her to defy him.

"I'll contact my landlord, Dean Drown, about the safety issues, and I have your number in case of an emergency. Don't worry. I'm not planning any big gestures to trap the killer. I'm basically a coward." She opened the door wider, a hint for him to leave. She needed to speak to Dahlia in the apartment, but would she answer?

He ignored her hint. "I know Dean. He's busy with his new building projects and hasn't installed any security into this one. You'd be better off staying in the hotel across the river where someone can't sneak in and leave you photos."

"It's a piece of paper. I'm sure I'll be safe once I'm locked inside." She had her gun.

The corner of his mouth turned down. "Think about it. I'll secure the downstairs and walk the outside perimeter."

"Good night." After he left, she snapped off the living room light, stole to the windows and pulled down the shades. She wanted to stay in a place where she sensed her sister's presence, from Dahlia's favorite brand of coffee to the sound of her voice.

But Rose wasn't about to act foolishly either. Groping around in the darkness, she tugged a chair from the kitchen table and jammed the frame under the doorknob.

Knowing she'd get little sleep tonight, she removed her gun from her coat pocket. She dropped down on the couch and pointed the weapon toward the door. She whispered a prayer she wouldn't have to shoot, but if her sister's killer believed she was going down without a fight, he was wrong.

"Dahlia? I need your help. I can't do this by myself. I never wanted to be alone." She closed her eyes, and her hand gripping the gun shook.

A feathery caress of comfort stroked across her fingers. She wasn't alone.

CHAPTER 3

At midmorning, Rose whispered a prayer that today would bring Dahlia's killer to justice and abandoned her attempt to sleep. She poured coffee into Dahlia's favorite mug that she'd found tucked behind a bottle of wine. Written on the two sides was the saying: Always borrow money from a pessimist. They never expect it back.

Did Dahlia think of her when she used the mug in this place? It was a miracle her sister had been able to keep up with her rent in Brattleboro, never mind leasing another apartment in New Hampshire. Neither Rose nor Dahlia was making enough from their shop to afford two places.

Rose's shoulders sagged as the warmth from the cup seeped into her palms. Her sister's mug she could handle. She couldn't deal with her sister's bureau sitting in the corner of the living room for her convenience. Maybe tomorrow she'd sort through her twin's belongings, but not today. Yes, definitely tomorrow.

She sipped the drink and stifled a yawn. Images of Dahlia and her faceless killer—he must have been the one who'd run after her on Main Street—haunted her throughout the night. Now it was almost noon. Since she was talking to Detective Lennox today, she needed to get a move on. He asked her for patience while they searched the river. Now they were done. Hopefully, he'd give her new evidence that would lead to an arrest. She gulped her coffee and then jumped into the shower. When she finished, she heard the beep of her phone and found a text from her landlord, Dean Drown, who assured her he was following up on her request concerning building security. Thirty minutes later, she was dressed and headed to the Police Station located at the opposite end of Main.

A brisk jaunt in the daylight would clear her head, and prove that she could walk down the street without glancing over her shoulder every few seconds. She carried her gun inside her purse in case anyone decided to play a deadly game of Pursuit.

First she had Dahlia appearing to her, now she had a murderer stalking her. Life couldn't get much better. Being in a witness protection program or a contestant on the cable show *Wife Swap* would be an improvement. Too bad she was single.

She reviewed her mental to-do list as she walked. Pinpricks of apprehension warned her somebody lurked nearby watching, and ruined her concentration. She was probably on hyper alert to anyone glancing her way, thanks to last night. But neither spirit nor man would stop her.

She paused before the polished stone building. The engraved sign which read "Ledgeview Police Station" hung above the entrance. The letters weren't as pretty as the sapphire font on her shop.

Rose remembered opening day of the Blues Sisters Boutique. They had stood in front of their red brick building. Dahlia wore her favorite paisley dress and a jean jacket. Her bracelets jangled when she turned to Rose in her white starched shirt and beige pants. "We did it!" Dahlia held up her palm for a victory slap.

Rose released the memory and pushed through the glass doors of the station. The hairless desk clerk dressed in uniform led her through the metal detector and into a large room of blues. The buzz of conversation, ringing phones and the click of computer keys, denoted the large work area. Her nose twitched at the pungent scent of a lingering cleaning fluid. Cops threw her glances and resumed their jobs.

The clerk ordered Rose to wait a few feet from a cubicle and then left. She stood near the workers. How long would she stand alone while the rest of the officers pretended she didn't exist? Hurry up, Lennox.

The tap, tap, tapping of the computer keys surrounded her. She turned away and wandered closer toward the cubicle.

"Pay attention, Lennox." A man's tight voice floated over the divider. "We don't need a flatlander who thinks he's hot shit coming in to second guess us. You blew in here and beat me out of this job based on your daddy's reputation. The whole department knows it."

She edged closer to the divider.

"Since you're caught up on the old ladies' gossip," Detective Lennox answered, "you've plenty of time to work on the Blue Case. Go to every store that carries electronics in the Brattleboro and Ledgeview areas. Show them Dahlia Blue's picture and find out if she bought a prepaid phone from them. Then write up and hand me your report by eight tomorrow morning. Got it?"

She couldn't decipher the grumbled answer. A middle-aged, plainclothes man suddenly stalked out from behind the barrier. She dodged to the side to avoid a collision. He slowed with a grunt and marched away, leaving behind the odor of garlic.

"Miss Blue." Detective Lennox, dressed in dark khakis and a light blue shirt with rolled up sleeves, stood a few feet from her. His gaze slid rapidly over her and back up.

Her insides jangled. She would have to be tazered unconscious not to notice the man now that her grief was under control.

"Come inside."

"Any big breaks in my sister's case, Detective?" she asked without moving.

"I'm afraid we're still investigating, Miss Blue. Have faith."

"I'm trying." She tamped down on the pressing sense of urgency. She hadn't really expected an immediate arrest, but she intended to make sure everything possible was being done.

She glanced at the cops ignoring her across the room and walked in front of him. "Friendly place, you have here. I was amazed over the large size of your department. It's big for such a small city."

"Are you a member of a taxpayers association, Miss Blue?"

She hesitated and blinked several times, clearing her mind. "No, I was struck by the number of people in the office. Not that I'm an expert on police forces. I like facts and figures." She was babbling while the detective observed her with a cool glance. If someone gave him a bottle of Maalox, he'd spit out the liquid and chew on the glass. At the moment, she'd prefer to guzzle its contents.

"I didn't mean to offend you. Please, call me Rose. And I'll call you...." She paused, and when he didn't fill in the blank, she added, "Lennox."

She continued past him and caught his aftershave. The pine scent reminded her of hiking in the woods. She wanted to inhale deeply but kept moving into the space crowded with a desk, folding chair and file cabinet. She settled on the cold metal seat.

The crammed area seemed to emphasize his largeness. He inched to his desk, closed up an open folder and set it on top of a pile of files.

"You've a lot of cases."

"Ledgeview hasn't put their old cases online yet." He sat. "Rose and Dahlia. Was your mother or father into gardening?"

She shook her head. "What I remember of my mother, she was more into Woodstock. She died in a car accident when we were seven, and then we lived with Gram, Mom's mom. Gram always said our mother was born in the wrong decade. As for our father, he wasn't into kids. We never met him."

"I'm sorry."

"My sister used to pick out fathers for us from our friends' parents. Thankfully, she never asked one to adopt us." Rose glanced at the picture of a uniformed man standing on a pile of files on top of the cabinet. The man's blue eyes were the same color and shape as Detective Lennox's. "He's a relative of yours, right?"

"He's my dad. My grandfather and father were both in law enforcement."

"I bet your father boasts about you all the time." She heard the twinge of wistfulness in her voice. *Stop acting like Little Orphan Annie.*

"My dad passed over a year ago."

Despite his bland tone, he stiffened and instinct told her she'd touched a raw nerve. What was wrong with her today? Nothing was coming out right. "It's my turn to apologize."

"I understand how it feels to lose a member of your family, Rose. Are you doing better this afternoon?" The change in topic relieved the pressure in his chest he always felt when his dad's death was mentioned.

"I'm fine. I didn't mean to pry about your family." Her face reddened.

"It's all right. I'm here to help with your sister." *And to check you out.* He'd run the background search. She had no record, and spent her time at work or at home. Today, he'd learn more about Rose Blue. He'd study the way she held her body, breathed and her slight body movements. All would betray her if she lied. He wanted a break, a suspect, but the right one. He couldn't afford wasting investigation time on Miss Blue if she was innocent. The balancing act had begun.

"I guess we have a few things in common." She slipped the purse strap from her shoulder to rest the bag in her lap and dug inside. "I wrote up a report about last night." She held out a handwritten two-sided page. "You already received my list of store customers though I'm not sure they'd approve of me giving you their addresses when I promised not to pass them on."

"They'll understand. We're not selling body part enlargements." He accepted the paper and skimmed it. "You work fast, considering what's happening in your life."

"My sister always complained I took life too seriously."

"Being a hard-worker is a good trait." He leveled his full attention on her, and the background noises faded away. During an interview, he always followed his dad's rule. Never let them know what you think, until you read them their rights.

Was she a devoted sister or cold blooded killer? He hid his doubts in politeness. "What can I do for you?"

She pressed her hands against her knees. "Today's the third day since the teenagers found Dahlia, and the investigation feels as if it's moving in slow motion. What's happening at the river?"

"The divers finished their search this morning without turning up any findings."

"That's not encouraging." The muscles in her jaw tightened. "What else do you have?"

"I reviewed other homicides in our state and Vermont, looking for similarities and possible leads. A woman around Dahlia's age vanished close to the Fourth of July. She lived in North Conway in New Hampshire's White Mountains. Her body was found in November, four years ago. If we can connect the two deaths, law enforcement can pool resources to track one killer versus two."

Surprise left her wordless for a second. "You think the same killer murdered my sister?"

"It's only one theory, but the fatalities contained likenesses. Listen, I'm bringing up the possibility because you need to heighten your safety measures, not trudge through the city like a defeated defense lawyer." He allowed his curt tone to show his annoyance. "The message wedged in your doorframe was pretty clear. We can't dismiss the idea a bloodthirsty hunter is out there preying on young women. You don't want your name posted next on the missing persons list."

Her fingers closed around the butterfly hanging on the chain around her throat. "I'm ahead of you. I notified my landlord, and he's working on security today. Apparently, the locks were manufactured in the day of Adam and Eve, and every Adam owns a key to it."

"Good, did you remember anything else about the person tailing you?" He glanced down at the report. "You noted height, ski mask and dark clothes."

"Sorry, I was too busy running for my life to notice more details." The shadow of a frown crossed her face. "What did you do with the news clipping from my door?"

"The lab is testing the paper for fingerprints. I'm waiting on the results."

"You don't really think he'd be dumb enough to leave prints? It sounds too easy."

"The odds are slim, but he'll slip up and we'll get him." Luke leaned forward, and the scent of her flowery perfume invaded his senses. He was suddenly drawn toward her, overcome with the urge to reach out and touch her.

He sat back in his chair, away from the fragrance of her teasing scent. "Tell me about your friends, people in the Brattleboro neighborhood where Dahlia lived. Any hold a grudge or a fascination with you or your sister?"

"She'd only lived in her apartment a couple of months, but she never complained about anyone. We lived in Gram's house until then. She died last year, and we sold the old place and my sister and I each rented a place a few blocks from each other."

"And did you have trouble with the people in your old neighborhood?"

"They were like family. Gram and my mom moved once, after Grandpa died from a heart attack, but Gram said it was one of her worst mistakes. She always used that reminder when the grass is always greener lecture didn't work with us."

He nodded. "What was your sister like?"

"Dahlia never met a stranger. She talked with everyone and was the life of a party. I realize now her behavior was more dangerous than I ever imagined."

"Maybe she accepted a ride from a new friend and never went home again. Other women have disappeared in the same manner."

She tightened her grip on her purse strap. "Don't get the wrong impression of Dahlia. She was a kind person, who sometimes shared her heart too quickly, but was the first to volunteer to help someone."

"Your sister's ex, A.J. Edwards, left Brattleboro. Where can I find him?" He picked up a pen and held it over the top sheet of notes on his desk.

"I've no idea. He left when their relationship ended, shortly before Dahlia disappeared near the end of February."

Luke lowered the pen and studied her. Was it possible she really didn't know where Edwards had gone? Nothing indicated she was lying. "Did he seem upset when your sister broke off their engagement?"

"He was devastated, but not angry. I can't see him as a murderer. Do you? Is that why you're asking?"

"I'm gathering information. Did he owe money or have a drug problem?" Either she knew nothing or was protecting the ex. He made a mental star next to the man's name.

"No to both questions." She blinked at him as though he wasn't for real.

"Did your sister owe money?"

"Dahlia kept up with her bills, though it was hard for her. Except..." Rose hesitated and broke eye-contact. "Recently, she messed up the boutique's account. We had a hard time paying January's rent. The *Blues Sisters* has always been our dream. Dahlia bored everyone talking about the boutique and her jewelry. She was an accomplished silversmith, a natural talent and we sold her creations at our store. I was more the buyer, behind the scenes person. When Dahlia was younger, she designed beaded bracelets for the kids at school, and I sold them. Some kids ran cold drink stands, we sold jewelry."

He sensed she was trying to bury the admission of Dahlia's error with another story. "What happened when your sister messed up your account?"

She lowered her eyes for a second.

He was onto something. "Go ahead."

She inhaled and her breasts under her gray sweater rose and fell with a sigh. His gaze skipped down and back to her face.

Rose wet her lips and admitted, "It was unusual. We're both good with figures. So we argued about the lost money."

"How much?"

She expelled a breath as though surrendering. "She stole two thousand."

"Yet, your sister paid three thousand dollars cash for her Ledgeview apartment's first and last month's rent plus security deposit." He spotted the slight jolt of her body.

"She did? I'd no idea."

"I reviewed her W2 Forms and bank records. The Ledgeview lease money wasn't from her savings." His pulse picked up. Something wasn't right here.

"Maybe she stashed away a rainy day fund." Rose avoided his gaze again.

"Where do you think she got her additional funds for the New Hampshire rental?"

"I don't know." Rose crossed and uncrossed her ankles and finally heaved a sigh. "All right, you might as well know though I've never discussed her problem with anyone. Dahlia helped herself to small items."

"She stole?" He was getting a different picture of Dahlia now, and one that might have led to her unhappy ending.

"Not exactly, she took little objects like pens or a salt shaker from a restaurant. She worked on controlling the problem. There's no way she'd steal the amount you mentioned."

"Her dishonesty must have caused problems for you."

Rose shifted uncomfortably in her chair. "Gram and I had a few tense confrontations with Dahlia and her victims. We always tried to watch her, encourage her and have her replace the items.

And as I said, they were small objects."

"She helped herself to a couple of grand from your business. It sounds like she graduated to taking larger amounts."

"The boutique theft was a one-time thing. In the past, Dahlia stole these small things to get people to see her for herself. She felt everyone saw us as a pair, a set." She shrugged. "That's what a counselor told Gram when Dahlia was first caught shoplifting. She was twelve."

Follow the money trail. "Who would loan her the rest of the payment for the apartment?"

"I can't think of a soul." Rose wrinkled her brow.

"The cash could be a motive for her leaving home. She met someone, maybe online, who was financially well off, and your sister came to meet her online friend. Then she took too many little things from her network pal, who punished her by a swim in the river."

Her face paled, and she shook her head. "You're describing a big time thief, not Dahlia."

"What about the stolen engagement ring?" he asked in a quiet, challenging voice. "I read the report. She stole it from the pawn shop, and it was worth more than a pen."

Rose sat forward on the edge of the chair. Her hands fisted in her lap. "I can explain.

When she and A.J. broke up, she returned the ring to her fiancé. He didn't want it, so he pawned it. When Dahlia spotted the ring in the pawn shop window, she was hurt. She didn't think. She just grabbed it."

"Did your sister sell the ring?"

"No, she cooled off and returned it the next day, but while she was at the pawn shop, a cop arrested her for shoplifting. Believe me, my sister's not a big crook." She paused and fanned her face with a hand. "Is it hot in here?"

She didn't' look well. Her face was the color of beach sand. She closed her eyes and her shoulders hunched forward as though she was in pain. A shiver shook her body.

"Miss Blue?" He jumped out of his seat and reached her in two seconds. "Rose."

She glanced up at him, her eyes glazed.

"I'll call a doctor." He reached for his phone.

"No, don't."

"What is it?"

She straightened in the chair and ran a shaking hand through her hair. "I just saw my sister for a moment. I'm okay now."

"Saw her where?" What was she talking about?

She waited a beat. "How about I give you unknown details about my sister's death?"

"You mean what exactly?"

Her eyes narrowed, and he felt her take an emotional step back for a second before answering. "I was there the night Dahlia died."

He had witnessed unexpected confessions when he worked in Buffalo, but he had to use all his willpower to keep his jaw from dropping. "You went with your sister when she was killed?" He sobered.

Was she a co-conspirator? He'd investigated the insurance angle. Rose received enough from the policy to bury her sister. Nothing else was left. Dahlia Blue possessed no funds to bequeath. She lived financially on the edge. Had the fight over the stolen boutique money prompted the killing? He stood in front of her. "Miss Blue, are you changing your story and confessing to murder or being an accomplice? Wait a minute." He shot a hand in the air. "Remember you have the—."

"You can save your Miranda rights. I'd never harm my sister." She folded her arms over her chest and sat back in her chair. "I'll explain, but you must try to believe me."

He nodded, unsure what was to come next. Resting his hip on the end of the desk he waited for her to begin.

"Remember, keep an open mind. I wasn't literally there." She swallowed several times as though the words refused to come out of her mouth. "Since Dahlia...died, I've been undergoing a few...paranormal experiences."

A ping of caution erupted in his chest. He worked to keep the surprise out of his voice. "Paranormal meaning–?"

"The night she died, I was with my sister because I entered her mind, but I couldn't make out everything, or I'd pinpoint the location."

Was she serious? Luke reconsidered her. Possibly, he'd let her attractive face mislead him. It wouldn't be the first time, but he'd sworn off pretty females long ago.

"You were in your sister's mind?"

"Kinda. I watched." She shrugged and held out her palms. "My explanation sounds odd, but we sometimes shared feelings, experiences—though nothing like when she was murdered. Last night, for instance, I saw Dahlia in a pond, the way she died." Rose paused and swallowed. "I believe Dahlia cried for help, and she brought me to her when she was killed."

The woman was original. At least she wasn't spouting the worn out my-controlling boyfriend-forced-me defense, or the Ledgeview River Monster did it. "Can you remember anything about the killer? Shoes? Tattoo?"

"I'd guess she was murdered by a man. His form was more of a shadow. I think he attacked from behind because I felt the blows." She laid a hand on the back of her skull and winced. "Then my sister fell down onto the rock. Her killer tied her up in duct tape."

"But you weren't really hit? Have you always been psychic?" If this story didn't work, would she claim aliens beamed down the information?

"I'm not. Except for the night I described, Dahlia and I always communicated in the normal way, and I've had no luck talking to her so far. Let me explain." She gripped the top of her purse. "Growing up, my sister and I experienced the usual identical sibling occurrences. We chose the same toothpaste, shampoo, but nothing like the night she died. Once Dahlia broke her foot, and I experienced the same pain although my foot was fine. It was a twin thing."

"A twin thing," he said, taking in the information.

"I've talked with a few people and found out not everyone develops their psychic ability at an early age or recognizes it. I'm guessing the fact my grandmother strongly discouraged us having our own twin talk or sharing mentally interfered with my psychic development."

"Sure." Had the woman told him anything truthful?

Rose gripped her hands together. "Gram was very religious and brought us up in her faith. Anything supernatural or in the psychic realm was against our beliefs. It was a sin. I wasn't about to go against Gram or our church. I always denied mental communication with my sister and passed it off as intuition, but now I realize the ability was always there. We often knew where each other were or felt without words, unless we were fighting or blocking the message."

"Were you fighting when she disappeared?" he asked, observing the nervous tightening of her hands.

"Yes." She shifted in her seat with discomfort. "We argued over the boutique's missing funds. Since the night Dahlia died, I've been trying to communicate with her, but I haven't made much progress."

It sounded like a crazy story to him, one he'd have to be crazy to believe.

A corner of her mouth turned down. "I can't clarify that horrible night's experience much better except I'm certain it happened to us, Dahlia and me." Rose stiffened when he didn't comment. "I'm not good at explaining what went on, but I swear I'm telling the truth."

"Describe the site of the murder for me." He picked up the ballpoint and notebook.

She stretched out her open palm. "Let me draw it."

He passed the writing utensils and eased back to wonder about her sanity and his own. The drawing would be the ultimate test. He was in a tight spot in the investigation. With the new ME unable to pinpoint the exact time of Dahlia's death because of the water temperature, he was left with only a weak estimate. Rose could have committed the crime and be leading him on a merry chase, starting with the sketch.

"My sister was the artistic one, but I'll give you an idea how it appeared to me." She bit her lip and set to work. The sound of the pen's tip scratching across the paper filled the cubicle, and all the background noises had long ago faded.

"Dahlia hated heights."

"I can sympathize with her. Flat ground is where I prefer my feet. How about you? As a twin, did you share your sister's fear?"

She stared at him, appearing to be judging him, deciding if she should share her secret. "I never reveal or discuss my personal fears, but since you're working my sister's case...spi—ders." Her voice wavered with emotion. "I hate them."

"Spiders?" Not an unusual phobia or what he expected to hear. "I understand. How's your drawing?" He bet it was a place that didn't exist and no one would find.

"I'm almost done. I'd guess the killer knew about Dahlia's phobia, bound and dragged her to an old, iron bridge. He threw her off to watch the ultimate horror on her face as she fell." Though the words were spoken softly, there was an underlying sadness mixed with revulsion in the rigidity of her body. She set the pencil down before flipping the drawing toward him.

"Dahlia was attacked on these boulders." She pointed to the ellipses, and then lowered her finger to the wavy lines beneath the stones. "This is the water below." She bent her head, breaking eye contact. "The bridge where he tossed her over seemed to be an old train overpass."

The picture on the paper leapt into his mind and grew until the matching scene came into focus. A granite ledge appeared out of the woods and sloped into the river below. A few yards north stood the remains of a deserted railroad trestle. A jolt of recognition hit him with a punch that nearly knocked him over.

"Besides my search of the Brattleboro area, I surfed the internet for hiking trails and campgrounds in New England. Nothing resembled my mental image of where she was murdered. My car was in the garage the week she disappeared, and I was limited to bumming rides to hunt for her. I should probably broaden my searches now."

"Rose, don't bother chasing down anymore sites. I know the exact place where your sister died."

CHAPTER 4

They'd had the perfect night at the perfect place. Everything had been a dream. Their evening together played over and over. In the daylight the rush disappeared and the daily grind took its place.

Now Rose had come. She walked the streets around Ledgeview. Lived in the same apartment.

Could a flower by any other name be as sweet as dear Rose? We'll meet soon in the spot your sister and I loved.

"You drew The Ledges that are on the outskirts of the city." Luke tried to hide his excitement and speak in a professional manner. "It's an unofficial recreation area. During the summer, families picnic on the boulders and swim in the river below the rocks. But after dark, they say the place is haunted. Only the local high school kids risk going in the evening for the occasional drinking party. The police chase them away, but unless they assign a cruiser to patrol all night, it's a lost cause. The teenagers make it a personal challenge to stake out a claim and sneak into the place after sunset."

"Let's go." Rose jumped to her feet, letting the picture drift to the floor. "You are available immediately?" She glanced at the files cluttering his desk. "If you're too busy, I'll drive out and search around for myself."

"You'd have better luck taking a cab to find Amelia Earhart. No one hangs out at The Ledges in the cold weather. The place is abandoned."

She bit her lip and seemed to consider his words while Luke

33

examined her hovering form. The gray sweater hugged the curvy shape of her slender body. Dark pants covered long legs that fit into low–heeled, black shoes. Waves of dark blonde hair fell around her colorless face and onto her shoulders. The lack of makeup didn't hide the fact the woman was a knockout, but something else about her held his attention. Although she'd controlled her voice when speaking about her murdered sister, her eyes told him a different story. When he gazed into them, he felt like he saw not only her pain, but her broken heart.

What was happening to him? He'd become soft, a marshmallow man, and that could be dangerous in his business. Damn. The woman could be playing him. If she'd done her homework, The Ledges was the perfect spot to pinpoint. Who would contradict her? Yet, she couldn't know about the fax he'd received about the currents from his friend, who worked for an ecological firm and ran a few quick tests as a favor. The results indicated The Ledges was the number one spot for the victim to have entered the river.

"I want to show you something." He stood up and opened a drawer in his metal cabinet. "This report came in a couple of hours ago." He drew out a file and tossed it on his desk watching her reaction to the report.

"I see." She lifted her chin and placed her hands on her hips. "Science confirms my story so you have to believe me." She dropped her hands.

The fire in her voice told him she didn't agree with skipping the trip or like his doubt. If she'd something to do with her sister's death, she covered her reaction to the latest news like a pro.

"Remember smart and caution are words I like to practice, and in your case, they should be the most important words in your dictionary," he advised.

"Got it, smart-on will be my words to live by." She gathered up her purse.

"Hold it." She didn't have a clue what a murder investigation detailed. "In a homicide case, everyone needs to prepare for difficult questions and unpleasant answers. You might not like what we learn. The truth can hurt. You can opt for a daily written report instead of hands on investigation."

She flattened her palms on his desk and leaned forward. "I'm not patient about sitting around and waiting for censored notes. You're also forgetting I'm your prime witness or victim's family or both, depending on how you view my role."

The woman was right. He'd never find a better eyewitness or a suspect, and he could observe and judge her truthfulness close up. "You've won me over with your persuasive discussion."

"I had you at *witness*."

"You bet, but if you think you can go on ride alongs or participate in questioning, you should know up front that's impossible. I have procedures and chain of custody and—"

"No problem, can we leave now and skip lecture number 5,029?"

"Is anyone else with you, waiting somewhere? You said you were alone but—"

"I'm traveling solo."

"The trail leads through the woods, and the snow sticks longer in the shaded areas. You should pick up boots for the trip."

"You're afraid of cold feet, detective? I don't have time to go shopping for footwear."

He pulled on his leather jacket. She was right. Daylight promised to last for only a few more hours. If they didn't head out soon, he'd find out if ghosts walked The Ledges at night.

Rose glanced out the window. "Can you fast forward or give me the short version of your speech? I want to arrive before midnight."

"I've one last reminder. I'm paid by the public to protect, and if I advise you to stay somewhere—"

"Smart-on, Lennox." A sudden smile lit her features.

Her grin changed her features, softened it and added a touch of vulnerability. If Rose Blue was a killer, she'd won his vote for best actress in the innocent role. "Let's go."

As he exited the front door, he ran into Buddy on the sidewalk.

Buddy Drown swiped a strand of dark hair away from his forehead. "Requesting clearance for entrance."

Luke paused next to Rose on the sidewalk. "Bud, we're on our way out. Were you coming into the station?"

"I'm afraid I need your detective skills for a couple of minutes. Sorry to butt in during your business hours, Luke, and Miss—?" He turned toward Rose.

"Miss Blue," she offered, clutching the strap of her purse and putting one foot forward.

She was anxious to leave.

"It's nice to meet you, Miss Blue." Buddy scratched his head. "Did we meet up before? You look familiar."

"She's new in Ledgeview, Bud. What's the problem?"

"I've misplaced my phone. Have you seen it? I might have left it in your car after the game the other night."

"I'll double check later. Now's not a good time."

"Gotcha. Guess I'd better phone Shauna before she starts worrying when I don't answer her call. We've three months until the wedding, and she already has the wife's where-have-you-been part down." He flashed a smile, revealing even white teeth. "Miss Blue, welcome to Ledgeview. Luke, don't forget you're coming over tonight to let me win our bet and all your money. Shauna's doing a night out with the girls and won't be manning the stove. We'll order out."

"As long as you don't make me eat your cooking, I'm in."

"You're safe." He slapped Luke across the back. "Glad you're home. It's going to be like old times around here again. Catch ya, later." With a nod to Rose, Buddy headed off.

"Sorry for the delay," Luke said to her. "Bud's an old friend."

"Sounds like you're close."

"He and I go back years. Buddy's the next best thing to a brother." He strode toward his car with Rose keeping pace.

"I have to ask one more thing before we leave. Do law enforcement officers gamble?"

He stopped at the corner. "The loser springs for a super sized meal at the local fast food. Do you have more questions for me?"

"Where's your car?"

"I parked in the rear." He led the way to the lot behind the building.

In the close quarters of the front seat, the scent of her sweet perfume teased his nose again.

He forced himself to concentrate on the traffic. His companion seemed deep in thought and oblivious to him. Luke broke the silence by pointing out his old high school, the local hospital and adding it was the biggest employer in the city. "Things haven't changed much since I left five years ago."

She tossed glances in the directions he indicated but remained quiet.

He changed the conversation, hoping for more of a response. "I understand you headed your city's Main Street Committee."

"Did you investigate me?"

"I look at everyone. It's my job."

"Good, I like thorough. As for the committee, I used to joke that Dahlia was my campaign manager. She won the election for me with her ability to schmooze with everyone. She also was my sounding board. I bounced all my ideas off her before I presented them."

"Did your sister swim or hike? I was wondering why she'd tramp around The Ledges in cold weather."

"Dahlia was more the indoor type. Her idea of exercise was walking to the TV set to push the on button instead of using the remote. As I said, I've no idea why she came here."

"In your visions, are you ever on the path leading up to The Ledges?"

"None that I remember."

"You never visited our city as a child or later?"

"I've never been here."

He was getting nowhere with his questions. "We'll need to be careful when we're walking around at The Ledges. The ridge can be dangerous and a bad place to slip or fall."

"I'm aware of the risk, and you're here to steady me."

"This is the first time a woman wanted to fall into my arms after one meeting."

"Don't flatter yourself, Lennox. I plan on keeping both feet firmly underneath me."

He mulled over the turn in the case and the possibilities. If Dahlia was murdered at

The Ledges, traces of evidence would be long gone after the last thaw. He was crossing his fingers for a one in a hundred shot. What would happen once they walked out on the boulders? Would Rose assume the role of injured sister or act like a psychic in the movies, pretending to see dead ones? He'd find out in about fifteen minutes.

After ten miles, he drove onto a narrow, winding road and parked on the dirt shoulder. "The state owns most of the land. It's largely floodplain and unbuildable. Wait here while I scout out the area." He pocketed his keys and swung the door open.

"Now's a good time to learn two things about me, Detective. I don't do windows and I don't do waiting around." Her hard countenance disappeared. "At least I don't do either one well. Besides you need my help to confirm the spot. How long is the walk?"

"If you insist on coming, we've a five minute trek through the woods to the rocks. Then you can verify if it's the place."

She slid out to stand on the gravel shoulder and studied the woods and road.

He grabbed sunglasses from the visor and imagined her view of the spot. No cars, houses or people were in sight. They were alone in an isolated locale. On top of the shrinking snow bank sat a half empty grape soda bottle. Well, not totally alone. Someone had passed through recently.

He hopped out of the vehicle. A black crow flew out of a tree with a loud caw and circled over their heads, protesting their intrusion before flying off.

"Nice welcome." Rose pressed closer to the car. She folded her arms around herself.

"Are you okay?"

"Sure." She dropped her arms and stepped away onto the dirt edge. "It's chilly today. Ready to go?"

Rose was one contradiction after another. She seemed fragile, weak and yet on the other hand, determined and tough. "I'm all yours." He marched toward the path with her scurrying after him. The tree branches fluttered in the breeze, and the cool air seeped through the warmth of his jacket. "Wait a minute." He retraced his steps, ducked inside the vehicle and dug out his camera from the glove compartment. He slipped it into his pocket.

She stood where he'd left her, blinking her eyes rapidly.

Was she having a vision? "All set or do you need a few minutes?"

"I can't wait. After you."

"The trail starts near the pine grove." He headed toward the track with her beside him.

Patches of snow clung to the ground as they headed deeper into the woods. The sound of their footsteps breaking through the crusted layers mixed with the creak of tree branches bending in the breeze. He reached a two foot snow bank, tramped over and stopped to work out a sliver of ice.

She hiked over the mound to join him. "You must know the trail. I can't see any signs of where to walk."

"I'm relying on instinct from the old, high school party days, but I'm letting you in on one of my dark secrets, Miss Blue. My dad would have ordered a military court-martial for me if he knew what I'd been up to. I grew up listening to his stories about the suspects and criminals he arrested. Underage drinking would have qualified me as one of his lawbreakers."

"My Gram was old school, too. I often thought that my mother was the opposite. She never outgrew her teenage rebellious years."

"How about you? Were you rebellious?"

"If you call being in the honor society and president of the marketing club defiant."

"They had a marketing club in high school?"

"You were too busy with your wild parties to notice." Rose slapped her hands against her thighs. "Okay, Squanto, which way do we go?"

"If we head toward the river we'll find The Ledges. I can hear the water running. This time of year, the melting snow feeds the current, and the river runs high and fast."

"Thanks for the warning. I'll cancel the dip."

"You should pay attention to my warnings."

"Just a little levity, Lennox. It helps when I'm nervous."

"Understood." He shot pictures of the area while she stamped her feet. Then they started off again. The scent of evergreens bobbed in the air. Sunlight filtered through the treetops, dimming the light as they traveled deeper into the woods.

"Recognize anything?" he asked over his shoulder.

She paused. "I'm positive I never walked through a forest in my visions." She jammed her fists into her jacket pockets.

"Don't forget. You can go back if you feel overwhelmed."

Maybe she needed an out.

"I can't forget. You keep reminding me." She shivered. "It's colder with the trees blocking the sun. Spring is two weeks away, and I still need gloves."

"Good old Spring in New England. Most people agree we slide out of winter right into summer, but they're forgetting the season in between."

"Spring?"

"Mud season."

"Ah, I understand why New Englanders visit Florida."

"My mother would agree. She loves to call and inform me of the temperature on the beach in front of her Florida condo."

"I'd be tempted to join her during a blizzard, but not today. Lead on, Detective Lennox."

They plodded forward. The ground sank under their feet in the muddy places exposed to the sunlight.

"Where are we? All I see are the tree branches in my face." She bent to avoid a low–hanging limb.

"Don't worry. A few more feet and we'll reach the end of the path. Listen, the river's louder.

She stood still. Her head tilted upward.

"Recognize anything yet?"

"Nothing."

She was going with Plan C, "see no evil." He dropped back and stayed glued to her side as they trekked out toward the brighter light. She focused her gaze straight ahead. Instead of the vulnerability he'd sensed a moment ago, there was only purpose. Was she as strong as she was acting? Cripe, he should have come alone and shown her the pictures of The Ledges when he returned; he'd been too anxious to disprove her bogus story.

"I hope I find something familiar." She sped up her pace.

"The clearing is after the curve."

They entered the tree line where she halted. Bushes and the few stubby trees grew between the woods and the rocks. Then she plowed ahead. He pushed on to catch up to her.

"Is this the place?"

"Dahlia didn't know the way either," she said, staring off.

Was she falling into a trance? His gut chilled.

"She followed someone to The Ledges." Rose slowed and

stretched upward on her toes. "I can't see the person, Lennox."

Relief poured through him at the sound of his name. "You're probably too nervous. Walk around a little." He raised an arm and pointed to the protrusion of granite. "Here's where people sun themselves in the summer." He strode onto the top of the gray, flat boulders. The familiarity of his surroundings chased away his suspicions. "If we could travel back in time, we'd be standing in the middle of the glaciers." He flung his palms out at his sides. "I'm always amazed by these stones."

"If we could travel back, we'd learn the truth about my sister's death." Rose sidestepped closer to him and massaged her forehead.

"Are you all right?"

"Small ache, no problem." She lowered her arm and focused on the drop–off.

Six feet away, empty blue sky melded into the rock as the ridge disappeared to slope downhill and meet water. The sound of the rushing current filled the cool air. "The daredevils dive off the edge into the river."

"Dahlia would never do that." Rose turned around in a circle while inspecting the ground. "We won't uncover any footprints on this ground."

"I'm afraid not. The sun has melted the snow out in the open. Does this location match what you've seen in your mind?"

"The stones are the same." She twisted her fingers in front of her.

"Take a few minutes. No pressure."

"No pressure," she mumbled, inching further onto the smooth surface before it slanted away. The rubber soles of her shoes scuffed against the rock and she wobbled for a second.

"Watch out." He jumped forward and slipped his hand under her elbow. Hell, all he needed was for her to faint or fall.

"Thanks. You can let go now. I'll be careful."

He released his grip, but remained glued to her side.

"I have to see the water." She edged out on the ridge, her mouth in a tight line.

He crept along at her heels until they stood on the crest. Below the dark river surged at their feet, snaking past with speed and power that swept chunks of ice and fallen branches along with it. He removed his camera and shot the water at different angles.

Biting her lip, Rose worked her way down the uneven incline.

He stuffed the camera in his pocket. "Where are you going?" Damn. He caught up and grabbed her arm. "It's not safe. We need to go back. Rose. Rose, are you listening?"

She stared upward. Her jaw dropped. "I see Dahlia," she whispered.

What! With the sound of the water roaring in his head, he must have misunderstood. "Your sister is here?" He scanned the empty rocks and saw only trees and sky.

Rose nodded.

"Where is she?"

"Up there!" Rose pointed to the rise above them.

He shot a gaze up to the ledge with moss but no ghost.

"She's gone." Without a warning, Rose started upward.

"This is dangerous, especially if you slip into a vision." He glanced down at the swirling water and imagined the river swallowing him or Rose within a second. He snapped his attention to her. "Wait up!"

She didn't answer, but kept climbing upward.

Damn, this was one of his worst ideas. He didn't care if she was for real or as big a fake as Bigfoot or the lip synching Grammy winners. Below the white, frothy white caps of the river almost dared him to fall.

"Here!" Rose shouted from the peak. "My sister stood on this ledge a minute ago."

"Great." He hiked up beside her. "Now, let's move to level ground."

"There's the railroad trestle." She pointed past his shoulder. "We should get closer to it."

To his far right sat the rusted bridge. "Most of the piers are rotted out. No one goes out there, especially me." He repressed a shudder.

She jerked her head toward the tree line. "Someone's coming."

A chipmunk scampered across the path and up a tree trunk. Sweat broke out on his palms. "Okay, this is enough. We found the place. Now we're going back to the car." He seized her hand, but she stayed cemented to her spot. "Rose, did you hear me?"

"He's almost here. He has a surprise."

Despite his better judgment, Luke peered into the woods, searching, listening.

"I'm waiting. Hurry."

Save me, she'd lost it completely. "Rose, we're leaving." She didn't respond. "Rose, am I talking to you, or are you Dahlia?"

She twisted around to him. "What?"

"Did you see Dahlia near the woods?"

She crossed her arms and rubbed her mittened hands over her sleeves. "Dahlia's gone, but I still feel her. She trusted him, the man who was coming."

"Did she expect more than one person?"

Rose shrugged. "She didn't know. She didn't understand."

"Try to see or remember. Who's coming? Is it a man? Is he tall, dark, young, old?"

Rose grabbed his arm, forcing him to face her. "Lennox, Dahlia didn't understand."

"Understand what?"

"The man is coming to kill her."

CHAPTER 5

"We're out of this place," Lennox said. "The Ledges gives me the creeps. I don't remember getting the same menacing feelings when I was younger."

"Sorry to ruin your memories." She kneaded the sides of her temple. "I need to go home and lie down. Then I'll be okay." Her gaze skipped to the old railroad trestle.

Dahlia, dressed in her pink parka with her hair blowing in the breeze, teetered on the edge of the railing. The wind whipped her blond hair over her face. She stepped off the side and disappeared into the air.

Pain stabbed Rose. She gasped and turned toward the path, blocking the image.

"I don't understand what's happening," he said, gripping her arm, "but we're leaving. Lean on me, and don't give me any guff."

It isn't real. It isn't real. Please, Dahlia, speak to me. The pressure of Lennox's arm drew her closer to his warm, firm body. "I'll be okay once I'm in the apartment."

"I vote for that one."

She stole a glance at the trestle. Dahlia was gone. Rose swallowed hard, her mouth drier than a month old bagel. On the trail, she crawled along at a tortoise pace to ease her aching head and used their earlier footprints as her guide. Lennox's arm fell away as they walked in rhythm. She wished he could take away the hammering. The reality between herself and Dahlia felt off-balance, blurred.

Lennox threw her glances but said nothing as they trudged through the lingering snow and the darkness of the woods. The path seemed to go on forever. She breathed a sigh of relief when they reached the road. Years must have passed since they first arrived. She wouldn't be surprised to stare into the mirror and find her hair turned gray. She eased into the car.

He sat silent, his brow wrinkling in apparent thought while she fastened her seatbelt.

"You might as well spit it out, Lennox."

He expelled a breath. "I wasn't sure who I was talking to when we were on the ledge."

"You and me both." She gestured toward the road. "Can we go? I'm afraid the worse has happened. I'm actually longing for the lumpy sleeper in the living room."

The engine rumbled to life, and they were on their way. Resting her aching head against the top of the seat, she welcomed the warm sunshine on her skin and closed her eyes. The purr of the motor was a soothing constant in the background.

"Rose. We're here. Rose?"

She sat upright. Her headache had disappeared, leaving a sense of exhaustion. Her building stood in front of them. "How fast did you drive?"

"I'm sworn to uphold the law and the speed limit. At the risk of sounding like a bad echo, how do you feel?"

"Tired." An image of the gray boulder from The Ledges edged into her mind. She blocked the picture by fastening her attention on him. "Since my sister died, I never sleep without dreaming, until right now."

"Are you accusing me of being so boring you dozed off?"

"Not quite, but since you mentioned it...." She pushed down on the door handle.

"Don't move."

"I was kidding, Lennox. You're not bor–ing." Her last syllable hung in the empty air.

He'd jumped out and was headed for the passenger side.

"I expect you'll whip out the wheelchair next," she said when he opened her door. "I appreciate your concern, but I don't need a nurse. Let me walk to my apartment or I might believe I'm helpless."

"I'll stay a pace behind just to make you feel healthy."

"You're thoughtful." She resisted rolling her eyes and fished inside her pocketbook until her fingers closed over her key. Rose held it up to him. "Ready." She started toward the front stoop aware of the handsome detective at her shoulder. "You'll wait until I get inside?"

"I'll do you one better. I'm walking up the stairs with you."

"That's not necessary." She shook her head and proceeded to the steps and paused. "What's on the schedule for tomorrow?"

"I'm going to talk to dad's former partner."

"How about *we* visit your retired officer now?"

"No, and he'll only know more when *I* see him."

"I'd like to meet him." She inserted the key into the lock. "Keep me in mind. I can be useful."

"Miss Blue," a man shouted to her.

She whirled around with a clenched hand in the air. Her heart hammered a warning.

Lennox's friend, Buddy, held up two fingers. His boyish next door looks softened her fright. "I come in peace."

"Sorry, I'm a little jumpy today." She lowered her fist.

"Is this what hanging with a homicide detectives does to the beautiful women in Ledgeview, Luke?" He pinpointed his gaze on Rose.

"Buddy, what brings you round, again? Ready to concede you picked losers for tonight's game and want to surrender your money ahead of time to avoid total humiliation?"

"You wish. Actually, I wanted to talk to Miss Blue."

At his constant staring and open interest she had to force herself not to back away.

"I met your sister."

"Dahlia?" Rose's chest tightened.

"You knew Dahlia Blue and never mentioned it until today?" Lennox crowded closer to his friend. "Why didn't you come forward sooner?"

"Take it easy. I mean met in the briefest sense of the word. It was a hello, nice to meet you and goodbye. Our get-together didn't reach the national security level. Let me explain." Buddy scratched the back of his neck. "Your familiar face bothered me, Miss Blue. The truth hit me after I drove by a minute ago, and I u-turned." Buddy paced a couple of steps away with nervous energy. "I hope you're not offended that I brought up your sister. I should have remembered when we first met earlier today."

At last, someone with news about Dahlia. "How did you meet my sister? Was she happy when you saw her?"

Buddy shrugged his shoulders. "I can't comment on the happiness factor. We crossed paths once at the Audi, the Ledgeview Auditorium, when I went to drop off donated clothes. She was answering an ad for a gofer at the theater. While we talked, Myra, the play director, appeared and convinced her to try out for a part in their latest production."

"What day did you deliver the clothes?" Lennox asked.

"It was March first, the day before my engagement party. Mom loaded me up with donations from her store for the Audi's costume department."

As he spoke, Buddy seemed to be watching and judging her every move or reaction. An uneasy quiver crawled across her back.

"How could you forget you'd met a murder victim and then happened to remember while driving past?" Impatience sharpened the detective's voice.

Buddy shook his head. "Blame it on pre wedding nerves taking over my mind, and the fact I'm about to take the big step. I never dreamed a two minute conversation was earth shattering. Your sister and I only exchanged a few sentences before someone directed me downstairs to leave the clothes. I found out she wanted a job and was going to try out for a role."

Rose mentally brought up the silhouette of her pursuer closing in as she raced for her apartment. Her would-be-attacker's height matched Buddy's. No, he didn't, or did he? She stepped away for a better view, afraid of what she'd find.

"Is everything okay?" Lennox asked her.

His incredible eyes were narrowed in concern for her. She could drown in his attention. Wait, what was wrong with her? First she was seeing ghosts and attackers everywhere and now fantasizing about a man. Of course her sister would crash headlong into a flirtation with Lennox, and when Rose disapproved, Dahlia would shake her head and lecture her on lightening up, enjoying life. Look where enjoying life had gotten Dahlia. "I need to go inside."

"I hope I haven't upset you." Buddy whipped out a pair of sunglasses from his pocket and perched them on his nose.

The pain in her jaw warned Rose she was gritting her teeth. "I have a lot to think about."

"Did you ever speak to anyone at the station about meeting Dahlia Blue?" Lennox turned his pointed stare on his friend.

"Why should I?" He shrugged twice. "I've no idea what

happened to her. Be real."

"The fact you might help the police never crossed your mind." Lennox's face tightened.

"Dean reported to Detective Conroy that he rented to the victim when she was first reported missing."

"Dean's a model citizen. I'll come to the station tomorrow and you can interrogate me." He directed his gaze to Rose. "Miss Blue, if possible, enjoy your stay." Buddy moved toward the street while talking and stopped. His shoulders sagged for a second before speaking. "Is your apartment working out?"

"You mean Dahlia's apartment." Why was he interested? She pivoted toward the three-stories. The building offered a shelter from the weather and a place to hide behind locked doors. Now, she took in the lower fake brick facade and the peeling, green window trim. The red vinyl covering the upper portion stood out against the other refurbished brick structures on the block.

Inside, the apartment's high ceilings, the wide planked floors and the long windows were features that drew Rose. In fact, the temporary shelter reminded her of Gram's house where she and Dahlia grew up after age seven. Their house had been old and needed work but a warm glow filled her when she recalled the rooms with Gram's doilies, handmade curtains and the whistle of the tea kettle.

Today, she saw her sister's rental as Lennox must view the place, easy to pry a window or door open in this aging structure.

"Is there another way in or out besides the front one?" she asked Buddy.

"The other exit is through the hall door near the stairs," he said. "You end up in the empty Chinese Restaurant, but the door was always locked. I bet the key doesn't exist any longer. No one will ever get rid of the fried rice odor."

In the restaurant's window, her reflection overlay the *For Rent* sign. As she watched, Buddy's image merged and then wiped hers out.

Her heart pounded a double beat, and she retreated a few steps. She caught Lennox staring at her with a question on his face.

"I hope Dad gave you a deal on the rent, Rose. I mean not everyone wants to live in the apartment of a murder victim."

Charming, a homicide in the building explained why Dean was eager to lease to her. Hold on. Dean, her landlord, the middle-aged man in the business suit, was Buddy's dad? "You're Dean Drown's son?"

"You're the only person in Ledgeview who didn't know." Buddy grinned. "Hey, Luke, did you ask my dad about his whereabouts for your investigation?"

"His statement is already filed."

"Figures. Old dad gets an A plus."

Rose held the image of Dean next to Buddy, searching for a resemblance. Mr. Drown was shorter and stockier than his son. He had an olive complexion Buddy didn't share.

"Are you in real estate too?" Rose asked.

"Not really, I'm Dad's gofer. He says he's teaching me the business. I'm really in-training for a secretary slash handyman job."

A white car beeped and pulled up to the curb. "Speak of the paternal devil." Buddy frowned at the vehicle.

"The sidewalk is getting a little crowded," Lennox observed as the older Drown parked.

"Your father's spotted you. Your get away window just slammed shut."

Stenciled across the white Cadillac's sides were the words: Drown Real Estate. Dean Drown hopped out. Unlike his son, he was dressed in a gray suit and overcoat. His clothing could easily hide a muscular man. Had he hauled up her sister's bureau by himself to the second floor from the basement where it was first stored after her sister's death? Dean had suggested bringing it upstairs for Rose to go through.

Could he be her late night pursuer? She compared the two men and gave a mental shake of indecision. Everyone seemed to match the size and shape of her mystery hunter. She needed to get away and clear her mind. Suspects were everywhere.

"It appears we're having a family reunion." Buddy gave a hollow laugh.

"Hello, Rose," Dean said, taking off his sunglasses. "Luke, it's good to see you."

"Dean, how's your new building on Fifth Street filling up?" Lennox asked.

"I've a bite for one of the first floor suites. Hey, Bud, your mom just told me you're coming to dinner next week. How'd she lure you over?"

"The meal's not for me. Mom wants to celebrate the return of the infamous Luke Lennox. She should have told you." Buddy fast shuffled toward his car.

Dean pivoted to follow his son's movements. "She was busy and filled me in quick."

An awkward silence hung in the air as Buddy opened his car door without acknowledging his father's last statement. Buddy's mouth was set in a mutinous, straight line. Finally he raised his head. "Bye, Rose. Luke, bring your wallet tonight."

The engine roared to life, and Buddy zipped away.

Dean's shoulders sagged as he watched the silver SUV disappear into the traffic. At about five-feet, eleven-inches tall, Dean was handsome in a rugged way. He had high cheekbones a model would envy along with a perfect square jaw. His only obvious physical defect was his thinning brown-hair cut long to blend in with his receding hairline.

He was still staring at the pinpoint of Buddy's SUV. He flicked a glance at Rose "Adult children, who can understand them?"

His voice reminded her of a radio broadcaster with a deep, generic accent. "They're always busy. You're too young to know what I mean." He straightened his shoulders and smiled, easing the moment. "I dropped by to let you know the locksmith changed the locks today. Here's your new key." He passed it to her.

"Thanks for your promptness."

"Your safety is a priority. Let me know if you need anything."

"As long as my main means of cooking–the microwave–functions, I'm happy," Rose said.

"Luke, guess we'll get together soon." Dean glanced down the street where Buddy had vanished and then back at Rose. "I'll drive over to my office. You have my number if you have any problems." With bent head, Dean trudged toward his parked vehicle.

"Mr. Drown, wait. Are there any other ways to get inside besides the front entry and the connecting door in the hall? What about the side and rear entrances?"

He paused with his hand on the car's handle. "The restaurant's doors are always bolted. The fire code requires a fire escape, and yours is outside the living room window. You'll find a release bar for the last flight of steps on the railing."

She'd seen the rusty stairs and vowed never to set foot on the death trap, but Dahlia's killer might sneak up.

"Anything else you wanted to know?"

She shook her head, forcing her immediate worry to the back of her mind. Dean climbed behind the wheel and drove off.

"Are you planning a fire drill?" Lennox asked.

"I'm making sure the place meets code. What's up with the Drown men? They seem to barely tolerate each other. Their office must be a fun place to work."

"Normal tensions between family members. Both Dean and Bud would go to bat for each other if one of them was in trouble."

"You didn't mention you were good friends with the entire family."

"Drown's Realty is known throughout the city. Good thing Dean showed up or you'd be locked out."

"Your job would be to help me, right?"

"I'll help now. Try the new key, Rose, and I'll enter first."

She inserted her key, and Lennox pushed the front door open. Inside, he circled the empty vestry. Pausing, he flipped on the overhead light in the dim hallway and walked to the edge of the floor beside the staircase.

She hesitated on the threshold with the cool air circling around her. "No slasher or masher is hiding inside. Satisfied?"

"My ex wife never thought so. Go ahead."

He had an ex, she mulled as he dogged her heels up the stairs. At her door, he insisted on inspecting her apartment.

This is a good thing, she told herself, pacing in the upstairs hall. Not every woman has a detective to inspect her apartment.

"Clear," he said reappearing.

"We're on for tomorrow," she reminded as he headed toward the stairs.

"No, *I'm* on for tomorrow. Lock up, Miss Blue." He nodded to her and left.

She bolted the door and threw her purse and coat on the kitchen chair. Finally she breathed a sigh of relief. She listened to a phone message from Cassie that all was well at the boutique.

A pain of homesickness tugged at her when she shut off her phone. At least her friend sounded happy. She bet Cass would marry a man like her father and enjoy a life with husband and two point one kids. Cassie was unlike the Blue women who seemed to find love in all the wrong places. Cassie's past boyfriends were regular upstanding members of the community. Although she had only brief relationships, they remained friendly toward each other. Dahlia's breakups were always traumatic for all involved. She'd cried for days over her breakup with A.J. and sobbed about how much she once loved him. Then she disappeared two weeks later. If she and A.J. had stayed together, maybe Dahlia would be alive today.

Since Lennox announced his suspicions of her sister's ex, Rose had begun to scrutinize and question every scene she could remember with him, seeking sinister motives. Where was he? Was he somewhere near Ledgeview?

She compared him to her pursuer. In his boots, A.J. would squeak by at five-foot-ten. The idea the man her sister had trusted and wanted to marry might have killed her set lose a panic. Rose closed her eyes, reining in the helpless feeling. Lennox could be wrong. She'd wait for him to produce proof of A.J.'s guilt. Then she could blame herself for giving her blessing to a killer.

From her suitcase in the corner, she pulled out her journal. In the galley kitchen, she sat and began to write the events of the day. After she finished, Rose massaged the tightened muscles in her neck. She tossed the diary into her suitcase, and zipped the top. She removed her butterfly necklace and tucked it away in the top bureau drawer closer to her reach.

Bed called to her. She yawned and dropped onto the couch, throwing the blanket over herself. She'd pull out the sofa sleeper in a few minutes, once she had some energy. A loud thud startled her. She stared into the darkness waiting for her vision to adjust. She must have fallen asleep. What was the noise? It sounded like somebody fell against her door.

"Who's there?"

The hum from the electric clock was the only response.

She sat up. The blanket fell away, and she hugged her arms against her chest. The room had turned cold. What happened to the heat? She stood and snapped on the light. A draft of air swirled around her ankles. The clock read 11:55pm.

It was freezing. She followed the flow of air to the space beneath the bottom of the door and cracked it open. The overhead light illuminated an empty hallway. A frigid breeze flowed toward her. The main entryway must not be closed. She'd bet the farm on Facebook her neighbor was responsible. The guy was strange. He rode his bike through the city with an attached boom box blasting away day or night.

She ran across the hall and banged on the door. "Hello, hello, you left the door open."

The silence from his apartment yanked on her nerves. Okay, she'd shut the entryway. She retreated to her kitchen and grabbed her gun. She remembered the motto she'd told Lennox. "Smart-on."

Back in the hallway, the quiet hummed in her ears. She tightened her grip on the weapon and sprinted to the top of the stairs. Below, the main door stood wide open. She was right.

Sounds of a vehicle passing on the street drifted inside. She hesitated. An uneasy feeling tempted her to retreat. No, she could do this in two minutes, and she was armed. She hustled down, keeping the entryway as her finish line. Putting on a burst of speed, she reached the door, slammed and locked it. Done! Lennox had no reason to worry about her.

She turned to find the door to the abandoned restaurant open.

What was going on? She crept forward. The outside streetlight lit the room. In the puddle of light on the floor, lay a severed hand holding a rose.

CHAPTER 6

Rose hovered near the stairs to her apartment. She gestured toward the empty restaurant. "I can retrace my steps and show you how I found the hand and flower."

"Stay where you are." Lennox crossed the hall and stopped at the open doorway. He reached inside and the click of a switch echoed in the empty room. "Electricity's not working. I doubt Dean would shut the service off. It's not good for showing a space to prospective renters." Lennox entered the adjacent room. "Someone removed the light bulbs. Answers the power question."

She climbed a couple of steps and stretched up on tiptoes to spy through the open doorway. What was he doing in there? Were more body pieces scattered across the floor? She pressed her fingers to her mouth and fought the urge to run upstairs. *Buck up, Blue.*

She drew her gun and crept into the restaurant. Lennox was shining the beam of his flashlight over the severed hand. Somewhere a handless person must be spouting a pool of blood. She gulped a deep breath and prayed everything would stay put in her stomach.

He turned around and crossed the floor to her. "You were to stay near the stairs." He extracted the weapon from her hand. "We'll head up to your place."

They walked in silence to the staircase where she couldn't wait any longer "What did you find?"

"Rubber hand, the type you can buy at a costume store."

"What? A sick-o left the body part as a joke?" She couldn't

believe it. "I'm not laughing." At least her queasiness disappeared. "How about the flower?"

"Fake too."

She cleared her throat. "You shot over to my apartment for nothing. I apologize." She pivoted around to go upstairs.

He cut in front of her, blocking her escape. "You're missing the big picture. Whoever left the presents wanted to scare you or worse. The perpetrator painted the fingernails *blue* along with choosing a *blue* rose for you. He was sending a message and not a friendly one, Miss *Blue*."

Nerves jangled in her stomach. "You think it's the same person who left the newspaper clipping?" She chewed on her last remaining fingernail. Had someone hidden in the defunct restaurant, left the gifts and watched her discover them? She glanced into the corner shadows, and her hand slid toward her empty pocket. She should retrieve her gun.

"I can't rule it out. Whoever dropped off your newest presents is at the least, a sadist who gets off on scaring women. Listen, I've a guest room at my house. You'll have plenty of privacy, and no one will bother you. I live alone, and I'm not home much. You can lay low until you find another place."

No, she wouldn't leave Dahlia. She had to try and talk to her and learn who'd killed her. "I'm sure it's all a sick joke. Maybe a teenager left me the hand and flower. My sister's story was in all the papers and on TV." Yes, that was reasonable. She felt better already.

"Does your answer mean you're rejecting my offer?"

"I am. I'm not giving that creepy person the satisfaction of thinking he scared me over a couple of pieces of plastic. Besides, this type of gag sounds like a kid's idea."

"You're aware of my professional opinion to the contrary."

"I get it."

"Then stay glued to your spot while I look around some more." He dug out a mini flashlight and stole back into the empty restaurant.

Her nerves tightened and twanged. She didn't like being alone after her new discovery. She skirted the doorway. "See anything?"

He moved closer to the restaurant's main entryway and shone

the light on the frame. "The lock was picked. Must be an amateur from the marks left. I can dust for prints after you're upstairs." He placed a gloved hand on the knob and gave it a twist. The door swung open with a creak of protest.

Rose crept forward. The musty odor followed her across the room. She swung a glance around the grimy dining area. A person could hide behind the long bar in the rear. A sick dread squeezed her chest as she inched toward the counter, and then, held her breath and peeked behind. A torn and dirty mattress lay on the floor. "A person's living here," she yelled. "I bet it's the stalker who chased me. If you hadn't shown up the other night..."

"Forgot how to stay in one place, Rose?" He was beside her in seconds. He flashed his light over the bedding. "The blanket probably belongs to a homeless person. The shelters close this time of year, but the nights are still cold. They search for cover wherever they can. It's not unusual to find them in an unused or a deserted business like this one." He rested his flashlight on the bar top. "When the weather warms up, they'll camp down by the river. The bank is a mixture of teens seeking privacy and street people hanging out."

"I hope you're right." A person who lived under the stars seemed harmless compared to a homicidal maniac hiding under her bedroom. "Though I'm not sure a street person living in a tent or makeshift house could afford to buy a plastic hand and a rose."

"Stealing or finding them in the trash are possibilities. I'm calling in my men. We'll work the restaurant. You need to leave." He grabbed her elbow and steered her across the floor.

"Lennox, you must have been a bodyguard in another life. I like it."

"I'm just doing my job, Miss Blue." He released his grip in the hallway.

"Some stranger holed up underneath my apartment makes me crave my gun."

He narrowed his eyes at her.

"I won't use it since I'll be okay with you downstairs."

"I want you to remain locked in your apartment the rest of the night. Don't wander out. I'll talk to Dean and find out if he knows anything about his uninvited guest."

"Don't worry. I've no intention of coming downstairs, and I don't sleepwalk. I hope you find who left the gifts." She headed upstairs with the detective ushering her from behind.

The sound of the main door slamming followed by shuffling footsteps sounded in the downstairs hall. Rose froze on the stairs. Lennox halted a step behind her.

Was her stalker brave enough to walk inside with law enforcement present? Had she deluded herself into believing he would stay hidden and away once he saw she wasn't alone? Her hand went to her empty pocket. She turned around and faced the detective. "You have my gun," she whispered.

"I know." He made no move to retrieve it.

The footsteps grew louder. She braced herself, gripping the rail and fastened her attention on the figure jogging up the stairs. He raised his head, and his step slowed when he spotted them.

"It's my neighbor." She stopped clutching the banister. The young man slipped in and out of his apartment across the hall at all hours. He was about twenty, tall and wiry. As he drew closer, he shifted green eyes toward her and slid them away with a blink. His bandanna–wrapped head bobbed an acknowledgement.

The guy was strange, no doubt about it. He always dressed in the same clothes: jeans held up by a black belt that appeared ready to fall off his slim body with one release of a belt hole. A gray jean jacket and a pair of scratched work boots topped off his ensemble. Around his neck, a cross hung from a chain and clunked against his chest with each step. The weight of the crucifix could easily tip him over. He was probably stronger than he appeared. The young man carried a boom box in his tattooed hand. His gaze landed on Lennox and flickered away.

He stopped two steps below Rose. "Did somethin' happen?"

"You tell me," Lennox said.

"I got nothin'." He shrugged and pointed above. "Gotta go."

The detective cut in front of him and held up his badge. "Remember me? I'm Detective Lennox. We spoke the other day about your former neighbor, Dahlia Blue."

He swallowed, and his Adam's apple bobbed up and down. "I hardly knew her. What's up? Did another person die?"

"I'm here about a break-in. We found the connecting door open, and the closed restaurant's locks picked. Have you seen any strangers entering or hanging around the building?"

"No." He shot a glance toward the entry and back to Lennox.

"Any ideas who broke in?"

"Nope. But book 'em." A grin spread across his face.

Lennox's jaw tensed. "This is serious. A woman died. The moment you see anyone prowling around inside or out, you call me immediately. You have my number. Use it. Do you understand?"

"Right, I sp-eye." He pointed to his eye with a grin that disappeared when Lennox glared at him. "I really gotta go now."

Lennox stepped aside, and her neighbor thudded up the stairs.

"Does he resemble the man who ran after you?" Lennox asked Rose, watching the young man disappear into the upstairs hallway.

The question set free the quivering in her stomach. "No, why would he bother to chase me on Main Street when he lives across the hall and could catch me coming or going?"

She caught the flicker of disagreement as he raised one brow at her. "I don't know much about him. We've never been introduced. I nicknamed him Bike Boy."

"His name's Todd Clark. He's twenty years-old, works as a fast food cook and lived on the outskirts of Ledgeview with an aunt until about two months ago when he moved into this building. After Detective Conroy and I interviewed your Bike Boy, we paid the aunt a visit. She knows nothing is her story. Todd claims he only saw your sister twice. Both times, he passed her in the hall without speaking."

"He could be lying."

"I believe everyone's lying until I find collaboration." He held out his palm for her to continue upward.

"Distrust in a police detective is a reassuring trait," she tossed over her shoulder. "No one will put something over on you." She ran up the rest of the stairs energized by the lure of security. No newspaper article met her at her apartment doorway. What a relief.

Lennox insisted on checking inside before she entered.

She waited two minutes and then crossed her front door

threshold. The odor from this morning's toast greeted her as she walked inside.

He reappeared in the kitchen. "You were supposed to wait for the all-clear from me."

"I feel safer inside the apartment. No monsters under the bed, I presume."

"Do not open up for anyone and call me anytime. Got it?" He handed her the key. "Your weapon is on the counter. The safety is on. Put it away."

"I will."

"Good." He turned to go.

Maybe she could delay him. "Lennox?"

He paused with his hand on the knob.

What should she say? I want you to stay with me? Her mind went blank as he skimmed a gaze over her face.

"Rose?"

"Sorry, I wanted to say, thanks."

"I'm—"

"You're just doing your job. I know." She shut the door and listened to the sound of his footsteps until they faded away. Detective Lennox would be easy to get used to having around. He was also great to look at, and his confidence added a sense of protection she lost when she was alone. At least he'd be nearby for a while. She paused, struck by her own foolishness. He was a policeman, not Superman. But what was the harm in a little fantasy? She needed a lift.

Not that he'd care about a woman who screamed when she found a plastic hand. She wasn't off to the best start in Ledgeview.

Stepping into the small living room, she walked past the sofa and chair covered by tan throws and crossed to her sister's pine bureau. Rose took out her silver chain with the butterfly pendant from the drawer. The small rubies decorating their wings winked in the light from the lamp.

Rose closed her eyes and felt the wet tears trickle down her cheeks. "I miss you, Dahlia. I prayed for you to come home."

The day she'd confronted her sister at their store crashed into her memory. Dahlia had denied stealing from their store to Rose's face. Rose had yanked off her butterfly chain and thrown it at Dahlia. "I can't believe a word out of your mouth. I don't want to see you ever again."

Afterwards, Rose found the necklace on the floor where her sister let it fall.

If she'd never said those words to Dahlia, she'd still be alive. Rose wouldn't be alone. With trembling fingers, she fastened the jewelry clasp around her throat. What had happened to her sister's necklace? Unlike Rose, Dahlia never removed her favorite piece.

Rose studied the butterfly in the mirror above the chest. "I will find Dahlia's killer. I won't let him scare me away."

Her image in the glass rippled and warped before suddenly clearing. "What—?"

She squinted at her likeness. Where was her jewelry? It was missing in the reflection. What was going on? She peered closer. A birthmark marked her chin in the mirror—Dahlia's birthmark.

A cold sweat popped out on Rose's forehead. With unsteady hands, she reached up toward her neck. The cold metal tip of the pendant against her fingertips told her the truth. She was wearing her necklace.

Her sister whispered, "We will be together. Soon."

The memory of the night with Dahlia was fading too soon. The urge for more haunted each night and day. But no hunt was needed.

She was here in Ledgeview. She'd come to him. Perfect.

Now the nights were filled with visions of Rose and waking up in a sweat, hard, anxious, wanting her, longing for her pain.

Don't hurry. Make it last. Soon, the appetizer would be the taste of fear on her lips.

CHAPTER 7

"A fan left the graffiti message, DEATH TO THE PIGS, under the station's sign. Is he in solitary on bread and water yet?" Buddy Drown slouched against Luke's cubicle wall. Dressed in jeans, leather boots and an open blue parka he seemed ready for spring skiing, not questioning in a homicide case.

"I missed the message. I came in the rear, but I'm sure a team member will canvass the area and remove our new ad right away." Luke sidestepped to the door and called out to Conroy. Where was he?

"If you're looking for that middle aged detective who's always eating, I heard him tell someone he was going out."

Great, Luke thought. Conroy was supposed to meet him this morning to plan their next step in the investigation. The man had skipped out.

Luke tamped down on his irritation and dug out his notepad from underneath the cold case files. "I'm surprised to see you so early. Have a seat."

Buddy sat on the chair in front of the desk. "I came to do my civil service, and don't worry about being assigned scrub duty. Some sublevel officer was cleaning off the graffiti when I arrived." His eyes lit with amusement. "You looking for me to pay up on the bet I lost? To be fair, since you canceled watching the game at my house, I think you should forfeit your winnings. That's the same as yelling uncle in the civilian world."

"We have an old family saying, Bud. Work gets in the way when you want to play." Lennox flashed back to late, last night. His men had canvassed the old Chinese Restaurant and then up at The Ledges searching for clues. The portable lights shone well into the late hours, but they'd come up with a big fat zero at both places.

"I bet you're hoping I suffered a breakthrough and can remember an earth shattering clue in the death of that murdered woman."

"You're here because you can help me track Dahlia Blue's movements. Think back. You arrived at the Audi on the first Thursday in March with the donated clothes. Where was Miss Blue when you first saw her?" He picked up the pen, ready to jot down notes.

"She was standing on the stage, waiting to talk to Myra who was ordering everyone around. I'd never seen the woman before so I was curious. She wasn't the Audi type."

"What do you mean?"

"They're frustrated thespians dying for a last chance on a stage. Miss Blue stood out."

"How?"

"You're serious? Okay, I can go with your Law and Order questions. For one thing, she had a life ahead of her that didn't include a Medicare payment in her near future."

"What did you say when you first met?"

"I said hello, told her my name and that I was delivering clothes. I explained about mom's store, told her to drop by and mention we met. Tia would give her a deal."

"You're always the salesman."

"I was taught by the best, my parents."

"What happened next?"

"She said she was waiting for a job interview at the theater. I wished her good luck. Myra joined us and sent me to the basement. I left the donated clothes and never saw the Blue woman again. She didn't stop at Mom's either."

"Did you send her to Dean's real estate office for the apartment?"

"Nope, she told me she found his advertisement online. Do you want me to swear on a bible I spoke the truth, the whole truth and nothing but what you wanted?"

"We'll skip that part today. If you think of anything else, let me know."

Buddy rose.

"One more thing, Bud. I'm asking everyone who had contact with Miss Blue to give me a calendar of where they were from February 25th to March 11th."

"Are you serious? I'm a person of interest because I said hello?"

"I want to rule you out."

"Shauna keeps a calendar. Since I'm with her all the time, I'm sure she can clear me. Am I free to go?"

"You were always free." Luke closed his notebook.

"Until the wedding and then I'll be saying, anything you want, dear." Buddy grinned and shoved away from the chair. "Wait until Shauna hears I'm a suspect in a murder case."

"Skip the torture part, Bud."

"The sleep deprivation was the worst."

"That's called staying up too late."

"You should know." Buddy shoved his hand in his pockets and left.

With his friend gone, Luke's thoughts wandered to Rose. Her image from last night refused to leave his thoughts. Her full lips were pressed together, trying to hold back fear while she gripped a gun. He held the picture in his mind and focused on her mouth, imagined tasting her lips. A surge of anticipation rippled in his nerve endings.

He shook his head and released his daydream. Forget the flavor of any part of Rose Blue. He'd enough grief in his life. *Don't get involved with another woman and mess up your life.* He'd keep his head down and do what he did best, solve cases. Still, as scared as she was, Rose had done what he'd asked. She stayed away from the evidence and called him immediately. He'd give her a gold star. That was until she seemed to get her second wind and started wandering around the old restaurant.

He blocked out the buzz of activity floating over the cubicle walls of his office and returned to the online search he'd begun before Buddy's arrival. First, he'd read about the psychic Jamison twins who'd become famous for world predictions, locating missing persons and solving homicide cases for the police.

They appeared legitimate. Maybe Rose was on the up and up.

If she could help solve the murder of her sister, he was willing to listen.

Then he reviewed information on psychic ability. Articles confirmed many people didn't develop their skills until they were adults.

At the sense of someone hovering, Luke spun his chair away from the computer. Over his shoulder, Conroy was reading his monitor.

Luke hit the sleep button. "You want to know what I'm doing? Show up for our meetings."

"I've been working." Conroy stood in front of his desk, his face pinched with tension. "Nothing's turned up on the hunt for Dahlia Blue's phone. Don't know where she bought the prepaid her sister claimed she owned." The detective's onion breath hit Luke's face.

"You came in for that? Where's your written report?"

Conroy shrugged. "I'll email you. What's the plan for the divers? Without warmer temperatures, we're done at the river."

Luke fought the urge to ream out the other detective instead of discussing the case. His father always warned him impatience was his worse trait, but Conroy's attempt to freeze him out of his own investigation needed to end.

"I expect you to show up on time for our meetings and then go to work."

Conroy smoothed his face into a bland expression. "Whatever you say."

Luke balled up a sheet of paper on his desk and threw it in the basket instead of at the other detective. "We're done for now at the river. If we'd come up with a scrap of clothing or the victim's necklace, I could validate continuing, but we didn't."

"Evidence of a weapon helps a homicide, too. I think the sister killed her twin" Conroy raised his head and glanced over the desk. "Do you have any donuts?"

"I'm not a donut shop." Luke tapped his fingers on one of the files. "Stay on topic, Conroy. I spoke to the members of the Brattleboro Downtown Merchants. They confirmed Rose was present during their planning meetings for the Main Street Spring Fling. The group met during the ME's estimated timeline for Dahlia Blue's death."

"The sister still could have driven to New Hampshire, killed her twin and gone back to Vermont in a few hours."

"Except, her car was sitting at a garage waiting for a part."

Conroy's forehead wrinkled in lines of concentration. "She rented a vehicle."

"I called the rentals in the area. None reported a woman with the name or description matching Rose Blue using one of their cars."

Conroy scratched his head. "She took a taxi or borrowed the wheels. Someone will step forward when they hear about the murder. I'll give the Vermont press a statement."

"Pass out the one we released to the Ledgeview News and you should re-interview some of the Vermont neighbors and boutique customers."

"What's the verdict on the foot search around The Ledges?"

"Unless the foot team finds a lead today to support expanding the area, we're finished up there."

"That'll make the men happy," Conroy commented.

"That's what I live for."

"Yeah, that memo got lost," Conroy said.

Luke sat back in his seat, forcing himself to relax. "While you're in Vermont, I'll interview the sister again and hit the theater where the victim was last seen. I'll grab the cast list. If anything breaks, I'll let you know."

Conroy grunted and headed out.

Luke pushed away his ire and fixed his attention on the notes he'd written about Rose. His exasperation faded. "Who are you, Rose?"

When she spoke about her sister, he sensed her vulnerability, yet she was confident and took center stage when she talked about her business. He'd spent part of the last few days, reading the interviews the Vermont police had passed onto him. They all described Dahlia Blue as full of life, creative, friendly, good sense of humor and enthusiastic about her boutique. She shared a close relationship with her twin.

Many of their friends and neighbors then launched into a description of Rose. They described her as 'dedicated, committed to her job.' One even went so far as to call her 'overzealous.' No one referred to her as their close friend or confidant. Instead, they used words like private, reserved and surrounded by invisible boundaries to explain her. He'd heard similar words from his ex wife about himself

He remembered the day she'd told him she'd spoken to a divorce lawyer.

"Why would you speak to him?" Luke asked, unable to understand what was going on.

"You can't be serious." His wife's lower lip jutted out, and she jammed her hands on her hips. "You're never home, and when you are, you think and talk only work. There's never been us time for a movie or a conversation in the last two years. We lead separate lives. If you'd paid attention when I told you we had a problem or how I worry about you on your job, we might be having a different discussion." She paused in her tirade and wet her lips. "I've tried to be patient, to be the cop's wife, but I can't do it anymore. I'm done. We, and I use that word loosely, are done."

He'd felt blindsided. After their painful split, he'd spent months examining his relationship. But it wasn't only women, his conscience reminded. If he'd paid attention to his father's feelings, his dad's life would have ended differently. Luke had skipped his dad's birthday, Father's Day celebrations and spent less than ten minutes wishing his parents a Merry Christmas on the phone for the past five years. Luke felt the familiar punch of regret to his gut. He wouldn't get caught in another relationship that would end in the same crushing hurt and doubts. It was a sad fact that he had a better connection to Old Charger. At least his car never let him down.

He switched his attention to the web search for Dahlia. None of the online social networks revealed a Dahlia Blue. Had she used a different name? "Didn't you want to visit Tweet land, Miss Blue?"

Forty-five minutes later, he clicked out and sat staring at the blank screen. Where was a clue, a lead? He swiveled away from the monitor and toward his printer. He swiped up the sheet from the feed with the article from the Brattleboro newspaper. He stared down into the face of Rose's sister with one arm around a dark-haired, husky man. Underneath their picture, the caption announced the engagement of Miss Dahlia Blue to Mr. A.J.

Edwards.

Holding up the nuptial announcement, he contrasted Rose with her sister. Rose's hair was a shade darker but otherwise the two appeared to be identical. Did these twins share the same tastes in food, movies or men?

Despite his earlier promise not to think about Rose, his thoughts stayed on her. He remembered the shape of her body when he'd pressed her close to his side at The Ledges. Afterward, the scent of her perfume clung to his clothes. For a moment, he imagined the flowery fragrance as he sat at his desk. He inhaled a deep breath and swore Rose's perfume was suddenly in his space.

He ran a hand over his face. The woman brought problems along with her perfume. At The Ledges, her wide, innocent hazel eyes were fixed on him while she announced unknown details about her sister's grisly murder. He could guess what would happen if word got out she was able to relay information from her dead sister to him. The guys at the station would love that one, and the Chief would be all over him, demanding physical evidence to back up each of her tips.

Lucky for him, the Chief was away for a few days at his daughter's wedding. When he returned from the celebration, he would want Luke's results. If Rose was lying and misleading him, he'd pay.

His gaze fell again on Dahlia's wedding announcement. Her ex worked as a mechanic on foreign cars. Luke would try tracing him through garages in the nearby states. It was too much of a coincidence that the guy disappeared when Dahlia did.

Luke grabbed his father's cold case files from his desk. No time to look for clues about his father's death today. Luke stuffed the folders into the cabinet and locked the drawer.

Frank was expecting him. He grabbed his leather jacket from the back of the chair, but stopped at the sound of the fax machine whirling into action. He stood waiting for the news to spit out. Finally, he snatched up the paper. One word leaped out at him: *Forensics*.

* * *

Rose paced the length of the living room, paused and glanced at her watch again. Lennox had called and told her he'd swing by to talk. His voice had sounded low and hurried when he announced he'd be there in less than five minutes.

She tilted her chin upward. "Gram, I sure hope Lennox found Dahlia's killer."

Rose shoved the blanket on the sofa bed aside and sat down. The fragrance of rose tickled her nose. Where was that scent coming from? She inhaled, trying to determine the source. The scent grew stronger. She rubbed her arms, feeling a draft. She leaped to her feet and spotted her.

Dahlia stood at the end of the room in front of the two windows with the shades drawn tight. Rose stifled a cry.

Dahlia's wet hair was plastered to an ashen face. She raised bound hands toward Rose.

"What do you want?"

Dahlia pointed at her.

"Me?" She struggled to breathe before she rallied. "Please, Dahlia, I need *your help*. I can't find the person who murdered you. Tell me his name."

Her sister's image dimmed against the white wall.

"Wait! Why did you come to Ledgeview? Why did you leave home? Who threw you off the bridge? Give me a name or a description. How do I find him?"

Dahlia vanished from the room. The rose perfume and the cold air disappeared.

"Okay, I've had enough." Her sister never cooperated. Rose stuffed the gun in her purse, scooped up her coat and left the apartment. She fumed over Dahlia as she ran down the stairs. Her sister always went by her own agenda, coming in to work late, leaving early. Outside Rose welcomed the ordinary sounds of traffic and people passing without disappearing or glancing her way.

Why was Dahlia haunting her? She must want to send her a message, or maybe her sister was playing a game to drive her crazy. Dahlia's sense of humor was often twisted or juvenile. Rose stomped to the other end of the walkway and zipped her parka to her chin though the temperature was close to fifty.

How long would her sister's ghost appear? Was her time short or forever? Rose stopped in front of the steps. Cars shot past, and the odor of exhaust mixed with the cool air. She paced the walk for several more seconds and scanned the street for Lennox. The back of her neck prickled. Someone was watching her. "Dahlia?"

No hint of rose cologne floated in the air. It wasn't her sister. The feeling was different, almost nauseous. Who was spying on her? Rose whirled around, searching the sidewalk, the fronts of the other buildings and the empty parked cars at the curb. Her hand went to the gun inside her purse. She closed her fingers around the weapon. Other than the vehicles driving past, she detected no other movement on the sidewalk or street. Was it her imagination?

A dull ache vibrated in her head. The street warped. Daylight dimmed. The apparition of the path through the woods raced in her mind. Footsteps crunched in the snow. A shadowy figure hovered over her sister, Dahlia, lying on the ground.

No, not now. Rose's hands dampened. She closed her eyes, forcing the image and sounds away. She needed to stay alert. She couldn't have a vision. She wasn't a TV. Perspiration broke out over her skin. She squinted at the traffic passing by. No one tossed a glance her way.

The image of Dahlia pointing her bound hands inched into Rose's mind.

She stepped closer to the building. The roar of the current filled her ears. The river, dark and gray, raced across her mind. She ran a hand through her hair and wished she could tear the scene from her brain.

The sound of wheels squeaking on the sidewalk grabbed her attention. A gray-haired woman pushing a shopping cart shuffled toward her. Beyond she spotted Lennox's dark car at the red light. The light turned green, and his vehicle headed toward her. She ran to the curb and jumped inside before he had a chance to cut the engine.

"Didn't your mother teach you to wait until the car comes to a complete stop before diving in?" Lennox asked, irritation raising his voice.

"Forget your coffee this morning? You sound a little grouchy, and my mother would rather teach me how to catch a cute guy's attention for a ride than lecture me about safety."

"Your mother sounds a little… different."

"She was different. She was a teenage mother who never grew up. Raising children wasn't Mom's forte. Even before her death, Gram was our main care provider. Mom was always leaving us with her to go off somewhere."

"Speaking of somewhere, why are you outside? I was planning on meeting in your apartment. Rose, your stalker could drive past and mark you for his next victim."

"I didn't want to stay locked up inside for days."

"You are supposed to lock yourself up."

She reached up and pushed the metal knob on the door. "I was getting claustrophobic in the apartment, and I couldn't stop thinking about my sister. I was starting to see things."

"What do you mean? Are you okay?" He leaned toward her. "Your face is almost gray."

"You're so sweet, Lennox," she said in a flat, disapproving voice. "I'm a little jittery. Scenes of my sister kept appearing in my head like a bad horror movie." She clicked in the seatbelt and crossed her arms over the front of her parka. "I needed some fresh air and went out."

"Did your sister talk to you again?"

"Sorry, nothing to report." She twisted the strap of her purse in her lap. "You do believe we communicate, don't you?"

"I'm skeptical by nature."

"Good, no one escapes your scrutiny as a suspect. What did you learn when you searched the restaurant? Did you find a lead? Was that the big news you hinted about on the phone?"

"We found a few candles near the mattress. Everything could have been left a year or a few months ago. I alerted Dean he had a possible squatter living downstairs. He called the locksmith and reamed them out for not replacing the side and rear entrance locks. My men and I nailed boards across the restaurant exits and entrances last night with Dean's permission. No one will get in again unless they carry a battering ram."

"I heard the hammering. What happened to the mattress and footwear?"

"A courier drove everything to the lab. The chance of getting a suspect's DNA from an old, well-used mattress is slim." He keyed the engine and backed into the street.

"I hoped you were about to make an arrest. Guess I was

dreaming. We're striking out everywhere, Lennox. Today has gotta be better. Where are we going?"

"I scheduled my visit with Frank, my dad's partner and a good friend. Since you're in the car, you might as well come along. But if anyone asks, it's a personal visit, not official police business. We can't risk having legalities questioned if we go to court in the future."

"Absolutely. Where does Frank live?"

"He's about eight miles out. But I wanted to talk to you about other news. First, I interviewed Buddy. He confirmed he only met your sister for a few minutes at the Audi and never again. More important, a fax came through from the state forensics lab a few minutes ago."

"Did we hit the jackpot, a lead to the killer from The Ledges?" Her seatbelt held her in place as she shifted toward him.

"Not quite. We discovered squat at The Ledges. No fingerprints or skin cells were found on the duct tape I found or the newspaper stuck in your doorway."

She sank against her seat. "Your news isn't encouraging. I thought you found something."

"No prints or skin cells from the North Conway victim either, but they analyzed the duct tape used on your sister and the other woman. The lab traced them back to the same lot."

"Which means?" She waved both hands in the air, hoping to speed him up.

"Duct tape lots have their own numbers, and minute similarities can be detectable in a lab. Since the tape used in the two homicides came from an identical roll then..."

"Okay, you're saying a serial killer murdered my sister."

CHAPTER 8

They'd all been perfect. Naïve, trusting girls who believed no one would hurt them. Rose was one of them. He saw it in the way she roamed the streets alone. Trust would be her downfall.

The police would search for her because it was their job. Then she'd fade from their memory, but not all. She'd always be one of 'the special girls.'

"Technically we don't have enough proof at the moment to label your sister's killer a serial, or that your stalker is the person who murdered Dahlia," Lennox said. "Here's what I believe. One assailant murdered both women and possibly more in the past, and if not stopped, will continue in the future. In these types of cases, there's often a pattern of physical similarities among the young women who died, and the most common thread is opportunity. You're Dahlia's identical twin. You can't stand around on the sidewalk like a target. You'll end up being his next victim."

Rose's hands shook. She folded them together and averted her face to the window to regain her composure away from Lennox's watchful eyes.

The pressure of his hand on hers snapped her attention back to him. She stared at his profile in surprise. He continued to keep a steady gaze on the road, and she fought the urge to link her fingers through his.

Lennox broke their contact to take a left turn without a comment.

She congratulated herself for not overreacting. He was simply offering a gesture of sympathy. He probably reacted the same with anyone who suffered a loss. She was lucky he didn't pat her on the head.

"When we visit Frank," Lennox said, "if you enjoy the flowers in the yard, be sure to tell him. He enjoys the compliments and works hard to earn them."

"Then I will be off to a good start with my name. How long has he been into his hobby?"

"Frank began gardening after his wife left him years ago. The guys at the station called him the Pansy Man. I'm going to ask him to unofficially join our investigation."

"What? Are you serious? You're bringing in a person referred to as Pansy!" She couldn't keep the shock from her voice.

"Even though Frank's officially retired, he did the work of two detectives and still gets the inside dirt. He's got connections to the station. He gets together with the guys for breakfast and coffee once a week at Joe's Coffee Shop, and people trust him. Frank starts recounting the old anecdotes about his wife leaving him while nursing his wilting petunias, and the women melt and pour out their stories. The older ones start thinking he could be husband material and the younger ones think he's the grandfather they always wanted. "

"I bet the men don't."

"Strange you should use that word, bet. Gambling is his one big vice. As far as the men, he utilizes a different strategy with them. Frank's a good listener who knows when to ask a question. He's a pro."

"If his questions solve the case faster, I'm for him. Solving the crime in a couple of minutes would meet my speed, but I'll settle for tonight."

"Thanks for the extra hours. I was worried for a second." He pulled into the driveway of a modest Cape Cod style house with peeling, white paint and sagging, green shutters. A black Chevy sat in front of the detached garage with a rusty rake leaning against the clapboard.

Lennox grabbed a brown paper bag from the rear seat. "There's nothing like a little refreshment while you discuss a case."

"You mean bribery, judging from the gift wrap. Do you bring

presents to all your friends?"

"Nah, it's a little pick me up for brunch. Frank doesn't want to miss all those vitamins and minerals at the most important meal of the day. Wait a moment, Miss Blue, and I'll get your door."

He hopped out of the vehicle and hustled around to the passenger side. She shook her head over his archaic, but charming manners, and walked beside him to the front steps. They paused on the top stair while he rang the doorbell. In the yard, patches of snow lay on the brown grass.

"Nothing's blooming yet," she whispered. "Guess I won't be able to sweet talk him with flowery speeches."

The door opened and Frank Ricci stood in front of them in his rolled up, brown flannel shirt sleeves. He appeared about fifty pounds overweight, but the mass fit the persona of a man who'd be more at home in a wrestling ring than a garden.

"Hey, Luke, you came back home. Too bad, it only took a recent homicide."

"Frank, thanks for seeing me today."

"I just finished combing my hair before I answered the door." He ran his hand over his shiny, bald head. His face glowed as he turned to Rose. "Going to introduce me to the beautiful woman by your side?"

"This is Miss Rose Blue."

She held out her hand, and Frank gave her a firm shake.

"Her sister, Dahlia, is the one I wanted to discuss with you," Lennox added.

Frank's light brown eyes widened. "Miss Blue, I apologize about the homicide crack. I didn't mean anything personal, ya know. Sometimes my mouth is faster than the old brain."

"Please call me Rose, Mr. Ricci. I understand a slip of the tongue. Besides, Detective Lennox speaks highly of you."

"You can drop by any time, even without the detective." He winked. "You'd better call me Frank. Come on inside. We're letting in a draft."

Lennox raised his paper bag. "I brought a little hair of the dog for the host."

Frank opened the door wider. "You can come in, too, since you brought the bottle. My cat's already in hiding. He doesn't like company and maintains a sixth sense about people showing up. I think he's smarter than the whole Ledgeview Police Force."

"Isn't the superstition that cats enjoy nine lives, not a sixth sense?" Lennox asked and followed Rose into the hall. "But I'll let that one pass along with the crack about the department since I'm feeling generous today."

"Six or nine, it makes no difference to me."

"My grandmother's allergy prevented us from having animals." Rose volunteered.

"You can always count on a pet to be there for you when others fail," Frank announced, locking his door. "I heard the guys aren't happy you're back, Luke. One half spouts off you're in Ledgeview to boast how you were a big shot detective in New York. The other half complains the chief hired you because he liked your old man."

She tensed and waited for Lennox's reaction.

"People say nepotism is the next best thing to twist off beer caps. What can I say about New York? I learned a lot at my last job. I left home when I was young and hungry to take on the world, and you don't always see what's in front of you."

"Agree. Sometimes we take a detour. Just prove to the guys what you can do."

"Are you going to let us sit down or keep us standing around while you flatter me?"

"Go ahead. You know the way."

Lennox nudged Rose toward the adjoining doorway.

"Flattery, criticism, sometimes it's hard to recognize the difference. Miss Blue, don't take our words seriously," Frank said as they walked into the next room. "I've known this young man forever. He's the best." Frank clapped a hand across Lennox's back. "I'd risk my life for him or his father. God bless him."

"Dad felt the same about you, Frank."

"Detective Lennox must appreciate your support." Rose walked into a rectangular room and stopped.

"We're all part of a family." The older man stopped near a pair of barrel chairs and a matching tan sofa.

A magazine featuring pictures of various size guns on the cover lay on a cushion. An old box style TV stood at the head of the room, and newspapers were spread across the coffee table.

"Bought a few new items for the war games?" Lennox asked.

She sent a searching gaze over the man's toys. An array of horses and cavalry figurines sat on top of the papers. An open set of paints and two brushes rested near the figures. The odor of paint tainted the air. What was going on?

Frank shoved the magazine to the side and capped the jars. "I expanded my army and won a few battles."

"Frank has a regular night for his war games in his basement where he sets up the battlefields," Lennox explained to her.

"Oh, nice, I guess." Was his activity normal for a retired detective? "And people come and move their plastic men around a miniature battlefield?"

"You got it, Rosie, my love." Frank winked. "Keeps the mind sharp, thinking of lines of attack to beat your opponent. And I'll let you in on a tip. I'm favored to win the Battle of Gettysburg next week. But enough about me. What's happening in your world, Luke?"

"Frank," she interrupted. "Detective Lennox told me you're the best investigator in Ledgeview, but unfortunately, you're not working any longer, which might explain why the police can't solve my sister's case."

"Don't discount Luke. His father taught him. Truth, our city has plenty of good men working on the force, but they can get stuck on the wrong track. I'm honored you think highly of me." He touched his hand to his chest. "Luke, she's bright and a head turner with that pretty face. Why are you guys still standing? Sit down, or do you want to run out the door?"

Lennox gestured for Rose to sit on the sofa and then sank down beside her.

Frank opened a drawer in the coffee table and pulled out a shot glass. He poured himself a drink from his gift bottle and set the glass on the newspapers.

"Detective Lennox told me you hear the local buzz," she said to Frank. "Have you heard anything unusual or memorable in my sister's case?"

"Sure, people are quick to point at the weird guy on the block or the strange kid from their school days. Myself, I'd study the usual names in the data base. You did that, right?"

"Yeah, past history of sexual and or violent crimes, done and no leads."

"Do you have any ideas, Frank?" she asked.

"Luke's school pal comes to mind."

"Come on, Frank." Lennox ran an agitated hand through his hair. "Buddy's never been convicted of a crime."

Buddy? Did they mean Dean Drown's son? A wave of shock hit her.

"Cause his daddy paid off the victim. He operates by his own set of rules."

"Frank, be honest. The girl lied and said she was the age of consent when she met Buddy. Even her father admitted she looked seventeen or eighteen when the officer interviewed him. The case of statutory rape was bogus from the start."

"Are you talking about *Buddy Drown*?"

Frank shook his head. "Something is wrong with that kid. He takes after his dad."

"You mean my landlord? What's wrong with Dean Drown?"

"Nothing," Lennox interjected. "Dean is his stepfather. He adopted Buddy when he was eleven. Buddy's mom, Tia, married a loser the first time. Buddy is nothing like his biological dad. He'd never beat a woman. I've seen him with his mother and girlfriends. Besides, Buddy's girlfriend emailed me a copy of their daily calendar for the dates Dahlia was missing. Buddy was at work or with Shauna. We're in the process of double checking each alibi like we do with everyone else we interview. So far, his life is about wedding cake samples and working at his father's real estate office."

Frank held up his glass. "Luke, you've a soft spot for the Drown kid because he took your side against those school kids who were trying to beat you up. Though I think Buddy was just showing off. He's the one I'd investigate, but I'll say no more about him." Frank set down his glass and rested his arms on his knees.

Rose managed to shove her alarm to the corner of her mind and ask her big question. "When you worked as a detective, Frank, did you ever use a medium, a person who could communicate with the dead?"

"You mean one of those fortune tellers?" He shook his head

several times. "I couldn't take the chance. If you made an arrest based on their predictions, you still had to convince thirteen men and women on a jury that you're not talking mumbo jumbo. It's too big a risk for a man with brains." He eased back against the barrel chair. "Luke understands."

She threw Lennox a glance and worked to keep the sarcasm out of her voice, "Does he?"

"You were Dad's partner," Lennox said without betraying an emotion. "I trust your opinion, except about Buddy."

"What's the next step, Frank?" she asked.

"Luke has lots of hours of foot and legwork ahead of him. I heard Sluggo headed across the border to meet with the cops in Brattleboro before he left our city and came up with nothing. He was working under the theory the murderer followed your sister to Ledgeview from Vermont. It's easier than admitting you're missing a killer who's in your hometown and under your nose."

"I'm not sure if your words are comforting." She clenched her hands and then relaxed them. "Who's Sluggo, Lennox?"

"The detective I was hired to replace in Ledgeview."

"Didn't he take another job?'

"That's his spin," Frank put in. "He hit the road before they threw him out."

"Charming," she muttered.

"I could use a person with your experience to bounce ideas off," Lennox admitted. "Are you interested?"

Frank shook his head, and his mouth twisted several times as though he kept changing his mind. Finally he answered, "I'm done with police work. I'm retired. The Chief was a little too happy to roast me at my retirement party and wouldn't like hearing I'm butting into a case."

"I'm just asking since Dad's not here. You're—"

"Geezum, you're hitting low." The corner of Frank's mouth sloped downward.

"I was going to say you're the best, next to Dad."

"You should run the ideas past your partner."

"Conroy's not the sharing type."

"You got to prove yourself. We all do. You're the head detective, but respect goes further than a title."

"Frank," she interrupted. "I personally would be grateful if you'd share any theories on my sister's killer that you hear or come across in the future."

Lennox shot her a look she'd expect on his face if one of the toy soldiers had knocked him over with their pretend gun.

A muscle twitched in Frank's cheek. "I guess."

"It's better than games in your basement," Lennox insisted, smoothing his expression and swooping in to control the conversation, "and you'd pretty much just be listening to my ideas. You'll still have plenty of hours to garden. And the Chief's away at his daughter's wedding."

"The boss's on vacation, huh?" A grin broke out on the older man's face. "As long as I have time to kill the weeds, I'm in."

The deal was closed. Lennox jumped to his feet. "I'll be in touch."

Rose stood up, and they walked toward the front door where she lingered near Frank. "Thank you for agreeing to help us. Dahlia and I owe you."

"You can come over to dinner any time. Luke, you can join us, too."

She walked outside while Lennox lingered behind with Frank.

"We must keep this young lady safe." Frank's voice carried down the sidewalk to her. "And away from Buddy Drown."

Had Buddy been the one watching her earlier today? She scrambled toward the car and safety. Inside, she locked the doors.

Lennox joined her in a few minutes. He tossed a file onto the rear seat and was stoic-faced as they headed away. "Frank gave me his personal notes on the Conway case. My dad's are among the nonexistent. My Mom could have found my dad's after he died and thrown them out, thinking they were useless."

"We're making a little progress, Lennox."

"Myra, the director for the Community Players, agreed to meet me this afternoon," he told her. "Since one of my men interviewed her already, we're paying her a visit, not police related business. She's an old friend of my Mom's from one of her women's group. I've known Myra all my life. She'll give me a cast list from the play that involved your sister. I want you to come. See if you get any vibes of Dahlia at the theater since the

Audi was one of the last places she visited in Ledgeview."

"I'm not sure how much I'll help. Dahlia's ghost has a mind of her own. She appears where and when she wants." Rose dipped her gaze. "She was like that when she was alive. Gram got her a job at the diner where she worked. Dahlia showed up for work when she felt like it or not at all. I can vouch that was not the career for her. Even with our business, schedules never worked for her. I took responsibility for opening and closing."

"If you'd like a less active role, you can stay in your apartment and—"

"No way, Lennox, I promised Dahlia and Gram the maniac would be arrested and jailed. I'm not passing up an opportunity that might lead to him."

They rode in silence for a few seconds. "I can imagine Dahlia on the stage," Rose said, breaking the quiet. "I avoided the spotlight, but she sought it." She fastened her gaze on Lennox. "You'd make a great actor. You have a poise or presence about you." He was definitely leading man material.

"I'll pass on the try outs. The theater is around the corner from the Court House." He flicked a glance at his pocket watch while he drove. "Unlike Dahlia, we're right on schedule."

They walked toward the theater's glassed-in lobby about five minutes later. He led the way through a set of double doors. "Let me do the talking. You know actors and their associates can be the temperamental types."

"Are you hinting I should be quiet because I can't flash a badge?"

"In this city, you'd do better to flash a Ledgeview birth certificate. People are partial to the home team. Come on."

Backstage, they found Myra, a woman in her early fifties, with a clipboard of papers in one hand and a pen in the other. The odor of fresh paint grew stronger as they approached, and an overhead track of lights threw long shadows over the cardboard trees. Myra turned and spotted them. "Luke Lennox." She hugged him, keeping her clipboard between them.

Rose moved in for a closer view when the older woman released him. The director's gel plastered hair and French manicure didn't shout serial killer. Cross off Myra on the list of suspects. She wouldn't risk breaking a nail by attacking her sister.

"Now, Luke," Myra said. "Be sure to let your mom know the card group still misses her." She skimmed her gaze over him. "If you wanted a role in our spring production, you're a little late. All the main leads are gone, but we could use help backstage. You're young and strong unlike most of the men around this place."

Rose drew nearer although the other woman seemed oblivious to her.

"I'll keep it in mind, Myra. I'm here to ask you a few questions about a woman named Dahlia Blue. I understand she was in your last production."

"The Angels Are Singing Different Tonight was my best show. I tapped the retirement community for the roles. Unfortunately, the play wasn't financially successful. Ledgeview audiences rather watch worn out, predictable productions instead of opening their minds to unique material."

Lennox crowded closer to the director, edging Rose out. "Myra, let's talk over here." He gestured to a few feet away from the scenery and the lingering painter.

Rose stood alone, the odd person out. Glad Lennox included her in the interview. The painter, an adolescent with pimples on his face and a paintbrush in hand, stared at her with open curiosity. Under his gape, she crossed the stage to join Myra and Lennox.

He turned to her as she joined them. "This is Rose Blue."

Rose extended her hand. "It's nice to meet you."

Myra gave her a nod of dismissal and turned back to Lennox. "As I was saying, I don't know much about Dahlia Blue. I hired her to take tickets and gave her a small part in our production. I had to replace her when she was a no show. It was very inconvenient."

Rose definitely didn't like this woman's attitude.

"I need a list of the actors for police interviews," Lennox said.

"As I told you, the play featured male and a few women residents of the nursing home." She huffed a breath. "Step into the lobby, and you can have the names." She turned toward her stage hand. "Horace, take the detective to the ticket booth and give him a copy of our last playbill."

The painter and Lennox headed up the aisle. Myra's high heeled shoes clicked across the floor as she disappeared behind the curtain.

Rose wandered toward the front of the stage and turned around in a circle until an open doorway to the side of the orchestra pit caught her attention. She walked to it and peered inside. A set of stairs descended to a lower level. When Buddy met Dahlia he'd left the donated clothes downstairs. She read the *Out of Order* sign on the banister and squinted down into the darkness. Damp, cold air wafted up from the blackness, and floating on the draft was the fragrance of rose perfume.

"Dahlia?" She inched forward searching, but the steps disappeared into the gloom. Was her sister lurking below? Rose grabbed the handrail. The support felt strong and firm. She reached her foot out toward the first step.

"Where are you going?"

She stepped back and whirled around.

Myra stood in front of her. The older woman's thin nostrils flared. "Didn't you see the sign? It's dangerous walking on those stairs. You can't use them."

Rose retreated to Myra's side. "Has the sign been up long?"

"It's been there as long as I can remember. You're lucky you didn't slip and fall. The door is supposed to be locked, especially if the fire deputy comes for a surprise inspection. I've no idea who opened it." She pinpointed her gaze on Rose.

She dismissed the woman's suspicion and inhaled. "What's the odor from the basement?"

"Mold invaded part of the cellar. We're holding a fundraiser to pay for its removal."

"No, the scent is sweet like a flower."

"You must mean my rose perfume." Myra patted her hair.

"You wear a rose scent?"

"Hey, Rose, are you ready?" Lennox strode down the aisle toward her.

"I'd better go." She started past Myra and hesitated to throw a glance down the stairs. The flicker of a shadow streaked past in the light from the open door and blended into the pitch black basement. Rose blinked, peeked again and saw only the darkness.

"Did you see something down there?" Myra's hot breath against Rose's neck startled her.

She turned around and wet her dry lips. "Did you?"

Myra was bent forward staring below. "It must be a rodent."

"You mean a rat?" Rose backed away with revulsion.

"I'll let Horace know he has to set up the traps." The tightness around Myra's mouth eased. "Oh, by the way, you didn't ask about your sister's part in the play."

Rose shrugged. "What was her role?"

Myra folded her arms over her chest and threw back her head like she'd accepted a challenge. "Keep in mind I'd no idea what would happen to your sister. She only played the role once in rehearsal, but—Dahlia Blue played the murder victim."

CHAPTER 9

Faded paper dragons decorated the wall above the booths of the Chinese restaurant. As Lennox and Rose walked past an elderly couple, the white-haired woman raised her head, ran her gaze over Lennox and then winked at Rose. He sailed past the woman without a glance.

Rose sat across from him and perused the menu. Within minutes, the waitress was taking their order and the food arrived. She inspected her meal. The lunch's consistency reminded her of dog food. Her hunger disappeared.

"You're not eating," he said. "Order something else. You're too thin."

"Gee, thanks. I'm more the straight hamburger type."

"Try General Tso's chicken. It's my favorite."

"Let's talk about Myra. She's not the friendly type, is she?"

"I've found people don't like questions from the police or advice. Note *vice* is part of the last word."

"I'll remember your ad vice. Do you want to hear what I learned from Myra while you were with Horace?" She couldn't wait for him to take her bait and blurted, "Myra assigned Dahlia the role of the murder victim in the last play."

"Maybe Myra knew more about your sister than we guessed."

"I don't think she was psychic, Lennox." Rose sat back and frowned. "Since Myra told me, I've envisioned Dahlia lying on the stage with her mouth duct taped." The hairs on Rose's arms stood at attention and shivered. "Then I picture her at the morgue." Dahlia's fixed glassy eyes would never see anyone again. Her frozen, blue lips would never speak. Rose swallowed the sob in her throat.

"Sorry, Rose," Lennox's low voice broke into her recollections. "My men will interview the cast now that I've a list of names. Horace told me he overheard your sister say your mom loved acting."

"That's right. Mom was a drama queen. Any local play and she was there. I remember Gram babysat us during those late evening rehearsals and productions. I think Dahlia inherited her gene. What did Horace know about Dahlia?"

"That was the extent of his knowledge."

"Don't forget Frank gave us Buddy as a suspect." She waited for his response, but he sat silent. She picked at the food while she continued. "I'd like to question him."

"You're not a cop, remember? And, I already interviewed Buddy. Until I've evidence that incriminates him, he's not a suspect or a person of interest. If I find a witness or a discovery that supports an interrogation, I'm all over him."

His words didn't reassure her. At the moment, she needed caffeine for reinforcement. She'd pay a hundred dollars for a steaming mug. "Do they serve coffee in this place?" Where was the waiter? "I'd like a pint of strong French Roast."

"Try tea." He poured the liquid from the pot on the table into her cup. "Any hints from your sister at the Audi?"

She sniffed at the pungent tea. "Don't worry. Myra won't be passing the Ghostbusters's number to me any time soon. Dahlia and I didn't speak."

"Forget Myra. When Dahlia reappears, get the name or initials of her attacker."

"It's not like we're texting or having a phone conversation." Frustrated, she tapped her fingers on the tabletop. "What's the bully story Frank mentioned?"

The corner of Lennox's mouth turned upward. "The story's not exiting. When I was a sixth grader at Ledgeview Middle School, a few eighth graders decided to beat me up because I was the son of a cop and it would prove they were tough. Buddy had just moved here from Maine with his mom and Dean. As the new kid he was out to prove himself by teaching the older kids they'd chosen the wrong victim. The next day, Bud and I went one-on-one on the basketball court at lunchtime."

She leaned across the table. "And you beat the bullies and Buddy."

"The odds were against us, five of them to two of us, but the fight was broken up by a teacher before a winner or loser was determined. School suspended me, and my father grounded me for two months. But Buddy and I became friends. We covered each other's backs and were always there for each other in and out of school."

"What about Buddy?"

"Bud and I called our game a tie when next period bell rang."

"I can't imagine you in a schoolyard brawl. You seem too...law abiding. Did you get in a lot of trouble?" She imagined a younger version of Lennox swinging punches and sporting a black eye. "I bet you could have beaten them without Buddy." Lennox could win with both fists handcuffed behind his back.

"I wish I'd seen you take on a bunch of bad dudes." She conjured up the image of Lennox walking down the school hall with her, his arm around her shoulders. She glanced at him, glad he wasn't psychic. "Any other brawls during your middle or high school years?"

"A few, I avoided them if possible. My dad taught me being a good law enforcer was about thinking and psyching people out, not punching them out."

"What about your mom? Was she in favor of your grounding?"

"She always supported my dad. They were a solid team. I haven't seen her much lately. After my Dad's death, she moved away to recover. She took his death hard. I rent the house from her. She didn't want to sell it, and the former tenants gave their notice when I snagged the job in Ledgeview. The timing was perfect. Why are you asking all these questions?"

"I'm just curious." She shrugged.

"I'm curious why you asked Frank to join the investigation."

She shifted and caught a strong whiff of the fried rice on her plate. "I decided he's not a lost cause if he thinks his cat's clairvoyant. How's your food?"

"The verdict's still out on the eats, but Frank's a unique individual."

"Your friend's a flatterer," she said, inspecting the meat. "Did he compliment too many females during his marriage or was his compulsive gambling the reason his wife left him?"

"You should join the force. You have a suspicious nature."

"I'd be good at interrogation. I should talk to Buddy, and it doesn't take an investigator to guess what happened in your retired detective's marriage."

"Frank always kept his betting under control. As for women, he appreciates a pretty face, but he never cheated. He believes in the laws of marriage."

"People call them vows in the real world." She waited a beat. "What about you? Did your ex wander?"

"Getting a little personal, Miss Blue?" He glanced at her over the table with those now icy blue eyes. "What's my former wife got to do with solving a crime?"

"I was thinking how life often throws similar people together. My ex boyfriend strayed, too, if it makes you feel better. He put the blame on me. He said I cared more about my shop than him. Turns out while I was busy doing my part to open my store, he was doing everyone he could find." Her lower lip quivered despite her best effort to control it.

"The guy was a pig. Glad you dumped him."

"Thanks, Lennox. You're sweet sometimes."

"I've arrested plenty of people who'd disagree."

"Who'd believe them?" She lowered her voice in case the elderly couple at the next table could overhear. "I don't think my ex and I were a good match though I didn't see it for a while. The Blues are cursed in love."

"You believe in curses *and* ghosts."

"I bet you're happy you met me." The memory of the breakup bit into her with fresh pain. She managed a brief smile to hide her sadness. "Now he's gone and the *Blues Sisters* isn't. None of the women in my family have done well in love. My Gram loved my Grandfather but he died of a sudden heart attack when my mom was in high school. Gram was like your mom, Lennox. When Gram's husband died, she and my mother moved away for a short time, but they missed their home and returned to Brattleboro."

Rose gripped the napkin in her lap, gearing up to ask the big question one more time. "So what was the story about your ex?"

"Mine?" He shrugged. "She never mentioned that our marriage was cursed, if that disappoints you."

"Funny." She tossed the napkin on the table.

"My ex wasn't happy married to me, a detective. She felt I gave all my energy to the criminals," he admitted between bites. "My hours off were pretty limited. She had a point. When I was home, I was usually thinking about the job and not her or us."

"I'd imagine a police detective's career is exciting. You solve mysteries, put clues together and shoot at people. I could never do those things. I'm better at ordering supplies, working on my budget or thinking up fund raisers for the business association."

"What about firing your thirty-eight?"

"You want the truth? When I bought it, I figured the sight of the gun would frighten people away."

"Here's a sure fire way to scare people." He bent forward until he was whisper away.

Her gaze fell on his mouth and a ripple of anticipation ran through her. "What?" she murmured and held her breath.

"Call-the-police." He straightened and clapped his hands together. "We've talked enough about us. Your sister's case is the topic I want to discuss." He gulped tea as though to wash the past conversation out of his mouth. "What was up with your sister and the online social networks?"

What was he digging for? Unease tensed Rose's shoulders. "What do you mean?" She focused on her food to avoid her nervousness. "What's the seasoning in the poultry? It's quite strong." She pointed at the serving.

"Asian spices. I can't find Dahlia's tracks anywhere on the internet. Things aren't adding up. How did her killer know she feared heights unless she shared the information with him?"

"Dahlia didn't like people to know about her phobia, but you've a point. Why would he drag her out on the trestle when he could have thrown her into the water from the ledge?"

"He could just be a creep."

"I know something creepier." She debated for an instant and then plunged in. "Dahlia always believed she'd die on a bridge. She'd drive out of her way not to cross one. I thought she was silly, but not anymore." Rose tightened her grip on the fork. "She must have trusted the killer and confessed her fright to him. He used all her fears to make Dahlia's death gruesome."

She sipped her drink. Bitterness lingered on her tongue, and she shoved the cup away. "You don't think they have spiders in this place, do you? It's kind of old and a few crawlies might live in a crack or two." She hunched forward and inspected the wall.

"Aren't spiders against the department of health guidelines for restaurants?"

"Spiders have a way of ignoring the health department."

"Let's get back to my questions. Your sister never told you, her twin, about online friends or joining a virtual group?"

He was fishing for something. "Dahlia didn't need to talk to faceless or long distance people. We owned a boutique with real live customers, and she had a fiancé."

"How'd she meet A. J. Edwards?"

Lennox was interrogating her. Her pulse picked up. "She met A.J. during the Christmas rush. He came into the store on his lunch break to buy gifts."

"I want to talk to the man. Do you have the addresses of where he sent his presents or any ideas about his whereabouts?"

"He was always cash and carry. He seemed like a sweet guy. You think he was a fake? That he met my sister to kill her?" Why were the Blues women blind to men's true character? Other women seemed to possess radar when it came to men who were bad for them.

"I believe everyone is guilty, until I personally rule them out. How did they feel about each other?"

"My sister loved him, and he loved her. They were engaged. You think he used the engagement to get closer to her? That he always planned on killing her?" Hideous. Now she really had no appetite.

"Your sister might have broken up with him because she saw more to him than she wanted to admit."

Rose stared at her plate, considering his point. "Dahlia accused him of not being supportive of her dreams, but Dahlia's dreams changed daily. You also need to understand my sister. She often fell passionately in love, but her relationships burned out quickly. Going for the long run was not her usual style. I'd hoped A.J. was an exception because I wanted her happy."

"Maybe he was angry over the breakup and wanted to get

even. Wouldn't your sister share her fear of heights with him when they were together?"

"I wasn't aware that she did, but I don't know every word they spoke either." Rose's eyes widened. "He could have gotten revenge by throwing her off the bridge."

"Describe the end of their relationship. What caused them to separate?"

Her stomach began to hurt with each new question, and her last fight with Dahlia hovered in the back of her mind. She inhaled and plunged into her sister's past love life. "I think the relationship was over, at least, for my sister when Dahlia began to have no time for A.J. He seemed to take the end hard, but I never guessed he'd want payback." In her mind, A.J.'s smile twisted into a sneer.

Lennox stared at her across the table with those perceptive blues. Was he guessing she was white washing the breakup?

"Your business kept her too busy for her boyfriend? I don't get the picture. You reported searching the local bars for her. Dahlia had time to go out and join others, but she couldn't spare an hour for A.J.?"

"Dahlia went to the local bars after they broke up. She didn't handle her pain well and used a few drinks to solve her problems and without considering the consequences."

"Her lifestyle sounds dangerous." He sat in silence, his expression dead sober. "I guess true love isn't meant for everyone, including myself. I do better dealing with other emotions such as retribution."

"From what I've seen, you can read people after a few words. You might have had the wrong partner in your marriage, but were too close to recognize the fact."

"You sound like you're scoping me out for your own reasons."

She watched his gaze plunge to her mouth, then slide to her chest and back. A small thrill zipped through her. She squashed the feeling. Likely he was thinking of giving her more instructions on watching out for criminals. Besides, her sister's murderer was on the loose. She didn't have time for imaginary hook ups.

"Relationships are tricky. I don't think I've ever understood them," she confessed with a burst of honesty. "I never dreamed of a future without Dahlia either." She paused to clear the lump from her throat. "Do you have any more questions for me?"

"Let's get back to A.J. Did you meet his friends?"

"He introduced Dahlia to his co-workers at the garage. He only lived in Vermont for about five or six months. He was from Rhode Island." Uneasy, she glanced at the sign labeled Exit, now her favorite word.

He lowered his gaze to her food. "Are you finished? You didn't eat much."

"I'm having a reaction to one of the ingredients."

He tilted her dish toward him and scooped up forkfuls.

"Help yourself. It was kind of you to ask." She tapped her foot under the table and stood up. "I'll hit the ladies room while you finish."

She spotted the waiter carrying their bill. "I left my purse in the car. Can you give me the key?" She'd better get her money before Lennox thought she was a freeloader.

"Not a good place for valuables, Blue." He pulled the key from his pocket and held it out.

"Lecture noted." She scooped up the key, strode past the indoor Koi pool and shoved through the door.

Lennox's car sat by the building. The sound of music blasted across the lot. On the road, a figure dressed in a black hoodie pedaled away on a bike. A blaring boom box was tied to the handle bars. *Was that her neighbor?* The bicyclist disappeared around the corner.

She started to cross to the car and stopped. Keyed into the passenger door were two words.

"Rose?" Lennox joined her in the lot. "What's wrong?"

She pointed at the message on the car. DIE PIG.

CHAPTER 10

"My stalker's here. He left me another message." Rose's gaze skipped over the parking lot. "How did he know where I was unless he followed us?" The goosebumps on her arms rose up and warned the coward could be hiding, spying on them.

"My car is fairly well known. Rose, are you listening?"

"Yes, your car etc. etc." She paced a few steps toward the dumpster. The creep could be behind the garbage.

"Stand there." He did a quick jog around the property's perimeter. "No one's around, and the graffiti is for me. I'm the pig. Someone spray painted a similar message on the station earlier today. A few people don't like the police. I know it's hard to believe when I have a winning personality."

She put her hands on her hips. "Are you sure the threat is for you?"

"You can't have all the Ledgeview whackos for yourself, Rose."

"I thought I saw my neighbor, Bike Boy, pedaling away when I came out."

"A camera at the station caught a figure with the same build as Bike Boy painting graffiti on the wall. Unfortunately, the lens didn't catch a picture of his face." Lennox crouched down in front of the damage. He ran his fingertips over the scratched area like a physician inspecting a broken arm.

"I'm sorry about your car."

"She'll be okay. Old Charger has suffered worse and always comes through."

"I thought cops named their cars Old Paint. Your name fits

though. Will the touchup be expensive?" She leaned against the side of the hood and studied the destruction.

"Forget the paint job. I'm taking care of you first." His dark expression would send a normal person searching for cover.

"If it wasn't Bike Boy who keyed your car, then the true sleezeball could still be around." She did a three-sixty scan.

"I'm on it. Sit in the car for a second. You look like hell."

"I'm fine. Though, if you spoke to your wife like that, I'm beginning to understand your relationship problems."

"No personal commentaries."

She flattened her hands against her sides. "Whoever keyed your car is a coward. He should come out and listen to the message I have for him."

"I'll pay the bill. Come with me."

"I'll wait by the car. How much do I owe?" She opened her purse.

"That's not how it works." He took her arm and propelled her toward the building.

"If the words on your car were for you, why do I have to go inside?" she asked, running to keep up with him.

"Because I'm always mistrustful, remember? I'm not leaving you alone."

He slowed once they entered the restaurant. He paid the bill, but not before ordering the host to refuse Rose's money. The man threw her a speculative glance.

"You scared him," she said as he led them to the kitchen. "He probably thinks I'm a counterfeiter."

"You're crediting him with too much imagination."

He quizzed the waiters, cooks and manager. All claimed they were inside working and never glanced outside. The elderly patrons spouted off on the dangers of public parking and reported to have seen a stray dog hanging around the dumpster before they entered.

"As usual, no one saw a thing, except a dog that can't talk and isn't around. We've no suspects," Rose noted as the exit door swung open for them.

A detective from the station strolled inside.

"Conroy, what are you doing here?" Lennox angled in front of him, drawing the detective to a halt.

Conroy's eyes widened. He readjusted his glasses on his nose. "Did the mayor pass a law against eating lunch?"

"Since you're never around when I expect a report, I'm surprised to run into you. Back from Vermont already?"

"The report must have gotten lost in all those files on your desk. I'm on my way out of the city in a few minutes." Conroy raised his chin and stared Lennox in the eyes.

"When did you park in the lot?"

"I don't have to punch in and out, but if it's any of your business, which it's not, I arrived three minutes ago. Mind if I order, or do you want to spring for my meal?"

"Eat yourself sick. Let's go, Rose."Lennox took her arm and they headed out.

She leaned toward him when they were out of earshot. "Doesn't he work with you? I saw him at the station."

"He's a Ledgeview detective."

"Would he key your car? He sounded angry the other day and not too happy today."

"Don't worry about Conroy. I'll take care of him." Lennox yanked open her car door and once he snapped his seatbelt in place, he headed toward her apartment.

She broke the silence after a few seconds. "Why did you come outside from the restaurant?"

"To make sure you were okay."

It had been a long time since anyone cared if she was all right. She was usually the one who did the worrying about people in her life. It was nice to have someone else do the fretting about her.

"So no vibes of Dahlia at the Audi," he said, slowing for a stoplight.

"I caught a glimpse of a shadow in the cellar. Myra claimed it was a rat." Rose swallowed to ease her discomfort. "Let me explain."

"I can't wait to hear."

"I found the door leading to the basement open, and I caught a whiff of my sister's perfume drifting up the stairs. I was about to investigate when Myra interrupted me, and then, you appeared." She leaned toward him for her big question. "What kind of perfume was Myra wearing?"

"Is this a trick?" he asked, turning onto Main Street.

"She was wearing rose perfume. Strange, huh?"

"Tell me more about the theater and your sister."

She studied his face to discern if he was hinting at something. As usual, his profile gave nothing away. "Myra reported no one used the cellar stairs, and the door was always locked. She seemed to believe I unlocked it somehow. What matters, Lennox, is your friend, Buddy, lied to us."

"I don't follow." The stoplight changed to green, and he hit the pedal.

"Buddy reported he left the donated clothes in the basement. He couldn't if the door was bolted because of the steps. We've found at least one hole in his story about meeting Dahlia and probably can find more."

"There are several rooms in the basement and another staircase to them on the other side of the stage. My high school held their awards ceremony at the Audi, and before the event, I had a first-hand view of the layout below. The auditorium's basement hasn't been renovated since I was a teenager. My memory vouches for the fact Buddy could have gone downstairs another way."

"Then you've no reason to be afraid to take me to the Drowns unless you've doubts about your friend. A few of my harmless questions over a simple meal can't hurt."

"I'm protecting innocent people from upsetting insinuations. Remember, these people are the closest I have to family in Ledgeview. I promised no one will be left out of the investigation. The Drowns are no exception." He steered the car down Main Street.

"Bull, Lennox. Take me to the Drowns. I want to observe Buddy."

"Rose, when you show me your license in psychology or degree in criminology, I'll reconsider."

The tightening of his jaw warned she'd entered the no-win zone. She decided to change the topic, but suddenly she became aware of how closely they sat. A few inches separated them. She could feel his body heat. She played back in her mind his earlier concern. If only she'd met him another time in her life. Now it was all about pain and grief. How had her life become so bleak?

She felt like she was caught in the middle of a horror movie without a happy ending in sight. She had to make sure her sister's killer was found. The throb in her forehead turned into a pounding. *I'm trying to help you, Dahlia.*

"Are you okay?" He threw her a concerned glance.

"We've not made a millimeter of progress toward capturing the killer." Her voice shook with hurt. If she was stronger like Gram, she'd will away this sense of failure and pain. Gram had been a single parent most of her life and then started all over and raised both Dahlia and herself. She survived on a waitress pay until she died of cancer. She'd believed she'd beat the disease and had a survivor's attitude to the end.

Rose fell silent with the tears blocking her throat. Against her cheek, she felt the brief warmth of a palm. She stared at him. Did Lennox, the tough guy, have a hidden affectionate side or was she overreacting?

He removed his hand and placed it back on the steering wheel. "*If* we go to the Drowns," he said, keeping his gaze steady on the street. "I'll ask the questions about your sister and only if they fit into the conversation."

"Absolutely," she said, brushing away a tear on her cheek.

"We learned one earth shaking fact today." His brows drew together in deep thought. "Myra wears rose perfume."

"If only that fact solved the crime. Don't forget you have another suspect. Let me know if Bike Boy fesses up."

"I'll keep you in the loop, but confessions are rare unless they're in the confessional." He detoured into a drive thru, ordered a salad and handed it over to her. "For you and don't give me guff. You didn't eat at the restaurant."

In five minutes, he pulled to the curb at her apartment and reached for his door handle.

She released her seatbelt. "Wait, I didn't thank you for changing your mind about dinner with the Drowns, and I'm sorry about your car."

Without thinking, she leaned over and stopped halfway between the seats. What was she doing? Had she lost her mind? He'd never indicated or sent vibes that he wanted her to initiate anything personal with him. In fact, his change of heart about the visit was most likely a pity action. And she was supposed to be the psychic one. Mother of Pearl, she was making one large embarrassing mistake.

She needed to extract herself from the situation, but how to do it with poise? He was throwing her a curious glance. She inhaled the scent of his leather jacket, saw each tiny whisker on his chin and—

His arms encircled her shoulders and tugged her closer, giving her no time to protest. She pressed her hands against his chest and the smooth touch of his coat cooled her palms.

"Rose?"

"Hmm?" He had gorgeous, blue eyes.

"Is there someone who'd beat me to a pulp if I kiss you?"

Her face heated. "Feel free, Lennox. I've a no strings policy."

"In that case...." He skimmed his mouth over hers, barely touching her lips in a teasing manner.

What was he doing?

He tightened his hold, and her heart sped up. He continued to linger, and then began exploring, claiming the pulse in the hollow of her throat with gentle nips. The brush of his whiskers glided upward and grazed her chin. She shivered against the sensual promise and pressed closer against his hard chest.

She should end this. But the moment was filled with such delightful tingling sensations. She didn't want him to stop, yet. As though sensing her uncertainness, he tipped her head up and deepened the kiss, extending the moment. The sounds and scenes of the street vanished. He cupped the back of her head, holding her in place while his lips became more demanding. His hand brushed over her breast. Her body quivered with a dizzy feeling and a sizzling heat. She was lost in the feelings, in him. She gripped his shoulders.

A siren went off and blared in her ears.

"What was that?" She pulled away. Was she hearing bells or sirens when they kissed? Sirens made sense, he was the law.

"The ambulance drove by." His tone reflected an unruffled in-charge expression.

Obviously, he'd heard and felt nothing extraordinary when he kissed her. How embarrassing. "I have to go."

"I'll open your door." He reached for the handle on the driver's side.

He could speak calmly? Breathe? "Never... mind." She jumped out of the car and ran to the building's steps.

"Rose, wait," he shouted.

No way. "Don't bother walking me in. See you later." She unlocked and bolted through the entryway in record time. She flew up the stairs before he could catch up to her. She'd kissed the detective in charge of her sister's murder case. She should have been reviewing notes, bouncing ideas or theories off him, anything, but *not* kissing him! Wrong time, wrong man. She was a true Blue, following in the footsteps of her mother and sister. They flitted from man to man choosing ones who wouldn't commit or were totally wrong for them. She couldn't be the next to follow in their footsteps.

She ran across the sidewalk and into the apartment with great speed. How fast would she run when their time came? Planning the moment when she disappeared was critical. Take her unaware when she was trusting like her sister and then vanish.

Rose, my ultimate catch. You will be all mine.

CHAPTER 11

Thursday, Rose showered and dressed in jeans and a turquoise, button down shirt to sit in front of her laptop. Nowhere to go, but lots to do. How cooperative would her sister be today?

"Dahlia, how am I going to help you?"

You can do it, Rose.

Rose's heartbeat picked up at her sister's response. "Help me. Who did you meet at The Ledges?"

Rose waited, but her sister didn't answer. Shaking her head, she booted up the computer. Her eyes burned from a restless night of little sleep. Okay, she'd do this the hard way. She'd find information about Buddy Drown's past encounters with the police, something to support her suspicion and Frank's. Show Dahlia she cared and was sorry she'd gone off course with Lennox yesterday.

After nearly an hour of searching the internet, Rose found nothing damaging about Buddy's character. Where was the news about his arrest for statuary rape?

She sipped on her third cup of Irish Cream coffee. The fighting Irish was just what she needed for energy. Her thoughts wandered to Lennox. He didn't have an easy job if this fruitless search was typical. She wished he was here. And then, there was the possibility of another kiss.

The hope of a repeat performance and his promise to take her to the Drowns for dinner kept threading through her mind. She couldn't wait. She gulped another mouthful of coffee and on impulse, typed in Luke Lennox. She hit the enter key.

The computer whirled and brought up a screen full of results. His name showed up in old stories about the Ledgeview High football and baseball teams. Buddy's name was listed beside his.

She read the final paragraph describing Lennox making the winning touchdown in overtime. *You were quite the athlete. What else did you do?* Scrolling downward, she came across the headline: John Lennox, Local Detective Deceased.

She clicked on the article and leaned forward. A picture of Lennox's father materialized next to the piece. She read through the section, taking in the basics.

Detective John Lennox died yesterday at his home. He was a member of the Ledgeview Police Force, serving as one of their lead detectives. John leaves behind a son, Luke, and his wife, Mary. He was fifty-seven.

Wow, what else could she find? She plugged John's name into the search box and chose the first link that appeared. The next piece reported John Lennox was born in Ledgeview where he attended local schools and graduated from college with a degree in criminal law. She read on: *The ME ruled his death a suicide from a gunshot wound.* Suicide?

He shot himself? What? She pushed away from the laptop, but the picture of Lennox's father that she'd seen in his office popped into her mind. Lennox was proud of his father; his death must have hit Lennox hard. She dismissed the image and was skimming through the rest of the online item when the phone rang.

Rose grabbed her cell lying next to the computer. The caller's ID told her to answer.

"Hi, Cassie, how's business?"

"Steady. How's everything in New Hampshire?"

"I wish the police had arrested someone, but so far...nothing. How's your mom? Remember, she gets a discount at the Blues Sisters while you're working for me."

"Mom has your store's name engraved on her credit card. We're still your best customers, and I'm your best stand-in manager. If I keep buying while I'm in charge of your boutique, you'll be able to retire early and rich. Hey, I called for a reason. Mom and I would like to help you by cleaning Dahlia's Brattleboro apartment. Are you okay with the idea?"

Rose sat up straighter in the chair. "I've been putting it off. I bet her landlord will charge for another month's rent if I don't get her stuff out before the first."

"We'll pack everything and bring the boxes to the store. Dad will help us too."

"Great. I owe you. Oh, and Dahlia kept skis in the backyard shed near the garage. If you can take those, it'd be great. I'll repay you when I'm home."

"Post my picture as your best customer on your store's website, and mention I'm single. We'll be even."

"Will do. You'll find a key to my sister's place in the top desk drawer in the office."

"Keep the faith. We love you."

Rose clicked off her phone and shoved away the touch of homesickness. With a sigh, she turned her concentration to the computer. "Buddy Drown, stop hiding your criminal past."

The thump of footsteps in the hall announced a person's presence. Her hands froze on the keyboard. The creak of a hinge confirmed someone was opening the door across the hall. It must be her neighbor. Lennox would interview Bike Boy and take care of him. She relaxed her hands and stared at the word suicide on her screen.

The buzz of the doorbell made her jump. It was probably a salesman, or a kid selling Girl Scout cookies. No, cookie selling was over. The bell persisted. "Sales people never rest."

Rose stuffed her feet into her shoes. She crossed the floor and hit the button. The buzz continued.

"Hello, let go of the button. What do you want?"

"Youuu. I want you."

"What?" She released her finger. Was this a joke?

The buzz became a persistent whine, clawing against her nerves. "Stop pushing the button."

The shrill filled the apartment. She put her hands over her ears for a second. Where was the connection? Where was it? She'd enough with suicides, murders and now the stalker or another crank at her door. She searched for the cable that linked the doorbell to her living quarters. Her fingers closed around the wire filament, and she tugged the line from the box.

The ringer fell to a distant whimper, but refused to quit.

Tension wound in her chest, tightening and twanging. Call Lennox. No, she could handle this. All she needed was to peek out the window and get a good look at him or her.

She crossed to the table and grabbed the gun from her purse. "Smart-on, Lennox."

She raced down the stairs. Halfway, she slowed. Stretching upward on her toes, she glimpsed out the rectangular windows at the top of the front door for any signs of the stalker on the stoop. She only caught a view of the cars parked at the curb.

Where was her bell ringer? She gritted her teeth. Was he accosting little old ladies and small children? Was the coward hiding behind a parked vehicle, in the rear a building or waiting for her on the front steps? Renewed anger propelled her downward. Her hand tensed on the butt of her weapon. Perspiration ran down the sides of her face when she reached the vestibule. Pausing, she strained to hear signs of movement through the door. He'd left?

She threw the entryway open with her gun raised and ready in hand.

No one was on the stoop. A light wind touched her cheek and whipped strands of hair into her eyes. Rose shoved them away and examined the sidewalk and street.

A black cat padded past. On the street, cars drove by. Rose whirled first to the right, and then to the left. Vacant space greeted her. Someone had buzzed her doorbell and spoken on her intercom. She hadn't dreamt it.

"Come out, wherever you are," she shouted, clutching the weapon with both hands. No one stepped forward. Lowering the barrel, she started to retreat inside when two young teenagers darted out from the alley.

It was only kids, playing a joke. She sagged against the doorframe and then turned again and caught sight of the doorbell button. A straight pin with a pink head and silver speckles stuck out of the bell. Rose grabbed the pin and dropped it in her pocket. A faint swell of relief swept over her along with a new reality. She'd destroyed the buzzer over a straight pin. It was the twisted kind of joke Dahlia would enjoy.

* * *

Luke sat at his desk running ideas through his mind. What

idiot thought process had taken possession of him when he'd agreed to arrange dinner with the Drowns tonight? Luke didn't search for the answer. When he'd looked into Rose's grief stricken eyes, the quick quiver around his heart should have warned him he'd cave to her.

He'd found himself agreeing to set up a date with his friends. Of course her eyes weren't the only thing about Miss Blue that held his attention. He remembered the quick inhale of her breath when he'd touched her and she fit snug against him when they'd kissed. Her breasts pressed to his chest. He'd curled his hand around the arch of her waist under her jacket and enjoyed the warmth of her body.

And then there was her dogged determination to question suspects. He didn't doubt her drive made her a successful business woman. No one could question her enthusiasm or dedication.

The memory of their kiss hurtled deeper into his consciousness. What happened after he'd kissed her? By the time he'd thudded to earth, she was gone. Why had she left in a hurry? He didn't even remember what he'd said, but he was sure he wasn't insulting. Women were a mystery. Tonight, he intended to keep his hands off Rose and spend a low key evening with his friends. Getting mixed up with a female even for a temporary fling was unwise. He didn't need another person leaving him like his father and wife.

Then there was the whole stalker aspect to the case. He'd assigned an extra detail to drive by her house every hour and finally ended last night sitting outside the building. Now he was running on adrenaline.

His gaze fell across his father's files piled on top of the corner cabinet. He'd file away the kiss like a cold case and deal with the issue later. Yeah, right. Who was he kidding? He was about to spend the evening with the woman he couldn't stop thinking about, and didn't want to. Although her eagerness to question Buddy left him uneasy. At least the dinner would provide a chance for her to learn Budd was at his worst, a little impetuous, but not a murderer.

Hell, he was fooling himself. Rose planned to cross examine his friend, and she wasn't always tactful. It was a part of her that intrigued and horrified him. Lennox could feel disaster coming like a meteorologist feels an approaching Tsunami. He'd have to run interference and keep her away from Buddy, which would be as easy as separating an alcoholic from his bottle.

He forced his thoughts back on his work. Today, he'd asked Frank to dig into his home office for any old personal notes or files on his father's cold case. And what about Edwards? Was it possible A.J. had relocated to New Hampshire, and Dahlia, for some reason, followed him?

Her motive for moving to the state could be part of her restless–soul pattern. The idea really didn't wash. Her past patterns consisted of finding employment in the city near her home. Besides, she and Rose shared a unique bond that transcended death, yet in this lifetime, Dahlia never informed her sister she'd taken an apartment in another state. Why?

"Lennox, I ran Dahlia Blue's former employers through the computer programs." Conroy tossed the dossier on his desk and stood with a scowl on his face.

Luke glanced at his watch. "Nice of you to show up two hours late."

"My watch must be slow."

"I'm busy now. Come back later."

"Come back in the middle of a homicide investigation? The chief wouldn't like that. Listen, I can yak about the time or what's happening in the Blue case. I've been following up the employment angle for Dahlia now that we've finished re-interviewing. One of the employers retired two years ago and lives in Florida. I haven't spoken to him yet. The rest had solid alibis for the nights the ME gave us as possible times of death. What was the deal with your interviews yesterday, Lennox?"

"Nothing new came up with the play director. I've got a list of the cast from the play the victim was involved in. That's next on the home front. We'll need you for the player interrogations. Do a phone interview with A.J.'s former employer in Rhode Island. If you turn up more, you can do a one-on-one afterward." Luke felt the tick in his cheek. "And here's a tip. Next time, knock before you enter."

The guy leaned over and knocked on the cubicle wall. "I'm leaving."

"Be on time for our next team meeting, Conroy," he tossed over his shoulder. A threat lingered on his lips. Luke forced it back. He shut down his computer, locked up his files in the cabinet, and shut Conroy's snide remarks out of his mind.

Phoning Rose for the second time, he reminded her to wait inside for him.

She called him a paranoid, but agreed. "What's happening with the scratches on Old Charge?"

"I did a quick touch up job when the department's insurance company reminded me of the deductible. Todd claims he was nowhere near the restaurant."

"The person I saw had to be him. How many bikers ride around with boom boxes?"

"Unless you saw his face for a positive ID, I'm letting it go for now. I'll see you in a few minutes." He shoved his chair away from the desk and grabbed his jacket. Usually he worked until at least midnight on an active case. A twinge of guilt bit into him when he stepped outside into the young night. The world was awake, and he was part of it. He should stretch his arms upward or shout alleluia. Instead he glanced at his pocket watch. He'd stop for a shower and a change of clothes before he picked up Rose.

"Luke." Buddy Drown stalked across the parking lot with both hands fisted at his sides. His body overflowed with anger as he stopped in front of him. "Call off your old dog."

"What do you mean?"

"That ancient cop who worked with your dad is following me, and don't pretend you don't understand." Buddy's face flushed with fury. "When you moved back, people talked about you and not in a good way, but I defended you. They said you left Ledgeview because you thought you were too good for a small, city police department and only returned to show off how great you were. I told everyone you weren't that kind of guy. Boy, was I stupid."

"Buddy, are you sure Frank Ricci was tailing you?"

"You want me to submit to a vision test? Don't pretend or deny you spoke to him yesterday. Everyone knows their neighbor and how they voted in the primary, and you were at the old guy's house. This is Ledgeview where people talk to and about each other. They all said you were an arrogant son of a gun who thought he'd show up and teach us a thing or two about police work." He charged forward until he stood toe to toe with Luke.

Bud's confrontational attitude triggered Luke's anger. "Are you saying that I should know a reason to have you followed?"

"Don't twist my words. Your senile detective tailed me all over the place. He's acting the same way he did when that crazy girl brought false charges against me. What's my crime, my stupidity? Guess our friendship means nothing. All the teams we co-captained, parties, fixing each other's cars. We even ordered our first beer at Tiny's Grill together, and you believe whatever that ancient fool said about me."

"We ordered our first legal ones if you're counting."

"Yeah, after today don't count on drinking any brews with me." Buddy stalked a few steps away before whirling around. "I never should have admitted I met Dahlia Blue. You think I killed her. Why did I trust you? You got my back, all right. You knifed me in it."

Luke's temper cooled enough to understand Bud's ire. "Buddy, you can trust me. I didn't know Frank was following you."

"I spoke two sentences to Dahlia Blue at the Audi, and now I killed her? The old guy's nuts. You must have repeated what I said and set him off, and I was trying to help you in your investigation. Instead I get grief and accusations. This is why no one wants to help the police." He stalked toward his car.

"Buddy," Luke yelled. "You're not under any surveillance. I'll speak to Frank. He won't bother you again."

"You do that, detective," Buddy spit over his shoulder.

"Hold on a minute."

Buddy stopped by his car parked on the street and watched his friend.

Luke fished out his phone, and within a second, heard the older man's voice. "Frank, stop tracking Buddy Drown. Got it?"

Silence marked the pause. "Got it. What else do you want?"

Luke's neck muscles tightened. "That's it. We'll talk soon." He shoved his phone into his pocket. "Satisfied, Bud? Frank won't bother you again."

"I could file harassment charges. I can't wait for tonight's family dinner." Buddy unlocked his door and hopped inside.

"I can't wait either," Luke mumbled.

"Luke."

Dean called to him from across the street. He held a brown bag in his hand.

I hope Frank's not following him, too. Luke waited for Dean to join him. "I thought you'd be at home."

"Tia sent me out for last minute refreshments. Was that Buddy who just took off?" Dean nodded toward the street.

"He was pissed over a police matter. I hope it won't interfere with tonight. Maybe I should reschedule."

Dean shook his head. "He's picking up Shauna first. She's good at calming him down. Buddy's temper rises quickly and falls as fast. Besides, you can't disappoint Tia. She's thrilled we're having supper together." He headed toward the corner. "Don't be late, or she'll call the police." He winked and raised a hand before he crossed with the walk light.

Luke headed home. Tonight was really shaping up. Buddy would be in a foul mood at his parents' house despite Dean's positive thinking. At least Shauna would be at the get together to counterbalance him. Bud was lucky she'd given him a second chance after their long ago senior high break up when he'd been anything but faithful. He'd continued to rack up a reputation for most of his twenties and early thirties as a love 'em and leave 'em type. What else was new in life?

He hung a left onto Main Street and found himself crawling through the after work traffic. Great, Rose had better stay inside until he arrived. Following a quick stop at home, he drove straight to her place. She wasn't outside. On her doorstep, he raised his hand to hit the buzzer when she opened up.

"What are you doing downstairs?"

"My doorbell's malfunctioning. Come up for a moment. I left my jacket and purse in the kitchen."

"Traveling without your gun?" He stepped inside, pausing to lock up.

"I have a secret place for carrying. Don't you?" She fluttered her eyelashes and grinned.

The idea filled him with lots of images of intimate pat downs of Rose. "Okay, Annie Oakley." He waved for her to go first.

On the way up the stairs, he spouted off the safety rules for weapons to avoid thinking about the sway of her hips. He finished at the second floor where he leveled his stare on her. "Understand?"

"Is this how you make small talk? I'm surprised anyone invites you to dinner, even the Drowns."

"What's wrong with reminding people about safety, and I get lots of invitations."

"To what, gun control conferences?" She wrinkled her nose. "Lennox, we should be discussing our strategy for the evening, not the Ledgeview Police Manual."

"Buddy isn't a fool. If you start interrogating him, he'll clam up. Besides he's not in a cooperative mood today. He showed up outside the station to yell about Frank following him."

"Doesn't sound like a covert operation on Frank's part." She led the way toward her apartment.

"He probably was taunting Buddy. Frank can't resist. He thinks Buddy is guilty of rape and he can't let it go. For all I know, he flipped Buddy off and considering Bud's earlier mood, he's going to be a great dinner guest. You should stay away from him tonight. Go and enjoy the dinner and company of the other Drown members."

"You're kidding. I don't go to parties to enjoy myself."

"Now you're joking."

"Networking is what it's all about, Lennox, not having fun. Let's talk about Buddy. Under pressure, your best friend could be showing his true colors. Consider the idea, Detective, and staying away from him would be hard if we're guests in the same room." She nodded her head in a knowing way and stopped in front of her apartment with the key in hand. "Someone pulled a prank on me last night. At least—" She paused and looked past him.

He followed her gaze across the hall. Her neighbor's door was cracked open, and his face peered out from the slit.

"Todd." Luke marched to his door. "Did you drop some money yesterday when you rode past the Commercial Street Chinese Restaurant?"

Todd pursed his lips and squinted like he was trying to see

the scene. "I told you. I never ride by there." He slammed the door.

"He's friendly, isn't he?" Rose asked and unlocked her door.

"Does he stare at you all the time?" Luke crossed into her apartment while throwing glances of daggers at her neighbor's door. "What kind of a pervert did Dean rent to?"

"Calm down, I barely see him. Didn't you run his name in your computer when you interviewed him last time?"

"He came up clean, which can mean he just hasn't been caught yet."

"There is something odd about him. I mean besides riding his bike around with a boom box blaring." She shut her door and slid the chain across the lock. "What do *you think* he does that's illegal?"

"I predict drugs, a little B and E. Call me the next time he bothers you."

"Is staring a misdemeanor or felony?" She tapped a finger against her chin.

"Watch out for him. Don't go anywhere with him."

She tossed her keys into her purse on the table. "He's rarely around the building. I can't blame him for glancing out when he hears noise in the hall." She faced him. "Come clean. Frank trailing Buddy is what's really bugging you. Do you think your old friend is trying to pull something illegal?"

"It's not Buddy or Frank. If I find evidence that implicates Buddy, I promise I'll be there when he's arrested." Luke scrubbed a hand across his face. He didn't want to admit he'd come up with squat on Dahlia's death, and the guy across the hall gave him hives. "Remember, I don't like anyone 99.9 percent of the time."

A smile touched her lips and chased the strain from her face. "You like me, or you wouldn't take me to the Drowns for dinner."

"I plead temporary insanity."

"I bet you can get a deal on therapy from the department shrink." She wet her lips and the teasing light faded from her features. "Are you upset about yesterday, when you dropped me off?" Her face flushed, and she twisted her hands in front of her. "I mean, no problem, I've already forgotten it."

"Forgotten what?"

"You don't remember driving me to the apartment?" Her hands fisted, and her mouth fell open in shock.

"Sure, I remember. You wouldn't let me walk you inside." He couldn't help but tease her a little.

"I can walk by myself." She let out an exasperated sigh. "How do I look?" She ran her hands down her red blouse and over the form fitting black skirt. "Well?"

He felt his eyes bulge out of their sockets. "Good."

"Good? Is that all?" She glanced down at her clothes.

"What's the problem? Good is really good."

"Tia Drown owns a clothing shop, which means she's up to date on all the fashions. I didn't bring a lot of trendy wear, and I can't show up dressed like some kind of waif. "

"Tia's not judgmental."

"What does that mean? I should have worn something else?"

"I knew this was a no win question," he grumbled and shook his head.

"Are you okay?" she asked. "You seem…different tonight."

"You must have finally noticed my sparkling personality." He wasn't about to tell her the truth. At the moment, his testosterone was pumping out in high gear. "I should be working, not socializing."

"You are working. We're keeping Buddy Drown under surveillance." She yanked on her jacket and slung the purse strap over her shoulder.

"Explain why you're stuck on Buddy being your sister's killer? I understand you want someone arrested, but we've no proof it's Bud."

She went still and faced him. "Buddy is Dahlia's type, tall, dark and handsome. He bears a resemblance to A.J., and the guy she crushed on in eighth grade. They're well-built and my sister falls for them instantly without thought of what type of person she might be hooking up with. If she met him at the Audi, she would have felt an instant attraction. If they started seeing each other, secretly, Buddy could be the last person who saw my sister alive."

CHAPTER 12

"You think Dahlia hooked up with Buddy?" Luke asked, narrowing his eyes at her with disbelief. "No, he wouldn't. Buddy's learned his lesson and is engaged."

"Dahlia led with her heart in relationships and let others worry about what type of person she'd hooked up with and their consequences. Your friend may have the same attitude. I'd hoped when Dahlia found A.J. she'd found the real deal."

"Makes it important to find her ex and question him," Lennox said. "If A.J. stalked her to Ledgeview, and then saw her with Buddy, he could have lost it."

"You like the idea because it supports Buddy as innocent," she protested.

"Keep an open mind about Buddy. Cut him a break at his parents' house tonight. If he's guilty, I'll nail him. I'll give you that he deserves the same scrutiny as any suspect, except at the moment, he's not one. Let's change to another topic."

"Good idea, someone stuck a pin in my doorbell, and I dismantled the wire to stop the ringing. When I ran downstairs, no one was there, but when I started to close the door, two teenagers ran away from the alley. Outside of that, nothing much happened. "

"Hold on." He held up his palm. "Someone—who you don't know—rang your bell and you answered? What time was this?"

"It was daylight. Before you lecture me, I brought my gun with me and looked outside first. No one was around."

"Why don't I feel better?" He shook his head. "Rose, you have my number for a reason. Do not answer the door at any time to anyone you don't know, especially with a deadly weapon in your hand."

"I solemnly swear to call you even if you're in the middle of a police raid and not to leave my apartment to do door duty."

"No more risks."

"I promise, Lennox, on my sister's ghost."

"My instinct is warning me not to believe you." He walked over to the intercom box on the wall and released a low whistle. "You massacred the poor devil." He tracked the shredded wire into the box and turned to her. "You need the bell. It's important to get it fixed as soon as possible. Get any messages recently from Dahlia about her night at The Ledges?"

"I asked who hurt her, but she didn't answer." Rose toyed with the strap of her shoulder purse. "I wish I knew how to communicate with her. I miss her, and she could send us in the right direction to arrest her killer." Her shoulders slumped, and she averted her face.

"We'll make the arrest." Before he could stop himself, he reached out and grazed her cheek with his knuckles. A pleasant sensation filled the pit of his stomach.

She bit her lip and blushed.

The brief break gave him the moment to get his mind on track. "I'll save the rest of the security talk for later." He moved away, seeking the safety zone, a place he didn't feel the urge to touch her.

"There's more? Never mind, I'll let Dean know about the intercom." She crossed the floor to the box and twisted the disconnected wire around a finger. "He can take it out of the security deposit."

"I'll remind him you can't be running downstairs to let me in."

"My landlord must have an extra key you can borrow. I'll vouch for your character." A slow smile lit her face and erased the awkward moment.

He wanted to keep the smile on her face, protect her from more hurt. "Rose, go home to Vermont, manage your store and stay safe. If you don't want written reports, I'll phone you every day."

"I can't." Her mouth hardened into a thin line. "You should

understand the ties to family."

"I'm thinking like a law enforcer. There's no alarm system in the building despite Dean's latest efforts. Your intercom needs to be replaced. Buddy's right: this place should be condemned." He paced in a tight circle around the living room, taking in the leaky window frames. A good push from someone on the fire escape would set the panes of glass free.

"Lennox, I can't leave." She shoved the phone into her purse.

"Explain it to me."

She met his stare. "I can't leave Dahlia alone. She's all I have left of my family. You should understand. You'd do anything for your mother. If something happened to her, you'd be all over it. Dahlia was my sister, my twin. This is my last chance for us to connect." She swallowed and clenched and unclenched her hands. "Sometimes, I feel a part of me died at The Ledges."

"Hold on, Rose. Dahlia's the one who's gone, and you can help her by protecting yourself. Dahlia would want you out of harm's way."

"My sister's here and needs me. I won't be scared away. It's the least I can do." Rose angled her chin higher.

He tamped down on his frustration. "I'm sure you'll be able to talk to her in another residence."

"You sound cynical about Dahlia's afterlife abilities, Detective. She's strongest in the apartment and at The Ledges where she died." Rose rubbed her arms as though chilled.

"Is your sister watching us now?" The idea was beyond spooky if it was true.

"I don't see her." She put her hands on her hips. "What's your problem, Lennox?"

"I don't like what happens to you when she's around. Let's call the discussion a draw for now and head to the Drowns."

"Wait a minute. Where's my lipstick?" She plopped her purse on the table and fished inside.

He released an exasperated breath. "I'm done the lecture for the moment, but I guarantee we're not finished."

"Count on it, Lennox."

"Having an argument with you is not how I planned to start the evening."

"What did you plan?" She stepped away from her purse and

faced him.

He lifted a fingertip and traced the curve of her lips, lingering over the indentation. She briefly closed her eyes and raised her face to him. He found her simple reaction excruciatingly arousing. Since he'd met Rose Blue, he'd been in a constant war of denial about his own emotions until yesterday when he'd given in to the kiss. He wasn't feeling much stronger at the moment, and why should he? He was officially off police business. The last idea set free his restraint.

He tugged her against him and cupped the back of her head, searching for hesitation in her expression. The hot sexual intensity on her face invaded the thin wall of his resistance, and heat surged through him. He bent and nibbled at the corner of her mouth. "Hmm, you taste sweet and sour."

"I hope you're not comparing me to our lunch at the ancient Chinese restaurant," she mumbled.

He silenced her complaint by running his tongue over her top lip. She tightened her grip. He slid his hands over the curve of her hips. The soft feel of the fabric slid across his palms and urged him to seek more.

He pulled her head back and deepened the kiss, pressing her body against him. Hot longing seared between them and shoved aside all his worries and thoughts about people except one. He wanted her. He craved the taste of her skin, wanted to inhale the scent of her...

The ring of a phone penetrated his hazy brain. He lifted his head. "Is that your cell?"

"Huh?" She blinked.

"First a siren and now your phone," he mumbled.

"I thought you didn't remember our kiss yesterday?" She threw him a wide-eyed glance and turned to dig her cell out of her purse. After a glance at the caller ID, she shrugged. "Sorry, it's my friend, Cassie, in Brattleboro."

"I read her interview with my predecessor. She was out of town when your sister went missing and claims to have little knowledge of A.J. Edwards or anyone wanting to harm Dahlia."

"Thanks for the rundown." Rose pointed to the phone. "I have to speak to her. She may have questions about the boutique."

As she left the room, the sway of her hips snared his attention. For two and a half years he'd thrown himself into his job and concentrated on surviving a divorce where his ex had asked for everything he owned except his mug with the coffee rings inside. Now Rose had gotten under his skin micro-inch by micro-inch until he was finding himself in a defensive position. Besides the obvious conflict of work, what was that warning in his gut about Rose?

Lots, he told himself. She talked to a dead sister who appeared and talked back. And if she wasn't really speaking to the victim, then how could Rose recite facts from the crime, which only the killer or victim would know? Worse, she had him dancing around her like a teenager hot for the prom queen or head cheerleader.

Any good law enforcer would know better than to get involved with her. Yet, he believed her story. He studied the windows again to distract himself. He whistled over the sight of the fire escape dangling in the air.

Rose walked back into the kitchen still talking on her cell.

"Thanks for the update, Cass. We'll talk again soon." Rose snapped her phone closed. "My friend, Cassie, wanted to review some orders that arrived." Her face sobered. "She also passed along sympathies from my customers. It's nice that people are thinking of Dahlia."

"She must be dependable."

"Cassie's a little flaky, but she's helping me by running the Blues Sisters while I'm away."

He approached her. "Now where were we?"

"I wish we could pick up from where we left off but—" She glanced at the clock on the kitchen stove. "We're going to be late."

He wanted to groan in protest. Instead he asked, "Are you ready to go?"

"As soon as I reapply my lipstick, I'll be set." She disappeared into the other room.

She was right. Now wasn't the moment to start something he couldn't finish. After the dinner, they had all night.

"Let's go," she said, reappearing.

"Rose, I want you to know something. I'm attracted to you,

but you and I together might not be the best idea." That wasn't exactly what he wanted to say, but it was better than confessing he was looking through the lens of a detective at their relationship.

"I'll be going home to Vermont once you make an arrest, and no one will remember me or us together."

Was he that forgettable? Her explanation irritated rather than reassured him.

She shrugged into her jacket, and they walked out of the apartment toward his car. She settled in the front seat, snapped on her seatbelt and then folded her hands together. "I can't wait to get into a warm house. Spring sure takes its time coming."

"The Drowns live in the North End, only a short distance." He turned the key, and the engine roared to life.

Within seconds, they were officially on the road and on their "date." Rose seemed absorbed in the passing scenery outside the window. Was this a good sign or bad? He drove past the downtown, hung a left up the hill by the Pizza Palooza and pushed the pedal to the metal. If Buddy hadn't calmed down, then the evening would take a different spin. No matter, the sooner they arrived, the quicker he could run interference with Buddy and end the first part of the evening, which meant they'd reach the conclusion at Rose's apartment. The last part of the night presented all kinds of possibilities he liked.

Finally he reached the neighborhood of larger homes with manicured lawns and mulch covered flowerbeds. Luke parked in front of the familiar beige Dutch Colonial with the three-stall garage. Buddy's silver SUV was nowhere to be seen, which was a minor relief. They strolled together along the walk lined by small evergreen bushes and had reached the front steps when the door flew open.

Dean stepped out. "Luke and Rose, welcome to the Drown Castle."

"Thanks, Dean." Rose glided over the threshold." I can't wait to enjoy a dinner with all of you. Is Buddy here yet?"

Luke stepped inside behind her. Dean might as well be the executioner welcoming them into the dungeon. Let the torture begin.

CHAPTER 13

Rose and Luke entered the gray tiled hall lit by an overhead chandelier.

"Bud will be along." Dean slapped Luke's back. "Hey, how about those Celtics? Come over and watch the next game on my new TV. The huge screen makes you feel like you're at the game. Rose, it's good to see you." He shook her hand. "Tia's taking care of last minute dinner preparations and will join us in a moment. We've planned a special announcement for you."

"For me?"

"Absolutely, I hope you'll approve." Dean paused a moment, and his smile faded. "I don't want to spoil the evening, but I'll mention the obvious once, and then we can forget and enjoy our dinner. Rose, I'm your landlord, and I'm responsible for the building's security. I want to apologize for what happened at your apartment. I've hired two men to install an alarm system. Of course, nothing is easy. The tragic news about your sister's disappearance and death set off a buying frenzy for security measures and a backlog for installation. The men will put in the system Wednesday. If I'm really lucky, the permit for the restaurant renovations will be approved immediately and remodeling can start in a day or two. Workers in the place will discourage anyone from thinking it's an easy target to break into."

"Glad you brought up the safety issues, Dean," Luke interjected.

Rose widened her eyes at him. "I'm not moving out."

"You're leaving?" Dean asked.

She shook her head.

"The safety measures in the building are poor." Lennox interjected. "The chain lock won't keep out a two-year-old, and the intercom is fried."

Rose's face flushed. "I'm responsible for the broken intercom. I'll pay for a replacement out of the security deposit."

"Thanks for alerting me. I'll work on the issues first thing tomorrow. Let me take your coats." Dean held out his hands.

They gave their jackets to Dean and he hung them in the hall closet. "You can leave your pocketbook inside." He nodded toward the open door.

"Thanks for the offer." Rose rested a hand on top of the purse slung over her shoulder. "But a girl always keeps her lipstick close. You never know when a touch up is in order."

She was carrying her gun. As long as she didn't whip it out and shoot Buddy, the evening would be a rousing success. Luke grimaced. His dream of a stress free night was vanishing faster than a celebrity's sobriety after rehab.

"Luke." Tia Drown stood at the edge of the hall.

She wore tan pants and blouse. Her brown hair was mixed with strands of red. As usual, the way she entered a room and held her head reminded him of Miss America strutting down a runway. She beamed her contagious smile, the one that Buddy had inherited.

"I'm happy you're back where you belong." Tia gave him a quick hug.

"Let me introduce Rose Blue," Luke said when she released him.

"Thank you for inviting me, Mrs. Drown." Rose stepped forward and offered her hand.

The older woman embraced her in her swift style. "Please call me Tia. I'm happy you joined us tonight. Ledgeview must seem like a place out of a horrible dream. I hope to show you decent people do live in our community. Dean, will you announce the news?"

Luke shot a glance at Dean. What was he up to?

Rose, my wife and I agreed to organize a Tip Crimeline of volunteers dedicated solely to your sister's case. They'll report directly to the police."

"And," Tia said, stepping into her husband's side, "we've donated a reward of three thousand dollars for anyone who has information that leads to the conviction of your sister's killer. Dean's spoken to the mayor, and he's already pushed through the red tape for the setup."

Rose stood still, staring, and then, bolted forward and hugged each of them. "I can't thank you enough."

Words left Luke for a moment. "That's...generous of you both." He calculated the hours, manpower and money needed for the project. Should he pen a thank you or lead a taxpayers' revolt?

"I hope you'll be involved, Luke. You can assign a man of your choice to head the committee, or do it yourself. The mayor raved over the idea." Dean clapped his hands together. "We'll work out the details after dinner."

"I can't believe your generosity." Rose blinked away tears of happiness.

Sure, she could play on their good natures for information on Buddy.

"Believe me. Lots of fine people live in Ledgeview." Tia smiled at her.

"Thank you, Mrs...Tia. Your gift is better than Christmas. I'll always remember your kindness," Rose said to her. "I've wanted to meet you for quite a while. Where's Buddy tonight? He's the only one missing."

"Don't forget dinner, Rose. The real reason we came," Luke added. Despite the Drowns' generous offer, Rose seemed determined to focus on his friend.

"Buddy and Shauna should arrive in about half an hour. She works until seven thirty at the bank on Tuesday nights, and Buddy picks her up." Tia lowered her voice. "She's like a daughter to me. Have you met?"

"I've never had the pleasure."

"You'll love her. Everyone does."

"Luke, let's leave the women to their talk." Dean clapped a hand on his shoulder. "I've plenty of cold ones in the bar fridge. What would you like?"

To avoid a disaster tonight. "If you don't mind, I'll stick with the women for a while." He edged closer to Rose, who narrowed her eyes in disapproval at him.

"Don't be silly," Tia said. "I want to show Rose the results of the clothing drive. You'd be bored to death."

"Right, Lennox, bored-to-death," Rose confirmed, widening her eyes at him. "Go with Dean." She walked with Tia to the hall.

Luke mentally swore. She was going to interrogate their hostess.

"When Buddy arrives, he won't waste a minute straightening out his father's version of the last basketball game."

"Does that annoy Dean?" Rose followed Tia into a cream-colored corridor decorated with photos of Buddy at different ages. What would these good people say if the tip line led to their son?

"Dean takes Buddy's corrections all in the spirit of the evening. Teasing each other is part of their relationship. Luke joins in when he visits. He and Buddy have been friends since middle school. They'd do anything for each other."

Or, be blind to each other's faults.

"They're close. In school, they were on every team together and inseparable. They were always at each other's house eating, supposedly studying or tossing a ball around. Luke's mother's a close friend of mine. I wish she'd move back to New Hampshire. I miss her." Tia paused by a snapshot of her son with his arm around a woman with long, dark hair and flawless, white skin. The young woman leaned into him.

"Here's Shauna and Bud's engagement picture. Beautiful, isn't she? Buddy is lucky. She's totally devoted to him, and he's crazy about her. They were high school sweethearts. You know first loves often find each other again."

"Again?" Rose raised her brows. Then she remembered Buddy had cheated on Shauna and she left him.

"They broke up before Shauna left for college. Buddy has dated lots of other girls." Tia inclined her head toward her son's picture. "He's a charmer when he wants to be. When Shauna moved back last summer, they started seeing each other, quietly at first. True love won in the end."

Rose studied the future Mrs. Drown. She gazed up at Buddy with open adoration in her eyes. Her face seemed to glow.

"Buddy's very handsome. I bet he broke lots of hearts when the engagement became public."

"Buddy had his share of girlfriends, but he didn't care much about them. Shauna was his first serious and only love. She was married briefly years ago, but we'll forgive her." Tia laughed. "They're perfect for each other. Sorry, I'm a romantic at heart and seeing them together reminds me of when I met Dean."

"How did you get together?"

"Not too many people know, but I was married before Dean. My ex and I said our vows the week after high school graduation. Buddy was born nine months later. The marriage was never good, but I was stubborn and determined to make it work. But as the years passed, I decided divorce was my only option to keep myself and Buddy safe."

"Going it alone must have been tough."

"Staying was worse. I thought I'd never marry again. Then I met Dean on a ski lift. By the time we reached the top of the mountain, we were a couple. We've been married close to thirty years. People thought we wouldn't last. I'm five years older, and had an eleven year-old when we got together."

"No wonder you're a romantic. Did Dean grow up in Ledgeview?"

"We lived in Maine. We moved to Ledgeview soon after we married for Dean to establish his business. Come this way." Tia switched on a light and led Rose through an arched doorway, into a twelve-by-twelve foot space. "This is my sewing room."

Piles of clothing covered most of the furniture and probably hid a sewing machine somewhere. The legs of a chair peeked out from under a load of shirts and skirts. "Your store must be a big success. You should rent a storage space."

"My shop is overflowing, but I don't rent. Dean owns the building."

"I forgot. Guess you have a good relationship with your landlord."

"Once a year, I collect clothes for the homeless. I admit I'm proud of my success." Tia put a finger to her chin. "Wait a minute." She grabbed a bag from the top of a pile and dug out a black garment. "Lovely, isn't it?"

Rose glanced at the fabric in her hostess's hands and nodded.

"Women are always searching for the perfect little black outfit, and today, one found its way to me. Can you believe it?" Sequins on the garb shimmered as Tia held it higher.

Rose nodded. "The ladies will be jealous when you wear it."

"The dress is perfect for you." She held the garment up and tilted her head to the side. "Want to try it on?" Her eyes glimmered with excitement. "You'll have to wear it to the celebration for Dean after he wins."

How much would the perfect little dress cost? She bet her hostess never carried a brand Rose could afford. She'd have to find a way to politely decline. Her mind groped for excuses while the last part of Tia's statement sank in. "Celebrate a win?"

"Dean's running for mayor. He believes he can beat the incumbent. A lot of people are unhappy with your sister's murder investigation. Ledgeview used to be one of the safest cities to live in. Now a young woman has been murdered in our hometown, and with no one under arrest, who knows who will be killed next?"

At least she wasn't alone in her fears. "I'm sorry my sister's death brought such fright."

"You're not to blame. Dean has picked out his platform for his campaign." She raised a manicured finger. "Elect a working man for the working people who puts safety first."

Tia beamed. "We're throwing a party next weekend to kick off the announcement. Of course, you're invited. Your presence will be a boost to Dean's campaign." She ran a hand over the piece of clothing. "Don't you adore the simple, clean cut lines? It's a classic." Her face brightened. "Luke can bring you to the party. You might not feel like a get together after what's happened to your sister, but Dean and I would appreciate your support as a guest."

She was acting as though she and Lennox were a couple, dangerous territory. "Homicide detectives don't take much time off, but you must be excited. When's the election?"

"The voting happens in the fall. Dean's announcing his decision next weekend to his closest friends. These elections require a lot of planning, time and money. My husband's been a city selectman for years. Mayor is the next logical rung on the political ladder, and he has what it takes. Dean's a hard worker, keeps his word and listens to people. He's a winner."

"How much is the dress?" Rose blurted out.

"It's free. Oh, dear, I hope you weren't worried about price. A customer of mine donated it to the drive. My clients drop off items from their closets to help me out."

Tia brought her to the room to give her a donated dress and further a match up with Lennox. Her own plan to learn about Buddy was nothing compared with her hostess's.

"The price tag was still pinned to the fabric when she dropped it off," Tia continued. "The previous owner probably thought she'd diet and fit into it before the truth sank in. She'd never be the right size. The dress was meant for you."

"Tia, you don't need to give me anything. You and Dean have done plenty by starting the tip line. I also haven't forgotten your husband offered me Dahlia's place and saved me hours of searching in a new city."

"Apartment hunting when you're upset is never good, especially when you're alone. Course, you can always talk to Luke. He'd understand your feelings. He dealt with his father's death, and I'm sure returning to Ledgeview hasn't been easy. People often like to remind you of uncomfortable moments from our past, for some reason."

Rose went still. "How did his father die? I read it was suicide."

"That was the final version." Tia glanced away.

"There were other stories?" This was news.

"He died a year and a half ago. His passing was listed as a suicide, but no one believed he'd take his life." Tia dipped her gaze for a moment. "Dean doesn't like me to talk about it because he feels I'm gossiping," she lowered her voice. "John Lennox would never commit suicide. He was never depressed a day in his life."

"What do you mean?"

"The M.E.—"

The door clicked open and Lennox entered.

Silence fell over the room for an uncomfortable moment.

"Am I interrupting the girl talk?" He searched their faces with raised brows.

"You surprised us," Tia said, recovering her composure first.

"Is something wrong?"

"I came to ask if you'd like me to check on dinner while you're busy. I'm a mean cook." He stepped closer to Rose as though he meant to herd her through the doorway.

She bet he wanted to cook up an excuse to get her away from Tia.

"I'm all set." Their hostess shook her head. "I wish Buddy would learn to use a stove. I've warned Shauna not to expect home cooked meals from him." Tia scooted over to the pile of fabrics and pulled out a paper bag. *Only the Best* was printed across the center of the flowery shopping bag. She slid the gift inside. "You can try it on at home."

"Good idea. Lennox, Tia told me Dean's making a big announcement soon."

"Really, what's that?" With hands stuffed in his pockets, he paced around the sewing room. His gaze traveled over the fabric as though searching for matching prints.

"He's going to run for mayor," Tia said. "It's still a secret from the general public."

"He's wants to be the mayor?" Lennox halted. His eyes widened in surprise.

"I bet Buddy's excited about his father's decision to enter the elections." Rose hoped Lennox wouldn't interrupt her chance to talk about the missing Drown.

"Buddy likes to stay out of the limelight of political affairs," Tia said. "But he enjoys a good get-together." The paper bag crinkled as she folded over the top. "Let me add how sorry I am about your sister." She patted Rose's arm and faced Lennox. "Everyone is on edge with a killer running around. No woman in Ledgeview wants to walk alone or drive by herself."

"We're going to catch the person responsible, Tia," he confirmed. "Until then, take precautions."

"I have faith in you, Detective Lennox." Tia turned and gave a startled cry.

"What is it?" Rose asked, trying to pinpoint a frightening object.

"Someone put the boxes of breakables on the bottom of the clothes pile. I bet my cleaning lady was responsible." Tia strode to a corner chair and lifted mound after mound of shirts, pants, and dresses like a forklift and transferred them to a heap on the floor.

"I can help." Rose's foot crunched on an object. She bent down and searched the rug. "I stepped on something." She picked up three straight pins with round pink heads. They were duplicates of the one stuck in her doorbell.

She rubbed her arms as a chill settled over her. Of course, stores must sell hundreds of similar pins. She slipped them into her pocket.

"Don't worry. I've sewing notions all over the place. Dean complains every time he comes into the room." Tia put her hands on her hips. "What a mess. I should limit people from dropping off their donations until the week before the sale." She swung the first box out of the way and bent for the second.

"Let me." Lennox stepped forward and grabbed the bottom container.

"Put it by the desk. I can manage the rest later."

He grabbed the box and frowned. "What's inside, brick knick knacks? He deposited the container on the desktop. "How did you lug this inside?"

"Once I married, I carried all kinds of things: a baby, sheetrock, deliveries for my store."

Tia's arms rippled with muscles underneath her blouse. She was a strong woman. Had she developed her strength out of self defense against an abusive husband, or the stylish way, working out at a gym?

"Let's join Dean and what's left of the appetizers." Tia rested her box on top of Lennox's. "He's probably in the kitchen stealing food out of the oven. He calls it sampling." She glanced at her watch. "I hope Buddy and Shauna arrive soon. Dinner's almost ready."

"If they're late, we'll serve them the leftovers." Lennox opened the door. "Ladies, first."

Rose carried her gift and walked through the hall with Tia. Lennox shadowed their heels. The doorbell rang as they reached the main entryway.

"I hope it's not someone wanting Dean." Tia's face scrunched up. "He's always working. You won't believe how rare it is to enjoy a dinner at home together." She peeked out the curtained side window in the entryway. "It's the police." Her lip quivered as she switched on the exterior light and opened up.

Lennox hovered beside Rose.

A young uniformed officer stood on the step. "Evening, Mrs. Drown. You probably don't remember me. I was in high school with your son. I'm Jay Lark. Buddy asked me to stop on my way home and let you know he's at the station."

Lennox stepped up. "Evening, Officer, is there a problem?"

"Detective Lennox, I didn't know you were here." He shrugged and blinked away his surprise.

"Is something wrong with my son?" Tia interjected.

"It was Miss Smith. There was an incident in the parking garage this evening."

"What do you mean? Oh, my God, was it that maniac killer?"

The officer bowed his head and shuffled his feet. His silent confirmation sent a quiver through Rose.

Tia stumbled backwards before Lennox steadied her.

"I'll get Dean." Rose squeezed Tia's shoulder and turned away. The killer wasn't hiding. He was hunting another victim.

CHAPTER 14

Luke escorted Rose inside her apartment and then found Buddy in the hospital where the odor of antiseptic greeted him. The white waiting room was strangely empty except for his friend.

"I didn't expect you." Buddy jumped up from his plastic seat and shook Lennox's hand. "Thanks for coming. The doctor's with Shauna."

Lennox was speechless. His friend never showed gratitude. It was his guy code.

Buddy sank into his chair. "I can't believe anyone would harm Shauna. She's a good person. How could the attack have happened?"

"Often these assaults are crimes of convenience such as a parking garage without witnesses but with an easy exit. What about the beat cop, did he see anything?"

"The patrol had already gone through."

"Are your parents around?"

"They headed home. Mom was too upset to sit in the waiting room. I promised to call them after Shauna's exam."

Luke sat down across from Buddy. "How's Shauna really doing?"

"She suffered a bruise on the side of her face that she doesn't remember getting and a sprained arm from escaping her kidnapper. Of course, she's shook up. She didn't want to go to the doctor, but my dad and I managed to convince her."

"You should have called me, Buddy."

"I wanted to handle the situation. You can imagine how my

dad acted. He rushed to the station and tried to take over. Shauna had enough to deal with." Buddy tapped his fingertips together in front of his chest. "The truth is—I… didn't want to call you because I'd acted like such a jackass earlier today." He bent forward, hung his head between his knees and swept his hands back over his hair. "I couldn't have been a bigger jerk. I hope you'll forget what I said."

"It's okay, Bud." Luke touched his friend's shoulder. "We'll always watch each other's backs just like when we played football."

Buddy straightened, blinking his eyes. "Thanks."

"How'd Shauna get away from her attacker?"

"She pepper-sprayed the guy."

"Did she see which way he fled or if he jumped into a car?"

"She screamed, ran for the exit and didn't look back. She was afraid he'd grab her again." Buddy collapsed against the chair and extended his legs in front of him. "What a night. She bought the pepper spray after the Blue woman was murdered, and I teased her for buying it, called her paranoid."

"Did she get a good look at her assailant?"

"She said he was about six feet, dressed completely in black with a ski mask and gloves. God, I feel awful." He ran a hand over his face.

"Describe the ski mask."

"Not much to say. Shauna said it was a black, knit mask with holes for eyes and a mouth."

"Did she notice anything about his clothes or a watch or any kind of jewelry?"

"No, she was trying to get away."

"Why did you meet her in the garage? Why not park in front of the bank?"

"The parking spaces in front of the building are taken by their customers. The attack's my fault. If I'd arrived on time, she'd be fine."

Luke wasn't about to absolve Buddy and let him off the hook until he learned more. "Why were you late?"

"I stopped at Tiny's Bar and Grill and ordered a drink. Then I heard my mom's voice in my head, complaining about me drinking before her dinner party. I canceled my beer and drank a diet soda. I was only a little behind schedule when I drove to the bank, but Shauna got out a few minutes before I arrived. If only I'd called and told her I was running late and to wait inside."

"You didn't phone her?"

"I haven't replaced my lost cell. I was kinda enjoying being outside of Dean's constant reach, and at the moment, a phone is the least of my problems." Buddy put his face in his hands.

Luke was tempted to ask why he didn't borrow someone's cell at Tiny's but decided to let up a little. "She's safe now."

Buddy met his stare. "She was a mess. Crying, she didn't want to see anyone. I had to talk her into reporting the attack and letting the doctor near her. The cops wanted to keep her longer. Dean convinced the officer taking her statement to let her go to the hospital. He also persuaded Mom to leave. She gets overemotional."

"I can't blame Tia, given the circumstances," Luke said. "When Shauna's calmer, she might remember something else. I'll speak to her then."

"Shauna's attacker must be the man who killed Dahlia Blue."

"We'll need proof."

"It must be him unless psychos have taken over the city. What's happened to this place?" Buddy fisted a hand on his knee. "This kind of thing never used to happen in Ledgeview."

Time to test Buddy's memory. "According to my father's cold cases, there was another young woman who died four or five years ago in North Conway."

"What's your point? New Hampshire was always a scary place?"

"Murders are big events in our state."

"The police better make Shauna's attack a big deal and catch the crazy guy today."

Luke stood. His questions had gotten him nowhere except to acknowledge a physical similarity to Rose's pursuer on Main Street. "We'll arrest him, Bud."

"You're always confident. It doesn't matter if you're shooting on the basketball court or pursuing a criminal." His angry expression fell away. "Don't pressure Shauna. I've told you everything she knows. She gave her statement and doesn't want to keep reliving it. She needs to rest."

Buddy didn't sound supportive of the investigation despite complaining he wanted the attacker arrested. "You must be taking her home soon."

"My mom insisted we bring her to their house so she's not alone when she's discharged. Shauna didn't want to call her parents in Connecticut and worry them."

"I'll read the report. Shauna can talk to me anytime. I'll come to the house, and we can meet in private away from the station."

"Don't count on it, Luke. She wishes tonight never happened and can't wait to put it in her past." The corners of his mouth lifted. "I'm going to sleep in my old room. We'll be one big, happy family at the Drown home."

Shauna was the victim and the one who deserved to be happy. Luke wanted to say, but the hospital was not the place for a lecture. "Give Shauna my love." He'd go over her statement at the station and catch up with her when she'd calmed down.

Buddy stood. "It's good to have you back." He held out his hand.

Luke accepted the handshake and remembered all the times they'd high fived over trouncing the visiting teams, eaten at each other's houses and griped about their teachers.

"You'll let me know as soon as you arrest the guy."

"You have my word." Luke left the waiting room and drove to Rose's apartment. A soft glow backlit the drawn shade in the front window. The temptation to visit her was strong. Maybe he could spare a few minutes.

He slowed and finally pulled over. The street was quiet. He could be upstairs in seconds.

Digging out his phone, he hit her number.

"Lennox?" Her voice sounded clear and close.

"How are you?"

"I'm fine, how's Shauna?"

He summarized Buddy's version of the attack.

"I'd hoped you'd get a lead," Rose said, her tone heavy with disappointment. "At least, she got him with the pepper spray and escaped."

"Once Shauna's over the initial shock, she may remember an important detail. I'll re-interview her. Sleep tight, Rose." He clicked off, and threw a last glance at her window. He wished he was joining her.

He imagined her running across the floor to answer his knock. Her hazel eyes would light with recognition, and a smile would spread across her face. Mentally, he skimmed over her full lips as she said hello and then downward to the curve of her hips where he'd slide his hand around her waist. Then he'd—

His phone rang, ending his fantasy.

"Lenn-ox," the Chief's voice barked. "What are you doing up there in New Hampshire?"

The image of his middle-aged boss gritting out each word while clenching a cigar popped into his mind.

"The Mayor and I have been playing phone tag all day. I finally caught him, and he chewed my ass off, informing me Dean Drown's future daughter-in-law was attacked in one of our garages that we've claimed are safe. Do I need to remind you the Mayor's up for re-election. Follow the domino effect. I also don't want to announce to my wife that her first vacation in thirty years is over. She'll miss the rest of her baby daughter's wedding celebrations because the man I hired for head detective can't keep our pledge to protect the citizens of Ledgeview."

"I'm on it, Chief. I'm trying to uncover a link between the attack in the garage and the Dahlia Blue homicide."

"Find it and start issuing warrants for arrests. Now. I don't have time to talk, but understand, I won't be happy to cut my family vacation short."

"Understood."

The click announced the end of the conversation.

The subtext of the phone call was clear. The Chief had gone out on a limb to hire Luke and not promote from within. Was it because he'd believed Luke was good at his job, or was it as everyone whispered—the chief's friendship with Luke's dad had gotten him the job?

Luke felt his limb of safety shaking and ready to break. The light in Rose's window glowed through the shade as he drove his vehicle down the street.

When he reached the Station, the building was quiet. In his cubicle, he saw the blinking red light indicating a message on his landline. Was the Chief calling again to fire him? He hit the button and retrieved a voicemail from Frank that asked him to call. Luke hit his friend's number.

"Hey, Luke my boy. I'm going to make your day. I nabbed another picture of Dahlia Blue's Old Lover Boy for you."

"You mean A.J. Edwards. Where did you get it?"

"I'm an ex detective. I drove to his high school in Rhode Island. Let's see. He was an only child." Frank recited A.J.'s birth date, place of birth and educational history. "The guy was big into sports but peaked during his teens. One of the women who worked in the school's office told me she remembered him when he attended classes with her son. She said he was the quiet type, and didn't socialize much, but he wasn't as silent as his cousin who he lived with. She rarely spoke. People used to joke the cat stole her tongue and sold it on eBay. Guess she spent a lot of time absent too. She dropped out of high school and sight."

"I'm not sure who is stranger, the cousin or the people making the statements about her. What else do you have?"

"A.J. Edwards's father went to jail for embezzling from the car dealership where he worked. That's when A.J. was ten, and he went to live with his silent cousin and her father. Guess A.J.'s mother couldn't provide for him when authorities sent her husband to the big house."

"I've a feeling about him. Find out more about the father and the rest of the family. We can interview them all. Maybe one of them lives in New Hampshire, and A.J. was familiar with our area because of the family."

"I've dug into his background. The uncle owned the town garage in Rhode Island but died three years ago. No one's been able to trace what happened to the cousin or Edwards' parents."

"Good job, and when was the last time you saw Buddy Drown?"

"I drove by his house before I left for out of state. I didn't see him. Want me back on his tail?"

"His girlfriend, Shauna Smith, was attacked in the parking garage next to the bank around seven thirty tonight. She spray peppered the guy and escaped with only bruises. She gave a vague description of her attacker. Here's my question. Was Edwards angry enough with Dahlia over their breakup that he followed her to Ledgeview and killed her? Then decided to stick around and terrorize more women?"

"That's a leap, but we follow them all. Pretty gutsy to attack in a busy downtown garage.

A patrol rides through every night."

"The patrol had passed through. The attacker probably staked out the lot and learned the times of the rounds."

"Any fights between the victim and your friend, Buddy?"

"You can't suspect Buddy Drown of assaulting his girlfriend, Frank. Besides he has an alibi. He was at Tiny's Bar where he ordered a drink. The story's being confirmed."

"There's always an alibi. Are you working the assault case?"

"I'm not the primary, at the moment, but if a connection to the Blue case comes up, I'm on it."

"I bet you get one."

"I hope so, Frank." He hesitated for a second. "I've a question for you. I recently contacted the witness, Mr. Simon Zinger, from the cold case in North Conway."

"Go on."

"Notes indicated Zinger might have seen the kidnapper's vehicle on the class six road near where he was fishing. The driver headed into the woods in a silver pickup. The victim's body was found two miles from the sighting."

"Did his memory improve with the years?"

"He wasn't helpful at first. During our little talk he mentioned something new. He'd spotted a bumper sticker on the truck: This car climbed Mount Washington."

"They give out thousands every year, Luke, and how does a sticker hook into Dahlia Blue?"

"It's another long shot, I know. I'm trying to tie the attacks together." He blew an exasperated breath. Was he inventing links to the recent homicide?

"No evidence confirmed that the woman's killer drove the vehicle, Luke."

"I'll keep working on it. We'll talk later, Frank." After he hung up, he replayed Frank's doubts about Buddy in his mind. Good thing Bud stopped at Tiny's and could produce witnesses.

He opened a manila envelope on his desk and dumped out the contents. The Vermont

Police had sent A.J. Edward's financial, phone and email records.

Luke circled in red several large sums of cash deposited and withdrawn on dates when he lived in Brattleboro and dated Dahlia. The phone records turned up nothing but he might have had a throw away. The emails raised more red flags. Many referred to business arrangements and meetings and were from ISPs from various states. What kind of trade was this mechanic into?

Luke punched in the number of the Vermont detective's private cell. The man answered immediately.

"I'm the detective on the Dahlia Blue homicide. I'm following up on your police department's report of A.J. Edwards. Any chance there's anything new to add?"

"No sign of him in our town. The report was written the first week of March when the Blue woman had been missing a week."

"When did you send the file?"

"I personally gave it to Detective Conroy while he was here re-interviewing a few of the neighbors. He said you'd read it right away. I guess with the change of commands the file got buried. Glad you're following up. We'll help if we can."

"I'll take you up on the offer if we need more manpower." Luke clicked off. Buried was exactly what Conroy had done with the file. He probably only produced it now because he was aware Luke was looking closer at Edwards and would start asking more questions.

Luke let out some choice words and swiveled his chair to the computer. He'd find Edwards despite Conroy. The mechanic was beginning to look more and more like a person of interest.

Luke booted up his computer. Within minutes, he'd signed into Facebook using his alias and posted a picture of a sweet, red Maserati. Next to the picture he typed: *Will hire a mechanic with a slow hand and a tender touch for my baby. I'm willing to pay extra for reliable service. Will travel anywhere in the state of Rhode Island.*

"We're going to have a face-to-face, A.J." Luke signed off.

CHAPTER 15

It was time to up the fun. She'd been in Ledgeview long enough. Now was time for Rose to learn she wasn't alone. Eyes were watching.

Time for a little personal moment. You know I care, pretty Rose.

Rose raised her head from the kitchen table and squinted at the clock. It was after eleven pm. She must have fallen asleep while writing in her journal. She wobbled to her feet. She'd pick up the diary later. Sleep called to her. In the bathroom, she got ready for bed and pulled on a T-shirt. Afterwards, she sank onto the sofa bed wishing Lennox was downstairs searching for clues in the old restaurant. His presence always made her feel protected.

Rose relaxed under the warmth of her blanket with visions of Lennox dancing in her head.

She woke a short time later when the cold penetrated the cover and chilled her feet and hands. What happened to the heat? She should check the thermostat, but leaving her cocoon seemed less appealing. Outside the wind howled, and rain beat on the window like a child throwing a tantrum. She tucked the edges of the blanket around herself and heard another sound.

Soft sobs mixed with the moans of the wind. Someone was whimpering in her apartment. Rose tugged the blanket beneath her chin and turned over to stare into the living room shadows. The chair and lamp took shape in the dark as she searched for the source of the weeping. She threw the coverlet off and sat up.

"Dahlia?"

The cries stopped.

Rose slid her feet over the side of the bed. The cool air infiltrated her flannel sweats. She grabbed the gray spread and wrapped it around herself and tiptoed across the room. The matted fibers of the rug scraped across the soles of her bare feet. She paused at the edge of the kitchen floor and snapped on the light.

Her door held by the chain was cracked open. What? Hadn't she locked it when she went to bed? She jumped forward, slammed and locked it. Rose shivered. Outside the rain smacked against the windows. The wind's moans grew louder and changed into the sound of tearing duct tape until the rip of the tape grew in her head. Rose grabbed her purse from the counter and dug out the gun.

She held the weapon with an unsteady hand and scouted the rooms where nothing was out of order. Finally, she sank into the kitchen chair. She laid her weapon down and stared down at her journal that she'd left on the table. One sentence was written across the page. She didn't remember starting another page.

She swept up the book. The new entry stared up from the paper. *Go home!*

The dot in the exclamation point was a heart, just like Dahlia had always used.

* * *

The next morning, Rose finished her breakfast and decided to walk to the police station to show Lennox the page. Everything seemed ordinary in the light of day and her message from beyond the grave seemed impossible, but then Dahlia appearing to her was not likely either.

Still, doubts ate at her. Had she somehow written the warning while she was half asleep? People walked and ate in their sleep. Why not write? The cool air whipped through her jeans, and she zipped up her parka. She hurried past the cupcake store on Main where customers lined up to buy their favorite flavor before the store ran out. Overhead, the bright sunshine held out a false promise of warmth. A piece of paper and dirt blew toward her, and she averted her face.

Resting her hand on the bulge of the gun in her purse, she

broke into a jog and reached police headquarters in six minutes. The uniformed clerk behind the glass took her name and told her to wait. She should have called Lennox first. Maybe he wanted to avoid her after their unofficial date at the Drowns. At least it felt like a date, until the end. Of course, Lennox wouldn't let a woman distract him from his job. Single minded or bull headed described him best. In Lennox, the characteristic was an admirable trait.

She found an empty chair against the wall in the station's waiting area. Two senior citizens were seated at the end of the row. A walker reposed in front of one of the men. Near the clerk's area, another elderly gentleman in a wheelchair kept watch on everyone entering and leaving. The clerk called a name and the senior with combed over hair grabbed his walker and wavered to his feet. He crept toward the metal detector while the officer held the door open.

"Some people seem to get more consideration than the rest of us," a short, pudgy man at the end of the row huffed.

What was the story with the elderly? She'd little time to imagine before the clerk called her name. Rose was admitted through the metal detector and then led toward Lennox's cubicle.

The large workroom was full of oldsters being interviewed. "Did someone mug a little old lady in the crosswalk or are they auditioning for a remake of the Golden Girls?" she asked, entering Lennox's space without waiting for him to invite her inside.

His taut face alerted her he hadn't slept much.

"Morning, Rose." His eyes warmed. "It's nice to talk to someone today who's not mad they canceled Murder She Wrote. Sit." He threw out a hand at the metal chair in front of his desk. "We're re-interviewing the cast of The Angels Are Singing Tonight. Myra included every breathing, elderly male of the Ledgeview Senior Citizen community."

"You're interviewing the entire cast?"

"We can't let anyone slip through." He sipped from a steaming mug, and the aroma of coffee floated into the air.

"You're drinking Espresso. It has a good bold taste that suits you." Rose inhaled the scent for a quick caffeine fix before she perched on the chair warm from the last body.

"Glad to have your stamp of approval, Miss Blue. I could use more. By the way, nothing forensic showed on the pin from your doorbell. They can be bought at any discount store with a craft or sewing department."

"Sorry. Did you hear any more about Shauna this morning?" She rested her purse in her lap.

"No word from the Drowns or Shauna."

"Too bad, but I won't take up much of your time." She fished in her purse and removed the journal. "I found a sentence I don't remember writing in my entry last night, and it's bugged me."

"I don't understand."

"I fell asleep and the last thing I remember writing was my name in my diary. When I woke up, this sentence was printed on the next blank page. She held out the journal.

He stared at the words, *Go home!* His face remained expressionless. "I'll have my handwriting expert examine it. If someone broke into your apartment—"

"The chain was on. No one could have gone in or out unless they were a shadow."

"Rose, your stalker could have locked himself inside."

"Inside?" Sick dread closed her throat, and she had to swallow to speak. "There must be a rational explanation."

"I'll install a new lock today."

She dragged an unsteady hand through her hair. "You could be wrong, Lennox. I mean no one was in my apartment this morning, and the chain was still on. It doesn't make sense. Besides, I've been thinking, and I figured out who wrote the words."

"Who?" His intense stare dared her to downplay the situation.

"My sister. She always hearted her exclamation point."

"Your dead sister wrote to you last night?" Both his brows shot up. "Now I really want my expert's opinion. I have a sample of Dahlia's signature from her driver's license and a shopping list found in her wallet. I'll bag the letter."

He thought she was crazy. She straightened in her chair, encouraging the anger to overtake her fear. "The message could be a warning, or she's angry with me. We fought over the stolen money the last time I saw her alive. See, she's never gotten over it. She's still mad at me and wrote me the threatening note." She paused. "You don't believe me."

"Rose, you have to admit it's a little out there."

She'd try her other theory. "Dahlia might have written the message through me and I don't remember. I've heard about it happening. What about the man who killed his wife in his sleep?"

"He was found guilty of perjury and murder." Lennox moved nearer to her and rested his hip on the desktop. "Let my experts examine the handwriting. It's possible it's a forgery."

She handed over the note. His disbelief hurt more than the idea of someone locked in her apartment. "Knock yourself out."

She turned to leave. The sooner she was away, the happier she'd be.

"Are you parked in the rear lot or out front?"

She paused at the cubicle exit. They stood so close together, her arm brushed against his chest. Despite her conflicting irritation and fear, the feeling of attraction enticed her nearer. "I walked."

"After what happened to Shauna and your experience last night, you should—"

"No police manual talks. I can't sit around, cowering in Dahlia's apartment. I came to Ledgeview to be sure her killer was caught and soon. I've a business and life to get back to. Staying inside my apartment accomplishes nothing and defeats my purpose. Right now, I'm going to the library. I want to reread the articles about my sister's death. I might have missed something."

He pinned her with a disapproving stare, and she stifled the urge to defend herself. Why did she have to want a man who didn't even believe in her? The memory of their kiss now brought regrets. "If any of the seniors flash back to a memory of my sister at the Audi, let me know."

"Listen, young man," a gravelly voice boomed over Lennox's portable wall. "I delivered her to heaven where she belonged. I confess. Take me away."

Lennox and Rose exchanged a glance and bounded around the divider.

Ten feet away, an elderly gentleman with white-hair thudded his fist against the plainclothesman's desk.

"What's happening here, Conroy?" Lennox demanded.

The other detective's mouth pulled downward.

The senior tilted his head back and the shoulders of his elbow-patched corduroy jacket sagged over his thin shoulders. "I was reciting my line from the play. It was a showstopper." His gaze landed on Rose. "Are we acquainted, young lady?"

"Me? No, we've never met."

"Did you meet her identical twin?" Lennox asked. "She was in the play at the Audi with you. Her name was Dahlia Blue."

"Excuse my confusion about our last meeting. I thought it was because I didn't take my Metamucil today." He winked at Rose. "Would you like to hear Othello's Soliloquy? I learned it when I was sixteen and have never forgotten one word." He dropped his voice to a confidential level. "The play was my first stage role at the high school."

"Sir," Lennox interjected. "Did you know Dahlia Blue?"

"I don't think so. Is she here?"

"Let's start again. What's your name?"

"Why, Othello, of course."

"Fred Melvin," Conroy said, tossing his pen on the desk with a shake of his head.

"I can provide you with a resume of my performances if you'd like." Othello widened his eyes in anticipation.

"Please," Rose cut in. "You must remember Dahlia. She was my identical twin."

"I'm sorry, young lady, I only remember my lines. I can recite personal references if you prefer, though I've not seen most of them in a dog's year or longer."

"Thanks for the offer, Mr. Melvin," Lennox said. "I have to escort the young lady from the building. Detective Conroy wants to learn more about your performances. Deliver a few lines to him."

"You're a big help, Lennox." Conroy's lips turned up in a pucker of disagreement.

"A gentleman always accompanies a woman to her destination," Othello called after them.

A small thrill went through Rose. For a few seconds, she'd pretend that Lennox was walking her out not because they were involved in a homicide case but because he truly cared about her, personally.

At the exit, he held the door and then joined her on the sidewalk away from the front desk clerk who'd watched them with interest.

She lingered near the building. "Othello or Mr. Melvin was too feeble to be a killer. I know you can't predict by someone's outward appearance, but I don't think he could have physically hurt my sister. I wonder what part he played in the Audi show."

"Fred Melvin was the Ledgeview High School drama coach when my dad attended classes, and he was still there when I was in high school. He used to hang at Joe's Coffee Shop until he went into the nursing home. Myra gave him a walk on in her play."

"I'm glad you're up on your facts."

"I'm sorry I didn't believe you about the handwriting. I believe in facts, but I'm trying to open my mind to other possibilities."

"I understand." Why couldn't he believe in her and never mind facts?

His hand skimmed over her cheek, and he smiled. "Good, let's go." He did his usual scan of the street and sidewalk before they started.

"Do you think you'll get a break in the case from the Audi players?" she asked, trying to forget the tingle from his touch.

"Unless you want tips on acid reflux, I wouldn't count on it. I've something else to discuss. I didn't want to mention it at the station since privacy was scarce."

"What is it?"

"Let's walk."

They strolled toward the library. A few shoppers and the early lunch bunch were out strolling to stores and restaurants. Her patience held for half a minute. "Okay, Lennox. What's happened?"

"I found out A.J.'s father embezzled funds from the car dealership where he worked. His father served time in the state prison for his crime and died shortly after his release."

"No wonder A.J. never talked about him." She paused near the Sneaky Sneakers Store as the news sank in. "What happened to his mother?"

"The family broke up when his dad was sentenced. A.J.'s mother died when he was about ten. He then lived with an uncle, who was a mechanic, and his daughter. The uncle passed away three years ago. We're still searching for the daughter. She could lead us to A.J. Any chance he spoke of her or places she lived?"

"I never knew she existed, which is strange. Dahlia told him all about our family: Gram, our absent father and our mother. I hope A.J is living with his cousin, and once we find her, you can interview and clear him or...arrest him."

"Remember, information about A.J. is confidential. I'm informing you as the victim's family. A team went down to Rhode Island this morning to A.J.'s old neighborhood where he lived and worked, and I expect to follow up on their results."

"I've been trying to remember everything he's said or did. I'll write it down for you. At last, we're going to arrest Dahlia's killer."

"Good, now we're working together."

Together. The word echoed in her head. This must mean she was officially off the person of interest list. He wouldn't work with a suspect. She bit her lip to hold back the bubble of laughter. Everything had turned around, and soon A.J. would be in jail or cleared. Hopefully it would all lead to Dahlia's killer, and Rose would be going home. But how would she live her life without Dahlia? At least now she spoke to her sporadically. She flicked a glance at Lennox. He'd be out of her life too.

"Have a good time at the library, Miss Blue."

His sudden dismissal surprised her. She headed off aware the detective was tracking her movements.

She tossed a peek over her shoulder when she stopped on the corner. Lennox was gone. At the screech of tires, her attention flew to the street. A car swerved toward her. She jumped back, her heart pounding in her ears.

The vehicle halted inches from her, blocking her path. What happened?

Her unsteady hand went for her gun while she searched for familiar features through the tinted car's windows.

"Rose!" Lennox yelled. He charged down the street.

The door of the car flew open.

"Put your hands in the air!" Lennox shouted.

CHAPTER 16

"Rose, it's me."

"Cassie?" Rose blinked and took in her friend's familiar light blonde hair. Her coral lips were drawn back in fright. Her eyelashes thick with mascara shot up and touched her fine, light brows.

"Hands now," Lennox raised his badge and reached behind his back.

Cassie put her palms in the air as people gathered a few feet away, hugging the safety of the store fronts. "Am I under arrest for stopping in a no parking zone? Really, it was an impulse. I saw my friend, Rose, and was totally into my surprise aspect. I forgot to pay attention to the parking signs."

Rose jumped forward and embraced Cassie before facing Lennox. "I know her. She's my friend, Cassie Raymond, from Vermont."

"What are you doing here?" he demanded of the visitor.

"Lennox, stop interrogating her. Cassie, what are you doing here?"

"Apparently, I'm going to jail. I thought I'd surprised you. You've had a tough time and I wanted to take you to lunch." She held out her fists to Lennox. "I'm ready for the cuffs."

He stuffed his badge inside his pocket and did a quick take on the area around them.

"Am I under arrest?" she asked.

"Both of you take a break." Rose wedged between them like a referee separating boxing contenders. "He's not arresting you. Lennox, Cassie's the person who's been in charge of my store

143

while I'm here in Ledgeview. Remember?"

"Got it."

"Good, I didn't recognize her car because I never expected her to be in New Hampshire." She pivoted around to her friend. "Is the Blues Sisters closed today?"

"Do you want me to drive home and open up?"

"Yup, she's my friend. Why are you here, Lennox? I thought you went back to your office."

"I'm a detective. I'm not always seen when I'm near."

"Is he your *private* bodyguard?" Cassie wiggled her brows and widened her eyes.

"This is Detective Luke Lennox in charge of Dahlia's case."

"I'm happy to meet you." Cassie stepped forward and gave him a dimpled smile. "I bet you'll catch the person who took away Dahlia and send our Rose home soon. I miss her."

"You'd better move your car," he said to Cassie. "You'll get a ticket for traffic obstruction."

Rose caught the curious glances and covert stares from the small throng collected around them. "A police detective shouting and running down the street was big news on a slow day."

Lennox seemed suddenly aware of the sightseers too. "Okay, the excitement is over. Move on." He made a sweeping gesture with his hands for people to disperse.

"There's a lot around the corner, Cass." Rose hooked her thumb in the air. "You can park there, and I'll meet you."

"Does this mean I'm forgiven for closing the store and can take you to lunch?"

"You are, unless Lennox detains you. How about it? Is she released into my custody?"

"Move the vehicle, and we're good."

"I'm on it." Cassie jumped forward and hugged Rose before driving toward the lot.

"I guess I'll skip the library for a while," Rose announced. Research could wait.

"The deli across from the library offers specials," Lennox told her.

"I get the hint. We'll stay close by and eat at the Black Cat Deli."

"Glad you liked my culinary tip."

What could she say to make him stay and continue looking at her with that concerned expression? Nothing popped into her mind. She trotted off to meet Cassie, but she sensed Lennox shadowing behind until they entered the eatery. A waitress immediately seated them.

Within minutes they'd ordered. As Rose waited for her veggie sandwich, she cleared her mind and listened to Cassie chatter about home. The stories revolved around a place where people were happy, without worries. All the stories felt like they came from another lifetime.

Her mind wandered as she took in the other customers. Most of the lunch patrons were dressed for the work day with mixed groups of seniors and young mothers and toddlers.

"Rose, are you listening to me?"

"Sure, you asked how I'm doing."

"Mom and I worry about you." Cassie bit her lip for a second. "Dad does too. He misses you and Dahlia asking for advice on frozen pipes or stuck doors."

"He's always been the best stand-in father a friend can have."

"I don't mean to pry or be too personal, but you didn't even cry at Dahlia's funeral. Are you okay? It's normal to be upset or mad after all you've gone through."

"Everything is personal when someone kills a family member. Your life changes forever." She clasped her hands together in her lap, praying Cassie understood and wouldn't press her. The constant talk about Dahlia's death brought a crushing pain to her chest as though someone was stamping on her heart.

She couldn't blame Cassie for asking. The three of them, Cassie, Dahlia and Rose had become best friends when they met in kindergarten. The trio had shared everything from sleepovers, make-up to stories about first kisses and boyfriends.

"My mom worries about you. Do you get lonely?"

Without Dahlia she'd always be alone.

Cassie touched Rose's fisted hand on the table. "Talk to me. Are you a little scared living by yourself in a strange city?"

Rose seized the glass of water to quench her dry mouth and gulped the contents before replying. "I can't sit around and do nothing. How can I face myself in the mirror if I don't do this for my sister?"

"Remember you can call me whenever you're down." A slow grin crossed Cassie's face. "You're not totally on your own. I noticed Detective Lennox ran to your rescue."

Heat flushed Rose's skin. "The detective is interested in me for whatever leads I can give him about my sister. I'm part of his job."

"I'm not sure I believe you." Cassie winked. "I wish some hunk would rush down the street when a car stopped in front of me. By the way, the Downtown Merchants Organization is cooking up great plans for Bargain Days. I know the group means a lot to you."

"I haven't given them a thought for weeks." The merchants group used to occupy a great deal of her after work hours and energy. She wasn't the same person who'd opened her store last fall with enthusiasm and excitement for the future. That person cared mainly about her committee, her boutique and focused on her margin of profits. She continued to listen to Cassie but refrained from commenting.

Cassie bit her lip and seemed to be searching for a topic. "Did I mention Sue Markey has a new boyfriend?"

Rose shook her head and glanced around the restaurant while her friend continued to fill her in on more home happenings. As Cassie talked, images of Brattleboro floated through Rose's mind: shoppers at the food co-op picking up their supplies, members of the church discussing the next fundraiser, friends and customers at the boutique browsing and chatting at the store.

She wasn't a part of their world any longer. Food and chats seemed trivial. No one understood that Dahlia's murder separated and marked Rose as different from others.

"I brought your mail from the store," Cassie said, finished with her last topic. She dug in her purse and produced a pile of envelopes.

Rose picked up the top one and read the personal note at the bottom of the card. *Your sister was a special person. She always greeted me and asked about my husband who was ill. Her concern for a stranger touched my life.*

"I've something to tell you," Cassie announced. "It's why I came today."

"Okay." Rose's throat ached with tears. Her gaze fell on the next envelope addressed to her at the Blues Sisters. She ripped open the flap. A picture of a rose bouquet decorated the card's cover. Inside she read the typed message: *I know your beautiful hazel eyes, your soft blonde hair. You can close this card, and I'll be gone. Or will I? Maybe I'm nearby, watching you at your shop or following you over the river to your Ledgeview apartment. I'm everywhere.*

Below the sender wrote a link instead of a name. What the heck was this? Her pulse leaped into high gear. She snapped the card shut and shot glimpses around the restaurant.

"What is it?" Cassie asked. Are you okay?"

She would stay calm. Some whacko wouldn't get to her. She held up the envelope. "This doesn't have a postmark."

"I found it under the boutique door a couple of days ago. What did it say?" Cassie bit her lip. "It must be bad. You look awful."

Rose tapped the card against the table. "This is one of those disgusting, unsigned, I'm watching you messages. I was shocked for a second, but I'm okay now."

"No wonder you're upset," Cassie's voice wobbled. "I should have read the greetings. A lot of mean people live in the world."

"Cas, have you seen A.J.? Is he still in Vermont?"

"A.J.?" She blinked several times and shook her head. "He's not around and doesn't have his old job or apartment any longer. Did you think he was back in Vermont and left the card? Why would he scare you? He didn't have anything against you, did he?"

Rose shrugged. "He just came to mind. I guess it could be from anyone."

"Give me the card, and I'll burn it. I feel responsible." Cassie held out her open palm.

"I'll destroy it." Rose's stomach churned. Cassie was right. Mean people lived everywhere. She stuffed the cards in her purse.

"I've one more thing." Cassie grimaced and drew in a deep breath.

"Before you bring up a new topic, I need to ask you something." Rose crushed the paper napkin in her lap. "I didn't mention this before because I didn't want to admit it, but, Dahlia helped herself to money from the boutique. Do you know why or what she did with the cash?"

"Wow, she stole from her own shop?" Cassie shook her head. "Do you think she took the funds for A.J.?"

"Why would she give money to her ex?"

Cassie's face whitened, and she shrugged. "I remember he talked about starting his own business, but I only heard him bring it up once. Maybe Dahlia wanted to get back together and thought the money would soften him up."

"She contacted A.J. after they broke up?"

"I guessed. I don't know why your sister took the money or if she ever saw A.J. again. Here." She pressed the glass of water into Rose's hand. "How about I order something stronger like wine?"

"Water's good." She gulped a mouthful before she spoke again. "It's so Dahlia. Help someone else at the expense of her family. Never consider the consequences of her actions."

Cassie wet her lips several times. "Don't listen to me. I've no idea what she did with the money."

Under the table, Rose tapped her foot.

Cassie shoved at the hair near her face. "I've ruined our afternoon."

"No, I asked and you told me what you thought. Don't worry about me. You drove a long way. What did you want to tell me before I asked about A.J.?"

Cassie played with the handle of her fork. "It's not important."

"Come on. What was your news?"

She chewed on her lip for a second.

Bad news. Rose tensed. "Whatever it is, I know you're a good person."

"It's...Mom caved and enrolled in cooking classes at the Woodstock Inn for ten days."

Rose unclenched her hands and relaxed in her chair. "I'm glad to hear a story with a happy ending. Was that your big news?"

Cassie nodded. "Dad paid for the lessons as a thirtieth anniversary present, and they're staying at the inn for a few days.

Sorry, it seems trite talking about cooking."

"Your story beats talk of death."

"I'll have to close the Blues Sisters a couple hours early on Wednesday until Mom returns to fill in for me. I'm taking an art class and have a big project due that will take hours of work. I'm sorry. I need to catch up."

"No problem, Cass, I owe you. The lessons and your project are a big deal."

The lines around her friend's mouth eased. "It's nothing compared to what's happening in your life."

"What's the class?" Rose shoved her sister's theft into the back of her mind and listened to details about Cassie's life. The rest of the hour zipped past as they splurged and ate cookies for dessert and drank iced teas. Soon they were paying the bill, and Rose struggled to shake off the touch of sadness when she walked with her friend to the parking lot. At her car, Rose hugged Cassie goodbye.

Her vehicle merged into the traffic with the toot of the horn and disappeared at the corner. Rose pulled out her phone. The URL written on the card burned in her mind. In seconds, she'd typed in the link. Her thumb hovered over the button.

Don't do it. He's playing a mind game.

She pressed it.

Her apartment building popped up on the screen. The bastard was spying on her and boasting about it. She wished he was in front of her so she could kick him in every part of his good-for-nothing body.

In the video, Bike Boy rode into view and chained his bike to the meter. He removed the Boom Box attached to the handle bars. Then he loped his way across the sidewalk and disappeared through the front door.

"The library's the other way, Miss Blue."

"Lennox?" She spotted him in his car, idling at the curb. How long had he been sitting there? It didn't matter. She ran to the curb and jumped into the front seat with her heart thumping from joy and fear. She slipped her cell into her pocket. "Have the seniors left the station?"

"They've gone home for supper. It's almost four." He merged his car into the traffic. "Where are you headed after your big lunch?"

"Home, please. I've something to show you when we park."

"I'm thinking it's not the restaurant bill."

"Good deduction." She held onto the moment of quiet. In a few minutes she'd show him her latest gift, and her life would bounce back into the shadows where she now lived.

As they drew up to the curb, she spotted a light blue van by her building. The words *Get Alarmed* were printed across the side. "The workers wiring the restaurant must have arrived to secure the side and rear entrances."

"Cassie brought sympathy cards from my customers." She fished out the unwelcome greeting and held it out. "Get your evidence bag ready, Lennox. A not so well-wisher stuffed a card with a creepy greeting for me under the Blues Sisters door. "

"Was it a threat?" He grabbed the greeting with a handkerchief.

"The sender included a link for a video. I'll show you."

He read and bagged the card.

She passed him her phone. "He put a webcam on my building. Can we track it and arrest him?" Was the camera next door or across the street? She twisted around and searched.

"Hold on. I'm watching the video."

He could be in the vacant apartment across the street. "Let's go find him, Lennox."

"Not unless Todd Clark, your Bike Boy, is wearing a coat of invisibility."

"What are you talking about?" She squeezed the handle, and the door cracked open.

"On the video, your neighbor's walking in your front door right now." He pointed to the empty doorway. "Do you see him in front of us?"

She did a double take. "It's not a live webcam?"

"The quality is poor too. My techies will get on it. I'll send the link to my phone." He finished and passed her cell back.

She hit replay. "You're right. I don't believe Bike Boy keeps walking inside over and over. Even for him, that's kind of strange. Sorry, I panicked and didn't consider it wasn't live."

"I'll ask Bike Boy a few questions. Here, you'll need this. Your new apartment lock is installed." He held up a silver key.

"You're a rock, Lennox." Her gushing schoolgirl voice made her cringe. She prayed he was tone deaf. "I also spoke to Cassie about the money that Dahlia stole from the boutique. Cassie speculated my sister gave the money to A.J. for some business he wanted to launch and to make up with him."

His jaw tightened. "You had quite the lunch. When did Cassie learn all this?"

"She claimed she guessed, but she told me he brought up the idea of starting a company. I never heard him talk about a business plan. Why wouldn't he mention the idea to me?"

"I'm more concerned about your friend's memory recovery. She never told the police about Edwards' company dream, which means she'll need to be re-interviewed."

"You're not going to charge her with a crime, are you?"

"Right now, I'll settle for the truth. I'll send someone to question her first thing tomorrow."

"Send someone on the sensitive side. Cassie doesn't do well with tough people."

"A cop who is sensitive…you do like challenges."

"That's why I like you. I'm ready to go inside."

"Wait a minute, Rose. I have something for you." He dug out a plastic bag from the glove compartment and handed it to her.

She stared down at her journal inside. "You tested my diary already?"

"I don't need a handwriting expert. I believe you."

He believed her. "Are you sure you don't want to keep the card?"

He gripped her chin in his hand and tilted her face upward. His eyes peered down into hers with a new light. "I've no doubt about what I want."

Her breath caught with surprise and yearning. His hand skimmed down the middle of her back, stopped and then pressed her closer. His other hand caressed the side of her breast as he whispered, "Very sure."

He buried his lips in the sensitive spot on her throat. Her emotions spiraled in longing and she breathed a sigh. He moved his lips to nibble at her chin and then crushed his mouth to hers. In a rush, she kissed him back, releasing all the pent of stress of the day, eager for more. She leaned forward in her seat to get closer.

He placed his mouth against her ear. "I know exactly what I want." He broke away. "We should go inside."

Unlike him, she wasn't sure ending the moment was what she wanted.

"Come on. I'll walk you into your apartment and talk to the workers."

She glided inside with Lennox thankful for the whine of a drill in the hallway, which prevented a conversation. She edged closer and peered through the open doorway and into the empty restaurant. Lennox interrupted the men to inspect their IDs and credentials. Cool air flowed from the main room and into the hallway, chilling her arms. The warmth of her apartment beckoned. She headed up the stairs. Lennox would follow in a few minutes. Maybe he'd stay for a cup of coffee or another kiss.

The rat tat tat from the workers repeated in the distance. Otherwise, the second floor was quiet. She started down the hall.

"Rose?" Lennox shouted and emerged at the top of the stairs.

He probably was going to lecture her on walking in the hall alone. The rattle of a chain lock came from the apartment opposite hers. The door opened a few inches. Her neighbor pressed his pasty white face in the space.

"Todd, I want to speak to you." Lennox closed the distance between the stairs and his new target.

Her neighbor's eyes widened, and he slammed the door. The slide of the bolt and the jangle of the chain lock announced the end of their conversation.

She turned to Lennox. "He's not feeling the friendliness today."

He marched to Bike Boy's door and banged on it. "I've a few questions for you. Open up. It's Detective Lennox."

The door creaked open. Bike Boy peered out with a can of grape soda in his hand. "Yeah?"

"I need to talk to you, officially." Lennox held up his badge.

"Is it about him?" He pointed down the hall.

Lennox glanced in the direction indicated, and Todd slammed the door.

"Hell, I can't believe this." Lennox thudded his fist on the door. "Todd, open up." He waited several seconds. "Stand back," he said to Rose.

"Are you breaking in? Is entering without permission legal?"

"Smell the odor in your hall? It's marijuana, and even if he has glaucoma, the drug is illegal in New Hampshire." He raised his foot and kicked the door. It flew inward and back with a crash. The useless security chain dangled down, swinging back and forth.

Rose darted forward.

"Stay." Lennox held out his arm, barring her before he disappeared inside with his gun drawn.

She charged after him.

Todd's sneakered foot disappeared through the kitchen window.

"He's on the fire escape." Rose rushed forward.

"Don't." Lennox seized her arm.

"But he's getting away." She pointed at the window and glanced back to him. His face was pale and his lips tight. "We'll catch him later." She straightened, sensing Lennox's resistance to venture out on the hanging steps.

"Those stairs are a death trap." He dug out his cell and pushed a button. "I'll call patrol."

Rose edged closer to the window. The fire escape swung in the air as Bike Boy leaped from the last step to the ground and kept on truckin'.

"The beat cop is on it," Lennox announced, clicking off his phone. "Stay here." He marched away.

"So close yet so far away." Rose sighed and studied the room. She was struck by a déjà vu feeling. The apartment was the mirror image of Dahlia's. Though Rose would never let anyone inside if hers was this messy. Dirty dishes filled the sink to her left. Empty donut boxes and bread wrappers littered the table. In the living room, shelves full of CDs and DVDs hid the walls. More DVDs and comic books covered the coffee table in front of the flowered couch. She walked over to examine them and ran her gaze over the clutter. The initials DB on a jewel case stopped her. A little red heart dotted each letter.

"He stole from my sister. Lennox?" She ran into the bedroom.

He stopped in his perusal. "What are you carrying in your

hand?"

"Guess what I found with Dahlia's initials on it."

"I'd say you found some kind of antique."

"CD s aren't that old. What's important is Bike Boy stole this one from my sister. She initialed the case."

"I'm sure he'll claim she lent it to him." Using a pencil, Lennox poked through the mail on the bureau. "Nothing here except bills and ads." He headed into the kitchen.

Rose followed him. "Lennox, be real. What's he going to say if I insist it belonged to Dahlia?"

"He'll probably claim his friend Daniel Boone lent it to him. Hold on, what's this?" He walked to the stove covered with unclean pots and pans and using a dishtowel grabbed a can. "Black spray paint. Wonder if he cooked up the police station's graffiti with this."

"Aha, he's guilty."

"I hope you're never on a jury."

"What else did he steal from Dahlia? Where's his stash?" She stalked around the room searching for her sister's belongings.

"Rose, you need to let me handle the situation."

She sniffed. "He must have been smoking up a storm."

"It's why he ran."

"He could have fled because he spray painted the station or keyed your car. What else?" She tapped a finger against her chin. "Did he drive to Vermont or have an accomplice there who left me a threatening card or—"

"Come on, Miss CSI. We're leaving."

"I want to see what's on the rest of the shelves. Don't you want to confiscate his marijuana?" She marched to the makeshift bookcase of plastic crates crammed with DVDs.

Lennox dogged her. "Don't touch anything. If we arrest and take him to court, we don't want evidence thrown out because of an illegal search."

"You mean put the CD back?"

"You've got it."

She bit her lip. "Okay, but what if Todd is the stalker and he killed my sister. I know you think it could be A.J, but either way we need proof. We should start with collecting the stolen items from his apartment."

"We'll do it legally." Lennox wandered around the room, taking in the clutter.

No way was that thief getting her sister's music. She stuffed the CD in her purse and took a moment of comfort in the sight of her thirty-eight weapon inside.

"Let's go." He slid his arm around Rose's waist and guided her toward the open doorway. "I promise you, we'll find Todd, the Bike Boy. Now, try out the new key and I'll go inside first. You stay in the hall, which means don't move."

Within a few minutes, he was finished with his walk through, and she stood in the kitchen while he lectured her to stay locked up.

"Is that all?"

He clamped her face between his large hands and crushed her mouth in a kiss. "Now that's all."

Her pulse was still beating fast from their kiss when he left. She threw off her jacket and dropped her purse on the table. She needed to clear her mind and inhaled deeply.

The scent of roses lingered in the air, growing stronger and stronger. Dahlia.

Rose followed the perfume's scent toward the bedroom where the fragrance grew stronger. She paused on the threshold. "Dahlia?"

She crossed into the room and stopped. Her eyes adjusted to the dim light from the one window. Her head began to ache. The maple bed on the bare floor distorted into odd shapes.

She ran a hand over her eyes and searched for the bed. It was gone and sitting in the middle of the floor was a casket. No! A light shone from the interior. She held her breath and peered over the edge. Her sister lay still inside, eyes closed. Water soaked clothes hugged her thin form. Her blond hair was plastered to an ashen face. Her lids blinked open. A cry strangled in Rose's throat. Her sister's sockets were empty.

"He's coming for you," Dahlia whispered. "Then we'll be together."

Dahlia and the coffin faded away, leaving Rose standing in the dark with tears streaming down her cheeks.

CHAPTER 17

"Come on down," shouted the announcer from Rose's clock radio. "Come on down to Players Restaurant today for beer, burgers and a game of darts. How can you pass that up? We also have Smith Blake from out west. Mr. Blake is a future presidential candidate and is getting the big jump on the NH Primary. He'll be at Players to answer questions from our lunch customers. Drop on by."

Rose tossed onto her side, hit the alarm button on the radio sitting on the floor and inhaled the scent of coffee grounds. At least she'd caffeine to keep herself sane. Thank the saint who'd invented the timer so she could wake up to her favorite drink. The familiar perk of the machine reassured her. In minutes, she was sipping from the mug and replaying Dahlia's words from yesterday in her mind.

Finally she shoved the morbid scene away and jumped into the shower. Within the hour she was ready for her day and wondering if Lennox had sent a man to interview Cassie yet.

Her cell phone rang out from its spot on the table. She scooped it up. The ID announced Lennox calling.

"Morning, find any signs of your neighbor?" he asked.

Lennox's voice zipped a wave of delight through her. "I'd bet Bike Boy is still sleeping somewhere and since the sound of a feather falling wakes me, I can vouch he hasn't entered the building. What's new on your end?"

"I heard from the lab," Lennox said. "Nothing usable on the mattress and on the sympathy card, the techie found zero prints. He thinks the video was filmed by a phone camera."

"I'm not surprised. What about the men who went to Rhode Island?"

"Interviews with neighbors who remembered him and his former employer confirmed what we already knew. No leads on A.J. or the cousin from his hometown."

"Our killer could be any perv from here to Vermont getting his jollies. Any word on Cassie's latest interview?"

"I sent someone with sensitivity training to speak with her."

"You did?"

"No, we're cops, Rose, but my man won't hammer her."

"Will you be searching Bike Boy's apartment?" What else was her neighbor hiding?

"I'll need more evidence to get a warrant," Lennox said. "I'd an interesting phone call a few minutes ago. Remember we interviewed the cast members of Myra's production?"

"How could I forget?" The memory of the station filled with the seniors flashed in Rose's mind. "The police station resembled an AARP meeting."

"Then you should recall the fellow named Othello. A nurse from the Ledgeview Home where he lives called me. He's doing better today and seems to have experienced a flashback he'd like to share with us."

"He knows something about Dahlia's death?" At last they had a lead. A feeling of hope expanded in Rose's chest. "When can we talk to him? You are taking me, right?"

"I've been instructed to invite the Blue woman."

"He remembered me." Her hope grew.

"I'll pick you up in four and a half minutes. Stay inside until I'm there."

"I'll be ready," she said.

Within twenty minutes, they were at the visitors' desk at the Ledgeview Nursing Home. Lennox asked for Othello's nurse, Miss Holloways. Rose kept her eyes glued on the hallway until a short, brown-haired woman appeared and announced she was the nurse who contacted Lennox. A warm smile lit up her freckled face while her wide brown eyes crinkled with curiosity. She seemed barely old enough to take high school courses, never mind take care of seniors.

"Your Othello, and our Mr. Melvin, is in his room. I'll show you the way." The nurse pivoted around on her white soled shoes and walked down the hall.

Lennox stepped aside for Rose to go first. The odor of evergreen air fresheners greeted them as they walked by rooms occupied by gray-haired people.

The nurse led them into a room with two beds. The first stood empty. In the second, near a window, lay Othello.

"Mr. Melvin, your company is here." The nurse laid a hand on his arm and the elderly man's eyes popped open.

He let out a sound that resembled a lion's growl, tossed onto his side and stared at them.

"He fell asleep waiting for you. I'm not sure he's in the mood for company now," his nurse said in a loud whisper. "He's often confused when he first wakes."

"Who are you people?" Othello yelled at Rose and Lennox.

He held up his shield. "Mr. Melvin, I'm Detective Lennox. We met at the police station the other day. Your nurse reported you wanted to speak to me about Dahlia Blue."

"I never met a Dahlia Blue." He waved a gnarled hand of dismissal and rolled over toward the window.

Frustration pushed Rose forward. "Mr. Melvin, I'm Rose Blue. My sister, Dahlia, had a role in the stage production of *The Angels Are Singing Tonight*. Remember? She played the murder victim and attended the first rehearsal."

He turned to them. "I know nothing about angels singing to blue women. I'm Othello." His eyes narrowed, and he pointed at Lennox. "This fellow's of exceeding honesty."

"My father and I attended Ledgeview High. Neither of us were in the drama club, but you might have seen me around the school."

"My recall fails me." Othello glanced at Rose. "If she be false, O, then heaven mocks itself!"

"I don't understand." Rose faced the nurse for an explanation.

"It's Shakespeare," Ms. Holloways said. "He repeats dialogue from the high school plays he's directed. I'm afraid he won't answer your questions. Once he starts reciting lines, he goes on for hours."

"But he has to talk to us." Rose clenched her hands together. "We need his help. Mr. Othello, do you remember Dahlia Blue in the play at the Audi?"

"She's gone."

"Yes, my sister was murdered."

Miss Holloways gasped from behind them.

"I am abused and my relief," Othello shouted and waved a hand in the air.

"He's performing a part." The nurse shook her head. "He's still into his character. You won't get anything out of him the rest of the day. I apologize for asking you to drive out especially after what happened to your sister. I didn't know."

Othello widened his eyes and pointed at Lennox. "I remember you."

"I'm Detective Lennox."

"Yes, you played Hamlet. The scene where your father's ghost appears and informs you that Claudius poisoned him was exceedingly well-performed."

Rose cringed and glanced at Lennox. His expression remained stoic.

He turned to the nurse. "What did he say before you phoned?" He took out his notepad.

The nurse wrinkled her forehead in doubt. "Maybe his order to call the cops was from a play. Shakespeare didn't write about cops, did he?"

"Highly unlikely," Lennox agreed. "You said he asked for me by name."

"He gave me your card with instructions to ask you to come."

"Repeat his exact words," Lennox insisted.

"He said he had an important message for you and the Blue woman." Miss Holloways narrowed her eyes as though digging the words out of her memory. "'The sins of the mother will be visited on the daughter.'"

"Was he speaking about me?" Rose was unable to keep the shock from her voice.

"I don't know. Isn't that a line from a play or a TV show?" the nurse asked.

"It's not from MTV," Lennox said. "What else did he say?" He poised his pencil over his notebook from his pocket.

"He was adamant about talking to you and became agitated when I didn't act immediately. I thought he was in his right mind because he called me by my name. When he's confused, he thinks I'm anyone from Amy to Zelda."

"Zelda was a beautiful woman," Othello roared from his bed. "Scott Fitzgerald was a fool."

"Let's step outside the room." Lennox headed for the hall.

"She was his Desdemona," Othello grumbled.

"I'll be back in a second, Mr. Melvin," the nurse reassured.

"I'm Othello, young lady," he sat upward in his bed and shouted.

"We should find Shakespeare's ghost to interpret for us." Rose sidestepped closer to Lennox outside the closed door.

He held out his card to the young woman. "Here's my cell number. Call me when Mr. Melvin recognizes his own name."

The woman studied his number before slipping it into the pocket of her uniform. "I apologize again for bothering you."

"Call me any time. It's my job."

"Is there a chance he spoke to another nurse today when he was lucid?" Rose asked.

"He's one of my patients. If he says anything at all, I'll write it down and fill you in immediately."

"Thanks." Rose didn't hide the disappointment in her voice.

"Ready." Lennox held out his hand for her to proceed down the corridor.

"I can't believe we missed our opportunity to speak to him," she mumbled as they walked toward his vehicle.

"Don't beat yourself up. We probably escaped a performance of all the roles in his last high school production." He grabbed the door and held it open for her.

"When Mr. Othello started talking about a father's ghost I hoped you weren't upset."

"I can't take a man with a failing memory personally."

"Do you think he knows something about our families? You heard him shouting about sins of the mother visited on the daughter. Maybe he talked to Dahlia at the Audi."

"Rose, the man spouts lines like a water fountain. Unfortunately he's not in his right mind, even if your sister used him as a family therapist."

"Othello counseling my sister is a stretch." She let out a sigh.

"Don't worry." He slid his arm around her shoulder and

pulled her closer. "I'll check on him every day in case he's having a good day, and I can question him. How about we stop for a late breakfast?"

"Sure, I could use a fourth cup of coffee." Did Othello know more than he was able to express? She wished she had Lennox's instinct to know if people were truthful. That was definitely another Blue deficit.

Lennox drove to the cafe at a nearby plaza. The aroma of cinnamon buns greeted them as they entered. He cut in front of her as they walked inside, bringing her to a halt. "Todd's aunt is at the counter. I guess it's my lucky day."

A woman dressed in denim with salt and pepper hair and wearing a gray jacket was counting her money by the register. She fixed a glare on Lennox.

"I'd say she sees you," Rose said out of the side of her mouth, "and she's not going to wish you a good day."

A young couple clutching brown bags left the café ahead of Todd's aunt who pocketed her money and marched across the room to Lennox. "I want to talk to you."

"I'm Detective Lennox."

"I remember. You and that other cop—"

"Detective Conroy."

"You," she aimed an accusing finger at Lennox, "and the other cop came to my house and accused my nephew, Todd, of killing a woman."

"We asked where he was during the time period when the woman first went missing," Lennox said, crowding closer to the woman as though he could drive her to the door."

"That's as good as saying he was a murderer. I read in the paper she was killed by someone who acted like a lunatic. My nephew's not a lunatic. I hired a lawyer to file a complaint against you. He's working on it. Todd didn't even know that dead woman."

"I want to speak to him. Is he at your place? He's not at his apartment." He reached around Todd's aunt and grabbed the doorknob.

"Keep asking and I might add harassment to the suit. Besides I haven't seen him in months."

"Are you telling me you don't know where he is?"

"I am."

"You should file a missing person's report."

Rose pushed between them. "I'm filing a complaint against your nephew for stealing from my sister."

The older woman's gray eyebrows jumped upward on her forehead. "Who are you? Are you with him? Are you a cop too? I can put you in my lawsuit."

"I'm Rose Blue. My sister, Dahlia was the murdered woman. Your nephew had one of my sister's CD's and since she barely knew Todd, she wouldn't have loaned it to him."

Todd's aunt pursed her lips and shrugged. "He probably found it somewhere. Or, it was planted on him. I want an investigation."

Rose felt the burn of anger building in her chest. "Or he stole her music before he spray painted the police station and keyed Detective Lennox's car."

"Thank you, Miss Blue." Lennox cut in front of Rose and faced Todd's aunt. "I agree we should deepen our investigation. For that reason, I'll send someone to your house and you can officially report him missing." He pushed the door open, and nodded his head toward it.

"I'm not responsible for Todd," the woman shouted halfway out. "He'd turned twenty-one before he moved into that Main Street apartment, and I'm still filing a complaint against you. My nephew wouldn't murder a woman, and no one can accuse him and ruin his good name when he's not around." The ring of the bell over the door announced her departure.

Lennox guided Rose across the floor to the counter. Customers seated at the cafe tables dropped their gazes as he raised one brow and dared them to say a word. A teen girl with pink hair stood by the register and gaped openmouthed as they approached.

"The woman's a real grouch when she misses her breakfast," he told the clerk. "We'll take two regular coffees to go. Large, extra caffeine."

"I don't think we have the last part," the girl said before turning away.

Rose waited to speak until the waitress crossed the floor to the coffeemaker. "Todd's aunt had her nerve speaking to you like that. You investigate homicides. What does she do for a living? Complain?"

His lips quirked upward, and he touched her hair, just a light stroke. She edged closer and felt his heat. The masculine scent of his soap mixed with the aroma of coffee beans.

"Remind me not to tick you off."

"Did you speak with Todd's boss, the burger shop manager, yet?" she asked him.

"He fired Todd two weeks after he started because he rarely showed up."

"I guess he wasn't up for model employee of the year."

"And his aunt wasn't up for model relative of the year."

"If Myra casts a Halloween play, I can make a recommendation."

"I'll be sure to let her know. In the meantime, I'll get a warrant to search for a missing Todd Clark and do an official search of his apartment." He walked away to collect their drinks.

* * *

Rose, come to the river. We're waiting for you.

"No," Rose mumbled, tossing on the sofa bed.

Rose, come. Then we can go home.

The whisper grew louder and louder until she snapped upright on the couch. The blanket fell to the floor in the empty living room. She brushed stray strands of hair away from her face. The tick of the battery powered clock on the wall echoed in the silence. It was four-thirty in the afternoon. She'd fallen into an exhausted sleep after Lennox brought her home.

Light slanted downward onto the floor through the window. The sun would set in less than an hour. She collapsed against her pillow and closed her eyes. *Please, Dahlia, let me sleep.*

Instead of peace, her sister's words repeated in her mind. What did she mean *we're* waiting? Was her killer there? Was Rose's mind playing a trick? She closed her eyes and prayed for everything to disappear. The spot where her sister's body had lain tangled in the bushes on the bank was the last place she wanted to visit.

Then we can go home.

The key to the murder was at the river. Now she understood. Rose slid from the couch, tugged on her parka and scooped up her purse with her gun. Outside, she welcomed the fresh air while her mind churned with anticipation. What would she find? She dug out her cell phone and hit the numbers for Lennox. The call went straight to his voicemail.

She listened to his familiar voice and studied the sky. Overhead, the sun battled a cloud and broke through to shine its last rays. She blinked into the sunlight. Days were short this time of year. She didn't have much daylight left, and no way was she walking near the water in the dark. She'd have to hurry.

When the beep signaled to leave Lennox a message, she blurted out she was down by the river, and she'd report back. She clicked off and started down the hill to Smith Plaza.

At the bottom of the paved road, she marched through the shopping center's half filled parking lot and past the concrete block stores. The shops would be closing within a few minutes. She sped up and jogged down the fire lane toward the dumpsters in the rear. The odor of something rotting greeted her.

Ahead lay the abandoned railroad track, and beyond was the hillside. The sounds of cars whizzing past on the distant highway floated toward her. She pulled out her gun, pointed it down and crossed over the tracks to the weed covered hill. The snow had disappeared on the sun warmed slope. Empty bottles and fast food wrappers littered the ground.

None of the street people had pitched their tents, yet. The sound of rushing water drew her downward toward the edge of the gray river. In the middle of the waterway, an ice floe refused to melt. A flock of pigeons sat on the frosty island with feathers puffed against the cold. Rose stopped, unsure. Was Dahlia's ghost down here? Lifeless bushes marked the incline. The wind blew and her skin chilled with sudden awareness. *Her stalker* was here.

Goosebumps broke out on her arms. She forced herself to pivot around, hunting for him or her. No one was within sight.

"Dahlia, are you here?" She wandered further toward the water, listening to the pounding of her heart competing with the roar of the current. *How long had her sister fought to stay alive in the icy river?* She shivered. The wind whirled and whispered Rose's name.

"Dahlia?" Rose forced herself to search the waterway.

A branch swept past, disappeared under the current, helpless in the force of the spring flow.

Why had her sister called her here? Her gaze skipped and skimmed over the dormant shrubs on the edge of the bank and found Dahlia.

"Dahlia!" Rose's hand tightened on the butt of her gun.

Her twin turned to her. Her wet hair hung lifeless around her bloodless face and hollow eyes. She turned away and walked along the river's edge.

Rose swallowed the acid lump in her throat. "Dahlia, come back."

Rose blew out a wobbling breath. She'd come this far. She headed toward her sister. The gnarled branches of the bushes grew low to the ground and snaked toward the edge. She wove through the underbrush and stopped on an overhang. Her sister's form faded and disappeared.

"Why did you call me here? What do you want me to find?" She closed her eyes. "Dahlia, please show me."

And then icy, gray water washed over her head, ending signs of daylight and land. Freezing. No air! Blackness closed around her. Confusion and panic took over. Which way was up? She struck out with her arms and legs. Air. She needed to breathe. Where was the surface? Help! She was drowning. Choose a direction. She flung her arms over her head and kicked her legs. Her lungs burned. Her body numbed, slowing her fight.

The chilly water invaded her bones, and weighed down her limbs and clothing. She could barely lift her hand. Her feet heavy as bricks towed her down, down. She was sinking, deeper and deeper. Her lungs wanted to explode. Desperate, she tried to propel herself upward before her last breath gave out.

CHAPTER 18

The frantic need to fill her lungs drove Rose to inhale. Frigid water flooded into her mouth and nose, choking and strangling her.

She sobbed and opened her eyes. She was lying on her back in the bushes. The low hanging sun blinded her. She coughed, sat up and sucked in the precious oxygen.

She ran her fingers through dry hair and dug her nails into the hard, solid ground. Her clothes contained not even a damp spot. The truth smacked her. It had been Dahlia in the river, her twin's last fight for life.

Rose drew her shaking knees up and hugged them to her chest. "It was Dahlia, not me.

Dahlia, not me. I'm okay. I'm not losing my mind."

Burying her face into her knees, she prayed a thank you for her life. She raised her head. "I wanted you to come home, Dahlia. I didn't mean it when I said I never wanted to see you again after you took the money. I didn't want you to go away forever. I love you. Did you bring me here to punish me?"

We rested here.

What? Her sister had washed ashore at this exact spot. She glanced down and flashed onto the image of her sister's nearly naked body twisted among the bushes. We? Was she next?

No! She leaped to her feet, grabbed her belongings and fled up the bank. Tears stung her eyes and blurred her surroundings. She had to get out of here. She ran faster. Her foot sank into a hole. She toppled forward. The gun flew from her hand. She closed her eyes. Not the water again.

Raising the binoculars, it was easy to spot her running up the hill. A spike of heat hit his gut and rushed through his blood. If only she were closer. Then he could touch her. He'd run his fingers down that slim, white throat and squeeze until the fear filled her eyes. Watch the horror on her face.

A surge of yearning abrupt and sharp hit him. Soon he'd make his next move.

Across the river he heard her scream and he closed his eyes in longing and glee.

CHAPTER 19

Rose smacked against the brittle, dry grass. *You're okay.*
You're okay. Rose lifted her head and stared into unseeing eyes.
A cry escaped her mouth. She shoved upright and stared down
into the face of her friend, Cassie. She lay in front of her, duct
tape wrapped around her mouth.

Rose screamed and scrambled to her feet, grabbing her gun
from the ground.

Was she going crazy? She dared another glance. Oh-my-God,
Cassie. Not Cassie. Was she real? Her open eyes stared up at
Rose. She was naked.

Rose leaned down and touched one of Cassie's cold hands
bound together by tape. She searched for her pulse. Nothing,
Rose jumped away.

The sound of laughter drifted across the river. Rose whirled
around. A figure darted into the grove of pines standing on the
shore across the river. The stalker was there. Was it A.J., Tia,
Bike Boy, Dean, Buddy or someone she didn't know, spying,
laughing at her and Cassie? He could have a high powered rifle
aimed at her.

Run. Faster. Her breath came out in pants and cries. At the
crest, she stopped. She fumbled for her phone pulled it out of her
pocket. With the other hand, she aimed the gun toward the
opposite bank even though the shore must be out of range.

Lennox's deep voice answered his cell.

"Thank God, it's you. Come right away. He's here. He's at
the river. I heard him laughing at me. Hurry."

"Rose, where are you?"

"I'm on the riverbank behind the plaza with the liquor store. He is watching me, Lennox...and it's Cassie." Rose headed toward the shopping center and then pivoted around to see if anyone was behind her.

"Who's watching? What happened to Cassie?"

"Dahlia's kill-er." She clamped her teeth together for a moment to stop the chattering. "He got Cassie. She's dead. On the bank."

"Did you see A.J.?"

"I wasn't close enough."

"Stay on the line. I'm on my way."

Pull yourself together. She swallowed hard and searched the bank for her friend. "Hurry." Rose turned away fighting the nausea, forcing its way into her throat.

"Rose, Rose."

"I'm...here." Stay alert.

"I'm in my car and on my way. Are you in danger?"

"I don't know. How could anyone hurt Cassie? She was a good person. She watched my boutique, drove for more than an hour to surprise me and brought me to lunch. Why kill someone who wanted to go to lunch?"

"Rose, focus. Where are you standing?"

"I'm at the top of the hill behind the stores. You're coming?"

"I'm almost there. Hang on. Go up to the liquor store, I'll meet you."

"Okay." She strode upward where the closed sign hung on the glass storm door. "The store's closed."

"Stay in the doorway. Take a deep breath. What happened to Cassie?"

"She's dead." Tears blocked the words. She wanted to dash off to her apartment, but she couldn't leave Cassie.

"Do you see any cars?"

She shook her head.

"Rose?"

"No...cars. I heard a man's laughter."

"Did you see any boats on the river?"

"No, he was on the other side of the water. Are you close?"

"Fifteen seconds or less."

She clicked off. Stay calm. Rose faced the slope. The coward was there. "You stole my sister and our friend. I hate you."

Lennox's car screeched around the anchor store and wheeled to a stop.

"The cavalry's arrived, Dahlia."

Lennox jumped out, and she sprinted across the ground and flung herself against his solid chest. He wrapped his arms around her waist and held her. Nothing bad would happen now.

He eased back. "Where's Cassie?"

"Go down the bank, straight ahead." She pointed and closed her eyes for a second. *Please, please be a dream, a horrible dream. I want to wake up.*

"Stay here and don't fire. Scream if you see anyone near." He hiked down the hill. Rose trailed him to the crest of the bank and stopped. A short distance from the river, he crouched down. He'd found Cassie. She wasn't dreaming. Rose turned away and gulped air. When she heard his footsteps, she faced Lennox.

"Is she alive?" she shouted to him. Maybe Cassie had fallen into a coma.

Lennox didn't answer until he reached her. "I'm sorry. She's gone."

Her lip quivered. Tears streamed down both her cheeks. "I should have helped her."

"You can help your friend by telling me everything that happened after I left you." Folding their hands together, he forced her to pinpoint her attention on him.

"I fell asleep. My sister woke me. She told me to go to the river. I left and walked along the edge. For a few minutes, I felt like I'd fallen in the water and was drowning. But it must have been Dahlia because I was lying on the ground. I ran up the hill. I tripped and found Cassie."

The image of Cassie's eyes glazed by death overflowed in her mind. Dizziness waved over her. "I need to sit."

"Come to my car." He slid his arm around her back and led the way across the fire lane to his vehicle.

Rose sat inside and faced the open door to inhale the fresh air. Lennox hovered near her. "He left her with all the litter."

Lennox crouched in front of her. "Rose, you should have called me before coming to the water by yourself.

"Dahlia told *me* to come right away. Lennox, how could it

happen? Cassie was on her way home. I saw her drive off. What happened? Why is she on the hillside?" Her mind cleared. "Do you think he hid in her car?"

"Did she lock her car doors?"

"She didn't at home." The scene of Cassie driving away, waving and happy while her killer crouched in the rear played in her head. *You monster, you'll pay.* Rose bent forward and rested her forehead on the steering wheel, willing herself better. *Don't let him get to you.*

"Backup should arrive any second." He laid a hand on her arm. "I need your help."

She sat back against the seat. "What can I do?"

"Give me the number and name of Cassie's nearest family members. I'll call them once we move her."

Rose mumbled her answer. Then she covered her eyes with a shaking hand. "I can't believe she's gone." Tears seeped between her fingers.

"I'll be on the embankment. Stay here."

She nodded, and he headed toward Cassie. In a few seconds he circled around her body, scanning the surroundings and finally crouched to study the ground. Rose brushed away the tears and wished he'd left the key so she could start the engine and turn on the heat.

Lennox trudged back. "Did you see anyone on your way to the hill?"

"I didn't notice a soul." She shook her head. "It's possible I walked by someone. I was paying attention to the riverbank."

"Explain again about Dahlia speaking to you."

She twisted her hands in front of her. "I was napping, but I heard her calling to me. So I came."

The sound of sirens screamed in the air.

"Is there a possibility Cassie stopped at the river on her way home? Did you mention where your sister was found?"

She shook her head. "I don't remember if I told her about the bank. She might have read it in the paper. After lunch, she was going home to Brattleboro. She never talked about visiting another person or place. I watched her pull out of the parking lot."

"Was anyone near her vehicle or following her when she

drove off?"'

"No one, Lennox, she waved to me. How could this happen to her?" She wiped at the tears on her cheeks.

"Rose, did Cassie mention threats or problems at home?"

"No, she was laughing at lunch. She came to cheer me up and talk about her art class. Look what happened to her." Rose closed her eyes and sagged against the seat. "Maybe I'm cursed like Typhoid Mary."

"I don't think a curse was her problem." He hunkered down in front of her and squeezed her hand.

"Lennox, do you think A.J. killed Cassie?"

"I wish I knew for sure. I'll speak to you in a few minutes. Don't move. I'm going to meet my men."

"I'll try not to run away," she mumbled.

The ambulance and two squad cars pulled up on the hill. A state cruiser followed behind an ambulance.

The trooper slammed his door and hiked over to meet Lennox. "The state's Major Crime van is on its way. I understand you have a possible homicide."

Lennox nodded and filled him in. A small army of men in uniforms and suits descended on the area. Rose watched the buzz of activity. *Buck up, Blue. You can't sit around forever.*

She walked over to Lennox and the group of uniforms. "What can I do to help?"

"Nothing, the men will do their jobs." He cut a glance at the new arrival driving to them.

"What is it?" She snapped her attention toward the vehicle.

"Frank's here."

The burly, ex cop slammed the door of his dented vehicle and spoke to one of the officers before he ambled forward.

"He heard already?" Did everyone know?

"I called him. Before you protest, listen to me." He took hold of her arms and peered into her face. "He'll take you home and stay with you until I finish up. I need to clear the crime scene to work it."

"I don't need a babysitter, Lennox."

"Humor me."

Before she could argue, Frank approached them.

"Rosie girl, I'm sorry for your loss."

"Thanks, Frank." She bit her lower lip to stop the quiver. "Lennox, do you want me to speak to Cassie's mom?"

"I'll contact her. Go ahead with Frank."

"Come along, Rose." Frank hooked his arm around her shoulders. "We'll let the young men work."

She sent one last glance toward the friend who'd come to cheer her up and instead lost her life. Yellow tape was going up to declare the area off limits. She should have told Cassie how much she meant to her. She should have asked more about Cassie's dreams and talked less about her problems.

"Ready, Rose?" Lennox asked.

She said a quick prayer and faced him. "Yes, take care of my friend."

CHAPTER 20

At her apartment, Rose poured steaming water from the kettle into her mug. "I need something hot," she said to Frank sitting across the kitchen table from her. "I'm freezing and can't stop shaking. Want a cup?"

"I believe I will." He reached into the pocket of his coat draped over the back of the chair. He came up with an airplane sized bottle. "My favorite warm up. I always carry one. Care for a touch?"

"No thanks." She set a mug in front of him. "I can microwave a bowl of soup if you're hungry."

"Don't bother. Your hot water is superb." He poured amber fluid from his bottle into his drink.

"I never dreamed my day would end this way." She held the cup between her hands, letting the heat soak into her skin. "I hope they find a clue on the bank that will finally put away that monster."

"I'm sure Lennox feels the same. Homicides can eat you up. The ones you can't solve are like cancerous cells destroying your faith."

Rose wrinkled her face. "Not everyone can hack being a detective. I wouldn't be able." She held out an unsteady hand. "I'm on the verge of crying again, but Lennox can handle it. He'll find who murdered my sister and Cassie."

Frank sat quiet, observing her.

"What is it?"

"I'm happy Luke has someone who believes in him. I'm afraid not everyone is so lucky, and tears don't mean you're weak, Rose. You're human with emotions. Crying can be how you survive to move on."

She rested her cup on the table. Now was her chance to find answers. "Frank, I need to ask you a question that's a little personal and has nothing to do with Cassie."

"Ask away. My life's yours for tonight only."

"I apologize in advance if it's none of my business, but I read online that Lennox's father committed suicide. Do you believe he killed himself?" She studied the older man's face, watching his reaction.

"Rose, my girl, you've touched on a sensitive issue." He stared into space for a second as though searching the past. "John was my partner and the best man I ever knew. I never believed he killed himself. I don't care how many Medical Examiners cut up and study his body. The man was murdered."

She forced out a word. "Awful."

"He was hot on solving the case where the young woman was strangled and dumped in a pond."

"Are you talking about the victim in North Conway?"

"No, this case was eight years ago, in a town near Conway and similar in makeup. Both towns offer lots of condos for weekenders or vacationers who enjoy shopping or sports, which gave us lots of transients to consider. John and the others working the case thought it was the same MO in both cases. Each investigation started with a missing person and ended in a homicide with a young girl's body disposed in water.

"How old was the girl in the older case?"

"She was about seventeen, a trusting soul and a little shy. She was not allowed to date. Everyone was horrified that such a sweet girl was tortured and murdered. John was friends with one of the detectives from the State Major Crime unit who worked the scene. The two of them used to kick around theories once the case went cold."

"Maybe the detective from Major Crime could help us with Dahlia's death."

"He died two years ago. Let's forget death for the moment." Frank chugged his drink. "You make great tea, Miss Blue."

"Heating water is a gift."

"I agree." He rested his mug on the table. "People don't

realize when you spend all your time living with heinous crimes, your life changes."

"And the life might kill you," Rose added, gripping her tea cup.

"Might is a big word and leaves a lot of room for doubt in my old partner's case."

She nodded and mentally said a quick prayer for Lennox. The desire to see him safe and sound seized her. She needed him out of harm's way at the river.

* * *

Not a trace of evidence remained on the girl. The river had taken care of that. Search all day and night. You'll learn nothing. I'm smarter than the whole Ledgeview Police Force.

You'll never catch me, even when I'm in front of you.

Sirens and flashing lights were drawing a crowd. The camera helped to blend in. People snapped and videoed the action on the hill. Murder was a big draw in Ledgeview.

I was here, but now I'm gone. Just like Dahlia, Cassandra and next, Rose.

* * *

Luke ordered the uniforms to establish the perimeter around the area. "Get the names of each EMT when they arrive. I want to eliminate or account for any DNA we might pick up. Then I want the name and address of each employee from the stores in the plaza. We'll interview each one."

The officers nodded and took off. The forensic techies were already garbed in their plastic booties, gloves and coats. In the distance a black sedan headed toward him. Conroy.

He halted his vehicle next to Luke's, flung open the door and headed toward the activity.

"What'd you find?"

"Victim is on the bank," Luke said. "She was a friend of the Blue women and drove over to visit Rose yesterday for lunch. Last seen headed home from Ledgeview to Vermont. I'd say she spent time in the river same as our last victim."

Conroy emitted a sound that was a cross between a grunt and a curse.

At the sound of an engine, Luke glanced up the hill. "The ME's arrived. She'll give us her opinion on how long the victim was in the river. Meanwhile, canvass the hill and the neighborhood."

Near midnight, Luke climbed the bank to his car. He'd contacted the chief and filled him in before the death hit the newscasts. Luke's gut churned with dread when he thought about the news conference ahead. The best thing he could do was to take a short nap before the morning. The past warned him that the few hours of sleep he was about to enjoy might feel like days by the time he made an arrest.

But first, he was stopping at Rose's. All night he'd wanted to touch base with her, hold and reassure her. Nothing would prevent him now.

The platinum-blonde blindsided him by stepping out of the dark behind a bright light, shining in his face. A thirty-something-year-old woman in a beige jacket held a mic in front of his face.

"Detective Lennox, we understand another murdered woman has been found in Ledgeview. What can you tell our viewers?"

Press, his wall of caution shot up. "At this time, I've limited information except a young woman's body was found near the river a few hours ago. I'll release a statement concerning the victim once relatives are notified." He started around the newscaster, but she jumped in front of him.

"Do you think this death is connected to the one at The Ledges?"

"I don't have enough information to answer. If you or any of the public have seen or heard anything suspicious, don't hesitate to call the tip line." He recited the digits. "I can confirm a reward has been posted for the person who comes forward with information that leads to an arrest and conviction in The Ledges Homicide."

"Do you believe there's a possibility the person who killed Dahlia Blue was involved in the death of the woman today?"

"I can't comment without more evidence. If you'll excuse me, I'm finished here." He started toward Old Charger.

"One more question, Detective. What do you say to the women of our city who are living in fear for their lives?"

"Take precautions, don't go out alone and call the police if you've suspicions. Report everything. We're following several leads in the Blue case, and we will arrest the perpetrator or perpetrators of these crimes." He'd had enough of her questions and stalked past to his car.

Her closing words to the camera floated behind him. "The women of Ledgeview continue to live in terror and like second class citizens who can't leave their homes. Who will be next? How long will it take our police department to capture a homicidal maniac who petrifies and holds our city hostage?"

Great, all he needed was a media inspired panic. He drove straight toward Rose's apartment. A nagging in his mind insisted he was missing something. He slowed his car and glanced in his rearview mirror. No one followed.

The feeling refused to be silenced until he climbed the stairs to her place. Walking past Frank into her kitchen, he concentrated on fighting the urge to take her in his arms.

She laid down her hand of playing cards on the tabletop.

"Don't ever let the woman play poker," Frank said, sliding the chain lock back in place. "She couldn't bluff to save her bank account." He grabbed his jacket off the back of the kitchen chair.

Rose stood up and fastened her gaze on Luke. He could read the hope in her eyes.

"Did you learn anything new?"

He shook his head and pulled the snack out of his pocket that he'd bought from the vending machine at the station earlier. "It's a Power Bar. Eat it." He pressed it into her hands.

Her shoulders tightened as she set the bar next to her tea cup. "How's Cassie's mom? Did you reach her?"

"She arrived an hour ago and identified her daughter. She's settled in a hotel for the evening."

"I should join her. She shouldn't be alone." Rose grabbed her purse and dug inside for her keys. "Where is she?"

"She's at the Hightail Hotel, but she needs privacy to grieve, and she's not alone. Her husband and brother arrived half an hour ago. They're all together. Speak to her tomorrow. Tonight's not a good time. The reporter from the local channel is circling the area even at this hour. She could have followed me and staked out the building. If you leave, she'll trail and hound you and Cassie's parents."

Rose stuck out her chin. "They'd better not bother her family.

Did you find any clues at the river?"

"We'll know more tomorrow when we process all the information." The last thing he wanted was to discuss the case. He wanted to run his hands over every inch of her body. He wanted her alive and breathing in his arms.

Frank gathered up the playing cards and stuffed them in his pocket. "Everyone will have a theory in the morning."

She nodded, dropped her keys into her purse and sank onto the chair. "What about my neighbor, Bike Boy?"

"I sent a uniform over to take his aunt's statement. She changed her story and claimed Todd's not missing, just visiting friends she can't name. She finally confessed she hadn't heard from him in over a month but waved aside our concerns about his safety. Of course she could be lying and know where he is. I put out a BOLO for him."

Frank pulled on his beige coat and walked to the door. "Now that we've got the changing of the guards, I'll hit the road."

"I'll lock up." Luke walked with Frank out into the hall and down the stairs. His mind refused to budge from the image of Rose waiting for him upstairs. In the entryway, he paused and put a restraining hand on Frank's shoulder. "Thanks for staying with her, and remember, don't go near Buddy Drown. I don't want to arrest you for stalking."

"I wouldn't dream of driving to his home and then sitting outside his house for the rest of the night. I'd lose my beauty sleep."

"I mean it, Frank."

The older man waved a hand in the air. "Did the pretty newscaster from Channel 23 follow you? I could get lucky and she'd interview me." He marched out the doorway and paused on the step. "Remember your own advice. Keep Rose safe and away from Buddy Drown."

"I won't forget, and don't let the blonde newswoman worm details out of you."

"I'd love her to try." Frank dropped his voice. "Don't let this investigation blind you to what's in front of you. Rose Blue isn't worth throwing away to prove you can solve a murder. Take it from someone who did it all wrong."

"Frank, I intend to make the right arrest. One more thing,

you're a great detective."

"I'm not talking about the job. Forgetting what matters most happens to the best of us. I'd hate for you to repeat the pattern."

Was he referring to his father or himself? The familiar urge to change the subject attacked him. "I'll do my job, Frank. The investigation comes first."

"Don't forget what's in front of you. That's all. Night, Detective."

Luke listened to the sound of his friend's footsteps. Lennox dead bolted the door and turned to find Rose in the middle of the staircase. Her tight face and stiff posture warned him she'd overheard his conversation.

"You're going back to work?"

"I can stay for a cup of coffee." The flare in her eyes and soft curl of her lips drew him up the steps. He followed her into her apartment. "How many pots of coffee have you had?"

"Two or eight." She raised one shoulder in a half shrug. "I don't have Espresso but you might like the French Roast."

"As long as it doesn't taste like mud, I'll drink it."

"Gosh, mudslide was my specialty." She set to work at the counter. "I'm sure Frank was happy to leave. I couldn't concentrate on the game. He must have wanted to give me one of those card games for dummies books." She measured the grinds, releasing their fresh fragrance before she poured them into the coffeemaker. "I've been thinking. I'm sorry about the way I acted down at the river. I was a babbling idiot." She turned to him, her hair falling in her eyes.

"You were in shock. Don't beat yourself up." He closed the space between them and brushed the strands from her face. Desire hit him sharp and deep. He wanted to kiss away her pain, and forget duty and regrets.

"I know the truth about Cassie's death."

He itched to touch her again. What did she say? She'd withheld information from him? "What do you mean?"

She fiddled with the v-neck collar of her shirt as though trying to loosen it. "Cassie died because the killer was following me the day she visited and probably saw you watching me. He took Cassie when he couldn't get to me. I should be the one on the riverbank."

"You're not making sense. No one deserves to be murdered. Your friend's death wasn't a competition." Rose was talking crazy.

"You misunderstood me if you think that's what I meant."

Luke edged closer, and before his brain could shout, stop, his mouth was on hers. His hands moved over her curves, the angles he'd longed to touch. He traced her full lower lip with his tongue, brushed her hair aside and kissed her earlobe.

Sensations curled through him, urging him to touch her everywhere. He took her mouth in a rough kiss. The hint of hazelnut lingered on her tongue.

"Luke," she murmured before he stole her lips away again. She hooked her hands around his neck and pressed her breasts against his chest.

He raised his face and cradled hers in his hands. "Rose, you should—"

She cupped her palm over his mouth. "Let me give you a hint." She dropped her hand. "Don't talk. I can't take any more rejection or hurt."

He didn't need any further encouragement. He lifted her chin and kissed her lips gently. She returned the kiss with passion as he slid his hand over her breast. Aroused, he backed her up to the wall. She gasped into his mouth. No, tonight he'd take time for her, for them. He forced himself to step away.

"What are you doing? Are you leaving?" She reached out to stop him.

"I'm all yours." He swept her up in his arms.

"Wait! Put me down."

She'd changed her mind? How had he misread her? Women, he'd never understand them. He lowered her to a stand.

She ran to the coffeemaker and pushed the off button. "We don't want to be interrupted by the fire department." She fluttered her eyelashes at him.

He grinned and held out his hand. She linked her fingers through his and led him to the sleeper. Together they laid down on the beige spread. The scent of freshness from the pillowcase and sheets lingered around him. For a moment, he stared into her large hazel-green eyes. She was gorgeous. What luck had brought her to him? Damn if he knew, and he wasn't going to waste time finding out. He skimmed a finger over her cheek.

"I've dreamed about us, alone, together," she whispered, snuggling closer.

"Are we alone?" He shot glances around the room.

Her lips twitched upward. "Dahlia's not here. I can't speak for your ghosts, Lennox."

"Mine are smart enough to keep out of sight."

Her amusement faded and her eyes narrowed with sadness. "Hold me. I can't get the last memory of Cassie out of my mind. Make me forget."

He needed no encouragement. His fingers traveled down her shirt, coaxing the buttons through their holes. He wasted no time admiring her lingerie except to note it was his favorite shade of blue. He unfastened her bra and kissed each section of her bare skin. She tasted salty like a good whisky sour. Her skin felt smooth beneath his palm as he ran his hands over the length of her body. Her body was soft and hot, hot for him, not the cold of death.

She whispered his name and pressed him to hurry while tugging his shirt away and off his shoulders. He lowered his hands to her jeans as she kissed his jaw, his throat. His anticipation sizzled and ran fast, pushing him to take more, now. He tugged on the zipper of her pants. It refused to budge. He pulled again and muttered an oath of impatience.

"Run into trouble, detective?"

The humor in her voice seemed like a challenge. He yanked the zipper down with restrained strength. The click of the metal teeth announced the success and he removed her last pieces of clothing before speaking to her. "Your turn. I'm at your mercy." He lay back with a gleam in his eyes.

She attacked him with unexpected energy, tossing aside his pants, shirt and boxers over her shoulder with a devilish grin. "It's too late for excuses, Lennox!"

"I can't think of one."

He rolled them over to her spot on the mattress. Something poked into his upper chest. Raising himself up, he saw the necklace around her throat. He reached down and picked up the butterfly pendant. The one she cherished. Bringing it to his lips, he kissed the ornament.

Her eyes glistened with tears, and she drew his head down to her. All thoughts left him except the fact he wanted her. He kissed her skin with his lips and teeth. Taking his time, he worked his way over every part to savor the taste of her. Her soft cries drove him until he couldn't wait.

With her legs wrapped around him, he plunged into her. He felt their bodies joined together when a wave of emotion hit him and he became lost in feelings, allowing her soft cries to drive him on.

When he could barely raise a brow he tugged her against his chest and held onto her until his heart calmed. Then he turned on his side, crushing her against him. This was right. This was as it should be. They lay quiet for a long time. She was his, all his. He forgot about dead women, warped killers and the world outside.

He listened to the beat of their hearts tapping its message of happiness. Was that what he'd felt, love, or was it simply old fashion lust? He loosened his grip. She increased hers. Love. He could fall in love with her.

"I can't stop thinking about you, Rose."

She squeezed his hand and smiled.

He wanted to say more, but caution whispered to not be a fool and enjoy the moment. Finally he gave up the struggle to speak his mind. He threaded his fingers through her hair and pulled her mouth to his.

CHAPTER 21

Luke woke to find the spot next to him empty. He glanced at the clock, five a.m. He'd overslept. When he worked a case, he went to bed after midnight and got up at four to arrive at the station before anyone else. He loved the quiet. He grabbed his pants and went to find Rose. She was seated and writing at the table. Her head was bent, and the sight of her blonde, rumpled hair around her face increased his craving for her.

She raised her mug and caught sight of him. "Good morning, would you like coffee?"

"You couldn't wait for daylight to inhale your first cup of the day."

"I plead guilty and an old nightmare woke me."

"Do you want to talk about it?"

"I've had the dream for years. My mother is tucking me into bed and when she leans down to kiss me goodnight, her eyes are gone." Rose's lips trembled. "I know the dream was caused by one of the kids at school who used to taunt me and Dahlia. He told us spiders crawled into my mom's coffin to eat her flesh, especially her eyes."

"Delightful." He'd love to meet the bully. "He's probably a serial killer now." "Congressman." She raised her head and grinned. "I got even though. One day I kicked him good between the legs when he started taunting us. The teacher kept me in from the next recess, but it was worth it."

"I understand your fear of eight legged creatures better." He put a hand on her shoulder and bent forward, enjoying her heat under her palm, the scent of her body after lovemaking and gave her a kiss.

She sighed and put her chin in her hand. "I used to hope if my Mom lived she'd be like my Gram. You know, sensible and a homebody who wanted to stay with us and not roam around chasing men."

He straddled the chair next to her. This was not the conversation he'd expected, but he'd go with it for a short time, and then he intended to start his morning with Rose Blue, not coffee.

"Do you speak to your mother?"

The corner of her mouth tilted upward. "Is this a sanity quiz? Afraid you slept with an unbalanced woman?"

"I can handle the idea." He leaned forward and kissed her. She tasted of cinnamon. "Hmm, I approve your coffee choice," he said, breaking away.

"Glad you approve." Rose gulped down a mouthful of drink and then continued. "My mother's too busy even in death to speak to me. Family was never important to her. If she talks to anyone from the grave, it's probably an old boyfriend. I'd like to think maybe it's my father, but no one knows about him."

"Your Gram didn't know your dad either?"

"If my mom did tell Gram his name, I'm not sure if she'd believe my mother was telling the truth. Gram used to lecture us not to turn into liars like our mother, but I honestly don't remember a lot about her. I think she'd sneak out a lot to party when she was a teenager." Rose shrugged her shoulders and fell silent, her brow puckered. Then her features smoothed. "Your confession time has arrived. Do you hear your father?"

"When I think about my dad, he's shouting advice at me. 'Dig deeper, Luke.' After a few seconds, I remember he's gone. It's a memory I'm recalling, not engaging in a conversation."

"I'm sorry about your dad, Lennox. If it's like losing Dahlia, I don't know how you stand it."

He tried to close himself to the ache brought on by her statement, but he was too late. The crushing blow of reality set free a pain worse than the day his wife walked out. To escape the memory, he fell back on work. "I've been reviewing my dad's last case. I'm trying to get into his state of mind before he died. I want to understand how he felt."

"Frank told me a little about your dad's cases and how he never forgot them. He was devoted to his job like you."

Luke picked up a packet of sugar and tapped it on the table. He was treading on firm ground again. His feelings were under control. "The former ME listed my father's cause of death as a suicide from a single gunshot. If I'd never left home and stayed around, I would have spotted his signs of depression and gotten him help. Now all I can do is try to understand his frustration or anger, and then, maybe I can comprehend why he died."

"Guilt is what I feel most of the time over Dahlia's death." Rose picked up the pen and clenched it in her hand.

He shook his head. "Your sex doesn't own a monopoly on the emotion. Working in New York didn't protect me from the loss of my father. I left Ledgeview to lead my own life. Here, my life was mapped out. I'd follow in the footsteps of the men in my family and go into law enforcement. Everyone already compared me to my father. It was a pressure I didn't want at the time. Today I see it as a compliment, a way to continue what he and my grandfather did."

"I understand. When someone close dies we take stock of our lives, and it doesn't matter where you live. Ghosts have a poor sense of geography. They follow you." She held out her open hand.

He linked his fingers with hers. "You need to help me with A.J."

The smooth skin in her forehead wrinkled "I wish I could break the case wide open. I want A.J. brought to justice yesterday, if he's guilty, and I want to understand why he'd kill my sister. I'm still not convinced."

"People do ugly things when they're angry, and life events serve as triggers. It's possible the end of his engagement was the event that set him off."

She bent her head over her notepaper, avoiding him.

"Are you okay?"

She raised her face. Her eyes filled with misery. "I'm trying to understand how a person loves someone one moment and destroys her, the next." She eased her hand away from his and ran a finger over the mug's handle. "Everything has changed since I came to Ledgeview. I look back and see myself as too involved with my own life, running a store, pretending I was business woman of the year while my sister became involved with a dangerous man right under my nose."

"Rose, you're not invincible. People end up in the wrong place at the wrong time, and no one can protect them. Did Dahlia take anything else from a friend or customer in your store? Would she have stolen for A.J. and changed her mind and refused to give him the stolen money?"

"Only A.J. can answer you, and no one else complained or accused her of stealing." Tears glistened in her eyes. "I need my sister, Lennox. Dahlia was the outgoing one. She was the one the customers wanted. She handled the dealings with suppliers and gave them cookies as a thank you. She was always generous. When she met a person who was cold on the street, she gave him her sweater or jacket. I was the practical one, who concentrated on the numbers in our bank account, who sent the cold person to the church's closet. Together we were a whole. Now she's gone, I'll never be complete again."

He slid his hand around her shoulder and tugged her into the crook of his arm. She fit perfectly into the curve. "You make my whole."

"You're a sweet talker, Lennox." Rose tilted her head up. "Women must spill their guts to you."

"My ex will vouch for my failures there." He paused. "Let's forget other people for the moment. I have to go to work soon. Let's take advantage of what's left of our time this morning."

A grin spread across her face. "I like your thinking."

He cupped the back of her head and drew her to him. She sighed as he left a trail of kisses across her cheek and moved toward her mouth. His tongue rimmed her full lips that tasted of coffee.

His cell phone rang out from his pocket. Damn. "Hold on."

"Detective Lennox," a woman fired his name into his ear. "Do you have a suspect in the Cassie Raymond murder or the attack at the garage?"

He recognized the voice of the local reporter from last night. "We're following several leads. I can't say anything further at this time. How did you get my number?"

"A friend passed it on to me when I did the garage attack

write up." She clicked off the phone.

"Reporter," he told Rose.

"He or she is calling early."

"She wanted the scoop on Cassie or the attack at the garage for the five thirty a.m. news show. She probably decided to gamble on my cell when I didn't show up at work at my routine time."

"How did she happen to have your number?"

"She said a friend gave it to her. I bet it was my friend, Conroy." He shoved away from the table and began to pace to ease his irritation.

"Lennox, I'd like to talk to Shauna. She's been on my mind and I'd like to see her. When I can stop thinking about Cassie, I start thinking about her."

"Lunch today. I'll set it up." He paused and let the new idea shove away his annoyance.

"I'm going to shower. Want to join me?"

She narrowed her eyes, and a sly smile slid across her lips. "Detective, are you planning on frisking me?"

"Count on it," he whispered.

* * *

At noon, Luke returned and picked up Rose, and they headed to the Drowns. The ride was uneventful. She seemed uneasy, shifting several times in her seat but remained silent. Was she having regrets about this morning or last night? "You okay?"

"I'm hoping Shauna will provide new details, woman to woman, and we're not wasting our time."

"Keep the focus, Rose. You're going to offer emotional support."

"I'll be gentle."

"I'm not reassured." He slowed for the turn.

Buddy's car was parked in the driveway next to Dean's white Cadillac. They walked side by side up the sidewalk to the front door of the Dutch Colonial. Lennox rang the bell. Hard to believe a few days ago they'd stood on these steps, waiting to enjoy a dinner.

"No one's answering," Rose said, walking backward to take in all the windows and signs of activity.

He dug out his cell and called Buddy. His friend appeared

two minutes later at the door, with a phone to his ear. He pointed at Luke. "Gotcha."

He laughed and dropped his hands to his sides. "Glad you called ahead, or I wouldn't have let you in. Rose, I heard my parents owe you a dinner. Come in. Mom's at work and Dad's on his way back. He stopped to pick up a contract."

Buddy raked a gaze over the yard before he held the door wider for them to enter.

"Thanks for letting us visit Shauna," Rose announced as they entered.

"Miss Blue, are you deputized?" His brows rose upward, and his lips broke into a grin.

"I'm here as support." She threw a glance at Luke. "I know how awful it is to be attacked."

"Do you? Sorry, I was unaware of your past." Buddy shut the door and dropped the phone into its cradle on the hall table. "Shauna doesn't want to talk to people, but I convinced her to let you guys in."

"I came as a friend," Luke said.

"I didn't recognize your undercover outfit."

"Buddy," Rose moved forward, catching his attention. "The man who attacked Shauna could be the same one who murdered my sister."

"Sounds like an official visit to me," Buddy grumbled. "We haven't heard zilch from the police since we left the station. I was wondering if they'd dropped Shauna's investigation."

"It's early in the case, Bud. Everyone is working on it."

"I bet you are." Dean emerged into the hallway. He was dressed in his suit and overcoat and held a brief case in his hand. "Good to see you both. I hope you don't mind, but I've a showing in ten minutes."

"We won't detain you, Dean," Luke said. "I hope all is well with the campaign."

"I can't wait to start stumping. Rose, thanks for coming by. Now if you'll excuse me." He paused at the door. "Bud, remember our meeting at two."

"It's the highlight of my life," Buddy deadpanned.

The tension in the room thickened as Dean stared at his son for a moment and then opened the door. "Everyone stay safe."

"You can always count on my father to bring up his own agenda." Buddy's lips tightened. "Shauna's upstairs. I'll talk to her first and ask if you can bring up the subject of the attack. She might give you the green light. Wait here." He turned and ran up the stairs.

Luke wandered to the window near the front door and picked up the curtain. The neighborhood was quiet. A few buds peeked out on a shrub nearby.

Rose joined him near the glass. "Dean and Buddy seem to get along like cats and dogs."

"At least we can count on their predictability."

"What was Buddy doing before he opened the door for us?" she asked. "He acted as though he expected Shauna's attacker to be slithering up the front walk."

"Bud loves drama. If you needed a spokesperson, you could count on him to be in your spotlight."

At the sound of approaching footsteps, Luke fell silent.

"She's ready." Buddy wound down to the hallway. "But she only wants to talk for a few minutes about the parking garage." He led them to the second floor and paused at the first closed door. He rapped and entered. Inside a floral wallpapered room, Shauna sat in a wide wing back chair, wearing a pink bathrobe. A lacy nightgown peeked through at her throat. The young woman's long, dark hair was combed straight around her face and emphasized the whiteness of her complexion. Her large brown eyes stared at them with curiosity and wariness.

"Luke," she greeted. "Buddy said you wanted to say hello and ask a few questions. I'm sorry I'm not dressed. Buddy said to pretend I was on vacation though I'm not good at forgetting the reason I'm really here." She picked at the crimson lap quilt covering her legs and waist.

"You're beautiful." Buddy leaned forward, kissed her cheek and straightened. "This is Miss Rose Blue. She wanted to meet you and extend her sympathies."

Rose hesitated by the bed stand with the vase of flowers. "What a beautiful arrangement. The florist included quite a variety. Does it contain any roses?"

"Roses? No, I didn't see any. Tia gave me the bouquet." Shauna held out a hand. "It's nice to meet you, Miss Blue."

Rose shook her hand. "I appreciate you speaking to us."

Shauna bit her lip, glanced at Buddy and back. "I...I'm sorry about what happened to your sister."

"Thank you," Rose said. "You had a terrible scare yourself in the parking garage. At least you were smart enough to carry pepper spray and escaped."

"After all that's happened in Ledgeview, she'd be foolish not to be prepared." Buddy sat on the arm of the chair and held her hand.

"I'm sorry about wrecking your evening with Dean and Tia. I understand you were all waiting for Buddy and me to arrive for dinner."

"Don't worry about the other night," Rose said. "We're happy you're okay, and if you describe your attacker, you might help us find my sister's killer. There's a good chance it's the same person."

"I talked to the police already. Besides, he's probably long gone." Shauna leaned into Buddy.

"I'm afraid not," Luke interjected. "Another woman was killed and found yesterday. There's a possibility the deaths are connected to your attacker."

"Another woman was murdered?" Shauna's eyes widened and she gripped the collar of her bathrobe. "You didn't mention someone else died, Buddy."

He squeezed her shoulder. "Don't worry, sweetheart. You're safe. So you believe it was the same guy, Lennox?"

"We're still gathering information. Did you remember anything else since the last time you spoke to the police, Shauna?"

"I—" Fear filled her eyes, and she met Buddy's stare.

"Go ahead," he urged.

Rose drew closer to the chair. "Please, we need your help."

"He was tall, dressed in black and wore a ski mask. I don't remember much, not even the color of his eyes."

"You're positive it was a black ski mask?" Rose insisted.

Shauna bit her lip. Lines creased her forehead. "Yes."

"Where was your attacker?" Luke asked.

"What do you mean? He was in the garage."

"When you first became aware of him, where was he?"

"He shot out in front of me. He must have hidden between the two parked trucks when I first entered. Yes, I remember. He jumped out from behind two pickups near the entrance. I don't remember details like models, but I couldn't see over them when I walked inside."

"The vehicles were by the main gate?"

"Yes, I was on the first floor because Buddy always parks and waits for me near the entrance." She wiped a hand across her forehead. "I can't think any more. I've a migraine."

Buddy jumped off the chair. "All right, your time is up. Shauna's health comes first."

"Stay with Shauna." Luke took Rose's arm and propelled her toward the door. "We know the way out."

"My mom wouldn't forgive me if I didn't see our company out of her house."

Rose hesitated. "If you remember any more, Shauna, call Lennox."

Luke decided to go for one more question. "Shauna, when's the last time you heard from A.J.?"

"Who?"

"A.J. Edwards, isn't he a friend of yours?"

She shook her head. "I never heard of him. Who is he?"

He felt Rose's questioning gaze on him. "I must have confused him with another bank employee. Rest up, Shauna." They walked in silence down the hall and the stairs.

"What are the chances you'll get the guy?" Buddy asked when they reached the entryway.

"We're moving forward," Luke confirmed.

Buddy shook his head. "Political BS, which means you have no suspects." He slapped Luke on the back. "Your secret is safe with me. Dad's going to campaign for the city to install at least two video cameras in the city garages. He figures it puts a positive twist on Shauna's attack." He opened the door.

Luke ushered Rose down the front steps.

"Positive twist on an assault?" she said under her breath and raised her brows at Lennox. "What was with the A.J. question?"

"It was a stab in the dark."

"Is Shauna always so hesitant to speak? She seemed afraid."

"Some people deal better than others with recent trauma, and

Shauna always defers to Buddy. The relationship works for them."

"Detective, can I speak to you?" The blonde reporter rushed toward them. Her videographer with the logo Channel 23 written on the camera's side tagged after her.

Luke shook his head, and he and Rose trotted for his car.

"Mr. Drown, how's Shauna Smith dealing with the aftermath of her attack," the reporter shouted, and the sound of running footsteps accompanied the media surging toward Buddy who appeared on his front step.

Two vans with Boston news logos on the sides pulled to the curb.

"Did someone call a press conference?" Rose slid into the safety of the vehicle.

Like turned to face another reporter and a camera.

"Detective," A thirty-something-year-old African American man with a mic approached Luke. "You're visiting the house where a young woman escaped an attack, and you're accompanied by the sister of another victim. Can you provide our viewers with a few facts about the recent attack or the Ledgeview homicides?"

"We're confident an arrest or arrests will be made soon in all cases."

"By soon, do you mean within the hour?"

Luke pushed his way toward the driver's side. "That's all I have to say at this time."

The newsman shadowed him. "Detective, is it true you were hired because of your father's past relationship with the Chief?"

He'd been ambushed. "The Ledgeview Police Department hired me based on my job performance on the force in New York. I'll continue to improve my record by arresting those who break the law." He stared into the camera. "Whoever committed these crimes needs to stand on alert. The Ledgeview law enforcement community will prosecute to the fullest extent any person or people who assist the perpetrator of these hideous events. No one will escape."

He glanced at the Drowns' house. Buddy stood on the front stoop, talking to the blonde reporter. Luke climbed inside Old Charger, and as he pulled away, the rest of the media flocked toward his friend. Luke threw glances in his rearview mirror. No sign of a news van trailing them.

"I bet they run to the TV Station to put Buddy's interview and a sound bite from you up for the evening news teaser," Rose said.

"Buddy will give them the interview they need for today." Suspicion kicked around in his mind. "At least we found out what Buddy was doing when he let us inside."

"Maybe he was being cautious after what happened to Shauna."

"He was hoping for a visit from the press." Lennox raised one brow and nodded his head. "The man breathes drama."

"Where did they come from?"

"They multiply like math teachers. Rose, I need the names of Cassie's friends, family, anyone who hinted of dislike. Mothers aren't always aware of all of their children's friends or enemies. I need to interview them all."

"When are you headed over to Bratt?"

"Don't get any ideas about tagging along with me or going off on your own. Frank will stay with you while I'm gone."

"I appreciate the concern, but I already planned to go to my boutique. The store's closed, and I've no idea what condition Cassie left it in."

He picked up her hand and held it while he drove. "You're important to me, Rose. I couldn't work if you were in danger."

Her face flushed. "I'll take that as the supreme compliment since work means everything to you. I like you too. We're a good team, right?"

"You still can't go."

"I'll show you the books Dahlia cooked if you take me to the Blues Sisters."

"I could get a warrant, but we'll compromise. Frank will drive you over, and I'll meet you at your store."

"I can drive myself, Lennox." She tugged her hand away, unzipped her purse and removed the small pad of paper. "I'll work on the names of Cassie's friends. I didn't know a soul who was mad at her." She bent her head and scribbled out a list on the paper. "Cass was always happy, smiling, humming. I can't believe how her life ended."

"That's why you won't be going alone to your store. I want you safe. Until we have A.J. thoroughly investigated and proof no pervert is still roaming around killing women, you'll take every precaution."

His conscience reminded he wanted her safe for other reasons. He couldn't forget the image of her in bed. The sensation of her fingers skimming over his bare skin, her blonde hair spread across the pillow and her hazel eyes staring up at him with trust.

He glanced at her sober face. He wanted to hear her laugh, watch the satisfaction appear on her face when she tasted her fist sip of the day's coffee and hold her hand and reassure her life would be okay while she whispered her fears.

He focused on the road, trying to understand. How did Rose get into his heart after he'd vowed never to let another woman in? For a man who was always on guard, he admitted, she'd ambushed him. He hadn't seen Rose coming, and he'd no idea where they were going.

CHAPTER 22

Rose played with the zipper on her jacket and watched the houses and stores zip past from the front seat of Lennox's car. In fifteen minutes they'd arrive at her apartment. She bit back the confession that burned in her throat. At last she gave up. "I want to tell you more about my fight with Dahlia before she disappeared."

Lennox tore his gaze from the street. "What happened?"

She tightened her fingers around the zipper pull. Might as well tell him. "I confronted her about the missing money. She tried lots of denial, at first. Then she realized she couldn't lie to me and was sunk. We had the 'big fight.' I mean I said terrible things to her. I couldn't believe she'd betrayed me by stealing from us. I wished she wasn't my twin. I wished I'd never have to see her again."

When he didn't respond, she wet her dry lips and plunged into the next part. "I told her we were done as partners and to keep her distance from me. I didn't even want to see her on the street. I threw my necklace at her." She let it fall on the floor." Rose twisted the zipper's pull tab and rushed on with her story. "A.J. came into the boutique during our fight, and when he asked how she could steal from her own sister, Dahlia yanked off her engagement ring and told him they were finished."

Rose studied Lennox's profile and tried to judge his reaction. As usual, he gave nothing away.

"It seemed the right move at the time. Now I view the fight from her perspective. She must have felt attacked by the two people she loved and trusted the most. I feel like I'm the one who betrayed her. I don't think she could exist without me. I know I barely function without her."

"Rose, you're blaming yourself again. Dahlia stole. That was wrong legally and morally. She was lucky you didn't press charges. You were her family. She knew you better than anyone. I'm sure she realized you'd calm down and want her back in your life. Were you and A.J. doing an intervention?"

The confession didn't push away the nausea threatening to climb up her throat. "No, the confrontation was unplanned. He frequently popped in. Do you think he pretended to love Dahlia to encourage her to steal and then pretended to be surprised by her actions?"

"I believe that's a possibility, but it's also possible she acted alone with subtle prompts from Edwards." He put on the car blinker and took the next left before speaking. "Keep in mind, the man who killed your sister is the bad guy."

"Thanks, Lennox. Why don't I feel better?" She blinked at the tears, filling her eyes.

"You haven't let yourself believe you're not to blame for Dahlia's death." Lennox slowed and parked in front of her apartment.

They walked to her apartment in silence. Her confession hadn't changed anything. She didn't feel suddenly relieved or free. Once inside her kitchen, he held out his hand to her, and she slipped into his arms. She rested her head against his chest, grateful for his presence and his strength. The dread and remorse that pressed down on her night and day faded away.

"Rose, I'm going to make sure nothing happens to you."

"Because it's your job?" She heard the ache in her own voice, muffled against his body.

He cradled her face in his hands. Anticipation rose in her mouth, sweet and tantalizing. His large hands moved over her backbone. *Say you care about me, Luke.*

His phone rang, demanding attention. He ignored it for a second, but then broke away to grab his cell and glanced at the caller ID. "I have to take this." He walked into the bathroom and shut the door.

His actions seemed ominous. In the short time she'd known him, Luke had never retreated into a closed room to answer his calls. Curious and disappointed, she took off her coat and put her purse on the table. She might as well do something useful. She sat and searched her brain for more names to add to Cassie's list.

Dahlia would have provided a longer list. She and Cassie spent time together shopping for jewelry and going to silversmith classes. Cassie and Dahlia had more in common. They chose the same style of clothes, music, and hung at the local bars. Sometimes Rose joined them, but usually it was just the two of them. Okay, reminiscing about Cassie wasn't helpful. Rose searched her mind for something about A.J. to help Lennox locate him.

Luke marched back into the room and paused to stand in his stance, feet braced apart, chin up. He'd reverted to work mode. Her hope for him to stay longer vanished.

"The Chief returned early. He wants me at the station. Will you be okay?"

"Of course, don't worry. I promise not to wander around despite who asks or calls."

"I'm including calls from the great beyond such as your sister. No trips to the river or The Ledges."

"Go see the Chief, solve the crimes and then—" She rose on tiptoes and touched her lips to his, lingering, sending him a message. The slow burn of desire curled through her before breaking away. "I'll be waiting."

The blue in his eyes deepened. She'd meant to turn away, but instead, she leaned into his arms and held on to him. She didn't care if their relationship was temporary. At least he was hers for the moment.

He stepped away without responding to her. Maybe he wasn't hers even for a split second.

He shrugged into his jacket. "Frank will check in with you."

The tenderness between them was gone. She scooped up the names of Cassie's friends from the table and handed them to him. Her defenses slid up, and she fell into her protective business manner. "When you come back, we're off to Brattleboro, right? I have to inventory my store before I close for a while."

"We're on." He stuffed the list of names into his pocket and gave her an absentminded kiss.

She touched her lips struck by the difference in their kisses. After locking the door, she paced the living room. Memories of her night with Lennox, the horror of discovering Cassie and scenes of Dahlia in her coffin flashed off and on like a neon billboard.

The ring of her phone was a welcome relief. She scooped up her keys for the front door as she answered. "Hello, Frank. I'm on my way downstairs."

"Rose?"

"A.J.?" The breath left her, and perspiration dampened her hands.

"It's me. Can you talk?"

"Sure." She sank into a kitchen chair, running a hand through her hair.

"I'm sorry I didn't call sooner. I couldn't. It hurt too much, but I just heard about Cassie." The fuzzy connection crackled in her ear for a second. "A.J., are you there?"

"I'm here. I can't believe what's happened. I thought Dahlia stayed away to sulk over our breakup and the shoplifting arrest. I never thought she'd…If I'd talked to her…maybe she'd be alive today."

"She's gone, A.J." Rose's voice came out hoarse. "Someone killed her and Cassie." Rose tightened her sweaty grip on the phone.

"I saw the news about Cassie on YouTube. One person murdered them both?"

"What do you mean?" Rose sat up straight. "Cassie's murder is on YouTube?"

"Not the actual murder. Someone put up an interview of the detective working on the case."

"Was it Detective Lennox?"

"He's the one. The poster wrote if you play his speech backwards you can learn the name of the killer."

"What a joke, I heard Lennox's speech. No way had he planted a hidden message in a video." She grabbed her laptop and scooted the screen in front of her. "How do I find the site? This is sick. Who posted it?"

"Don't get worked up. The poster was named Sure Lock. That must be a clue about him."

"Yeah, he lacks imagination."

"How are you, Rose? Are they close to arresting someone? Any suspects rounded up?"

Was he fishing for how close they were to arresting *him*? "A.J., where are you? I want to see you."

"I'm fine, Rose. Seeing you again would be hard. You understand with all the memories of Dahlia and you being twins."

"A.J., I'm worried. I need to talk to you."

"I'm sorry. I can't. It's too hard right now. I keeping asking myself why would someone kill Dahlia? I can't believe she's gone. I...I loved her."

"A.J. we need to get together. Where are—"

Pounding on her door jerked her attention away from the conversation. "Hold on." She lowered the phone. "Who is it?"

"Frank."

"Wait a minute." She returned to A.J. "Tell me where you are. I'll meet you."

"I'll phone again when we can talk. Bye, Rose."

"No, don't hang—" Dead air hummed in her ears.

Rose tossed the phone down and shoved to her feet. She unlocked her door and swung it wide. "How did you get inside?"

"Having a bad day, Rosie?"

"Sorry, Frank. I'm glad you came." She stood aside to let him pass. "But how did you get in?"

"I have my illegal ways, and I ran into Luke at the door. He let me in. We exchanged secret passwords and then I came up."

She drew the dead bolt.

"I called your phone, but it rang and went to voicemail."

"A.J. called me."

Frank slammed to a halt by the table. "Edwards? Where is he?"

"I don't know. We talked for a few seconds, and he hung up. I didn't get a chance to find out where he was. He told me someone named Sure Lock uploaded Lennox's interview about Cassie's death to YouTube and told people to play his words backwards to learn the name of the killer."

"Sounds like garbage. Can you bring up the number of the last caller?"

"Sure I can with a little presto change-o." She hit the redial button and a recording informed her A.J. was out of the reception area. "No luck at the moment," she said to Frank. "I'll try again later, but here's his number."

Frank punched the digits into his key pad and tucked his phone in his pocket. "Let's take a look at YouTube." He leaned over and dragged the laptop across the table to him.

"The Chief returned and called Lennox to the station. Do you think he's in trouble because of the video?"

"Play the interview, Rose, and we'll find out."

* * *

Luke sat across from the Chief in his office. For a busy man, the boss's desk and small space were neat and organized, not a paper clip out of place. The older man stared at Luke. His thin lips disappeared inward, a tip off to the tone of their meeting.

He'd skip the niceties of inquiring about the Chief's vacation and his daughter's wedding. "You must want a report on the Blue and Smith homicides."

"Save it." The Chief opened up a laptop resting on the desktop, hit a few keys and shoved the monitor around until the screen faced Luke.

"You're watching YouTube? I never look at the stuff." Luke raised his brows, and waited for the boss to explain.

"This isn't up for an Oscar." The Chief clicked on the square black screen, and Luke viewed himself speaking to the reporter the night of Cassie Raymond's death.

When the video finished, the Chief hit the sleep command. "I don't care what you did in the big city, but in Ledgeview, no one gives public interviews without clearing them with me first. From now on, no comment are the only two words reporters will hear from your mouth."

"Yes, sir."

The older man's thick brows drew together into one line. "The Mayor called me this morning, and it wasn't to offer congratulations. He said the news of the last homicide is stirring up a panic in the streets."

"Panic in the streets? Do I live in the same city?"

"Save the sarcasm, Lennox. The Mayor wants results, and he wants them yesterday. He's put the press off but knows sooner than later he needs to make a public statement. He wants to announce we're arresting a suspect when he declares he'll run for a second term."

"We're working on it."

The Chief waved away Luke's answer. "Anyone can see through the language you used in the last interview. We've nothing, and it stinks like month old salami." He ran a hand over his thinning, brown hair and patted it down. "And the nonsense about playing your interview backwards to reveal the name of the killer is the biggest piece of bull this year."

"What?" Luke bent forward. "I outed the murderer online? Who was it?"

"Glad you can joke, Lennox. Your sense of humor can help you on the unemployment line, which is where we'll be if you don't make an arrest." The Chief opened his desk drawer and drew out a white bottle. He unscrewed the cap and gulped a swallow. Then he slammed the drawer shut, leaving the bottle on his desktop. "Let's talk about where we are and where we're going with the investigations."

"Yes, sir." Luke reviewed their progress and his plan to head to Vermont to interview everyone connected to Cassie Raymond. "A.J. Edwards is the main person of interest in both homicides. The victims and suspect were friends who lived in the same city. The first victim was engaged to Edwards and the second woman killed was her best friend. I've put out an ATL for him. We haven't received a response yet. I believe he's circulating between Vermont and New Hampshire with a possibility of holding a job in Rhode Island."

"Sounds like a lot of traveling, but possible. What about the attack in the garage involving Dean Drown's future daughter-in-law?"

"The garage could be an isolated occurrence. She didn't give us much of a description of the assailant, and she doesn't have a connection to Edwards."

"We could have a copycat in the second homicide." The Chief grabbed a piece of paper from the top of his desk. "Twenty hours of overtime from our uniforms to search The Ledges plus Major Crime did a sweep. What was the tip that led you there in the first place?"

"Research on the river conditions such as current, water level and location of Dahlia Blue's body when she washed up led us to believe she entered the waterway at The Ledges."

The Chief nodded. "At least I've answers about the budget for the search."

"And Rose Blue reports she's psychically in contact with her twin, the first victim, and identified The Ledges as the primary site."

The Chief sat back in his chair and stared at him in silence.

He was letting him sweat.

"Alibi?"

"Rose Blue worked every day until seven. We've collaboration from several business people who work on Main Street. We verified her car was sitting in a local garage the week of the murder waiting for a part, and she begged rides from friends to search for her sister. Customers and phone records established she was at her store or looking for her twin during the time the murder occurred. Several local business employees stand by their statements that she was in their establishments during the time window of the murder going door to door with flyers. So far nothing indicates she benefits from the murder emotionally or financially."

"I've read the new ME's report. We could be off on the time of death. Keep Rose Blue on the radar. She might have hated her twin despite what she says. She knew Edwards, I take it?"

An uncomfortable lump grew in Luke's throat. "She did, but there's no evidence of co-conspiracy between Edwards and Miss Blue. In fact, he most likely is stalking her for his next victim."

The Chief leaned back in his chair. "I've investigated a lot of frauds in my life, Lennox. Many of them claimed to be into this psychic malarkey. I've yet to meet a real one. Keep the woman under close surveillance. Sooner or later, we'll learn if she's a con, an intended target or both. We don't want another death."

"I believe the sister's been truthful. If you want proof, there was the TV show based on the real life psychic who helped police in Texas."

"More BS I don't watch." The Chief sucked in his cheeks, a sign of his disapproval. "If the sister goes public with her so-called special abilities to the press, we'll contend with more problems than the full-of-crap play-it-backwards nonsense. Knowing reporters, your quotes will be the opening for the six o'clock news. Forget the no comment statement. Don't open your mouth when the media is around. I will attend all press conferences."

Luke tightened his lips. He needed to prove himself immediately. "I'm on my way to Vermont and then to Rhode Island."

"Get every name from Edward's high school class. Have Conroy canvass the retailers around the parking garage again. Work together. I don't need any lone-wolf hero antics, Lennox. Find out how or if the two cases tie-in. Keep on the twin sister."

Together was the key word that caught Luke's attention. "No problem, Frank Ricci took a little trip to Rhode Island and obtained the yearbook and background information on Edwards."

"Frank?"

"He's working on his own, no pay."

"Keep him away from the case, beginning now. This is not an investigation for retired detectives who play games with plastic men. If he's a source, describe him as one, but nothing else. Got it?"

"Gotten, but he's capable and—"

"I want him far away from our investigation." The Chief's face reddened. "We're under the microscope. We can't afford a mistake, and I can't explain one made by a man who's not even on the force. How would his involvement look to outsiders? If Frank made a break in the case, the anti tax group will want to cut our department and fill it with senior volunteers."

Luke bit back the urge to contradict the analysis of Frank's situation.

The Chief drummed his fingers on the desk. "Did your source interview anyone from the suspect's yearbook?"

"He talked with the school secretary, who gave us history on A.J.'s family and an ex girlfriend. We followed up with an interview of the prior girlfriend who swore A.J. never abused her or other women."

"Neither did most of the serial killers we've put away. Most of their girlfriends are in denial and will protest the monsters' innocence while they sit convicted, waiting for the juice to light up their chairs. What's the family background?"

"A.J. Edward's father was an accountant for a car dealership and embezzled from it. While his parent was imprisoned, A.J. and his mom lived with his uncle, a mechanic. His mother worked low wage jobs and moved around a lot. She finally abandoned him at his uncle's. The mother and uncle are now deceased. We're trying to locate the uncle's daughter, Edwards' cousin. They were once close and she may know where he'd go."

"Edwards grew up in a family where a role model was a thief." The Chief shook his head. "What are you waiting for? Get on it."

Luke scrambled to his feet.

"Remember, I hired you because of your experience and recommendations. Don't make me regret it. Confidence in oneself is good, but overconfidence leads to mistakes. Solve the case with your men. Now."

"I will, sir. We'll get our killer." The Chief's assessment of his personality grated on his nerves. He fought the urge to argue. "One more thing before I go. While you were gone, the Mayor approved a tip line that's running with volunteers and a donated reward for information leading to arrest and conviction specifically in the Blue homicide. I nominated Mike Conroy to head it."

"I'd prefer we gather tips for both homicides through our lines, but as long as we pay nothing toward it, I'm in favor of it. Conroy can gather the information from the volunteers on his free time. What are you waiting for, Lennox? Need a tip to go back to work?"

"No, sir, but Chief, I'm going on record as saying Rose Blue didn't kill her sister, and I'll prove it by arresting the person who did."

"I don't care if Miss Blue's a princess from Jordan. If she's guilty arrest her. If she's not, arrest whoever is and do it immediately. Then I can alert the Mayor that he can give his news conference that we've captured the homicidal maniac."

Luke turned to leave.

"And Lennox, get a haircut and shave before the press

conference."

"Yes, sir." He headed for his cubicle and caught the snickers of Conroy with a group of uniforms crowded round a computer monitor a few feet away from the Chief's office. One of the uniforms slapped Conroy on the back. "Way to go. Play it again."

"Hey, Conroy, I've got something for you."

Conroy walked away from the group and stood in front of him. The hint of amusement in his eyes faded, and his bottom lip stuck out. The aroma of a weak coffee emanated from the paper cup in his hand. "Have a nice chat with the boss?"

Luke's mind whirled with suspicion. "Been watching YouTube?"

"What? I don't have time for computer videos." Conroy slid a glance at the men who burst into grins.

Yeah, the guy couldn't even lie. "Never mind, I've a hunch about the attack on Shauna Smith. Come into my office." Luke marched to his cubicle aware Conroy lagged behind. "The Chief wants you to re-interview everyone around the parking garage and give me the report to read before you brief him."

"If the Chief wants confirmation, I'll do it today."

Luke grabbed A.J.'s yearbook off the file cabinet. He handed the book to Conroy. "I need you to research all of A.J.'s classmates and interview each one. Give me your team's findings by the end of the week. We're also on the hunt for his cousin, Nancy Burger."

Conroy stared down at the thick yearbook. His smirk faded away.

Luke shoved the book into the man's folded arms. "Knock yourself out."

"I'm on it." Conroy snarled and turned to the exit.

"Wait. I almost forgot the most important news. You're now the head of the new tip line. The Mayor is thrilled. Be sure to offer training for the volunteers. Chief wants you to set it up on your free time, and he'll expect a daily report. Have a good one."

"Daily?" Conroy let out a gruff sound and stomped from the office.

"Don't spill your coffee." At least, Luke had a suspect for the source of his YouTube problems. No surprise there. Conroy was probably emailing the link to everyone on his wife's Christmas list. At his desk, Luke opened his laptop and was about to search for directions to A. J.'s hometown when the urge to go to his Facebook page struck him. He signed in and clicked on his wall.

A few postings loaded on his page. One caught his attention. "Recommend Al James in Narragansett, Rhode Island. He worked on my baby and now she purrs."

"Alan James or A.J., I guess I better pay you a visit." Luke called Rose and learned Frank was at her apartment. "Is it calm on your end?"

"Not really, guess who called me today?" Rose couldn't wait for his answer. "A.J."

"What did he want?" Their main suspect was calling Rose. The Chief would add that to the evidence of a co-conspirator list.

"He found out about Cassie, and I've his number."

"With luck, I've already zeroed in on him. He's in Rhode Island." Forget the conspiracy theory. If A.J. was guilty and calling Rose, he could be done toying with her and setting her up for his kill. Luke wasn't letting her out of his sight. "I'll pick you up in fifteen minutes. Put Frank on."

"I will in a minute. I wanted you to know. I called Cassie's mom. She's devastated. She's having a small private funeral next week and emphasized I wasn't invited. I sensed she blamed me for her daughter's death. She kept repeating if only Cassie hadn't come to visit me she'd be alive." Rose's voice tightened and sounded hoarse.

"It's grief. Don't accept the responsibility."

"Right. Here's Frank."

"Hey, Lennox," Frank's deep voice boomed over the phone.

"Frank, sorry, but as of today, you're back in the civilian ranks."

The older man didn't answer. Hell, he was taking it hard. "I talked to the Chief—"

"No problem, Luke, I need to start planning my garden. The crocuses popped up yesterday. Spring's arrived, and the flowers won't wait for me to clean up my yard."

"Frank, if keeping you on was up to me..."

"Don't worry. When I heard the Chief was back, I doubted I'd be on your case much longer. The Chief is a by the book type of guy, and he doesn't use old geezers on his investigations. Most people think we should be playing board games."

"As long as you can make the winning chess moves, you're good. Take care, Frank."

CHAPTER 23

Rose met Lennox in the alley of the Blues Sisters Boutique. The afternoon sun beat down on her and promised warmth. She'd swap out jackets while she was home.

Lennox walked down the narrow lane to her in his familiar leather jacket and jeans. Now that Frank was back in the civilian ranks, it didn't make sense to expect him to guard or babysit her any longer. Besides, she was a capable adult. Despite Lennox's protests, she'd insisted on driving herself, and he insisted on following her.

"Welcome, Lennox, to my shop."

"Love the view." Green dumpsters lined the curb near the brick buildings.

"I'm putting it on a postcard. Most of the buildings house specialty stores on the street level and apartments on the second." She dug out her keys. "Usually when I open the boutique, I get a rush thinking what the day will bring.

"Today, when I think Cassie spent her last days inside, I'd rather visit a nest of spiders."

She twisted the key in the lock.

"The local uniforms have cleared the building. You're safe."

"I hope I don't get images of Cassie—imaginary or real—when I go in."

"She liked your shop and loved you. Only good vibes are here."

Rose pushed the door open and waited for him to cross the threshold. "Knock yourself out, Lennox. I know you want to inspect every corner."

"I want to test the locks. You're not staying alone if your security is like your protection at Dahlia's Ledgeview apartment."

"Blues Sisters boasts an excellent alarm system." She walked into the back room and halted. In the daylight pouring through the open door sat rows of boxes piled to the ceiling.

He gestured to the twelve-by-fourteen foot space packed with boxes of various sizes. "Is this the order your friend accepted"

"I hope not. I'll be broke. You can visit me at my cardboard shelter by the river." She browsed through the stacks. "These are marked Dahlia's apartment rooms."

She flipped on the overhead and pulled the door shut. "Cassie and I spoke on the phone about packing my sister's belongings. I never guessed she owned so much."

"Did she have a big place?"

"She rented a three room. Her closets were small, but she could be a pack rat. She loved to save things." Rose bent to a short stack of the boxes at her knee level. "This one is sealed with tape and was mailed to Dahlia."

Lennox removed a knife from his pocket and slit the tape. Rose dug into the containers and held up a flimsy, crimson teddy with the price tag still attached. She flicked the ticket over and read the name of the store. "My sister couldn't afford their prices. I don't get it." She read the tag again. No she hadn't made a mistake.

"Maybe the lingerie was a gift."

"From who?" Rose felt her eyes pop wide.

"Try this one." Lennox slid a box off the top row next to him and laid it at her feet. "The label is addressed to your sister, and the return address lists the retailer your twin couldn't afford."

He slit the seal and opened the flaps. Inside lay lingerie of various colors and styles but all in the same size, Dahlia's. "I can't believe my sister spent money, probably our money on …underwear!"

"We found out what your sister did with at least part of the money she stole from you."

Rose scanned the labels of the closed two-by-three foot cartons resting on their break table and threw her arms out. What was going on? "The store must have delivered them to the wrong address, and Dahlia wasn't home to return the merchandise. Cassie brought the boxes here when she packed."

"They keyed in her order enough to fill at least six boxes and never noticed the mistake?" he asked, browsing through the rows.

"I guess that's not the answer." Rose shook her head and grabbed another container to search. Inside were thongs of sheer fabric in a multitude of colors. "I can't believe it." She clenched the fabric in her hand. "Dahlia, what did you do?" Her sister was never satisfied or happy, and Rose or Gram were always stuck trying to get her out of her mess.

"The question is why she bought the lingerie? Did she have a fetish or a plan to add them to you store?"

"She should have mentioned if she wanted to add to our clothing line."

"Did she ever model?"

Rose shook her head. All of this was Dahlia's. "My sister almost financially ruined the Blues Sisters, but if you added up what she spent on panties and bras, plus the two apartments she'd bleed red." Rose sank on top of the lone box at her feet. The light pressure of his hand on her back reassured and calmed her first round of panic. "Why didn't Cassie let me know about all of this?"

"Maybe she knew you wouldn't approve, or she thought you were aware of Dahlia's buying spree."

"I can't believe Cassie didn't bring up the subject at lunch. She must have noticed the address on the boxes when she brought them over."

"Maybe she planned to tell you and changed her mind. Did she know Dahlia had a problem?"

"She was aware of some theft episodes. I don't know how many."

"Don't you find it odd she drove a couple of hours to eat with you in the middle of a work day?"

"I thought she was worried about me. Do you think she really came to let me know something about Dahlia and her purchases?"

"It's a good possibility." He swept a hand over his overgrown hair.

"Cassie did at one point want to say something important." Rose searched her memory. "Then she talked about closing the store early one night a week. I guess we'll never know the entire truth." Rose jumped up and dug out a flimsy red bra. She dangled it from her fingertips. "Of course, Dahlia ordered top of the line. Only the most expensive was good enough for my sister. Never mind, we might go broke. What was she thinking?"

"At least she had good taste."

Rose shook her head and read the date stamped on the label. "This order was mailed while she was engaged. It's not like she went off the deep end when she and A.J. were over and dealt with her breakup by shopping."

"I bet when we speak to A.J. he can explain her purchases."

An ache formed in Rose's chest. How much debt had her sister gotten herself into? The flimsy red panty seemed to answer her, and she sank onto the box. "Maybe she developed a lingerie fetish."

"Think motive. Why did your sister buy boxes of underwear?"

"Some of the garments must be her normal clothes from her apartment." The idea didn't help her feel better. At least Rose wouldn't have to help Dahlia figure a payment plan, though Rose would need to work on a return arrangement.

An old memory crashed back into her consciousness. Rose was fourteen and in the two bunk bedroom, staring at the small statue of the unicorn on her sister's nightstand. A warning rumbled in her mind.

Their next door neighbor kept a unicorn on her coffee table and called the statue her lucky charm. Dahlia had headed to their house to babysit yesterday.

The unicorn's presence meant one thing. Dahlia was stealing again and from people who trusted her. Dahlia had lied to Gram when she told her she'd beat her problem. The old episodes were starting again. Rose would have to tell Gram and somehow return the unicorn to the neighbor's. The sick feeling cramped in Rose's stomach.

Now her sister was older and she'd moved on to other problems. "My sister was a thief. That's her motive. I bet she bought the lingerie with our store's money. I'm going over our books again. Maybe Dahlia charged her purchases to the Blues Sisters and left town because she couldn't pay her bill and knew I was about to discover the debt." She wove between the boxes to the computer desk in the corner.

"We need to trace the source of her money."

Rose dropped into the work chair. "When Dahlia stole from the boutique, I had to apply for a short term loan. I was sweating the end of the month bills." Rose flicked the on switch for her monitor. While the machine booted up, her mind searched for other reasons for Dahlia's purchases.

"Rose?" Lennox stood next to her and pointed. "Does this door lead into your shop?"

She grabbed her purse off the desk and dug out her key ring. "It's the gold one. Knock yourself out."

He disappeared into the other room.

She brought up the figures for the boutique's last three months. She'd done the same thing when Rose confessed to stealing. None of the missing money equaled the amount Dahlia paid for the fancy lingerie, rents and deposit fee.

"What did you do, Dahlia?" Rose put her head in her hand. Closing her eyes, she concentrated. "Answer me. What's the truth?" Did dead women lie?

"Rose?" Lennox stood in the doorway.

"Did you find anything?"

"No boxes in the other room. Any changes in your finances?"

"I didn't discover anything new." She swiveled the chair toward him. "I'm going to call the department store and return whatever I can. I'm not sure how much they'll accept. I wonder if the bill is on her credit card with my name. I'm calling the bank. I don't want to be charged for her purchases."

"I went through all her credit statements from the last two years. Nothing popped out. She's paid up and no big purchases were due. As you know, no luck finding her laptop or outstanding emails from her ISP."

"Thank goodness, your news is the one good piece of information today." She bowed her head for a second and closed her eyes tight.

People who steal are punished when they die, Gram always lectured.

Was Dahlia's horrible death her punishment?

"Rose." The touch of Lennox's hand on her shoulder drew her attention to him.

"Finish up," he said in his quiet steady voice, "and we'll head home. We can stop at the store where Dahlia bought her fancy underwear. Then I'm driving to Rhode Island."

"I'm going with you, Lennox. We can drop my car off at my place. I live a couple of blocks away, and we can pick it up on the way back." She slipped her hand into his and stood up. "We'll find A.J. He must know something." Thank God, she had Lennox.

"*I'll* get him. You're staying safe."

"I can ID him for you and how much safer will I be than with you, unless you're planning a shoot out?" She tilted her head and waited.

"You stay in the car."

She jumped to her feet. "Let's go."

In half an hour, they'd dropped off Rose's car at her Brattleboro apartment, and headed to the store where they learned Dahlia personally bought all her purchases with cash. The sales clerk remembered Dahlia, always alone, came twice during a two month period, explaining the merchandise was for her business, but the clerk offered no other information.

Once they finished their brief conversation with the clerk, Luke drove toward Narragansett. The traffic on I-95 was heavy and from the number of boats being towed; Luke guessed people were anxious to get an early jump on the boating season. "When we arrive at the garage, I'll speak to A.J. Remember, you stay in the car."

"Lennox—"

"I'm in charge."

"I'm using my smart-on. I won't cause trouble."

Her lack of argument left Luke suspicious. She sat quietly with her eyes closed. She looked small and tired, and he longed to comfort her. He swallowed past the knot of unexpected emotion wedged in his throat. Feelings for Rose popped up at the worst moments like on his way to question a possible killer.

He glanced at his GPS. In five minutes they'd arrive. A street sign signaled him to turn right at the next street for the Foreign

Car Specialists. Luke drove down the hill to a large garage where various vehicles sat in front of the rectangular, concrete building. He parked in a vacant spot on the side of the three bays.

Rose stirred when the car stopped. "Are we in Rhode Island, yet?" She peered at him through half open eyes.

"We're at the garage. You're tired. Rest, while I go inside."

She unfastened the seatbelt. "I'm always tired. I'd have to wait for the next century to catch up on my sleep. Luke, you should reconsider and let me talk to A.J. first, soften him up."

"I don't want your presence to alert him something might be up, which you appearing out of nowhere would do."

"You brought me along to keep an eye on me?"

"No, I brought you as my personal sex object."

"Funny." She rolled her eyes.

"I don't know how this will go. I'll let you ID him when I'm sure it's not dangerous like when he's behind bars."

"That's useful." She folded her arms over her chest.

"I can't worry about you and a suspect at the same time." He slammed the door before she could protest and marched to the garage. He surveyed the front exits, three bay doors and one entrance for the office. There was one in the rear where he entered. The odor of grease filled the cool air, and the soft sound of an air compressor threatened to interfere with conversations.

"Can I help you?" A heavy set, middle-aged woman shouted from behind the counter.

"I'm here to speak to Al about my Maserati. He expects me. Name is Joe."

The woman gazed at him over blue framed glasses perched on her nose. "He's working. I'll see if he can come out." She pushed the buzzer of an intercom and spoke into the mouthpiece.

Luke wandered toward the windows that separated him from the work space. One man dressed in a green jumpsuit was on the wall phone. Lennox studied his profile. Dark hair, long face, it could be A. J. He needed a better view.

"It's not him." Rose sidled up to him and nodded to the figure beyond them.

"Did you forget how to wait again?"

"Lennox, I just—"

"Sir, sir," the woman behind the desk whipped off her glasses and yelled to him.

He glanced back at the man in the jump suit. The man had hung up the phone and returned to the sports car on the lift.

Rose stepped in front of him. "Lennox, listen to me."

"Later," he told her. When would she listen to him? He crossed the concrete floor to the receptionist.

"Al went home sick. We've another mechanic, but he's behind schedule and can't work on your car today. Do you want to make another appointment?"

Luke flashed his badge along with a picture of A.J. at the receptionist. Her eyes widened as her gaze bounced between Lennox's shield and the picture he held on his phone.

"Is this Al?" he asked.

"He must be in trouble." Her eyes squinted as she focused on the photo. "He's cleaned up and younger in the picture, but yeah, it's him. What did he do?"

"How long has he been employed at the garage?"

"He's worked for us about two months. He's reliable, always comes to work on time except for the one sick day. What did he do? Kill someone?" She laughed nervously until she caught his grave expression.

"When was he sick?"

"The first week, the boss had to dock him a day."

"I'll need his address and the date he was out."

"It's always the quiet ones." She pulled out an index card from a gray metal file and scribbled on the back.

"I've arrested plenty of noisy people." He grabbed the card, glanced at it and headed to the exit with Rose.

At the door, she lurched in front of him. "Are you ready to listen to me, Lennox? I saw A.J."

CHAPTER 24

"A.J. drove off. He must have seen or heard you asking for him and been suspicious. You do kinda walk like a cop."

"I'm sure A.J. would know."

"If you'd let me talk a few minutes ago, we'd have him already."

She was right. "I'll work on letting you forgive me later." He ran a fingertip across her cheek and dropped his hand. "We better go."

He sped to A.J.'s address. A decade old car sat parked at the curb of a gray three-decker building. "It doesn't look like A.J.'s car," Rose pointed at the ancient vehicle.

"If he did ID me as a cop, he might be hanging low. Let's find out. You'd better come with me in case Edwards is sneaking around."

They ran up the front steps and entered the building to stop at the first door. Luke banged on it. A rail thin, gray-haired woman opened up and claimed to be the landlady.

"I'm looking for Al Edwards. Where is he?" Luke held up his badge.

"It's a free country. I don't keep track of my tenants."

Luke's impatience threatened to get the better of him. "Cut the attitude. Where's Al?"

Her thin shoulders in the worn blue shirt seemed to cave forward, and a frayed belt held up faded jeans around her toothpick size waist. A hand marked with age spots gripped the doorknob. Was it for keeping her balance or to slam it in their faces? "Talk to the people at the body shop where he works."

"They told us he left for home," Rose injected, standing beside Luke. "The drive takes five minutes. He should be here."

"I can't help you." The landlady wrinkled her nose in a sneer. "I got to go. My grandbaby will wake up in a minute."

"There are two young women who will never wake up and maybe more if I don't find your tenant. Now answer my questions or I'll take you in for obstruction of justice. Does Edwards stay home sick often?"

"I'm not obstructing anyone and he never misses work. He's no trouble, goes to his garage every day."

"Any females visit Mr. Edwards?"

"Two dropped by when he first moved in. I'd never seen either one before or after. One came inside. He didn't stop by and introduce her."

"Describe her."

"She was blonde, thin, and kinda attractive, but wore too much eye makeup. What man goes for that type?"

"Did she drive or did he bring her here?"

"She drove and the other woman waited out in the car. I only glimpsed the one outside when she put down the car window to talk to her friend. I can't describe her except she was blonde."

"How long did Al's visitor stay?"

"I'd guess five minutes at the most. She and Al fought. I couldn't hear their exact words, but she ran down the stairs. I opened my door to see if she was okay and all. She stopped at the bottom of the steps and yelled up at him."

"What did she say?"

"She said, 'Don't forget. It's your last chance.'" The woman's nostrils flared. "She sounded like she was warning him."

"What did he say?" Luke asked, snapping out the words.

"He didn't answer. I heard him stomp away. He left her standing in the hall, and then I heard his door slam. That's when she went back to her car and talked to the other woman. I couldn't hear what they said either."

"When did she visit?"

"I don't know. I was writing my grocery list when she arrived. She mighta come at the end of February or the beginning of March. I can't remember."

"Did the woman who warned him resemble the person

standing next to me?"

The landlady tilted her head to the side and stared at Rose. "She was blonde like her, but she's not the one who came inside."

Luke dug his phone from his pocket and pushed a button. "Was this the woman?" He held up the image of Cassie Raymond.

The older woman pushed her nose up to the screen. "It's her, but she put too much powder on her face in your picture."

"She's dead," Luke said. "Her name is Cassie Raymond."

The landlady flinched and retreated a step. "Did she die from a cosmetics overdose?"

"She was murdered."

"And my tenant killed her?" The woman's mouth fell open, revealing a blue stained tongue.

"We're investigating her death and another person's. I want to check on Al in his apartment. The receptionist at his job told me he left because he was sick. He could be upstairs, too ill to answer his door."

"Like I already told you, he's not home and never comes back during the day." The landlady rolled her eyes and pulled a key out of her jean pocket. "I'd be able to hear him if he was upstairs. The ceilings are thinner than plastic wrap. But I don't suppose you're going to leave until I let you inside. If he's upstairs hiding, I want you to take him away. I don't want murderers living above and killing me when I'm asleep." She shut her door and climbed the stairs, complaining about her rheumatism. On the second floor, she stopped at the first door. The hallway was dim and the air stale.

Luke banged on the entry. "A.J. Edwards, it's Detective Lennox of the Ledgeview Police Force. I want to ask you a few questions." When no one answered, Luke turned to the landlady. "Open it. He may need medical attention."

"How do I know you're a real cop?" She pushed her glasses up on her nose. "I bet you can buy those badges in the toy department."

"We're dealing with an ill person, life and death," Luke said. "Unlock the door."

She tightened her lips and inserted the key with a twist. The sound of a lock popping announced they were free to enter.

He held up a hand to both Rose and the landlady. "Stay out here."

"Sure, I'll guard the hall from whoever lives here." Rose's gaze skittered over the doorways.

"You've nothing to guard here but dust balls. I don't have time to clean up after everyone." The landlady gave a sniff.

Luke removed his gun, entered the apartment and crept forward as he followed police procedure for entering a residence with a suspect inside. The rooms and closets showed no signs of a person hiding. A.J.'s belongings hung inside, waiting to be worn. The refrigerator contained fresh milk and bread.

Luke holstered his weapon and walked into the hall. "He's not home."

"I told ya he wasn't upstairs." The landlady crossed the floor to the steps. "Push the button on the knob, and lock up after yourself. I got to tend my grandbaby." She shuffled downward. The worn steps creaked under her light step.

"I want to walk through again, Rose. Keep up the lookout."

She slapped her arms against her sides. "Hurry, it's creepy out in this hall."

Luke made his way back into A.J.'s and hunted for signs of the man's timetable. The towels in the bathroom were dry. A clean Formica counter showed no signs of recent use in the kitchen. Above the empty sink, sun poured through the slats of the blinds. He turned to go into the next room and brushed against the wall phone. He dug out a pen from his pocket and pushed the recall. Surprise nipped him as he recognized the number. He finished up by taking pictures. Minutes later, he escorted Rose from the building.

Luke waited until they hit the highway to mention the phone call. "A.J.'s last call on his landline was to you."

She raised one shoulder in a half shrug. "A.J. called days ago. Remember? Are you sure? I was his last call? He owns a cell phone and talks a lot on it."

Luke's hands tightened on the wheel. "Repeat everything A.J. said when you spoke."

"He'd heard about Cassie's death from the YouTube video. He apologized for not calling before. He said he was too upset to talk about Dahlia. I asked where he was but Frank showed up and interrupted us. That's when A.J. hung up."

"Why would Cassie visit A.J. and not bring up the subject at your lunch?" New suspicions formed in his mind.

Rose shook her head. "I've no idea. When I heard that Cassie and Dahlia drove to Rhode Island, I couldn't have been more surprised if you told me the landlady was Miss America. Cassie never said one word about visiting A.J."

"She never told you about the boxes in your store either. She was a woman with many secrets."

Rose was silent for a second. "What if she really wanted to confess that she drove up to visit A.J. and wimped out before she could bring up the truth?"

"Maybe she thought you'd eventually figure out what was happening and save her a confession." Luke flicked a glance at the vehicle in the passing lane and breaking the speed limit before he answered. "Was it possible A.J. cheated on your sister with Cassie?"

"No, Cassie was Dahlia's best friend."

He wasn't convinced of Cassie's faithfulness to her friend, but he'd try a different theory. "Possibly Dahlia wanted to get back with A.J. and stalked him when he refused. Cassie might have been assisting your sister. The visit set A.J. off, and he killed your sister and then Cassie because she could lead the police to him."

Rose pushed herself up straight in the passenger seat. "No one knows better than I that Dahlia could be annoying, but she'd never stalk A.J., or follow him unless he offered encouragement. My sister didn't dwell long on the past. I bet he contacted her first and then changed his mind."

"Cassie must have stayed in touch with both of them."

Rose folded her arms over her chest. "Do you think the day A.J. was out sick was the day Dahlia died?" She bit her lip and her face paled to gray.

"We need to find your almost brother-in-law. He's the one who can answer our questions."

Rose cracked the window and tilted her face to the opening. After a few seconds, she seemed recovered from her fear. "I'll try calling him again to set up a meeting."

"A meeting is not a good idea, Rose. I'm predicting we'll be arresting Mr. Edwards soon, and he could be dangerous. At least two women have died in Ledgeview. I'm not aiming for a third. I need his location. I'm the detective, not you."

"We'll work it out tomorrow." She shut the window.

"Not on my watch, Rose. Forget about talking to A.J. I'm not taking risks with your life."

She stared straight ahead. Her lip jutted out in disagreement.

She wasn't taking his last order well, but no way was another person who he cared about getting hurt or leaving him.

Hell, what was he thinking? Of course she'd leave. She had another life. He shoved the fact away. He'd concentrate on keeping Rose alive and within his reach. And he was going to arrest A.J. Edwards for murder.

CHAPTER 25

A chill crawled down Rose's spine. She tugged up the blanket and turned over on the sofa bed. An icy sensation traveled across her skin.

Rose cracked open an eyelid and lowered her cover.

Dahlia peered down at her in the early morning light. Rose froze.

Dahlia fingered Rose's butterfly ornament. "He's here. For you. I can't stop him."

"No!" Rose shot upward. Her hand clutched the pendant around her throat. The sound of her uneven breathing filled the empty room. Dahlia was gone, or was she dreaming? Rose forced herself to inhale calming breaths.

She collapsed against the mattress and ran the warning through her mind. The digital alarm clock showed 6:45 am. Rose got up and padded across the cool floors, looking in each room. No one was here.

Relieved, she showered, pulled on jeans and a green jersey and finally settled at the table to drink a mug of coffee. Her nerves calmed. She dug out her journal and was writing her fourth page when someone rapped on the door. Her heartbeat picked up. "Lennox?"

"It's Tia Drown."

"Tia?" Disappointed, she hesitated and then slid the chain bolt enough to open the door for a peek.

Tia waved at Rose. "I hope you don't mind my dropping by early, but I'd like to come inside for a minute?"

Rose swung the door wider. "Is Shauna all right?"

"She's still recovering" Tia said, walking inside. "We're doing everything we can to help her forget her terrible ordeal. It's part of the reason I dropped by before work."

"How did you get into the building?"

"I helped myself to the emergency set of apartment keys. Please, don't be mad. If Dean found out, he'd lecture me about privacy rights, but I needed to speak to you today and this was the fastest way."

"Come in and sit down. Would you like coffee? I always keep a hot pot."

"No thanks, I'm cutting back." Tia's black boots tapped across the floor as she entered.

"Let me take your coat." Rose held out her hands for the turquoise garment.

"I'll keep it on. I won't stay long." She glanced at Rose's open journal.

Self-conscious, she swept up the book and put it on the counter. "Take a seat."

Tia slid into the kitchen chair and rested her black designer purse on the tabletop. She removed one black leather glove. "I can't forget our disastrous dinner. I wanted you to have a pleasant evening, a break from all the terrible events in your life, and the night turned into a fiasco." Tia blinked several times, and a tear rolled down her cheek.

Rose twisted her hands together. "You meant well. Don't worry. I enjoyed seeing your home, and your gift, the dress, was generous. What matters is Shauna's okay."

"I added to your troubles." Tia bent and opened her purse to tug out a tissue.

"You didn't." Rose shook her head. "Besides, you couldn't control the events of the night."

"No need to be polite." She waved the hand clutching the hankie. "I want to make it up to you. Remember, my husband plans to run for mayor?"

"Of course I do."

"Well, we're having a small dinner at the Audi with a group of Dean's closest supporters tomorrow night. It would mean a lot to me and my husband if you came and enjoyed yourself for a few hours."

The idea of going out to celebrate with strangers didn't sound enjoyable or appealing. "Has Dean announced his candidacy yet?"

"After the attack, we thought we should hold off, but now, we're going ahead with Buddy and Shauna's blessings."

"Tia, I'm not really up for a party. I'm flattered you wanted to include me."

"I promise the evening will be low key."

"Where do you hold a dinner at the Audi?"

"A small banquet hall was added off the side a few years ago. In fact, Dean and I led the fundraiser to build the addition. The room's the perfect place to give an intimate dinner, and you must come. Believe me, sitting at home doesn't help. I learned the truth when I stayed holed up in my house after my divorce. I felt like a failure and didn't want to see people. I was foolish. I know that now. And where else can you get a free meal?"

"Food is always enticing—"

"You can leave after the dessert."

At least she could slip away with a clear conscience. "I suppose I could attend for a couple of hours if you don't mind that I leave early."

"Perfect." Tia stood and tugged on the leather glove. "Cocktails will be at seven. The community party will be held later when Dean makes his public announcement." She opened her purse, dropped in her tissue and snapped it closed. "Shauna will appreciate your support, too. Tomorrow night will be her first outing since the attack at the parking garage. You can inspire her."

"Me?" Rose laughed and then sobered when she saw Tia's serious face. "I'm not the inspirational type."

"If you attend the event after all your hardships, you'll be a role model."

"Shauna and I only met for a few minutes, Tia. I don't think she's aware of my activities."

"She knows what you're going through because of your sister. You will give her courage. Don't forget your presence will mean a lot to me and Dean. As I told you, we're happy to provide one evening where you forget all your problems." She drew out the black gloves. "Of course, Luke will be there."

"Lennox?" Tia was matchmaking. "I doubt he has a spare minute since he's investigating the deaths of two women."

"Nonsense, he has to eat. He can leave after the meal with you." She faced Rose in the doorway and hugged her. "He'll love you in your new dress."

The woman's perfume reminded Rose of a strong ocean breeze. No flowery scent for her. Tia released Rose with a smile.

"I'd appreciate it if you didn't suggest to Luke that he bring me to your dinner. I don't want him to feel obligated." A small panic rose in her throat. He might think she'd instigated the setup.

"He won't. I've seen him with you." Her voice held the hint of amusement. "You didn't believe his story about helping in the kitchen at my dinner party, did you? He came in because he couldn't stay away from you."

Rose struggled not to choke over the truth. He was worried he'd miss stopping her inquisition about Buddy was more likely.

Tia turned to leave and then pivoted back. "I almost forgot. Give me your phone number in case any last minute details come up. It will save me from lifting the apartment keys for a chat." She winked and jingled the keys in her pocket.

Rose recited her number while Tia pushed the digits into her cell.

"I really doubt Lennox will take time off even for a meal. He's working day and night on the homicides."

"Don't worry. If he can't attend, Buddy and Shauna will escort you. I won't expect you to drive yourself. No woman should be out alone in this city, I'm sad to say."

"I don't want to be a third wheel."

"Nonsense, you're a friend. Friends watch out for each other." The older woman turned and walked through the open door. "Don't forget to wear the dress," she tossed over her shoulder.

"I'll go downstairs with you." Rose grabbed her keys from the table and escorted Tia to the main entry where the woman hugged her goodbye again. "Luke or I will let you know who to expect as an escort for tomorrow night. Take care."

Rose ran up the stairs to her apartment. Tia's matchmaking was obvious. What was Lennox doing today? After following her from Brattleboro yesterday, he'd left without mentioning seeing her again. His silence left her wary, and she found herself analyzing their night together. She needed to accept the fact they'd enjoyed each other, but he had a job to do. She wasn't a clingy why-aren't-you-by-my-side type.

Rose spent the day making calls to thank her customers who'd sent her cards and kept the words of the menacing greeting tucked in the back of her mind. Finished with that task, she phoned the store where Dahlia bought her lingerie. There wasn't time when she and Lennox had stopped to arrange everything. Speaking to the right retail clerk wasn't easy. Returns of personal belongings were a big no-no in the world of merchandise. Rose worked her way up the management chain until she had an agreement for the store to accept Dahlia's unopened purchases.

Next on her list was setting up the meeting with A.J, but she couldn't move forward without Lennox. She should call him. This was legitimate police business and not an excuse, she told herself. She hit his name on the speed dial. His voicemail answered. She left a brief message to call her and clicked off. Now what? Her attention wandered to the bureau where a few of Dahlia's belongings were stored. It was time to brave it and go through the drawers.

The phone rang. She recognized the number and grabbed it. Lennox. *Stay calm and friendly.* "How's everything going with the true blues and the men in black?"

"I'm following a couple of leads. I heard you had a visitor and an invitation."

Tia's scheme was in motion already. "If you're too busy, don't feel obligated to pick me up. I'm afraid Tia was matchmaking. She told me she's a romantic at heart and the story about meeting Dean on a ski lift and falling in love instantly." Okay, she was running off at the mouth. Be cool.

"I'm afraid I am too busy, Rose."

The weight of disappointment pressed on her shoulders, and she sank into a chair. "Of course, solving homicides takes precedence. Did you find out anything about A.J.?"

"Not yet, I'm on it."

"But we have to plan so I know what to tell him. Be

reasonable, Lennox. I can help."

"I'm on his trail. You stay out of it. Tia will arrange a safe ride for you to the party. Promise me you won't go unescorted."

"I'm crossing my heart."

"I'll see you as soon as possible. The cases take up all my hours."

"I understand. I can help with A.J. He trusts me."

"When I have more information about him, we'll talk. I gotta go, Rose. Trust me.

"I do."

"Good bye." The click announced he'd hung up.

She sat tapping her foot. Well, that was not encouraging. She wished he'd at least given her a hint what was happening. She set to work cleaning the middle bureau drawer. Soon she found herself lost in memories of her sister, only interrupted by doubts about Lennox and herself.

Frank surprised her at supper time with an order of fast food and news that Lennox was working nonstop. She spent the rest of the evening with the older man, losing two games of poker and listening to stories of the good ole days: the barbecues with the guys from the station, their card games and John Lennox spending hours on a case just deciding where to go next.

"He was great at looking at all angles of an investigation when you thought you'd hit them all. He was like a bulldog refusing to let go. That's why he spent time going back over cold cases like the North Conway one. He couldn't let go."

Finally around eleven, Frank left. Rose settled down for the night on the sleeper and resisted the temptation to call Lennox. She didn't need another lecture on staying safe, and he didn't need her as a distraction, especially at this hour.

The sizzling memory of their hot, sticky bodies in the darkness hurtled into her thoughts. She imagined the feel of his lips tingling against her skin. His whiskers brushed against her chin as his palms caressed each inch of her skin and traveled lower and lower.

She bolted up and took a deep breath before punching her pillow. *Concentrate on other things, or it was going to be a long night.*

The next day, she returned to the computer search about

Buddy Drown without results, and she managed to hold off until suppertime to speak to Lennox. He answered on the second ring. His clipped, tense voice warned her he couldn't talk.

This was a disaster. After reassuring him she was fine, she quickly hung up. She tossed the cell in her purse and then headed for the shower to get ready for Dean's big party. She stuck her head under the showerhead's spray, wishing she could rinse away her feelings for Luke Lennox.

She'd made big mistakes with him. Number one at the top of the list was the belief she could handle sleeping with him and then trot off into the sunset. *Face the truth.*

He was a detective who breathed and lived his job and she was his job for the moment. He had an ex wife to show for his lifestyle. When Dahlia's killer was found, he'd concentrate on the next investigation. She'd go home and run the Blues Sisters, and forget Luke Lennox. What did she think would happen to them? They'd marry and give birth to little detectives? Besides, Lennox was probably used to tough, bold police women who kicked in the doors of criminals and entered with guns drawn, ready to fire.

Don't count on a man and you won't be disappointed, Gram often told her.

"Sorry, Gram, I should have listened."

After the shower, she wriggled her damp body into the dress from Tia. She brushed her hair, wove the strands together and pinned the piece to her head.

Rose's phone rang. "Hi, gorgeous, are you ready for your date to drive you to the big party?"

"Buddy? Is Shauna with you?"

"Sure, she's sitting right here. Did you think I was hitting on you? Shauna, talk to Rose. The woman has no sense of humor."

"Hi, Rose, this is Shauna. We'll be at your place in a few minutes. "

"I can drive myself. The Audi's only a few blocks away."

"It's too dangerous. Please, come with Bud and me. Tia told us you might want to go home after the dinner. That's not a problem."

Shauna's worried voice yanked on Rose's sympathy and touched on her common sense. "Okay, your virtual arm twisting worked. Come pick me up."

"Good, we'll be at your place in about ten minutes. That way we'll be a stylish fifteen minutes late when we arrive."

Ledgeview had style? She learned something every minute. "Don't worry. I'll be ready." Rose skimmed a hand over her upswept hair and down the slinky fabric of her skirt that clung to her hips.

"Excellent," Shauna said. "From my past experiences with Drown productions, everyone will be in Oscar style outfits."

At least she wasn't nominated and expected to give a speech. Rose hung up. She paced and watched the minutes click by. She looked in the mirror and checked her makeup and finally the safety on her gun. She was past ready, she thought, and shoved the weapon into her purse. Throwing on her jacket, she headed down the stairs.

Buddy pulled up to the curb as she locked up and ran to the SUV. He stepped out of the vehicle. "You don't have to run. I won't take off."

"It's a habit." She climbed into the rear seat, and he slammed her door and jumped inside the front.

"Hello, Rose." Shauna shifted around to smile at her. Her makeup hid a pale face and sadness lingered in lines around her mouth. "Thanks for coming with us. When Buddy leaves to talk to his father's friends, you and I can dis'."

Buddy stared at Rose in the rearview mirror. "My narration of all the sport replays bore her. She's thrilled you agreed to come with us tonight." He steered the SUV into the street traffic.

"Tia's told us a lot about your problems and the strength you've shown," Shauna said. "I admire you."

"I haven't done anything."

"I get to escort two beautiful women to my father's celebration." Buddy let out a whistle.

Shauna leaned over and kissed him on the cheek. "You're a lucky man."

"Ready for all the excitement tonight, Rose?" He glanced at her in his mirror.

"I can't wait." Why had she agreed to the dinner? Oh, yeah, Tia had begged her to go and show support for Dean. Though with all his connections, her absence wouldn't make a dent in the guest list.

"The cops promised extra protection around the area where people park and walk into the dinner," Buddy announced.

"The security is comforting and scary." Shauna clutched at the collar of her black coat with a manicured hand.

"You're safe with me, babe." Buddy winked.

"*Don't* talk about my attack when we're at the party."

Rose's interest picked up. What was with Shauna's harsh tone?

"Don't worry, honey. No one will bug you. Everyone will be talking about my father, not you."

Shauna sat staring ahead. A tense silence fell over the car. Buddy turned right toward the Audi. Two uniformed police officers directed the traffic, but Rose saw no signs of Lennox.

"I never expected this many people," she said as they drew to a halt in a long line of vehicles waiting to enter the parking lot. "Tia told me the dinner was for close friends. Who are all these people?"

"These are my father's close friends."

A young man dressed in a valet uniform approached them and offered to park the SUV. Buddy threw the vehicle into gear. "It's show time, ladies."

"I hope your father hired our wedding band to play tonight," Shauna said. "I love listening to them. Rose, wait for us."

Rose threw her door open before Buddy or Shauna popped their locks up. She paused in the chilly night and gazed ahead to the Audi while her escorts climbed out. A warm glow lit the windowed atrium and lured her forward. Guests were entering or lingering near the main entrance to chat.

"Hey, Bud Drown." A couple joined Buddy and Shauna and cut them off from her view.

"I'll wait in the lobby," Rose tossed over her shoulder.

Before they could answer, she trotted off across the lot. Her foot touched the sidewalk as someone grabbed her arm.

She whirled around to a man dressed in a dark windbreaker jacket with a black scarf wrapped around the bottom of his face. His dark brown eyes stared down at her.

"A.J.? What are you doing here?"

"Walk with me away from the crowd."

Her stomach jittered. She hung back.

"I'm sorry if I scared you," his voice softened. "Give me a couple of minutes. Okay, Rose? I drove a ways to talk to you."

"I only have a minute."

"That's all I want." He released her and shoved his hands into his pockets. "This way." He inclined his head toward the rear of the building.

Rose debated. Near the parking lot, Buddy and Shauna were busy talking and oblivious to her. Ahead shadows surrounded the backside of the Audi. Coldness trickled through her. "Let's talk now. How…did you know I'd be here, A.J.?"

"I'll explain." He gripped her arm and guided her away from the guests. "I followed you when you left your place. I don't want to say more until we're away from the crowd."

Uneasiness slid down her back. "About what?" Her mouth went dry with dread.

His fingers dug into her arm, steering her forward. "Keep walking. We're too obvious standing in the middle of the sidewalk, and I don't need an audience."

"Let's head to the lobby." No one noticed them as they passed. She'd be all alone with him in a few seconds. What did he have planned? She pulled in a breath and released it shakily. "I think we've gone far enough."

"There're too many people everywhere." He was nearly running now, his iron hold forced her to keep up with him.

"A.J., what's going on? What's with all the secrets? I'm not going anywhere until you answer me." She yanked her arm away. "You're acting like a fugitive."

He stopped outside the reach of the lights and stepped onto the frozen grass. Laughter and voices floated across the night air. "I need to talk to someone, and you're the only one who'll listen." He threw a hand toward the shadows. "I don't know where else to go."

Were those real tears in his eyes? Rose shoved her hand into her purse and gripped her thirty-eight. "Talk to me, A.J. Why are we skulking around in the dark?"

"The police were at my job and my apartment. They spoke to the receptionist and my landlady. Both women now think I'm the new Jack the Ripper and Dahlia's killer. When I tried to enter my place, the landlady called the cops. I left fast. I don't know if they followed or contacted the New Hampshire authorities to be on the lookout for me." He ran a hand over his face. "Everything's all mixed up. I've been living in my car, driving around, trying to figure it out."

"Why didn't you tell me Cassie and Dahlia visited you in Rhode Island?" she demanded.

His mouth fell open. "You knew?"

A cold, sick dread settled over her.

He kicked the ground. "Right after I moved, Dahlia started calling every garage in Rhode Island until she found me."

"Why did she want to find you?" Rose inched backward. Her fingers cramped around her weapon, dreading the moment she'd need it.

"Dahlia wanted to get together again. When she wanted something, she was resourceful. That's not news. They drove to my apartment two days after I settled in. She sent Cassie inside as her messenger. Dahlia stayed in the car. I guess she would have come in if I'd asked. I was still angry with her and nixed the idea. I'm sorry for cutting you out, Rose. I should have spoken to you sooner and not left you out of the loop." He shook his head. "You were my friend, almost my sister. I didn't mean to hurt you. I was upset and didn't think things through. You believe me, don't you?"

He sounded sincere. The tension in her chest eased a centimeter, but kept her hand on the gun. "You should have told me you saw her when you called me."

"You're right. I loved Da—" His voice broke. He touched her hand with cold fingers. "Rose, I have to tell you something. I know you'll be upset."

"Just tell me." This was it!

"A.J. Edwards." Lennox appeared out of nowhere. "You're under arrest for the murder of Dahlia Blue."

CHAPTER 26

"Lennox?" What was he doing here?

He marched toward them. "Al James Edwards, you have the right to remain silent."

"We don't want him silent," Rose cried. "He was going to talk to me."

Lennox continued reciting A.J.'s rights. Out of the blackness, a host of policemen descended on them.

"Let him talk. Give us a minute." Where had all these men come from?

"Rose," A.J. said. "Go home. We'll talk when I get out in a couple of hours."

"Don't count on it." Lennox yanked A.J.'s arms behind his back. "Rose, stand aside. You're not involved in this."

"Yes, I am. I want to speak to him. If he killed my sister, I deserve to hear why." She glared at Lennox, daring him to defy her.

"I didn't kill Dahlia," A.J. said while Lennox tightened the last cuff. "I loved her. Honest to God, I wouldn't hurt her."

The uniforms blocked him from her sight before they rushed toward the building's rear, away from the guests.

Lennox clamped a hand on her shoulder. "Don't follow him. You can't do anything. Go to the party."

"Party? I can't walk inside and pretend to enjoy myself now, Detective."

The muscle in his cheek tightened, and he lowered his voice. "Stay away from Edwards for your own well-being."

"I have to know the truth. She was my twin sister."

"Don't get involved in his arrest. You know what people will think."

"What do you mean? I'm guilty, too?" The idea sent a shock wave through her. "You do. You think I helped kill Dahlia."

"Rose," he pitched his voice low. "I know you never would have hurt your sister."

She turned to search the empty spot where the cops with A.J. had disappeared. She'd been close to learning the truth about her sister. She still would. She'd walk to the police station and talk to A.J. with or without Lennox's approval.

"I'll get someone to drive you home," he said.

"What happened to keeping me informed, Lennox? I was caught totally unaware tonight."

"Rose? Rose?" Shauna's voice rose out of the gathering.

"I was busy tracking the man who murdered your sister." The flash of anger in Lennox's eyes alerted her to his ire and the danger of crossing him. He took her arm, drawing her closer and away from others.

Conflicting feelings battled inside of her. Reason told her he didn't have to tell her anything when he investigated, but her emotions roared that was wrong. They meant something to each other and that meant trusting one another.

He released her but didn't back away. "I went to A.J.'s apartment with a search warrant. I found Dahlia's necklace."

Rose's mind slammed to a halt. Her hand went to the pendant. "You mean...the butterfly?"

"You told me your sister created the jewelry for your birthdays, and they're unique."

"Where did you find hers?"

"A.J. hid the necklace under his mattress, not too original. I need you to identify the one we recovered."

How had he gotten the necklace unless he'd killed her sister? Dahlia never took it off. Rose felt faint. She leaned against the granite building. "A.J. killed her."

"He ingratiated himself. He made you and your sister trust him. It's not your fault. He was a pro."

It was true. Why hadn't she recognized his character sooner? She was another Blue trusting the wrong man. "You always felt he was the killer, didn't you, Lennox?"

"I deal with evidence, not feelings."

"Dahlia appearing to me is not a fact. I can't prove it in a court of law." She'd shared Dahlia's after-death materializations with him when all he wanted were tangibles. "I bet you *never* believed in my sister's spirit either."

"I can't discuss the situation now." He let out a frosty breath. "Outside a party with people wandering around isn't the place to have a discussion."

"I want the truth. Do you know why A.J. killed my sister?"

Lennox tightened his lips and glanced over her head. "We found pictures, S and M pictures at his apartment. Dahlia was in them. I believe the videos we seized contain more proof of a motive. The end of the engagement was the end of his business."

"My sister was in...." She shook her head. "You mean like whips and chains and...sex?"

He nodded.

"What about Cassie?"

"I don't know all the details yet."

Her head felt fuzzy, almost numb. She needed to get away and think. In her heart, she'd always expected some nameless person to be Dahlia's killer. She pivoted around on her heel and walked toward the front and the light.

"Rose, stop." He caught up to her and grabbed her arm. "Listen. Right now, you have to trust me."

The man was crazy. "When did you trust me, Lennox? When we went to The Ledges because of the report on the currents, not what I reported? When you thought I just happened to stumble over Cassie's body or tonight when you were sneaking around after me?"

"I study all the angles. It's my job."

His low tight voice warned her she was headed for trouble. She didn't care. "You were spying on me. You had no idea where A.J. was, and you lied about keeping him under surveillance. Why didn't you let me know the truth?" Anger roared in her ears. She'd been betrayed by her old boyfriend, her twin, AJ and Lennox. Add them all up, and she was a fool.

His hand fell away from her. "I'm a detective, Rose. I'm solving two homicides."

"I'm leaving, but I will speak with A.J. Then I'll be done with him." She marched to the front of the building and smack into a group of guests who watched her stalk around them. Lennox tailed her. "Rose, let the police department handle Edwards."

"It's too late to stay uninvolved," she tossed over her shoulder, unable to keep quiet in the presence of the gawking guests.

"Rose, Rose." From the sidewalk, Shauna ran toward her. Buddy trailed behind. "I've been searching for you." Lines of worry marred her perfect face. "Someone said the police took away a guest? Did you see what happened?"

"Lennox arrested A.J., my sister's ex fiancé. Can you bring me home? I'm not feeling well."

"We can take you anywhere you want," Buddy confirmed. "Who'd they arrest? What was the charge?"

Rose paused to glance back. Lennox was gone. "A.J. Edwards for murder. He followed me to the party."

The five minute trip to her apartment felt more like an hour as Shauna and Buddy seemed stunned into silence. Rose answered the few questions they threw at her, and she felt relief at the sight of her building.

In her kitchen, Rose sank down on a chair and put her head in her hands. What a horrible night. Her meeting with A.J and confrontation with Lennox repeated in her mind. She analyzed each man's reactions, trying to understand his motives, feelings.

A.J. might have an explanation for Dahlia's necklace. If only she could talk to him. The idea she'd encouraged him, a possible killer, to be with Dahlia made her want to vomit. All the time, he'd lied about loving her sister.

Happy Valentine's Day, Sis. A.J. smiled and handed Rose a box of chocolates.

Valentine's Day, the day Dahlia had accepted A.J.'s proposal. Now Rose saw each of A.J.s' moves, every word as part of a murder plot. What a mess. She dug her phone out of her purse and pushed the numbers.

"This is Rose. Can you come to my apartment?"

CHAPTER 27

A.J. sat across from Luke at the interrogation table in the eight-by-ten concrete walled room. The camcorder in the ceiling was recording them. All Lennox needed was the confession to be thrown out.

"Edwards, do you understand your rights?"

"I know them." A.J.'s folded hands on the table shook. "I don't need to wait for my lawyer. I already told you. I didn't kill Dahlia Blue. I loved her. We were in business together."

"What kind?"

A. J. wet his lips and shrugged. "I explained before. We ran a start up on the internet." He squirmed in his hard seat. "We sold women's lingerie online."

Luke's interest climbed. "Who modeled your items?"

A.J.'s Adam's apple bobbed in his throat. "Dahlia volunteered. Her friend Cassie wanted to join us. She didn't because our company fell apart when I learned I couldn't trust Dahlia as a business partner. She had a problem with stealing, which could sink us. I didn't want to share my bank account and worry she'd wipe me out."

"What did Dahlia do that made you distrust her?"

"She was a thief who embezzled from her own boutique and had been shoplifting since she was a kid. She confessed when her sister caught her robbing them."

Luke leaned forward. "What was the name of your online business?

"*Sweet Dreams*. Dahlia named it."

"Dahlia was into online porn?"

"She'd never do that."

"We've seen your homemade videos."

A.J. averted his head and Luke's hard stare. "They were harmless. She had no contact with the men on their computers. They paid and I sent them the password to get into our site and watch us act. It wasn't real, and Dahlia enjoyed it. She liked acting. No one was hurt. I'd never let anyone hurt Dahlia. I loved her."

"You loved her so much you lured her into pornography."

"You don't understand. We created a business arrangement to go along with our personal life. When we broke up, we didn't want to work together. The business collapsed. Poof." He expanded his fingers in the air.

"You know what I think about your story, Edwards?" Luke placed his palms on the table and leaned closer into A.J.'s face. "That's the biggest load of crap I've heard in years, and you're the lowest example of pond scum I've ever met. You call what you did love? We found your pictures of Dahlia with other men. They weren't playing patty cake. These men paid for sex and to act out their fantasies." Luke shoved back his chair. "We're done here. You can return to your cell and rot."

"Hold on. Didn't you hear me? I put restrictions on the deals. I wouldn't let men take advantage of Dahlia."

"What's the real URL?"

"You won't find it, I took it down."

"Sure, you took it down after you killed Dahlia. We did some investigating. The site's name was *Hot and Heavy Dreams*. You're a liar, Edwards."

He opened the file on the table. "We traced your phone calls and interviewed some of your customers. They want to cut a deal. They don't want to be prosecuted."

Sweat dripped from A.J's forehead. "You're forcing them to testify with threat of jail."

"We persuaded them. They don't want pictures of themselves with a dead woman posted in their local paper. You alone or you and Dahlia together developed a quick, get rich scheme. When she wanted to quit the business or wanted more money, you got angry and ended it by killing her. What triggered the murder? Was it when she quit or you wanted to pimp her out more?

Maybe she wanted to be a mother her children would be proud of and decided your games were over."

A.J. swung his head from side to side. "I didn't kill Dahlia."

"How much money did you give her?"

He covered his face with his hands. His shoulders slumped. "You don't understand. The money wasn't all for me or Dahlia. She agreed to help me."

"You gave it to the orphans."

He dropped his hands. "I gave it to my cousin. She needed cash to keep her son."

"Was she into porn too?"

"No, she lost her job, her house. She and her son were in the women's shelter under an assumed name. She was divorced and her ex was going to take the kid away if she didn't get on her feet soon. They've been hiding out." A.J. wiped a hand over his eyes. "I couldn't let what happened to me, happen to my nephew. No place to go, no one wants you. I lived that life when I was his age."

Luke's mind whirled with facts from A.J.'s history. He ripped a piece of paper out of his yellow pad and handed a felt tip pen to A.J. "Write down her name and address. You better hope her story and the facts support yours."

"They will." He scribbled a name and address. "Am I free?"

"No. What happened with Dahlia Blue? Did she threaten to turn you in when you pressured her to continue the business?"

"Why won't you listen? I never hurt Dahlia. I loved her. You arrested the wrong man. I'm innocent."

"You stole her necklace, didn't you? That's why she and Cassie found you and drove up to your place. You loved her so much you kept what she loved out of spite."

A rap sounded on the door and it opened. "This is Mr. Edwards' lawyer from Legal Aid." Conroy announced.

"Mr. Edwards is finished answering your questions, and you can drop the charge of murder." The lawyer, a skinny middle aged man in a gray suit, rushed in swinging his scuffed briefcase. "We'll need the date of the crime so my client can give you his whereabouts." He clamped a hand on A.J's shoulder.

"That's interesting councilor. We're interested in one day in particular when Mr. Edwards wasn't at home or work."

"I was gambling at Foxwoods. You can confirm my location with my credit cards and the videos from the casino."

"You were gambling?" Luke stared at the man. Was he for real?

A.J. sat back with a smug grin, ignoring his lawyer's attempt to budge him.

Luke shoved away from the table. "Don't take any bets that you're off the hook yet." He leaned into Edwards face and lowered his voice. "I hope you smiled for the camera, Edwards, because we'll be all over that video."

Frank had taken her to the station and they'd waited over an hour to learn A.J. was in the hands of his lawyer and wouldn't be talking to anyone else tonight.

"Let's go home," Frank encouraged. "We can learn more tomorrow."

"I just wanted to ask him face to face if he killed Dahlia."

"Do you think he'd be truthful?" Frank asked.

"I've always hoped the A.J. I knew will appear and I can believe him." Frank was right. A.J. was probably more concerned with escaping arrest now.

"Are you all right?" Frank was staring at her.

"Sure," she lied. A.J.'s begging whirled in her mind and added to her confusion. She knew one thing for sure. She'd never be okay.

Frank escorted her home where Rose assured him she'd be fine. Another lie, she thought.

Throwing her a look of concern, he left.

She kicked off her shoes and sank onto the sleeper. Lennox's appearance out of the dark and their last angry words at the Audi played in her mind. No, she had to focus on A.J. She replayed every scene with him and her sister through her head, trying to detect a nuance she'd missed, a signal between them that they truly loved each other, but beyond smiles and teasing glances, she found nothing.

Her head hurt. She closed her eyes tight.

He wants you, Rose. I can't stop him. Go home. Run.

She shot up in bed. Sweat soaked her blouse. "Dahlia?" She threw the blanket aside and swung her stocking feet to the floor.

She focused on the light from the kitchen spilling into the room. She'd fallen asleep.

Whack!

She jumped at the smack against the window pane and whirled around, expecting a ski masked figure outside her window. Her heart pummeled in her ears. Instead, only the invisible wind and rain banged against the glass. Swallowing, she searched the room. No signs of an intruder.

She crossed the floor to the coffeemaker and flicked the switch before sinking into a kitchen chair. She might as well do something since she wasn't about to sleep. She turned on her laptop. While it whirled to life, she leaned her head in her hands and pictured Luke Lennox swooping out of the darkness to arrest A.J. He'd staked her out like she was a co-conspirator. And she'd slept with him. Idiot. She mentally slapped her forehead.

Well, what did she expect? He was committed to his job, not to her. She was the dumb one. For a short time, she'd secretly hoped they might have a future together. They'd have what she's always wanted, a real family. No more looking through photo albums and imagining she had one. No more Dahlia pointing out strange men and whispering, "Do you think he's our dad? We have the same nose."

But, Rose had been lying to herself. A hearth and home were not in her future. Okay, she'd handle it. Lennox solved her sister's murder. Their relationship was at an end. She should move home and drive back for the trial. Reopen her shop. Go on without Dahlia.

Dahlia. How could her twin do what Lennox told her and post her actions on the internet? Images of men with whips standing over a scantily clad Dahlia hurled into her mind. Had she had sex with these men? They weren't paying to just playact.

The realizations hurt her stomach. "Why Dahlia? Why couldn't you be happy with our boutique? Why did you have to do those things?"

Dahlia didn't answer, but it didn't matter. Her sister had led another life, and Rose had learned one thing from this tragedy. Love definitely wasn't worth putting yourself out there. She needed a drink. Forget the coffee. Wasn't there wine in the cabinet? She found the alcohol and reached for a glass. No, she'd drink straight from the bottle.

* * *

Conroy strolled into Luke's cubicle, stopped and rapped on his desk where he was studying Edwards' timeline. "What's up?" Luke asked, glancing at Conroy. The man never showed up when morning meetings were planned.

"Why don't you ask the voodoo woman?"

"What?"

"The sister of our victim, Dahlia Blue, she claims to see dead people. Ask her to talk to the victim's ghost and find out what's happening."

"Where'd you hear that rumor?"

"You're back in Ledgeview now, Lennox. We don't keep secrets from each other. Everyone knows you're under her I-See-Dead-People influence."

"What do you want Conroy?"

The man handed him a file. "I've the interviews with the bank employees next door to the parking garage where Shauna Smith was allegedly attacked."

Luke felt the prick of curiosity followed by annoyance. "You finally finished? How long have you held onto them?"

"I don't know what you mean." He dropped the file on the desk and left.

Luke repressed a retort, threw open the folder and read. In the middle of the first page, the sentence stood up and waved to him.

"Conroy."

The detective reappeared in the cubby opening. "Practicing your beck and call voice?"

"Read these three lines." Luke held out the page and pointed to the place on the paper. "It's from the bank supervisor, who stepped out for a smoke.

"It was the end of the night, and the employees had just left. I needed a cigarette before I went home and stepped outside. I didn't see or hear anything." Conroy handed it back.

Luke thumbed through the folders until he found the file he wanted. He threw it open and skimmed the report for a second. "Now read this line from Shauna Smith."

"I was screaming and running for my life." Conroy lowered the sheet.

Luke leveled his gaze on him. "The bank's next door to the garage."

"I'll re-interview the supervisor about the evening."

"Shauna exited the bank five minutes after seven. She was exact on the time." Someone was lying or suffering from a bad memory. "Re-interview everyone. If Shauna Smith was screaming in an area of the downtown, we'd expect one witness."

After Conroy left, Luke returned to his paperwork. He'd wasted no time finding a judge to issue a warrant for the casino's video. One of his men was on his way to pick up the tape. He sat back in his chair and reviewed his first theory. A.J. Edwards convinced Dahlia Blue he loved her because he perceived her as a girl who wanted everyone to like her, and she was willing to go. Now A.J. wanted Luke to believe he'd identified with his down-and-out cousin's son and ran the porno business to earn money for the kid. If the story was for real, then maybe this was the part of him that Rose and Dahlia had first seen. Luke threw down his pen on the desk.

He rummaged through the desktop files and opened up Frank's aged personal notes on the North Conway murder. The information was similar to his dad's. He flipped to the next page and stopped. The handwriting on the page was his father's. They'd shared notes and ideas so it wasn't preposterous that a sheet had gotten mixed in.

Luke read through the lines. Nothing was new except the town North Conway was underlined several times. He'd keep that idea in the back of his mind. He shut the file. *Stop procrastinating and move onto the next item on the agenda, Rose.*

He'd let his guard down and become emotionally involved with her. He'd made a mistake. He didn't possess the qualities women wanted—time and devotion to love them above all else. A repeat of his painful, failed marriage was the last thing he wanted.

He picked up the desk phone. This was a call he dreaded, but the chief had insisted. He pushed the numbers.

"Rose Blue. Leave a message."

"Hello, Rose. We—"

"Lenn–ox," Rose answered, sounding breathless. "Are you still pressing the charges against A.J.? Did he give you any explanations or new information about my sister?"

"A.J. confessed he used your sister for an illegal online business venture. He claimed to have given part of the profits to his cousin who was homeless." When Rose didn't respond, he pressed on. "He's still under arrest for your sister's death. That hasn't changed."

"Did A.J. admit to Dahlia and Cassie's murders?"

Luke ground out, "No. We're tracking down the cousin and the alibi story at the moment."

"What was their business?"

He heard the hope in her voice and hesitated for a second. "He was into pornography like we thought. The site's been disbanded. He was putting together a new one when he was taken into custody. I'm sorry, Rose. Remember you're not responsible for Dahlia. She was a consenting adult."

"You don't understand, Lennox."

"Explain it."

"If A.J. is the killer, and he was caught, why did I dream that she wants me to leave because her murderer is still out there?"

Frustration stretched his nerves. How could he get through to her? "Rose, they're dreams, not reality."

A long pause told him she didn't like his answer. "I'll be at the trial. Bye, Lennox."

"Wait." He ran a hand through his overgrown hair. "We'd like you to come down to the station to speak to our psychiatrist."

"You think I'm crazy?"

This was as bad as he'd thought. The pressure in his chest grew. "I don't. The defense may try to use you at A.J.'s trial. We want to provide proof you're legally sane. Our psychiatrist can speak to you this afternoon at four."

"Fine." She hung up.

Damn. He clicked off the phone. He'd call her back. What should he say? He drummed his fingertips on the desk, seeking the right words. What the hell were they?

His phone buzzed.

"Detective Lennox," the station's desk clerk spoke to him.

"I've a Mr. Lorenzo who'd like to speak to you about the Shauna Smith case. He asked for you by name."

"All right, I'll set up a meeting." Within seconds, they agreed to meet at two.

"I'll be here," Luke said and hung up. *Mr. Lorenzo, I hope you're not a waste of my time.* The man was full of hints and insisted he needed to speak in person with Luke about the evening.

He flipped open a file and began to re read his notes, waiting for his mind to automatically connect all the lose threads in the Dahlia Blue case. Five minutes later, he stopped. The pieces refused to join together. He had the M.E,'s best estimate for Dahlia Blue's hour of death. He had Rose's statement with the last times she'd seen her sister physically. The problem would be if A.J. Edwards' alibi for the day and night proved true. They'd need to scramble to prove he committed the murder on another day. They also had nothing concrete to connect him to the murder. No DNA, no witnesses for the night of the murder besides the version Rose offered. The whole case could fall apart.

But his bigger problem was Rose. He believed her, but what would the shrink say? They had their own biases. Rose's hurt voice echoed in his mind.

Concentrate on the pieces. No witnesses came forward to support Shauna's story and now what would Mr. Lorenzo add?

He stared at the phone, wanting to push Rose's number and restore her good faith in him. He couldn't do it sitting at his desk. What would his father do? Luke knew what he'd say.

Look at all the angles.

He strode out the rear door and past the reporter at the corner taking a cigarette break. Once he jumped into Old Charger, his confidence grew. He maneuvered by the media vans with their satellite dishes. He glanced in the mirror. No press followed. To be sure, he'd take the long way up to The Ledges.

He dug out his sunglasses to shade his eyes against the bright sun. The air had warmed to a balmy fifty-five degrees. On instinct he drove to the Audi and asked for Myra.

Horace led him to a tiny closet where Myra sat at a spic and span desk, frowning over a sheet of paper. She started to rise, but

Luke gestured for her to sit.

"I heard about the big arrest behind the Audi last night," she said. "Everyone was hoping someone saw it and could fill us in."

"I didn't want to upstage Dean's night, but today, I need your help." He pulled up

Edward's picture on his phone and held it out to her. "Have you seen Mr. Edwards anywhere near the Audi when Dahlia was alive or since her death?"

Myra shook her head. "Never saw anyone who resembled him."

"Did Dahlia mention the name of any man?"

"I'm sorry, Luke. Our conversation was brief but…"

He raised his brows and waited.

She frowned. "When I first met Dahlia, she wanted to know if I'd ever met her Grandmother. She said I reminded her of the woman. I was little put out to be compared to someone's Granny and told her I never met gram."

"Did she say how you would meet her?" Did her Grandmother have a connection to someone in Ledgeview?

She shrugged. "We didn't pursue the topic after I reminded Miss Blue that discussion of age at an interview was illegal."

"Isn't that the age of the interviewee?"

"Fair is fair. The girl was disappointed, but she seemed to understand she'd touched a sore spot. I admit I don't care to admit how old I am. What woman does?"

"And you didn't know how you'd know her Grandmother?"

"No, I took it that her grandmother visited once, but you understand, Luke. Ledgeview seems like a small town, but if someone keeps to themselves, I wouldn't meet them unless they lived in my neighborhood or joined the theater or church."

"Thank you, Myra. Call me if you remember anything else."

He walked out to his car. Dahlia thought Myra might have known her Grandmother. Was the city the connection in this crime? He hopped in Old Charger again. Water streaked the road from the last melting traces of snow. What if Dahlia came to Ledgeview to look up old friends from the time of her Grandmother?

Another question pushed to the front of his thoughts as he drove toward The Ledges. How had Dahlia reached the outskirts?

She rode with her killer or drove herself. Either way, where was her car? No one had stepped forward when the article in the paper announced the police sought the vehicle, and a computer search found no one had registered a matching vehicle in the New England area. He'd have to investigate the other regions and the possibility the killer sold it to a chop shop.

Seven miles past The Ledges, he hit the border of the police search for Dahlia. He pulled over and changed into his hiking boots. His phone buzzed. When he finished with his boots, he checked his caller ID. It was the Chief. Luke pulled up the voicemail and listened. The Chief planned a meeting in two hours and Luke better be there.

Great. He had Mr. Lorenzo to interview at the same time. He'd better get started. He grabbed a map from his glove compartment and tramped off.

A half hour later, he paused on his trek and fished the folded map out of his pocket to reread it. An abandoned fire tower stood on top of the hill. He'd get a different view from up high. He tucked the map away and headed off. In twenty minutes, he stood on the crest, surveying the landscape. No signs of tire tracks in the dirt or traces of oil from any recent vehicles showed up on the hard ground. He climbed up the rickety metal stairs. He paused to survey the view when he reached the last step. In the distance, the river and the rocky formations of The Ledges were recognizable. He turned his attention to the view in the opposite direction.

The roofs of a few buildings peeked out from the woods. One appeared to be a farm. He glanced at his pocket watch. If he left right away, he'd have time to drive back to the station and meet his appointment with Mr. Lorenzo and then hit the Chief's meeting. Luke wound down the metal stairs and the hillside path.

His hike had revealed a big fat nothing. Drawing out his map, he ran a thumb over the blue bodies of water. Soon as the weather warmed up a few more degrees, he'd bring the divers back to search for Dahlia's car in the river and a nearby pond.

The urge to find a clue, a scrap of clothing drove him. He started off one last time. Within thirty minutes, he'd reached the driveway of the buildings he'd seen from the tower. He read the name on the mailbox and ran through the list in his mind of people interviewed. The name didn't match any. Lennox glanced at his watch. He should head back to the station. The Chief would have his butt if he wasn't there. The farm owners could have seen or heard something the night of Dahlia's murder. His men should have interviewed them but often more info comes out on a second round. Look at Myra and with luck, the bank manager.

He turned and jogged down the drive. The closer he drew to the buildings, the more ramshackle they appeared. Luke approached the front door and gave the knob a twist. It was locked. The boarded up windows confirmed the lack of human presence. He circled the building before giving his attention to the barn. The roof of the peeling red building showed missing shingles and sagged in the center. He yanked the barn door open. He pulled out his gun and entered. Dust floated in the sunbeams poking through the holes in the roof and reflected off the metal roof of a vehicle.

Excitement rose into his throat as he stared at the Vermont license plate. He pulled out his notebook and flipped through until he found the page with her plate number. Then he called the station. "Conroy, I've found Dahlia Blue's car. Brief the Chief."

"He's not here. The Mayor called him over to the palace for an emergency meeting. What do you bet the boss won't be saying I love my job when he returns? Where are you?"

"I'm near The Ledges. I need you to meet with a Mr. Lorenzo, who wanted me to take his statement about the garage attack. He'll be at the station at two."

"Hope he's legit. I'll join you soon as I'm done."

Lennox gave directions and hung up.

Dahlia Blue had driven out to The Ledges. Had she left her car inside the dilapidated barn? More likely her killer had moved the vehicle to the spot to hide it.

CHAPTER 28

Rose's brain was fogged-in. Squinting at the clock, she read 1pm. She'd napped for over an hour and had three more before she went to the appointment with the police head shrinker. Okay, she was never spending another minute sitting around whining or wine-ing. She was throwing out the attitude.

She shuffled into the kitchen and emptied the remainder of last night's wine down the drain. No police psychiatrist would call her a drunk. He could label her crazy maybe, but not a wino. Already she felt better.

Crossing into the living room, she yanked out the bottom bureau drawer to dig out Dahlia's clothes. They were going to the women's shelter. Her fingertips scraped against paper as she grabbed the last pile of jeans and shirts. She dropped the clothes on the sofa bed and picked up the printed sheet stuck to the bottom of the drawer.

Holding up a printout, she read *The Ledgeview Local News*. The piece was written last summer. The headline: *Ledgeview High Drama Club Celebrates Fifty Dramatic Years* was splayed across the page. A picture of Mr. Melvin or Othello from the Nursing home smiled at her from the page.

Rose sank onto the couch. Why would Dahlia want or keep an old Ledgeview news item? Rose skimmed the article to the last few sentences: *The drama club is still seeking fellow thespians to invite to the gala.* The first name stopped her from reading further.

Laurie Blue headed the list. Her mother attended Ledgeview High? When? Gram lived in Vermont all her life, except for the one year after Grand dad died.

Ledgeview. At last, Rose had found the missing piece. Dahlia had chosen Ledgeview because Mom and Gram had lived here once. Rose dug into her purse lying on the table. Pulling out her phone, she hesitated and then pushed Lennox's number. She listened for two rings and hung up. She'd a better idea. She'd talk to Othello or Mr. Melvin. She threw on her jacket and slung her purse over her shoulder.

Grabbing her gun from the counter next to the coffee maker, she stuffed the thirty-eight in her pocket. I'm still using smart-on, Lennox.

Minutes later, Othello's nurse greeted her at the desk. "Miss Blue, Mr. Melvin will be happy to see you. Today is a good day for him."

"He's coherent?"

"He called me by my name. Course, he might have run out of other names and said it by mistake." She frowned.

"Can I see him now?"

"Follow me. He's in the dayroom by the windows." She led Rose through the large space where seniors congregated together in small groups talking or working at the puzzle tables. Othello sat alone near the bank of windows. Sun streamed in through the glass behind his arm chair spotlighting the senior.

"Mr. Melvin." Rose walked past the nurse who indicated a seat for her across from Othello. She perched on the edge and rested her purse on her knees.

Mr. Melvin raised his head. "Young lady, are you here for an audition?"

Her hope died for a second, and then, she rallied and dug out the article. She held it under his nose.

He glanced at the paper but refrained from a comment.

Why didn't he speak? "I found this piece from a few months ago. The article was about the high school drama club celebrating their fiftieth anniversary. They listed missing members at the end." She pointed to her mother's name. "What role did Laurie Blue play?"

"I think she played...." The light in his eyes dimmed.

"Please, Mr. Melvin."

"My name's Othello."

"Mr. Othello, this is very important. Try to remember Laurie Blue. She would have been in the drama club twenty-eight years ago. You were still teaching, right?"

He chuckled. "They used to say I'd be buried under the stage and haunt the administrators who cut my budgets. I memorized their names."

"She was a student in one of your plays."

"I'm sorry, young lady. My mind hides at times." His shoulders sagged, and he seemed to shrink before her eyes. "I'm afraid I can't help you."

Rose leaned forward and touched his hand. "Please, try to remember."

He smiled. "She was in love. I remember her now, but it was ill fated."

"Right, she was in one of your plays and had a boyfriend." Anticipation held her on the edge of her seat.

His smile faded. "The course of true love never did run smooth."

He was reciting another useless line. Even if he recalled her mother, the memory could be faulty. "Thanks." She might as well leave. "I have to go." The trip had been pointless. She slipped out of the chair. Sadness for Othello mixed with her frustration.

"Don't give up, young lady. You'll get the lead next time."

"I won't give up." She trudged to her car and drove toward her apartment. Now what should she do?

She turned into the parking lot behind her building and cut the engine. Should she talk to Lennox? No, she'd continue by herself. She'd find someone else who could remember her mother at the high school. A search on the computer for classmates would be the next step. Once she learned a fact or clue she'd turn it over to Lennox.

She hopped out.

"Rose!"

She whirled around.

He'd tracked her all morning. Now she was right in front of him. Who was watching? He scanned the rear of the buildings and the lot with a handful of cars. It was still risky. Someone in one of the apartments could glance out a window and see them. His heartbeat pounded in his ears and adrenaline overflowed. He'd never get a better chance.

She smoothed blonde hair away from her face and stuck out her chin. So like Dahlia. A wave of wanting hit him. Grab her now. It was a perfect day to visit The Ledges.

CHAPTER 29

Dean leaned out the window of his white car and skidded to a stop a few feet from her. He motioned her over. "Luke found something of your sister's. He needs you for a positive I.D. and asked me to bring you to him. He doesn't want you driving alone." He threw a glance at her car. "Did you go somewhere?"

"I went to the nursing home. Where is Luke?"

"He's out near The Ledges. Get in. He expects you."

His words drove a skip of hope through her chest. She slid into the vehicle. The clicks announced the locking of the doors. "He didn't hint at what he found?"

"All information is top secret with the police." Dean scooped up her purse. "I'll put this in the back and give you more room." He stretched his arm over the seat and dropped her bag behind them.

"Didn't Luke arrest your sister's boyfriend at my party? He stole a lot of the night's excitement, but I'll forgive him since he found the Ledgeview killer and people are safe again." He threw her a smile.

She clasped her hands together tightly. "With two homicides, there could be two killers."

"That's why we have detectives like Luke. Criminals are masterminds at fooling people."

She shook her head. "Why would A.J. kill Dahlia in Ledgeview and not at home?"

"He probably thought no one would connect him to the crime if she died in a different state." He patted her clenched hands. "Everything will work out."

At his cold touch, she resisted the urge to shudder. What was wrong with her? She should be happy that Luke had made a discovery. "I wonder who attacked Shauna."

"What do you mean?"

"If A.J. killed my sister, why would he attack Shauna, a stranger?"

"You've hung around Luke too long. You sound like him. At the trial, we might learn the reasons someone is stalking the women of Ledgeview."

His words didn't comfort her. The sun disappeared behind a cloud, and the day turned gray, matching her mood. The city grew smaller in her side view mirror.

Dean's phone rang. He dug it out of his jacket pocket. "Luke, we were just talking about you. Yes, she's with me. We'll be there in twenty minutes. We'll meet you, good luck."

"Let me speak to him." She held out her hand.

"He hung up." Dean tossed the cell into the console between the seats. "Don't worry. You can talk to him in person soon enough."

"Did he give you a clue of what he found?"

"He was tightlipped as always. I guess he wants to keep a lid on the investigation until we're with him."

She surveyed his brown jacket, pants and work boots. "You dressed differently today."

"I changed when Luke asked me to bring you to The Ledges. An overcoat and dress shoes don't cut it in the woods."

He had time to change?

Besides, I love the outdoors—hiking, skiing. Do you like to ski? You should go up to the White Mountains and try some of the trails. I can tell you the best ones."

"I'm going back to Vermont soon." The car bounced over the secondary road for the next fifteen minutes. "The pavement is worse in the spring with the frost heaves."

A ding, ding chime rang from the dashboard.

"What's happening? Are we running out of gas?" Rose glanced over at the fuel gage.

He stared down at his control panel. "My rear tire is low."

"Are we almost to Luke?" How close were they? All she saw were trees and road.

"Don't worry. I carry one of those instant air cans in my trunk. If needed, we'll call Luke to pick us up, or at the worst, we'll walk. We're about two miles away. I see a place to pull off." He glided onto an overgrown path in the woods.

The goose bumps on her arms rose and cringed. "Why didn't you park on the shoulder?"

"Did you see how narrow the edge is? All we need is a teenager speeding around the curve, and I'd be a dead man." He smiled. "I'll get you to Luke."

He grabbed the keys and climbed out of his car. His footsteps crunched on gravel. The tree branches pressed against her window, and the overgrown trail narrowed and disappeared into the forest. The memory of the path at The Ledges filled her mind. The ache in her head warned of images pushing into her mind. Images she didn't want.

She grabbed her purse and jumped out of the car. The vision powered over her. She bent toward the passenger door, fighting the vision.

Footsteps crunched against the gravel "He's coming." Dahlia ran across the boulder and searched the path. Then she saw him emerging from the woods. He was dressed in work boots and a brown jacket and as he strode forward he lifted his head and she smiled at him.

"Dean! I've been waiting for you."

Dean! Panic sunk its sharp teeth into Rose.

From the rear came the whine of the trunk flipping open. "Rose, I need an extra pair of hands," he called. "It's worse than I expected."

She shot a glance at the ignition. He'd taken the keys.

"Rose, are you coming?"

Run, Dahlia whispered.

Rose whipped around and fled.

"What are you doing? Rose, come back. You'll get lost."

The sound of his thudding footsteps told her he was in pursuit. Adrenaline gave her a burst of speed. A whoosh of small barbs shot past her arm. She screamed and stumbled over a downed tree. The phone fell from her hand, but she stayed on her feet. *He had a taser!*

She sprinted forward. Branches scratched her face, grabbed

her arms like tentacles stretching out of the woods.

My gun! She yanked the weapon from her pocket and rounded a curve. The directions to fire scrolled through her brain as she performed each step. Ready, she whirled around to surprise him and struggled to control her breathing.

His heavy footsteps crashed louder through the underbrush. He'd catch up in seconds. Perspiration soaked her clothes and burned her eyes. She gripped the firearm with both hands. Hold Steady. Any second he'd round the bend.

His brown jacket! She gasped and squeezed the trigger. The gunshot echoed as he came into full view. Astonishment crossed his face. "You shot me?" His hand went to his earlobe, now dripping blood.

She'd fired too soon, too high.

"You bitch." He lunged forward.

"No." She spun around and fled. The land pitched downward. She skidded. She slowed to regain her footing. She had to get ahead. Take a stand. Shoot again. Aim lower. Wait longer for her target. She leaped away from the trail, stumbled over a root, recovered and felt a pulsation. A thousand hits pricked her funny bone, shot through her body. Her muscles went rigid. She tumbled toward the ground.

She couldn't put out her hands to stop. The gun flew from her fingers. The earth rushed up and smacked her face, her chest and legs. Dirt tunneled between her lips. Pain vibrated through her body. She hit the ground and lay on the edge of a rise. Below the river flowed. Its current twisted and surged. Terror pricked every nerve. She couldn't move. She couldn't yell. Dean's boots thudded toward her.

CHAPTER 30

The Staties and the Ledgeview Police Department swarmed over the farmhouse and yard. Luke stood on the edge of the yellow taped area.

"The place belongs to a Homer Holmes," Conroy reported, closing up his cell phone and crossing the yard to Lennox. "I spoke to him. He bought the property a year ago to convert into an auto salvage business, but the renovations cost more than he planned. His idea stalled, and he hasn't been able to raise cash to get the project off the ground."

"Check his background yet?"

"Guy comes up clean. His real estate agent can give us the name of the previous owner."

"Yeah, who's the realtor?"

"Dean Drown is listed. Holmes said the plow took down the sign and it hadn't been put up again."

Dean?

"Didn't you go to school with his son?"

Pieces spun around in Lennox's mind: *Dean, realtor for the farm, Dahlia's landlord, Ski, North Conway, Ledgeview, murders.*

Luke needed to speak to Dean right away. "Send a squad car over to the Drown house and one to his real estate office. I want the former owner's name and bring Dean Drown here."

"I'll send someone from the station over." He marched off.

Luke pushed Rose's number and heard her voicemail. He left a short message and called Frank. "Hey, do me a favor. Find Rose and stick to her."

"I'm out the door."

"Call me as soon as you're with her. She's not answering her phone." Luke stuffed his phone in his pocket and turned to the uniform approaching him.

"The tow truck driver wants to talk to you about hauling the car to the state lab."

Luke nodded and followed him to the barn where he spoke to the driver. Five minutes later, Dahlia's car was headed to the state lab. His phone rang. Glancing at the number, he distanced himself from the searchers.

"Frank, are you at Rose's?"

"She's not around. She didn't answer her buzzer or door. I helped myself inside, and the apartment is empty. I'm sitting in the parking lot next to her car."

Where was she? "Go to Drown's Real Estate and call me if Dean's at his office. Then ask Tia at her store if she's seen Rose and stop by the library. She could be at either place." Where else would she go?

"I'm on my way."

"Call when you find her." He hit the end button. A few minutes later, the phone went off.

"Luke, I called the library and Tia's, no sign of Rose. I'll drive by and verify she's not at either place."

Luke hung up and called the station to put out an APB for Rose Blue. Think. Think. She might go to her store in Vermont. It was a long shot. He hit the numbers and spoke to a Brattleboro Detective who promised to go straight to the boutique and would let him know if Rose was there. When Luke finished, he notified Conroy he was in charge.

Conroy raised his brows. "Taking a lunch break?"

Luke didn't bother to answer. He'd swing through Ledgeview and search himself. Within minutes, he was in Old Charger and bumping over the frost heaves. A woman in a long black coat dashed out from the trees. He slammed on the brakes and yanked the steering wheel to the right. His car skidded and halted on the dirt shoulder.

Rose? He blew out a breath of relief. It couldn't be her. Where'd the woman go? He inspected the area. No one was in sight. His heartbeat slowed to normal. Why was she in the middle of nowhere crossing the road? Why had she run off into the woods? He rolled down his window and yelled, "Hello? You okay? Rose?" Luke yelled. A crow flew overhead and cawed loudly.

The woman's profile reminded him of Rose, but she was blonder. Dahlia. It couldn't be. He stepped on the gas. His tires spun with a loud whine, and his engine strained. "Come on, Charger." The car rocked back into the rut.

Hell, he was stuck. Welcome to mud season. He leaned out the window. "Dahlia!"

His phone rang. Lennox grabbed it.

The Chief's voice shouted through the receiver into his ear. "I just suffered through a two hour meeting with the Mayor, and we're taking a new course, one of action"

"I found Dahlia Blue's car near The Ledges. It's on the way to the state lab."

"I know. Conroy left me a message. Put him in charge. We need to talk. Be here in twenty minutes."

Luke hung up. He'd have to call a uniform from the farm to pick him up and drive him to his meeting; he'd be late.

The ting of his phone alerted him to a text. Now what? With his luck, it was the Chief changing his mind and firing him on the spot.

Rose lay on the ground. Dean paused and she heard the zip of the backpack. *Just like Dahlia. This is how I die.*

Dean bent and bound Rose's hands and feet with gray tape, round and round.

Terror flooded her chest. The tape covered her mouth and threatened to suffocate her as it climbed toward her nostrils.

Breathe. Keep breathing.

His hand stroked her hair. "You're as pretty as your sister. She came willingly to The Ledges." He grinned, and then, his smile faded. "This isn't right. We're in the wrong place."

He grabbed her shoulders. "Get up. Up."

He was going to shove her down the hill into the river below. Her throat closed up. She concentrated on breathing through the prickles of terror.

Instead, he removed the pack he was wearing and slung it

over his shoulder. Then he heaved her over his back. The coppery odor of blood on his shirt filled her nose. He started off.

She forced herself to focus on the trail, searching for anything familiar. He continued parallel to the river, and the truth smacked her. Dean was taking her to The Ledges.

Minutes passed. She moved her fingers. Control over her body was returning. She squirmed but wriggling did nothing to slow Dean on his death march. *Dahlia, help me. Please.*

He broke through the trees and crunched across the boulders of The Ledges. The sound of the river grew until the flow roared in her head. He paused and tossed her to the ground with a grunt, knocking out her breath. She was in the place of her visions, her nightmares.

He opened the pack and crouched down in front of her. Reaching inside the knapsack, he dug out a knife. He drew it across his thumb, and red bubbled out. "Nice."

She shoved her heels into the ground and managed to push herself a few inches.

"Now, Rose, be good." His mouth twisted into a smile, and he ran a hand over her breast.

Her cry came out muffled.

He bent and licked her flesh beneath her chin. She wanted to scream.

"So delicious. I loved watching you. Sometimes I believed you were a mirage, and you were Dahlia who survived to trick me. You're not her, are you? You're not playing games with me?" His hand tightened on a clump of her hair and yanked. "Are you?"

She shook her head, unable to drag her gaze from the long blade in his hand. Fright shook her body. *Stay focused. Get ready. Block. Duck the knife.*

He hummed a little song. "Do you know those words? Double your pleasure. Double your fun with Rosie Blue, Dahlia Blue. They are the one."

We are one, Dahlia's voice whispered.

The point of the knife aimed for her throat. Rose couldn't stop her trembling.

"Answer me. Have you heard the song?"

The tip pressed into her skin, pinching, promising more pain.

She shook her head.

"We'll do it a little different this time." He raised the knife to her mouth.

He wanted to cut off her lips! Rose flinched and dug in her heels to shove away.

He pressed his knee against her chest, crushing her into the stone. "Your generation knows nothing about fun." He slit the tape across her mouth. "Go ahead and scream. Dahlia couldn't, and I missed the pleasure. I won't this time." His cold smile sent shivers fleeing up her spine. "We'll have lots of private time."

She closed her eyes. *Dahlia! Gram! Luke! Oh, Luke, I'm sorry.*

"That's right. Say your prayers before we have a little fun. God can't save you." He ran the side of the cold knife down her cheek, over her neck and to the top of her blouse. He licked his lips as he opened her jacket, slit open her blouse and the front of her bra. She closed her eyes again and felt his calloused hands roam over her body.

She tried to slow her gasps, grab control.

He stopped and sat back on his haunches. "Don't like it? Think you're too good for everyone? Your sister was the same way."

Anger and panic twisted inside of her.

"But," he added, his eyes gleamed with coldness, "in the end she changed her mind. In fact, she told me, incest was the best."

What? Think about escape. The knife was resting on the ground. Could she grab it with her teeth? Think.

The slap across her face stunned more than hurt.

"Listen when I speak to you. I'm your father. That's why Dahlia came to Ledgeview. That's why she loved me. And, I taught her things no one else did or could."

Father? Dean was their father? She searched his face, searching for a resemblance, some sign. Where was it?

He laughed. "Kiss your daddy."

He leaned toward her, his lips open.

His hot breath hit her face. She sucked in her cheeks and spit.

Her salvia hit him between the eyes. A big glob dangled from his nose.

"You little—" He swiped at his face, swearing. "I've been too good to you."

He grabbed her bound ankles and dragged her across the pebbles strewn over the boulder. The rocky surface scraped across her clothes. Her jacket and shirt rode upward. The gravel bit into her skin, burned her flesh.

Where was he taking her? Then she knew. The trestle loomed ahead. He was going to throw her off like he did Dahlia. The image of her sister falling filled her vision. She closed her eyes and opened them to a new scene.

He lifted himself off Dahlia, not bothering to zip his pants. He yanked her up. She felt the bridge sway. Terror clawed at her insides. She tightened her muscles and fought with all her strength against the restraints. Nothing loosened.

"Dahlia, how about a better view of the water?"

Dahlia's screams echoed inside Rose's head.

She forced her body to go limp to weigh herself down as he dragged her toward the trestle. The tape cut off her circulation. She couldn't feel her hands. She couldn't kick her bound legs.

The bridge drew closer, closer.

"Dean Drown. Stop!"

A shot whizzed through the air over their heads.

Dean halted and turned around.

"Let go of the girl, put your hands up and step away."

Rose tilted her head back to catch sight of her rescuer.

Frank stepped out from the trees about twenty feet away.

Frank! Tears of hope filled her eyes.

He held a gun with two hands and stalked toward them. "Do it, Drown."

"Whatever you say." Dean bent down, lowering her feet with one hand. His other swept the underside of his jeans cuff.

"Gun," Rose yelled.

The shot vibrated through the woods. Frank tumbled to the ground.

"Frank!" she screamed.

"Stupid old man was always in the way. You and I need to have our fun, but not here. We'll have our moment on the bridge. I've dreamed about it."

Rose glanced at the still body. "Frank?" Tears streamed down her cheeks. *Please, God, help us.*

Dean raised his pant leg and stuffed the gun into the top of his boot. He tucked the knife into his belt and dragged her forward.

The railroad trestle grew larger and larger. She was going to die. Panic paralyzed her. She couldn't breathe.

Dean paused and flung her across his shoulders. He strode onto the abandoned railroad bridge. The ties shook with each step. She glimpsed the frosty white caps below.

He lowered her to the tracks and reached into his belt. He removed the knife.

"No. Stop! Help!" She writhed on the ground. The tracks jabbed into her. Below, the wail of the river cried for her.

"No one's here to save you."

This was it. Her life was over. She closed her eyes and whispered a prayer.

He knelt in front of her. His knife went to her waistband, and he began to cut away her jeans.

Spiders crawled on the track toward her. *Not my eyes!*

"Dean! Rose!"

He jerked upward. "Luke?"

She turned her head and blinking focused on Luke crouched beside Frank.

"Good thing you came." Dean straightened. "The old geezer was trying to throw Rose off the trestle. He charged me with his gun. I had to shoot him."

"Help! Smart on! Sm—"

The sole of Dean's boot came down across her mouth and nose.

"She's hysterical. I could use you out here, Luke."

Rose squirmed beneath the boot's sole. The crunch of stone alerted her that Lennox had started toward them. *Please help us.*

"Hurry," Dean shouted. "The trestle's not safe. She might fall."

The spider scurried past her face. Rose fisted her hands tied at the wrists. Now. With all the effort she had left, she drew her fists upward and struck Dean in the crotch.

He swore a stream and jumped to the side.

"Run!" Rose screamed. "Run!"

The point of Dean's boot smacked against her skull. The world blackened.

Shots fired in the air.

"Come off the bridge with your hands up," Luke yelled from the woods.

She rolled to her side and blinked against the throbbing, gray pain.

Dean squatted down behind her. "I'll kill her. Don't be stupid."

A shot whizzed over Dean's head. "You'll hit the girl. Give it up."

"I didn't come alone. My men will be here any second. Raise your hands, Dean."

"Forget the old ploy," Dean shouted. "You can't have both of us. You might take me in, but our precious, little Rose will be going for a swim." He nudged her toward the trestle's side.

Below the river wailed and swept past. Rose's heart slammed against her ribs. She'd easily fit through the missing rusty railing. She squeezed her eyes shut and mumbled another prayer.

"You're dead if you hurt her."

Dean's mouth tightened. "You want her instead of me? I'm surprised, Luke, but I could see it in your face. She got to you. So we'll play it that way. We'll compromise. I'll leave and you get Rose." He grabbed hold of her arm and paused. "Throw your gun in the river."

Luke stood his ground.

"Having second thoughts? Made the wrong choice? It's now or never. One good push and she's gone."

Rose couldn't stop her body from shaking.

A shot fired. Dean's eyes widened, and for a fraction of a second, stared down into hers. His grip tightened and then relaxed. He pitched forward over her. She screamed.

He plummeted into the fast moving current and disappeared before resurfacing a few feet away. The water carried him forward and then yanked him beneath the darkness.

"Rose! Rose!"

Luke was racing toward her.

The bridge shook underneath her with his weight. He hunkered down beside her.

"Lu–ke." Her teeth chattered and chills raced over her body as she looked into his whiskered face and wide blue eyes.

"I got you." He scooped her up.

The wind stung her face. She pressed herself into his wide chest. The breeze picked up, and the bridge swayed. Tears bit into her eyes, blurring the landscape. She curled her numb fingers against her palms as he trudged forward on the rickety structure.

The granite boulder grew closer and closer until he stepped off the trestle. He lowered her feet first to the ground. Bound, she leaned against him, feeling his strength, listening to his pounding heartbeat. She was alive. They made it.

Perspiration dotted his white face. "Are you okay?"

She could only nod and sank to the ground.

He removed a small knife from his pocket and worked in silence, slicing the tape from her wrists and ankles. Then he fitted his jacket around her shoulders. "I need to check on Frank"

She shook her hands, hoping to end the lack of sensation while Luke trudged to the prone man and bent over him.

"He's alive."

Thank God. She felt her chest rise up and down with each breath. Luke's voice floated across to her. He was on his phone. She rose and wobbled to the edge and stared into the raging current. No signs of Dean. She turned and headed across to Luke and Frank. She sank down next to the older man.

"The ambulance will arrive soon. They'll take you both to the hospital. I'll ride with you."

She struggled with the words. "Dean said...he was my father."

Sobs poured out of her. She couldn't stop them. Luke slipped his arms around her waist and held on, whispering words of comfort.

Finally, she controlled her crying. She closed her eyes and murmured, "Gram, I kept my promise."

CHAPTER 31

Two days later, Luke walked into Drown Realty.

Buddy sat behind Dean's desk. He glanced up from a pile of papers. "If you came to offer condolences, you should speak to my mom. She's holed up at home."

"I read your interview in the paper. You said you were moving?"

Buddy leaned back in his seat and put his hands behind his head. "Shauna wants to live in Connecticut close to her parents. Once we're in a new place, we'll be able to put the nightmare of Ledgeview behind us. My mom is coming too. She's relocating her shop. We'll be selling all the buildings. Are you in the market for real estate?"

Luke observed the clean desk. "Getting rid of everything? You're not waiting for the results of the search for Dean?"

"Email me, but not at the office."

He kept his eyes on his friend. "The office is where Dean trained you?"

"Don't even bring training up. I never wanted to follow him into buying and selling properties."

"I didn't mean real estate, Buddy. You anonymously texted me the day Dean took Rose to The Ledges. You warned me that Dean kidnapped her. Did he mention his plan or were you familiar enough with his patterns and actions to guess he was going for her?"

Buddy dropped his arms. "You must be out of suspects to name me. When's the last time you slept? Did the Ledgeview budget committee find you in a dark alley and chew off your ear about the cost of the investigation?"

"If you hadn't acted frenzied when you went into Egore's Electronics and used their phone, I would never have tracked the call to you."

"My phone was lost, and I didn't bother to replace it because it was always someone calling for me to do something for them. Besides you're wrong. When I went in Egore's I called Shauna to smooth things over. I missed meeting her for lunch, and she was going to chop off my head."

"I'm not wired, Bud. This is you and me talking. People might not understand why you didn't turn Dean in. I understand. He was your father, blood or not, and that's not a bond you can break, even if you wanted. We're programmed from birth to love, honor and most importantly, to obey our parents."

"I didn't commit a crime."

"I dug into Dean's past. No father listed on the birth certificate. He was in and out of foster homes while his mother suffered from a mental illness. I don't have all the details, but I'd guess he endured a lot of abuse at her hands and wasn't fond of women."

"Do you get paid to make up stuff for the DA or did you steal lines from a bad detective movie?"

"Here's a fact, Bud. I contacted the local college. You're not enrolled. Shauna believed you were taking business courses and that you had a future career, but you had nothing."

"I changed my mind before classes started. I knew she wouldn't take it well, and didn't let on to her. Can you see me spending my day worrying about quotas? Come on."

"Yet, you always had money."

"Hello, I worked for my mom and Dean."

"Errand boys don't earn much of a paycheck. Dean paid your bills. I went through your finances and kept asking myself. Why did Dean take care of a grown son's bills when his son was nearly forty-years-old and capable of finding employment?"

"Okay, I lied to Dean too. He didn't mind helping me out while I was in college, and I let him continue believing I was attending. Arrest me."

"No, Bud, you were his paid co-conspirator and not in academics."

"Lack of sleep makes you conspiracy crazy. You should go to a sleep clinic or get therapy. I recommend both."

"Here's how I see it, Bud. You or Dean met Dahlia Blue when she arrived in Ledgeview. My guess, she ran into Dean first because she needed a place to stay. She shared her reason for visiting, trying to locate her father. Dean decided she was too easy, too good to pass up. She was without friends who'd miss her and she was estranged from her only family member, Rose. She was hoping to discover her dad, a role he'd already adopted with you. I don't know what story he fed her, but I'll guess. He was married when he fell in love with a teenager, who was Dahlia's mother, or he hid their affair because of the differences in their ages. Only you know."

"I know you've lost it." Buddy stood, hands fisted.

Luke edged in front of him. "He introduced the two of you. You were the big brother she'd never met. It was the perfect lure. She thought she'd found a family. In fact, you're the one who led her to The Ledges the day she died. You probably offered to show her the secret meeting place of her mother and father. Did Dean agree to give you a bonus for bringing her?"

"Luke, you're insane."

"You might work a deal with the DA on sentencing in exchange for information. But why, Bud? Why did you go along with his plans? Was it only for the money? Didn't you have a conscience?"

Buddy's lips folded inward. He appeared to be holding himself from blurting either another denial or a confession. Finally he yelled, "You're the hot shot who knows it all. Why would I?"

"I can speculate. Tia's first husband was violent. She chose Dean another abuser, following her pattern. You were programmed for cruelty."

Buddy shrugged. "Why didn't Miss Blue just phone Dean instead of sticking around?"

"Dahlia had put together her mother was a teenage parent, and lived in Ledgeview before she and Rose were born. Dahlia figured her father was from our city when she found the reunion article. She was desperate for family, a connection. Her grandmother passed away in the fall. Her sister never wanted to see her again, and her future husband turned out to be a pornographer she couldn't stand any longer. She thought you and Dean were the answers to her dream. If she'd only known, meeting you was the worst thing that ever happened to her."

"Speculation doesn't hold up in a court."

"Dahlia told you about her fear of heights. She was sharing with her brother, letting you into small family secrets. You talked to her a lot and not just at the Audi. At first the evidence pointed to A.J., but now, I realize the scare tactics used on Rose fit your profile, your style."

"My profile shows off my best features." He smirked.

"To you, the fake hand with blue nail polish was humorous while the ploys were bizarre."

"Luke, give it up. If you had evidence, you wouldn't waste time taunting me with your fantasies."

"I've found proof of lies, Bud. My men interviewed the employees of the law firm next to the garage. They rent the first five spaces in the parking garage. None of them drove a truck to work or parked one inside the garage the day Shauna was attacked. Her story about the attacker hiding between the pickups wasn't true."

"She was confused and stressed. Give her a break."

"The other problem was her story about the attack. A witness stepped forward who saw Shauna leave the bank and jump into your car the night of the dinner party at your parents. I wasn't able to interview him until today. Funny thing, he didn't see anyone attempt to assault her."

"Obviously the man confused his dates or needs glasses."

"He insisted he had the right day. He told me he always picked up his daughter from dance class on Tuesday at the same time and that's the only day he uses the garage. His vision is perfect. He's also a bank customer and recognized Shauna."

"A good lawyer will rip his tale to pieces."

"He won't. Shauna was never attacked. She lied for you, to mislead us. That's why she didn't want to speak or visit with anyone, not even her own family. Her conscience bothered her. Did you threaten not to marry her if she didn't help you? Did you cause her bruises?"

"Lennox, you're way off. I love Shauna. I'd never call off the wedding."

"You panicked when Frank followed you. You were desperate to shake suspicion. I'll also remind you filing a false police report is a crime Shauna won't be able to hide from."

Buddy's face tightened. "You'd better leave, or I'll file a report of police harassment."

"I can talk to Shauna next."

A vein above his eyebrow bulged as his face reddened. "You always were the hard ass, Luke. I'm not going to be a virtual notch on your daddy complex belt."

"I wanted to believe in you, and you did show one glimmer of hope."

Buddy's features slid into curiosity. "I helped an old lady cross the street?"

"You got Frank to follow you out of the city when you realized he was tailing you. You were worried the text wasn't enough. When you arrived at The Ledges, you hid your car but let Frank follow you on the trail. You stayed ahead of him, and then double backed to home when he found Dean and Rose. It would have been all over for her if Frank hadn't interrupted Dean first. You saved Rose." Luke debated bringing up his next topic.

"I want you out of here, now." Buddy retreated behind the desk.

"I've one more question. You lived in the White Mountains before moving to Ledgeview. Did Dean drive your mother or you up the Mount Washington Motor Road?"

"Did the police find a woman murdered at the Mountain's Weather Station, too? You want to connect Dean and me to every murder and every day of bad weather?"

"Do you remember?"

Buddy angled his head at the exit.

Luke held out the warrant. "Buddy Drown, I'm serving you with a search warrant for the Drown Reality, your apartment, electronic devices and car. One has already been served to Tia for the house, contents and vehicles."

Buddy ripped the paper from his hand. "I loved you like a brother," he shouted.

"My brother wouldn't help kill people." As soon as Luke

walked out, his men ran inside. He was out of the investigation by the Chief's order, who told him he was too close to the case, and they needed to "protect against bias." Conroy would handle Bud now.

Luke hesitated by his car at the curb. All the years with his friend had come to an end today. The door opened, and a couple of uniforms rushed Buddy to a nearby patrol car.

"Hey." Detective Conroy walked up to him and gave him a mocking smile. The fragrance of his last taco meal hung around him. "Are you finding it hard to watch pretty boy go to the station for questioning?"

"As long as you read him his rights when we finish building our case, I'm fine." Luke pivoted around to leave.

"I've one more thing." Conroy's mouth twisted several times as though he bit into something sour.

Luke braced for a hit. "I've bad taste in friends?"

"Good job. So far." Conroy turned on his heel.

"Conroy," Luke waited for the detective to pause before adding, "you too."

Conroy walked away into the real estate office.

"Luke!"

He shielded his eyes against the sun and glanced toward the end of the block. Rose hurried toward him.

She halted on the sidewalk a few feet from him. She wet her lips and forced a smile. Both her hands were stuffed inside her open parka's pockets. Her shoulders were tensed. "I hope you don't mind me calling you by your first name now that the case is over. I was going to the station but found you on the street like a common beat cop. What's up?"

"I was about to drive to your apartment. Sorry, we haven't had time to speak privately. How are you?" He fought the urge to touch her, reassure himself all was okay.

"I'm fine." She shrugged and cleared her throat. "I understand A.J. will make bail although he's charged with other crimes related to his internet business."

"He'll be out today."

She nodded. "With today's newspaper with the dramatic headline, The Killer Hidden among Us, I'm sure his ex internet business will make him a hot topic in Ledgeview."

"The Ledgeview News has sold a lot of papers thanks to Dean Drown."

"How could Dean have fooled us? He planned to run for mayor. People believed in him."

"He ingratiated himself into the world with good acts like the tip line, supporting the clothing drives for the poor and his desire to do good by running for office. No one wanted to scratch beneath his shiny surface."

"I wish Dahlia's death was a dream." She heaved a sigh.

"Buddy's answering questions at the station. They'll search for emails to and from Dahlia. Don't worry. They'll prove he was Dean's co-conspirator for your sister's murder."

"Do *you* think he helped Dean kill Dahlia?"

"Bud and Dean met your sister when she arrived in Ledgeview, searching for her father. *They* took advantage of her."

"Dean and Buddy, I'd like to forget I ever met them." She glanced down and twisted the end of her jacket. "I wished I'd never found my father if he's Dean Drown."

Luke took her hand. "Dean was a liar. Don't believe him."

"I hope you're right." She stepped away, breaking contact with him and kept a distance between them. "I was going to speak to Tia about giving me a personal item of Dean's for a DNA test."

Her reaction to his touch confused and irked him, but he didn't want to upset her more by quizzing her about her actions. She had bigger problems. "Don't worry, a lawyer can help you."

"I just want Dahlia's pain to end and to understand Buddy's role." She blinked several times before continuing.

"He was raised in violence with his father and then his stepfather. Dean loved power and control, and he enjoyed the high and false sense of both when he killed. I can profile both Drowns for you, but you can figure out the rest."

She waved a hand. "I've heard enough. I'm headed home to Vermont today."

"You're leaving?" He felt a punch to his gut. He hadn't counted on her quick exit.

"It's time. I want to thank you."

"Rose, I—"

"You were just doing your job." She smiled briefly. "I understand, Luke. Don't sweat it. You were brave out there on the bridge. I'll never forget you saved my life."

"You've come a long way from the woman who called the police over a plastic hand. Dahlia would be proud of you. I'm proud of you too." He inched closer, driven by the urge to say something. He wasn't sure what except he didn't want her to go.

His phone rang and the number popped up. "It's Frank. Excuse me for a moment."

"Luke, my boy," Frank's voice boomed into his ear. "I was released today from the hospital, and now that the case is closed, I wanted to invite you over for a war game."

"Are you sure you're up for games already?"

"I can't wait to face your men."

"Good. I read your interview in yesterday's paper."

Frank chuckled. "People always think seniors are too old to do anything."

"I never did, Frank."

"I showed them. You're a smart one, Luke, like your father."

"Thanks, that's the one compliment I won't forget. Dad was the best."

"Hey, did ya notice my favorite picture next to my interview?"

"You mean the one with the Chief shaking your hand while you lay in a hospital bed?"

"I'm framing it. I bet he shook yours too."

"The Chief told me it was about time I solved the case."

"He was over the top with praise. The piece has gotten me lots of attention from the women. My next door neighbor, a lovely, single lady, has volunteered to bring me supper for the next week."

"You're the man, Frank. I'll be over Tuesday." He hung up and turned to Rose. She was gone.

He surveyed the street without finding a sign of her. Should he try to catch her? He wanted to speak to A.J. before he was being released. He'd catch Rose later when he figured out what to say. He drove over to the County Jail where a clerk directed him to the discharge desk. Luke found A.J. shoving his belongings into a paper bag.

He stiffened at the sight of the detective. "Afraid you can't gloat today. I'm out on bail. I sold a few pictures of Dahlia to a news agency for the money. They didn't mind dealing with me. Besides all the new evidence proved I'm not a killer. Shouldn't you'd be home licking your wounds, Detective. Did you enjoy my picture at the Casino?"

"We saw you. Don't go anywhere yet." Luke crowded up to him. "I'm betting the Drowns were customers of yours. Did you connect them with Dahlia?"

"Dahlia didn't deserve what happened to her at The Ledges." He wiped at his tearless eyes. "Did you come to torture me? Dahlia's dead. I'm sorry. I loved her."

"Cry me a river and build me an overpass, get over it. I came to tell you to stay away from Rose Blue."

"Don't worry. I'll never speak to her again."

"If I discover you're active in the porn business while you're out, count on immediately going back to jail. I'll be watching the internet for signs of your activity. I don't care where the money goes. And remember, speak, email, text or go within ten miles of Rose, and you'll regret it."

"Isn't threatening innocent people a crime?" He grabbed his bag. "So long, and don't look me up."

Luke left and drove to Rose's without a prepared speech. Time had not given him the words, but he had to see her. He rang the buzzer. She didn't answer. He used his bump key and entered.

Upstairs he found a note on her door. *I cleaned the apartment. If you need to contact me, call the Blues Sisters. R*

She was gone.

CHAPTER 32

The scarlet butterfly landed on the grave marker and fluttered its wings.

"I love you, Dahlia. I always will," Rose whispered. "I hope you Blues Women are behaving in heaven."

She unzipped her blue fleece. Spring had finally arrived and brought the long anticipated warmth. She turned from her sister's grave and spotted him. Luke Lennox, dressed in his worn leather jacket and faded jeans, was leaning against his car, at the entrance of the cemetery.

Hope filtered through her. No, he hadn't come for her. Her personal time with him was over. He'd probably driven to Bratt to question her more about Dean. His name brought her near panic.

She did a quick breathing exercise. Dean had no power over her. He was dead.

On the path, Luke was walking toward her in his familiar gunslinger stride, stirring up memories that hurt worse than ever. Her car was too far away for a quick escape.

She'd faced a killer. She could speak to Detective Lennox. She forced cheerfulness into her voice. "Hello, Luke. I didn't expect to see you. Did you hear I received the results of my DNA test? Dean wasn't my father."

"I never believed him."

"I've done my best to research what happened in my family. Apparently Mom and Gram moved over the border to start over in Ledgeview when my grandfather died. Mom enrolled in the high school and followed her already established pattern of sneaking out with boys. Voila, she became pregnant with us. They moved back home to Vermont, maybe to be with friends during Gram's trying time of dealing with an unwed teenager."

"I'll guess she was against abortion. Adoption?"

"They must have ruled the option out. All I know is the mention of their move brought up bad memories for Gram, and she never spoke of Ledgeview. I've found nothing on our true father, but I'm not looking for him. At least, I'm not today."

"You could never be a Drown." He held out the paper coffee cup he was carrying. "For you."

She blinked in surprise and took the cup. The sweet aroma of spiced coffee teased her nose. "You know what they say about men bearing gifts."

"Call nine-one-one?"

"Not quite." She gulped her drink in her nervousness before she spoke again. "I wish Dahlia had gone the blood test route before she ran off to The Ledges to meet Dean, but it's too late for her." Rose's chest tightened with regret. "I see you had time for a shave and haircut."

"I was celebrating the end of the investigation with shorter hair. On a personal front, the Medical Examiner ruled my father's death undetermined with the theory the death may have been staged. His case is officially reopened and the mayor has appointed a team to investigate. The new results spurred my mom to book a flight home for a visit. Everything is changing."

"Luke, I'm so happy for you and your mom." She fought the urge to wrap her arms around him. How long would these cravings for him last? How long would he stay and she have to pretend she didn't miss him, ache for him?

"How are you doing?" He fixed those blue eyes on her.

"Dahlia's at peace, and she and I are in... harmony. She doesn't visit much anymore. I don't have nightmares of her from the river." Rose glanced at the butterfly flitting across the grass to avoid his stare. "I think she wanted me to forgive her too." She shrugged, feeling uncomfortable. "I've forgiven myself."

"You weren't guilty, Rose. You're one of the most loyal people I know."

"Next you'll be calling me a saint." She dipped her head, but felt her face flush with pleasure. Keep the conversation casual and friendly. Soon he'd leave. He had to.

He stuffed his hands into his jacket pockets. "I saw Dahlia up at The Ledges the day Dean kidnapped you. She ran in front of my car and stopped me in the mud."

"Dahlia was there? You never told me."

He rubbed the back of his neck. "I'm slow at digesting some information. Sorry, I know for sure it was her. I went looking for her in the woods and found you. I'm sorry for doubting your story about her."

"My sister was always there for me." Rose fiddled with her butterfly necklace and tried to keep her tone neutral while she asked the big question. "Thanks for telling me. What else brings you here?" She stiffened, prepared for an emotional blow. "Did they find Dean's body or is evidence missing in your investigation?" She slid her gaze to his face.

"A hiker found Dean on the riverbank a few miles from The Ledges. He was identified and buried. My team is still digging into Buddy and A.J.'s participation in their crimes."

"I'm relieved, but it must be hard for you to deal with Buddy. I never understood why he texted you or brought Frank to The Ledges."

"Loyalty was Buddy's redeeming strength and weakness. He wanted to remain loyal to me, yet he couldn't break away from Dean, the man who'd been his father. He was caught in his family dynamics, good and bad."

"I'm sorry about Buddy; though I'm glad he won't be stalking any more women or helping his father in his plans. How are you dealing?"

"Conroy handles his case. I wish the final arrest had ended differently. I can't lie."

She relaxed her shoulders, and the tautness in her neck eased. "I was afraid you wanted me to identify Dean's knife or came to explain a snag in an upcoming trial. I wouldn't have been able to get away if you needed me in Ledgeview. I'm scheduled up this month with talks at the area schools. I've arranged a series of art scholarships for elementary kids at the Community Center. So many people in town sent me donations to support the search for Dahlia. I wanted the money to go to good use."

She was babbling. Get control.

"Good to hear you're back on your committees, and don't be surprised by the support. People care about you."

They strolled across the grass and onto the gravel road. To anyone passing, they must seem like a couple without a care. If only their appearance was true, a few more feet and he'd be at his vehicle. "You still haven't told me why you're in town and why you're at a cemetery. Are you tracing a suspect? Don't tell me Bike Boy's in Brattleboro."

"Funny you should bring him up. No more graffiti has sprouted up since he's been missing. His aunt called the station last week and wanted the uniforms to remove him from her house where he'd crashed and helped himself to her credit card. He's in jail until he can make bail. Your old neighbor won't be bothering anyone for a while."

Anyway, I was on my way to your apartment when I drove past and recognized your car."

"I don't understand. You could have called."

He fished in his pocket and held out a white, square box. "I brought you a present."

A rush of pleasure warmed her as she took his gift. "I'm afraid what's next. I hope you're not preparing me for bad news." She set her cup on the ground and removed the box's lid. Inside laid the silver butterfly with the ruby jeweled wings. "Dahlia's necklace," she whispered and held the chain against her heart. "Thank you, Luke. Dahlia's creation means everything to me."

He stepped closer, too close. She recognized each angle of his imperfect features, the ones that continued to invade her dreams once her guard was down. She could see the hint of whiskers on his angular jaw, the dark blue specks in his eyes, and his wide mouth that had kissed her with heat. The familiar, breathless rush returned. She tightened her lips together, afraid of what would leak through them. If only he'd mailed the necklace instead of delivering it in person. Now his presence brought on the familiar pain of losing him all over again.

"Let me." He slipped the necklace around her neck. His fingers brushed against her skin as he secured the fastener.

Quivers of pleasure danced over her. When he finished, she stepped away as fast as possible. "I was going to bury her necklace by her stone, but maybe the two butterflies should be together." She touched the pendant, still not quite believing it was found.

"I need to talk to you, Rose."

She nodded, unable to speak past the lump lodged in her throat. Was A.J. getting off, moving to Vermont?

"I haven't done well in relationships. That's not news. My ex complained I never talked to her. She was right. I was all talked-out from work and asking questions. When I went home that part of me shut off, and I'd stopped listening and feeling. When my dad died, I didn't understand why he left me, what I'd done. I couldn't get involved with anyone after the divorce and my father's death. The pain was too much. Another part of me cut off the possibilities in my life."

"I understand." Where was he headed with his confession?

He angled in front of her, forcing her to meet his blue eyes. "I should have listened when you voiced your fears about Bud. I should have explained the plan to follow you to the Audi the night of Dean's party and not sprung the trap on you."

He'd come to apologize because he felt guilty. She'd deal with him, and then, he'd leave and end her torture. "You were doing your job the night of Dean's party. I understand now, and Buddy is in custody. As for your father, you'll find who took his life." There, she'd tied it up for him. All over except for the final good bye. She fisted her hands.

"Today is about you. I don't have the exact words, so I'll just say what I think. I was wrong not to believe you, and if you forgive me, I promise I won't keep any secrets because I trust you and you're more important than anything in my life, including my job."

Did he say she was more important than being a detective? How could that be? Her heart skipped a beat. "You think we should stay in closer touch? I guess we could email daily." She bit her lip and considered the possibilities of contact with him.

He shook his head. "No, Rose. Let me explain." He took a step toward her and grasped her forearm. Despite the pressure of his fingers, she was held by his intense stare and the other emotion in his eyes that made her heart flutter.

"When you first showed up in Ledgeview, I asked myself,

who is this woman? Now I know. You're my heart. I can't let you go."

A light headedness hit her. She was having a dream, a hallucination.

"I love you, Rose. If you let me, I'll prove it to you every day. I want us to be together. I haven't figured out who does what or where, but we'll tackle one problem at a time, together."

Tears burned her eyes.

His fingers wove through hers, linking them together. "Will you give us a chance?"

She inched away from him and swallowed the lump in her throat. For the first time since she'd left Ledgeview, she felt the dizzy feeling of hope. "First, I have to say something."

"What you're going to say can't be that bad. Is it?" Doubt tinged his voice, and he lifted one brow.

"I love you, Luke." Tears spilled down her cheeks, but she had to finish. "I'm not an expert myself on the girlfriend role, but..." Her throat tightened. She couldn't speak. She could only show him what was in her heart. She slipped her arms around his neck and kissed him with all the passion she could muster, willing him to understand the words she wanted to say. Finally she broke off the kiss. "I don't want us to be apart either."

He gave her a broad smile, keeping a firm grip on her. "I'm taking that as a yes to my question."

Rose's pulse increased and she slipped her arms around his waist. "A Blue woman finally chose the right man."

The butterfly circled above their heads and disappeared on the breeze.

THE END

A WORD ABOUT THE AUTHOR...

Dead Women Tell No Lies is Nora LeDuc's tenth published book. She is hard at work on her next one in her New England home. She lives with her husband, cat, and dog, who inspire her to write.

She would love to hear from you.
NoraLeDuc@yahoo.com

And be sure to check Nora's website:
NoraLeDuc.com

If you enjoyed *Dead Women Tell No Lies*,
please leave a review at Goodreads.com

Or at your favorite e-book store.